Love and Lament

ALSO BY JOHN MILLIKEN THOMPSON

The Reservoir

Love and Lament

a novel

JOHN MILLIKEN THOMPSON

OTHER PRESS

New York

Copyright © 2013 John Milliken Thompson
Production Editor: Yvonne E. Cárdenas
Text Designer: Chris Welch
This book was set in 10.75 pt Caslon by Alpha Design & Composition of Pittsfield, NH.

10 9 8 7 6 5 4 3 2 1

Library of Congress Cataloging-in-Publication Data

Thompson, John M. (John Milliken), 1959-
Love and lament : a novel / by John Milliken Thompson.
p. cm.
ISBN 978-1-59051-587-7 (pbk.) — ISBN 978-1-59051-588-4 (ebook) 1. Young women—
Fiction. 2. North Carolina—History—19th century—Fiction. 3. North Carolina—
History—20th century—Fiction. 4. Domestic fiction. I. Title.
PS3620.H68325L68 2013
813'.6—dc23
2012030141

Publisher's Note:

This is a work of fiction. Names, characters, places, and incidents either are the product
of the author's imagination or are used fictitiously, and any resemblance to actual persons,
living or dead, events, or locales is entirely coincidental.

In memory of my grandparents

Mary Myrtle Siler Thompson

and

William Reid Thompson

Ah my dear angry Lord,
Since thou dost love, yet strike;
Cast down, yet help afford;
Sure I will do the like.

I will complain, yet praise;
I will bewail, approve:
And all my sour-sweet days
I will lament, and love.

—"Bittersweet," GEORGE HERBERT

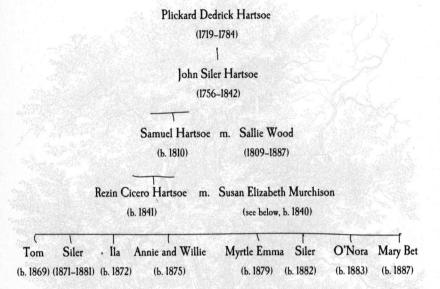

Plickard Dedrick Hartsoe
(1719–1784)

John Siler Hartsoe
(1756–1842)

Samuel Hartsoe m. Sallie Wood
(b. 1810)   (1809–1887)

Rezin Cicero Hartsoe m. Susan Elizabeth Murchison
(b. 1841)   (see below, b. 1840)

| Tom | Siler | Ila | Annie and Willie | Myrtle Emma | Siler | O'Nora | Mary Bet |
| (b. 1869) | (1871–1881) | (b. 1872) | (b. 1875) | (b. 1879) | (b. 1882) | (b. 1883) | (b. 1887) |

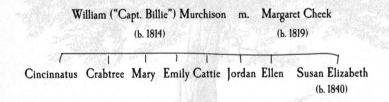

William ("Capt. Billie") Murchison m. Margaret Cheek
(b. 1814)   (b. 1819)

Cincinnatus Crabtree Mary Emily Cattie Jordan Ellen Susan Elizabeth
(b. 1840)

~⊃ CHAPTER I ℃~

1893

THE DEVIL WAS coming for her, of that she was sure.

He was riding a big gray horse, and he was all dressed in black, from his slouch hat to his long swallowtail coat to his black-stock tie and pointy hobnail boots. He had a black handlebar mustache, and though she couldn't see his eyes under his hat brim she knew he was the Devil because the horse's eyes were red. She was standing by the dusty road clutching her dolly by the arm, her thumb stuck in her mouth. She had come outside to see the thingum, because her mama had told her she should. And now she knew why she'd been afraid to come out. It was because Mama had also told her that someday the Devil was going to get her.

He slowed as he came up, and lifted his hat. And just then came the clang of a horseshoe striking a rock in the road like a bell. She was too scared to do anything but stand there, trying to go invisible, her free hand pressing into her pinafore. His forehead was high and shiny, but there was black hair hanging long in back, and thick eyebrows that raised. He had a flat smile, if it was a smile at all, and she thought he looked fine, until she remembered who he was.

She shook her head. "I won't go," she said.

He brought his horse to a stop and leaned over until he was covering the sun and the trees. "Won't go where?" he said. He had a deep smooth voice like molasses pouring from the jar.

"I won't go with you."

He laughed. "I expect you will someday, and you'll be glad to." He put his hat back on and continued up the road. She watched until his black hat disappeared over the rise between the woods and the cornfield, and he never once turned around. She crossed her heart the way Ila had taught her and ran inside, a breeze lifting the hem of her pinafore so that she thought he was still out there trying to snatch her.

"'Twasn't the Devil," her mother told her. "It was the circuit preacher. Presbyterian, by the sound of him. You'd know if it was the Devil, now go wash your hands and make yourself useful. There's beans to snap."

The Devil was a Preacher; the Preacher was the Devil. You had to be good or the Devil would take you away forever and you would never see God. But God could punish you, the same as the Devil, and you had to be especially mindful in church, because God was there, listening and watching. He could help you, but you had to be good, and you couldn't work on the Sabbath.

Mary Bet would see that Devil Preacher at night sometimes, riding up the road, or standing in a field waiting for her with a flat smile on his face, haunting the edge of her dreams. But she knew he was real. And that someday he would come for her.

SHE WAS BORN the year the railroad came to Haw County, her arrival associated by her family with that greatest of events yet known in the area, a harbinger, like the railroad itself, of a good and prosperous future.

The more she puzzled over it as a young girl, the clearer it seemed that the railroad brought the misery as surely as the heavens turned in the night sky, as certain as death itself, the hulking black engine an unholy smoking beast on straight and narrow rails of steel. And yet who could deny the excitement the railroad promised, the freedom of movement out beyond the fields and hillocks of the piedmont to the endless blue horizons of the mountains and the seashore?

Mary Bet's grandfathers were men of substance in the decades after the War between the States. Grandfather Samuel, an austere and avaricious grandson of Plickard Dedrick Hartsoe, who'd emigrated from Germany, had but one child, Mary Bet's father, Rezin Cicero Hartsoe. It was as unusual in those days to have only one child as it was to give property to anyone but that child. Samuel had done well with his mill and wanted his son to know the feeling of making his own way. He'd done well by turning over the milling to younger men, leaving to others the breathing of corn dust and the wrangling of two-thousand-pound stones. The life of a mill owner was much preferred to that of a miller, and Samuel Hartsoe squeezed every penny from his mill that his stern voice and tight-ruled balance sheet allowed.

And then Samuel became an old man and at seventy-one years of age wanted to be remembered for his civic beneficence, and so when there was talk of the railroad coming through Murchison Crossroad, as the town was then known, he offered a slice of the land he owned to the north.

There was at that time an innkeeper named Captain Billie Murchison who lived in the center of Murchison Crossroad. Captain Billie was Mary Bet's other grandfather. The fact that he owned and occupied the house of Samuel's father, John Siler Hartsoe, was to some minds an offense that Samuel stored silently in his heart— that his own father would sell his house, the first in the county to have glass windows, to a loud, boorish upstart like Billie Murchison, and sell it for a song, had to rankle.

It was in Murchison Crossroad that the stagecoach heading west from Raleigh intersected with the stage from Guilford Courthouse heading south. Captain Billie bought the house he turned into a stage stop from John Hartsoe in 1842, when he was twenty-eight years old. The war was but a minor interruption to Captain Billie's business, which prospered even more afterwards.

Likewise Samuel Hartsoe's gristmill, which lay a few miles south of the village. His one surviving child, Mary Bet's father, Cicero, joined up with the Haw Boys, Captain Billie's militia. He did not particularly want to fight, nor did many of his acquaintance, but when it became clear that his future standing in the community might depend on military service to his state, he enlisted.

He came back early from the war with a wooden stump beneath his right knee, and was happy to have come home with so much. He married Captain Billie's youngest daughter, Susan Elizabeth Murchison, who was one year his senior, and they had nine children: Tom, Siler, Ila, twins Annie and Willie, Myrtle Emma, Siler (after the first Siler died), O'Nora, and, finally, on a hot June day in 1887, Mary Bet. By the time Mary Bet was fifteen, nearly all her family had died.

Cicero had earned himself a captaincy just before being wounded, but he insisted people call him Mr. Hartsoe, or just R.C., instead of Captain Hartsoe. "I didn't do a thing as captain but get myself shot," he said. He stumped quietly back to the general store he had operated for his father before enlisting, and, against his father's will, offered credit to farmers trying to get back on their feet after losing their slaves and their able-bodiedness. In a few years he had prospered so much that he was able to buy the store from his father and build a fine house on ten rolling wooded acres. The place already had a nice little two-room cottage, which he spruced up and made into an east wing of his two-story clapboard house. He bookended the house with two common-bond brick chimneys, and embellished it with hip roofs, four-over-four sash windows, and expansive porches with chamfered posts, spindle brackets, and an intricate balustrade. It showed what he had accomplished, while others around him were failing.

Samuel's wife died two months before Mary Bet was born, but her other three grandparents were still very much alive. As were her parents and seven of their eight other children. Their second, Siler, died of typhoid when he was ten years old. Annie, their fourth, contracted the disease when she was eighteen. Mary Bet was five at the time, and her earliest memory was of Annie, who had been a second mother to her, lying in bed too frail to get Mary Bet a glass of milk. If she could get the glass of milk, Mary Bet thought, then she would be all right.

"She's susceptible," her mother said. For Mary Bet the word became shrouded in the somber rituals and attentions of the sickbed; to be susceptible was to be so ill that one could only lie in bed from morning until evening, waking just enough to drink chicken fat soup held to your lips by your mother or your sister (because Essie the maid was superstitious about typhoid fever, even though the doctor said it was not contagious). Then the clammy sheets would be changed and the chamber pot taken out, and Mary Bet would come in and comb Annie's long, light brown hair so that it lay flat across her pillow. She would do this quietly with great attention and devotion, the rhythm of her hands through the silky hair soothing and mesmerizing her as she looked from the hair to her sister's face, the broad almost comical nose and the deep lovely eyes and the soft skin now pale and unanimated save for a wispy smile, so that she felt she could go on combing and combing the entire day. Then her sister would take a sharp breath, which meant she was asleep, and her mother would tell her they needed to let her rest.

Sometimes Mama would sit in a rocking chair and read aloud from the Bible or a book of Illustrated Stories, and Mary Bet would lie on the brown braided rug and disappear into the sound of her mother's voice as it opened the door into a world where girls drank tea and went to boarding school and wore pink taffeta gowns at costume balls. Her mother thought it wrong to waste time on such frivolous literature, but she made an exception for a sick child. Susan Elizabeth did not believe in coddling her children, and was not affectionate with them past the age of five or six. She wore plain dark skirts with few ruffles, a high collar, even though they were no longer fashionable, and no jewelry, and she sat in her rocking chair, stern knees together, eyeglasses on the end of her flared nose, her voice unwavering when the story got to the place where the girl was reunited with her father who'd been lost at sea.

After two weeks Annie developed a rash and the doctor said her condition should start to improve if she kept her strength up. But they couldn't get her to take much nourishment. She lay in bed now, her eyes half-open, staring at the muslin curtains waving in a late spring breeze. Mary Bet still combed out her hair every day, but it had become brittle and lost some of its color. More of it came out in the tortoiseshell comb, and Mary Bet was afraid to keep combing. Annie seemed unaware of her presence, or of anything except the curtain.

One week Annie was so racked with coughing that the doctor worried she would break her ribs, and he gave her a daily spoonful of laudanum, which made her sleep so deeply and peacefully she looked to Mary Bet like a pale, blue-skinned angel, her pulsing temples the only sign she was alive. It became a room of dreams, filled with the spicy aroma of camphor plaster and their mother's low voice, turning the Psalms into word pictures.

After they found blood in the chamber pot, Mary Bet was not allowed to go back into her sister's room. She saw people going in and out—the doctor, her mother, and one or two neighbor women. And then one Sunday morning she heard her mother crying and she knew that Annie was in heaven. The undertaker came and moved her onto a wooden cooling board and drew a sheet up over her face. Mary Bet wanted to say good-bye, but they were already taking her out and her mother wouldn't let them stop and pull the sheet back. Mary Bet could see Annie's yellow nightgown through the little holes in the cooling board.

She was too young to attend the funeral. But she was allowed to go to the burial, and she stood between her mother and her sister Ila, her bony knees locked, while her father threw a handful of dirt on the coffin. She wore the black tulle dress that Ila had made, and she held Ila's hand and wished she had stayed home after all, because everybody was crying.

The earth was open and raw-smelling as it swallowed her sister. But there was no evil in sickness or in dirt, just the terrible hollow feeling of grown-ups not knowing what to say. The Devil had no part in it, because God had taken Annie. Yet Mary Bet could feel him lurking, watching, somewhere along the edges of the church-yard, over where the green trees rustled in the wind.

~ CHAPTER 2 ~

1893

ICERO WAS BACK at work in his store the following day.
.Hartsoe's offered seeds and medicines and dry goods and can-
dies and housewares of all sorts, and he pulled all the bottles
and gallipots of medicine down from the shelf and threw them into
a wooden flour barrel that served as a wastebasket. He didn't mind
if the glass broke and the medicine spilled. Men came in for their
usual twists of tobacco and took up seats near the Franklin stove to
watch the proceedings. They said not a word.

He kept the lycopodium, which worked on cuts, and some cas-
tor oil, and Bellingham's Stimulating Unguent for the hair and
whiskers, which his brother-in-law Crabtree Murchison liked. He
looked in the wastebasket and saw an unbroken bottle of swamp-
root tonic, which he himself had used on occasion. He pulled it out
and put it back on the shelf. "The rest is quackery of the vilest sort,"
he said, "and I'll not have it in my store."

Thad Utley, a fat overall-wearing man with stained teeth as crooked as old headstones, said, "You're right, R.C. Them nostrums never did me any good. Old Doc Slocum said—"

"You can tell your Doc Slocum to go to the Devil," Cicero cut in. "He's no better than any of this." He gestured at the pile of glass and rubbish in the barrel.

"R.C.," said Robert Gray, "why don't you take the day off? The world will get along without you for one day. You've suffered a terrible blow." Robert Gray was a retired lawyer who dressed in a suit every day of the week.

"No, sir," Cicero said. "I've never taken a day off, and I don't aim to."

"You never heard of a vacation?"

"I don't care to vacate." Cicero had worn his black suit to work, but was now jacketless, sleeves rolled up, suspenders bulging over an impressive middle-aged paunch. He smoothed his mustache with a thumb and finger and regarded his cronies—over beside Thad sat Oren Bray, a farmer with a growth beside his nose that looked like a second, melted nose. His face was as shriveled as a dry peanut, and he wore his usual gray pants and jacket with the letters "C.S.A." stitched onto the collar. Cicero never wanted to see his own uniform again—his wooden leg was enough of a reminder. And yet he pitied other men's bondage to the past.

"I'm feeling aggrieved is all," he said. "Willie's taken sick, and if he has the typhoid I don't know how Susan Elizabeth can stand it."

"Has Dr. Slocum seen him?" Robert Gray asked.

"That damn foo— no, he hasn't, nor is likely to. I could treat him better myself with what I just threw in the trash." Cicero grabbed the broom and began sweeping just to have something to do. He stopped and scanned the neat shelves, those not stocked with medicine, as though to see what needed ordering. Hardware, candles,

ropes, coffee, flour, beans, biscuit meal, twists of Red Meat tobacco, yellow boxes of Arm & Hammer soda, barrels of molasses,
bolts of cloth, gunnysacks of animal feed from his father's mill. The
men behind him had gone quiet. From next door came the metallic
banging of the smithy who rented his place from Cicero; one door
over was the livery that Billie's son Crabtree had been operating
since closing his curio shop—he, too, rented from Cicero.

"I reckon things could be worse," he said. But he didn't believe
it. The grief he felt was like pain—it was exhausting. He had just
enough energy to get dressed and come to work and throw away
the old bottles in a fit of anger, with none left over to talk to his
friends. He spent the morning in the back of the store, and after
going home for his midday dinner he went to bed complaining of
stomach trouble.

MARY BET COULD see him, her father, standing at the mirror in
his room after Annie's funeral. He was holding a small glass down
at his side, the amber liquid glinting in the late afternoon light
from the window, and he was making strange faces at himself and
pulling on his chin so hard she thought he would pull his beard out.
It was the long mirror with beveled edges, set in the walnut wardrobe. He suddenly jabbed a finger at the mirror and said, "I hate
you." He turned and glanced out the window toward the pasture,
then looked back in the mirror. "I could kill you. Why don't you,
then? Shut up! No, *you* shut up!" He walked away from the closet,
and once more turned back to look at himself, shifting the glass to
his right hand. He threw the glass against the mirror.

She would sometimes try to remember what had happened after
that, and it was like trying to remember a thing that hadn't yet
come to pass. As if her memory was what had called it into being.
Or as if she had buried the memory beneath layers and layers of
other dreamlike memories, where she could later retrieve it, if she

could remember the way back. There must have been a shower of glass, a terrific and horrible shattering noise, and perhaps she ran off and hid beneath the house in the dirt where the dogs lay on hot days. She was sure, though, that he had broken the mirror, because she returned to his room once and saw the blank space in the wardrobe, and later she had come back and seen a new mirror, exactly like the first, and she had thought, "Nothing happened at all . . . but I know it did." And she thought that seven years was a long time to have to worry about bad luck—she would be twelve years old, and a lot could happen in that time.

It was shortly after this that she had found the baby rabbit in the woods behind the pasture. She was back there looking for orchids, mindful not to go beyond the' fence to the neighboring pasture where there were bulls. She wouldn't have noticed the movement at the edge of her vision if she hadn't been watching the forest floor with sharp eyes. It was just a flicker of white, and she came over and squatted beside a little round burrow in the soft weeds. There was a baby rabbit—only one, and no mother about, nor a cover for the nest. She knew that mothers sometimes left sick ones behind to die. But this rabbit looked healthy enough; its gray-brown fur was glossy, and the white-tipped hair inside its ears was like cotton. It sniffed her hand.

It was alive.

WILLIE'S COUGH WORSENED during the summer, and Cicero finally resorted to asking Dr. Slocum to stop by. The doctor arrived at suppertime, and, after filling himself with biscuits and cold chicken and dumplings, lumbered upstairs to the room that Willie shared with his brother Tom.

The doctor said he thought Willie just needed to eat more and get more fresh air and exercise, that maybe working in a barn all day wasn't good for his breathing, and that after bathing at night he should keep the windows closed on account of the night vapors carrying germs into your open pores. He *had* lost some weight recently, Cicero and Susan Elizabeth thought. But he seemed to be eating right along. He was tired a lot, but perhaps he was working too hard. They decided to send Mary Bet to her grandparents' for a few days, just in case. She liked the old house, and didn't care that they'd "let it run down," as her mother said.

It was a narrow frame house with a nogging of rock and brickbats between the inner and outer walls, to protect the original owner, John Hartsoe, from rifle fire. It was not known from whose rifle he was protecting himself in 1803, unless it was rebellious slaves or irate neighbors. The second-floor roof was more steeply pitched than the symmetrical roofs over the front porch and back wing, giving the house an angular, tightfisted appearance. After Captain Billie bought the old place, he repainted it, replaced the sagging roof over the porch, and planted fruit trees all about. Before the war, the Governor's Guard appointed Billie captain of the local militia, and he formed a unit he called the Haw Boys. Every Saturday they held drills on his property, no matter the weather. Billie himself was too old for fighting, but when war broke out his unit became Company H of the Twenty-Sixth North Carolina regiment.

Twenty-two years after the war, and one week after the birth of Captain Billie's last grandchild, Mary Bet, the first passenger train came through and stopped at Murchison Crossroad. A café opened up at the train platform, and Captain Billie and Margaret no longer served big meals to hungry travelers. Nobody had time for such things anyway—the train passengers ate on board, or they might get a ham sandwich at the café and take it back on the train. "It was time for us to cut back," Billie told people. Margaret's line was, "Not all progress is progress." Their unmarried son, former postmaster Crabtree, who had been almost single-handedly running the business the last few years, kept it going as a curio shop, selling postcards and rabbits' feet and wooden whistles and other little gifts, and he served Brunswick stew to a few loyal patrons from town. Billie got it in his mind that he could've sold his property to the railroad and become a millionaire. He decided that the Hartsoes had somehow convinced the railroad to bypass his place and so tricked him out of a fortune.

Mary Bet and her mother arrived on Saturday evening, riding the mile in the top-buggy. Grandma Margaret greeted them and ushered them back to the dining room, where Captain Billie and Uncle Crabtree were sitting. Mary Bet's other uncle and aunts had homes of their own. She liked the doting attention of her grandparents, and the way her uncle Crabtree would show her doll how to scale fish. She didn't know that he'd lost some of his hearing—and nearly all his motivation—in a bombshell explosion at Cold Harbor that killed two of his fellow soldiers.

"You're just in time," Billie said, rising unsteadily to his feet. He'd already been downstairs to sample the latest supply of Tennessee sour mash—half a dozen jugs every month, four years now after his business had closed. When the county banned the sale of liquor the last year he was in business, he'd declared his property a municipality, appointed himself mayor and his son treasurer, and the whiskey continued to roll in.

Billie was glowing with goodwill and charm. "The boys are coming over in a little while," he said, "so we'd best pass judgment on your grandma's chess pie before they get here."

Margaret scowled at her husband, and Mary Bet caught the look and the fact that it was meant to be unnoticed. "They need their supper first," she snapped. She smiled graciously at her daughter and granddaughter, determined to continue hosting perfectly as she had for decades in this thin old house that they'd let go to seed until it was in worse shape than when they moved in. She'd covered holes in the walls with photographs of better times, but there were places where you could reach in and pull out chunks of brick and stone if you cared to.

Mary Bet had never been over during one of her grandfather's poker games, but Captain Billie was not about to interrupt his greatest pleasure in life for a small child, no matter how much his wife pleaded and cajoled. "If you get liquored up down there," she warned, "I'll turn them all out. See if I don't."

The men came over after supper. There was Thomas Thomas and his son-in-law Alson Thomas, farmers from out in the country, who came from two different lines of Thomases. Alson tousled Mary Bet's hair and said, "I've got a boy about your age, but no girl. How'd you like to come live with me?" Mary Bet shook her head and half hid behind her grandmother while the men laughed and said what a pretty little thing she was. And there was a man with a big belly and a white beard whose name was Mountain Danny—he had an Irish accent and talked about his preacher father. And, finally, a quiet, baldheaded man named Robert Gray, who never said much, but liked to jingle the coins in his pocket.

The men went down to the cellar, and Mary Bet was sent upstairs to bed. She was staying in her aunt Cattie Jordan's old room, with pretty tulip-patterned wallpaper and lace doilies covering every surface; she was afraid she might break something after her grandmother told her not to touch Cattie Jordan's things. She lay there trying to picture a game that only men played. After a while, she got up and went to her open door. She crept out into the dark hallway and sat on the top step, and imagined that if someone came she'd just say she was scared.

The voices of her mother and grandmother rose from the parlor, twisting and intertwining in a way that was peculiar to them, her mother a soft wind against which her grandmother's high, creaky words were like swift blackbirds sure of their course. Her mother was worried, but tried to sound as if she weren't, and her grandmother flung a pitter-patter of sound against the worry, which only made the wind rise. Mary Bet bumped her bottom down a step, then another. From farther below, as though from deep in the earth, came the muffled voices of the men at their game—a gruff laugh, a jolly whoop. Mary Bet had just learned to tie a bow and she tied and untied the green ribbon on the front of her nightgown as she sat there, bumping down one step after another.

When she was at the bottom she got up and swung herself around the newel post, then walked down the hallway, quiet as a cat. She reached up and fingered the latch to the cellar door, opening it a crack and letting in a whiff of dank air tinged with cigar smoke. She slipped in and took a seat high up the stairs so that by leaning over she could just see the men at their table, perched at angles on loose cane-bottomed chairs. A kerosene lamp, hanging from a joist, cast coal-miner shadows across the men's faces. The pale yellow glow extended not much farther than the table, though she tried to see what was in the dark corners.

"You horse's ass," her grandfather was saying, "you surely don't expect me to fall for that." He was holding some cards, as were the other men, and there was money in the middle of the table. They were drinking whiskey from glasses that sparkled like gold in the lantern light, and sometimes they'd pour more from a brown bottle. "The Devil's own medicine," her grandmother called it, though Mary Bet did not know why. She watched with fascination, not paying much attention to the talk. Then Captain Granddaddy roared, "Goddamn if I ain't the luckiest son of a bitch since Jesus met General Lee," and drew all the money toward himself with two big hands.

Mary Bet sat there feeling her face flame, waiting for the Devil to come take her grandfather away. Surely he would hear the cussing and come for his medicine—how foolish her grandfather had been. She thought it possible she herself would be turned to stone for hearing such a thing. She wanted to leave, but now she was afraid to move and she sat there like a block of ice, hoping that no one, not even the Devil, would know where she was. Her head burned so, it must be close to the furnace of hell already. "God," she prayed, a tear rolling down her cheek, "I promise never to leave my room at night."

The card dealing and wagering went on, with the piles of money growing in front of some of the men and disappearing in front of others with an unseen logic. They kept drinking and getting louder and cussing more freely, and Mary Bet grew so used to the words that they no longer bothered her. She thought the men were like big goats with their beards and something always in their mouths, whether it was cigars or chewing tobacco or whiskey, their heads up and bleating when they wanted something they didn't get. She almost laughed. Suddenly the room got very quiet.

"Son of a bitch did not say that!" Captain Billie drained his glass and poured himself some more, eyeing Alson Thomas the while.

"He did, Captain Billie," Alson said. "As sure as I'm sitting here." He exhaled a stream of smoke from his cheroot.

Billie took a big swallow. "Samuel Hartsoe told you if he was in this game he'd snatch my coat?" He shook his head. "That rat-faced black bastard—why, I thought he spent his Saturday evenings counting his gold." The men burst forth in laughter. Mugs and glasses were refilled. "That old miser's been trying to figure a way to get this house ever since his daddy sold it to me. He thinks it's his."

"Would've been, wouldn't it?" said Thomas Thomas, who was good at pointing out the obvious.

"If his daddy'd wanted to give it to him, he would've," Billie said. "That's Hartsoe business."

They went on with their game, the talk and stories getting more descriptive as the room grew more fogged in smoke and the piles of cash ebbed and flowed. After he'd lost fifty dollars, Robert Gray got up abruptly and left out the back entrance.

Captain Billie became thoughtful. He leaned over and whispered something into his son's ear. "Fellas," he said, "how about we break for a spell. Crabtree's going to fetch a replacement for Robert. I'm feeling prosperous tonight."

Pretty soon Mary Bet could hear his horse trotting down the road toward town, the soft cool air of early fall breathing through the slant-open cellar window, along with a thinned-out chorus of crickets. The men sat and talked about their crops and their animals and the falling price of everything, except for tools and stoves and painted clocks and other such things that were shipped in from the North—you never saw any drop in those prices. She fell asleep, waking up some time later when she heard the clomp-clomping of two horses. She watched as Crabtree came back into view down below, followed by an old man she recognized as her other grandfather.

Samuel Hartsoe was much smaller than Captain Billie, and he moved with the quickness of a younger man. He wore an old black suit, worn through to the lining at the collar and cuffs. His face was a ruin of etchings, his mouth caved in over teeth he had refused to replace, and his long veiny nose curved down and off to the side as if searching for something of value. He kept a gray beard trimmed tight to his face, yet his white eyebrows raged violently across his brow. From where Mary Bet sat, he looked like a dwarf from a fairy tale, and she thought he must know she was watching. The few times she'd seen him in church he'd given her a stern look and said, "Have you read your book, your book?" and then, "Don't be proud, proud." She was scared to say anything, because she wasn't sure what he had really said—her mother told her he had a German accent.

Not until he was seated did Samuel glance at the other men, and then it was only a quick, indifferent look that took in numbers, not faces. He removed his hat, nodded briefly to the others, and pushed back his few strands of yellow hair. "Gentlemen," he said.

"I heard you were in town on business," Billie said, casually. "Thought I'd ask you to join us."

Samuel managed a thin smile. "Draw or stud?" he asked. Now he looked like a skeleton in clothes, gripping the table with a claw. Mary Bet knew he ran a mill where corn was turned into flour and grits. She thought of him as rich, but at the same time, in her mother's words, "as mean as Satan."

He watched as the cards were dealt around. Captain Billie poured him a small glass of whiskey, but he didn't touch it. He picked up his cards and clutched them to his chest, shielding them from view with his other hand. When it was Samuel's turn to deal, Mary Bet was amazed at how nimbly he shuffled the cards, his gnarled hands like a wizard's. She nearly nodded off, listening to the flipping and flopping of the cards against the rough pine table, but she came alert again when there was a hush in the room.

Her uncle was now asleep on a pile of burlap sacks in a corner, and only Alson and her two grandfathers were still playing, piling more and more money in the middle. Then Alson quit and it was just Captain Billie and Samuel Hartsoe, facing each other over their cards. There was lots of talk back and forth, and then Captain Billie said, "I'm staking my property to this hand, Hartsoe. What about you?"

"Let's see the deed," Samuel said.

Captain Billie leaped up from the table, his chair tumbling away. Reaching for the table, he managed to get himself positioned so that he could stagger over to the stair rail. Alson jumped up and went after him, "For godsakes, Captain Billie," he said, "come back here and put down your IOU."

Mary Bet saw her grandfather coming and tried to shrink into the wall. She nearly cried out before he saw her, his eyes narrowing in confusion. But he just pulled past, opened the basement door, and headed into the hallway.

Now she could hear a commotion behind her, while down below Alson was trying to talk Grandpa Samuel out of the bet. "He's not in his right mind when he's drinking," Alson said. "Let's just call it a night. You boys split what's in the pot and that'll be that."

"I didn't ask him to drink," Samuel said. "Matter of fact, he invited me to this game. And, more to the point, ve don't know vhat cards he's holding." He pointed a bony finger to the five over-turned cards at Captain Billie's place. "How can you say who's taking advantage?"

From off beyond the open basement door came the rising voice of Mary Bet's grandmother. "William Murchison, if you go up those stairs you'll be sorry!" There were muffled pleadings from her mother, then the pounding of footsteps and her grandfather roaring back something profane and indecipherable that ended with, ". . . the whole burdensome goddamn lot of you!"

Captain Billie came tearing back down the stairs, stumbled, but caught himself on the handrail. In his free hand was a worn brown envelope, which he smacked onto the card table. He caught his breath. "There's my house, Samuel Hartsoe. I call you."

Grandmother Margaret Murchison then came skipping down the stairs like a young woman. She went to the half-open jug nearest the table, pulled the cork out and pushed it over so that the mouth cracked on the cement floor and amber liquid began leaking out. "There's sin in this house," she said, as though to herself, "and I aim to get it out." She struggled with the cork on the next one, another two-gallon jug, and, failing to loosen it, just turned it over and watched as it rolled toward her husband's chair, off which it bounced before continuing on under the table and coming to rest on Samuel Hartsoe's foot. He had some difficulty pulling himself free.

"What in God's name?" Captain Billie said.

"There's no God in here," his wife said. "So you can cuss him all you want. He won't hear you atall. Go on." She had managed meanwhile to uncork a smaller jug and then decided to just drop it, and she watched satisfied as it broke across the already whiskey-wet floor. Too cowed to interfere, Captain Billie could only stand there as his wife went one by one to the jugs parked against the wall and assaulted them as best she could. When the floor was a smashup of glass and whiskey and rolling jugs and bottles, she paused for breath, hands on her narrow hips, her gray-black hair fallen over her face.

"Well," Captain Billie said, "at least you saved me some."

"Get out!" she yelled. "All of you, get out of my house now!" She pointed up the stairs, where Mary Bet and her mother were huddled, too stunned to move. "And don't you ever come back. You hear? I'll get the constable!" She grabbed the envelope from the table and stuffed it into her blouse, then stood waiting for the men to collect themselves. They traipsed up, heads bowed like scolded boys; Alson paused on the steps to touch his hat to his head. He started to offer an apology, but Margaret cut him off. "Keep on stepping," she said.

Samuel Hartsoe could not simply leave more than two hundred dollars for Billie Murchison, nor could he dip into the pot to extract his share. He glanced down at the two hands of cards, then up to Billie. Billie nodded at him, almost imperceptibly, and as the two men reached for their cards, Margaret threw herself on top of the table, scattering cards and money all over the sticky floor.

The men went down on hands and knees, grabbing up what bills they could, not caring how wet they were, and stuffing them into pockets. "For shame," Margaret said, "for shame."

Crabtree woke up. He rolled over, sniffed the pool of whiskey in front of his face, and regarded his father and Samuel Hartsoe crawling around on the floor. When Margaret saw him, she went and stood over him a moment as if undecided. Then she bent down and tugged at his elbow. "Come on, son," she said. "Get you upstairs." He rose and walked with his mother to the steps. The last thing Mary Bet saw before her own mother whisked her off to her bedroom was her two grandfathers getting up, brushing themselves off wordlessly, and looking at each other as if there was nothing they could ever say about what they had just done.

In the morning the house was so quiet all Mary Bet could hear when she came downstairs was the ticking of the tall-case clock. She opened the cellar door and slowly descended. Shafts of light from the half-window revealed a clean-swept room that looked as though no business of any sort had been conducted there of late. There were things she didn't want to remember, but they were inside her mind and so they had to be real.

∽ CHAPTER 3 ∾

1893–1895

MARY BET STAYED with her grandparents for two weeks, during which her brother got sicker and sicker. It began to seem as if Willie had always been sick. He was eighteen and a string bean, their mother said, and he could walk on his hands and recite *Julius Caesar* at the same time, rolling over when he came to "all of us fell down." He had green eyes and he brought home orphaned squirrels and rabbits and other animals he found out in the woods.

Finally, on an Indian summer day in late September, he died, and there was another funeral to attend. This time Mary Bet was allowed to go to both the funeral and burial, and she could not understand why she had not been allowed at the funeral of her sister—it was just like a church service, except that her mother was crying, as were her sisters, O'Nora and Myrtle Emma. Myrtle Emma, who was fourteen and a good singer and pianist, let her play with her cameo brooch, which made Mary Bet very happy, though she could not help crying a little herself because Myrt seemed so sad.

On Sundays they went to the new Baptist church in town, but for funerals they went to Love's Creek north of town, where the ancestors were buried. The preacher said that Annie had been so lonely in heaven that her twin brother had to go up there and keep her company. Mary Bet pictured God calling Willie from a magnificent bank of sunlit purple clouds, and Annie there waiting for him. Outside, the men lowered the coffin on ropes and then everybody came back to the Hartsoes' for refreshments. The women brought platters of fried chicken and roast beef, sliced ham and biscuits, vegetable casseroles, deviled eggs, cucumbers, and pies and cakes, and Essie, who had attended the funeral, was back in the kitchen in her apron stirring pitchers of iced tea and lemonade. But hardly anybody touched the food.

"There's a reason for everything," her mother said. "Everything under the sun is God's will and we have to accept it." Usually something had gone wrong when she said this, and her lips would tighten, as they would when she didn't approve of things.

Mary Bet still thought of her family as the ten fingers of her hands—her father was her right thumb, her mother the left. Then there was eldest sister Ila (a beautiful young woman engaged to be married to the eldest son of Robert Gray) and big brother Tom (the tallest finger), both on her right hand, then Willie and Annie—the weak fourth fingers who were in heaven. Myrtle Emma and Siler were younger, so they were on the left hand; Siler was special because he had come to replace the other Siler who was in heaven, and he was also deaf. O'Nora and Mary Bet were the baby fingers.

She still prayed for Willie and Annie in her prayers at night. It felt to her as though something were missing, her own fingers or her hand. She felt as if God had robbed the family, but she didn't like to talk about sad things, because it made other people sad.

Everyone wore black for a long time after the funeral, and the person who wore it the longest was Mary Bet's mother. It seemed as if she had always worn black and always would—long black dresses and black high-shouldered jackets on Sundays and black pleated skirts and blouses around the house. So that it came as a surprise to see any bit of color at all—a navy blue blouse, or a bit of purple in her scarf, as if a long winter was finally thawing and the crocuses were coming out again.

Willie had brought home a crow with a broken wing. The bird would hop along a perch Willie had fashioned from a green stick and nailed to an eave in the hen coop. It would chortle at the hens, eyeing them with its head tilted. Sometimes it would flap down for some grain, scattering the chickens, and then use its beak and feet to climb the wire mesh back up to its perch. It was given a separate, smaller enclosure. Since she was now six years old, Mary Bet inherited the job of taking care of the crow, which merely meant giving it fresh water, because whoever grained the chickens would toss some grain over to the crow.

She was afraid of the crow, but she tried to be brave because it was an honor to do something for her departed brother. The crow would see her coming and would watch her out of one beady black eye. She discovered that she could wait for several days before adding more water. When the crow sickened and lost its luster, no one said anything but that it missed Willie and, anyway, they never expected a wild bird to live long in a cage.

She spent a night at her grandmother's and when she came back she was busy with her new hobby of threading needles and sewing patches together for a doll quilt. When she went near the coop, the bird gave her an accusing look, and she was afraid even to use the stick to turn the old water out.

After a while the water turned stale and green. The crow sat on his perch and no longer squawked at her or at anything. Sometimes he rustled his dull feathers in the sun. She decided that the crow was sick for some other reason and that when he hobbled about his cage, eyeing her with his now milky eye, he was blaming her. Then one night she heard a long low *caaaaw*. The next day she thought she might have dreamed the sound, yet when she went out to the crow's enclosure it was empty. No one said a thing at breakfast, but later on Siler told her, in his back-of-the-throat voice, "Ya caw's daahd." No one had ever called it hers before.

"Do the chickens need fresh water?" she asked, thinking that he would never guess why she was asking.

He looked at her, his dark brooding eyes piercing her, and pointed to her lips. She repeated it while he held her jaw, then shook his head in confusion. He touched his open palm, "Show me." He was five years older than Mary Bet and already skilled with his hands. He could repair chairs and tables and fashion toy tops and soldiers as quickly as anybody. His tutor had given him some basic signs so that he could talk with his family. At the deaf-and-dumb school in Raleigh, if he used his hands to talk he had to sit on them; if he used them again that day the teacher rapped him on the knuckles with a ruler, or tied his hands behind his back. He was sent home halfway through the term for hitting a baseball through a window and refusing to say "I'm sorry."

Siler studied Mary Bet's lips, held her jaw and made her repeat the question. She pointed to the well, then to the chicken coop. She dropped her arms and pouted. You couldn't ask a roundabout question of Siler—you had to say what you meant. His eyes brightened, then narrowed as he studied her. He nodded, "Yah." He put bird-beak fingers at his mouth, crooked a finger down, then touched W fingers to his lip. "Birds need water."

Though she had just begun to learn her own alphabet, she knew what he meant. His whole face explained that it was a stupid question, that of course they needed fresh water, every single day.

It was the next spring when the hanging of Shackleford Davies took place on Gallows Hill in Williamsboro. It also happened to be a market day and so Mary Bet was allowed to ride the thirteen miles over to the county seat—starting at six in the morning got them there just past nine. The frost on the ground had melted by the time they arrived, but they still needed coats and sweaters and bonnets.

When they got there, carriages were already parked solid half a mile west of the courthouse. Cicero found a colored boy to mind the horse, then they began walking, the crowd getting thicker as they approached. They took their time, Cicero limping along with his peg leg and walking stick. The courthouse looked to a small girl like a castle, its cupola rising in three layers from the roof; but its pillars and pediments sent a sterner message than the turrets and arches of fairy tales—justice was the center of the county, not silly romance. And today there was punishment and revenge in the air, and the excitement frightened her.

They began walking north. Throngs three and four people deep lined the wooden sidewalks along the two blocks of downtown and spilled into the road. Mary Bet asked her father to lift her up on his shoulders so she could see, but he was crippled and she knew better than to ask.

Then shouts arose and people said he was coming. Mary Bet worked her way through the sea of legs until she was at the edge of the street, and she could hear iron wheel rims grinding, hoofbeats drumming closer. And right then came two men mounted on big black horses, one of the men wearing a metal star on his jacket, and behind them a cart pulled by a mule. In the cart sat a man in a black suit and a wide-brimmed hat. His face was shaded so that Mary Bet could not see his eyes, but he seemed to be squinting into the sunless sky. She shivered when he looked in her direction. It was the Devil again, Mary Bet felt certain. But then she was not so sure, because his hands were bound together in his lap. She watched him as he swayed, perched on a long yellow pine box.

Some people yelled out mean things, but most watched and talked and laughed, as if they were at a parade. Mary Bet felt a shivering tingle run all the way from the back of her neck to the base of her spine. Maybe he *was* the Devil, and he wouldn't die from the hanging. People said he'd come from the west, from Tennessee, where he'd been a preacher, and he'd gotten a job on a farm up near Silkton. But he wouldn't do what the farmer asked him to, and when the farmer told him to leave, he took a hand ax and chased him out to a field. Then he chopped him until he was dead.

Mary Bet could see this man wasn't the same as the preacher in the road, because he had lighter hair and he was shorter and thicker. But the Devil could change shape, and it could be that he was after her for killing the crow. Now she was back with her family and they were caught up in the crowd as it followed the bad man's carriage. She took Myrtle Emma's hand—Myrt was her favorite now that Annie was dead. Myrt scolded her for running off.

Her father chuckled and said, "I thought they'd taken you to Gallows Hill."

But Mary Bet didn't think it was funny and she blushed. She was guilty, and if she didn't mend her ways she would end up just like the bad man. "Do they ever hang girls?" she asked her sister.

Myrtle Emma laughed and said, "What a silly question, Mary Bet. Of course not. They don't hang women either, unless they're very very bad."

"What do you mean?"

"I guess if a woman killed somebody, she could be hanged, but I don't want to think about it."

"Neither do I," Mary Bet said, but she did think about it. She knew that Shackleford Davies was guilty of murder, as well as robbery and incest. "What's incest?" she asked.

"Hush now," her sister said.

"I don't want to go to the gallows," Mary Bet said, for she was worried now that they would follow the crowd. It was sure to be a long walk, and she did not want to see a man hanged from a rope.

Myrtle Emma laughed again and lifted her sister up by her armpits so that she was looking straight into her face. "You're as good as pie," she said. "You're never going to the gallows, ever."

She wanted to tell her sister about the crow. But she was afraid. Perhaps Myrtle Emma already knew and had forgiven her, or perhaps the family had met and decided it was not her fault after all. She was still the baby, and always would be.

Myrtle Emma took her father's hand and said, "Can we go to Pfifer's?"

Cicero slowed and looked at his children, his beard like a buffalo's, and said, "Isn't it too early for ice cream?"

"We should go now before all that crowd comes back," Myrtle Emma suggested.

"That's a right smart idea," he said. "I promised your mother I wouldn't take you to any hanging, and here we were going along like we were off to the circus." The crowd surged by.

And then they were heading back into town, Mary Bet riding like a possum baby on Siler's back. There were other people who didn't want to go see the hanging. Her father stopped and talked with several men wearing nice clothes, jackets and ties, not like the farm people in tattered clothes who had been surrounding them. But there had also been nicely dressed people who wanted to go see that horrible ugly thing. Why would they want to?

Siler stood straight, until she was clinging to his neck, her pink dress up over her knees, and she no longer felt like a possum baby. "Pigback," she said, but he had shaken her off and she had to walk. And then they were in Pfifer's, where the floor was all tiny white and black tiles, and there were fans high up in a white pressed-tin ceiling. And they sat in a big wooden booth and ordered fancy ice creams. All five of them—her father, Myrtle Emma, Siler, O'Nora, and herself.

"Don't tell your mama about this," her father said, winking at her. Then, "You want chocolate this time?"

She shook her head and said, "Vanilla." Which made him and the others laugh, and she blushed. She thought she should be more grown up next time, but she liked the eggy-sweet taste of vanilla. And when the cone came she forgot that she was embarrassed, and she licked it to a smooth ball like Siler did, except without the slurping noise, because her mother said it was rude but that Siler couldn't help it. Her father was talking about the price of milk and how corn and wheat and cotton were falling dangerously, and she thought it had to be one of those things that grown-ups worried about. Maybe somewhere corn and cotton were falling, but she could see out the window that they weren't falling here. She closed her eyes quickly and thought, "Please, God, don't let corn and cotton fall, amen."

Siler tried to follow what the others were saying. He was the only boy at the table, Tom having stayed at home because he was grown up and had a job, and Ila because she was visiting with her fiancé. O'Nora said that if the farms failed the factories would fill in. Cicero tilted his head in that funny way that made everybody laugh and said, "How does a ten-year-old girl know more than the idlers down at my store?"

Mary Bet was sure it was something O'Nora had heard at school, and now Siler wanted to know what it was. Cicero turned to Myrtle Emma, who could spell with her hands faster and knew more signs than any of them, and she translated. Siler nodded and smiled his thin-lipped half-smile, as though he understood everything, whether he did or not.

Market day was ending with ice cream, when it could've ended with a hanging. Mary Bet was bursting to tell everybody how happy she felt. She wanted to tell about the crow and the bad man and how cold it had been, but how after they had turned back to the confectionary the sun had started coming out and it had made her feel safe and hopeful. Her mother had recently stopped tucking her in at night and kissing her forehead and saying, "I love you, darling." Her father still called her "baby girl" sometimes, when he was in a happy mood. She wanted to say that she loved her family and her place in it, and that she loved being alive on such a nice day with friendly people all around. Finally, she said, "This is a nice outing after all."

Her father laughed and pinched her cheek a little and said, "Yes it is, but you oughten tempt fate." He rapped his knuckles on the table, and she picked her father's hand up in both of hers. It was heavy and warm, mottled and bristly on the back but worn smooth as a river stone on the palm. If only she could protect it from danger and worry—and anger, too—then she would feel safe.

ALL THROUGH THAT summer and fall and well into the next spring, no one was sick in the Cicero Hartsoe family. Ila's wedding was fast approaching, was, in fact, only two weeks away when she took to her bed with a fever. When it was clear she was not going to make a quick recovery, the wedding was put off a month. Robert Gray's son visited every day to see how his bride was faring. She would smile and lift her head from the pillow, and take his hand in hers. Mary Bet combed her hair out for her the way she had for Annie. Though she had never felt as close to Ila as to Annie—for Ila was a grown woman with her own concerns and more often than not away in some village teaching poor children how to read—she did admire her oldest sister. She had long jet-black hair, the same color as her own, and Mary Bet had decided to let her hair grow down to her waist, if her mother would let her.

It was at this time that Mary Bet's mother, perhaps feeling that her purpose in life was over (her childbearing days past, and child-rearing nearly so), took to sitting on the porch in a rocking chair with not so much as a pot of snap beans to occupy her hands. She would stare down toward the little valley the creek made just north of the house, as though she could see fairies playing there.

Cicero took it upon himself to try to cheer her out of her spells. "You can't help it, Sue Bet," he'd say, "your father had his spells." It was well known that Captain Billie had run out of his house during one drunken raving, hollering, "Boys, it's time! Grab your guns!" And once he went outside to feed his chickens in nothing but boots and an umbrella. But that was all before he nearly gambled his house away; since then, he'd reformed. And his earlier episodes had been put down to drink, not actual lunacy. The real craziness in the family was rumored to be buried away on the Hartsoe side.

The spells that had suddenly descended upon Susan Elizabeth seemed to Cicero a case of preemptive melancholia—staking out the blue arena for herself meant that no one else, particularly himself, could indulge in sadness. It also was a way of telling God to pass over this house—there was enough suffering here. "I don't know what I'll do if Ila dies," she said, rocking and staring, rocking and staring. "I just don't."

"Hush now," Cicero said.

"I ought to be doing some needlework," Susan Elizabeth said. "Something with my hands, but I just cain't make myself do a thing. Do you have anything I could take?"

"Nothing that works," he told her. He sometimes wondered if she felt she'd been a disappointment to him, with the Murchison name falling out of favor around town. He'd had to reassure her many times that she was a good wife and that he didn't care a fig about the reputation of her father, one way or the other. He had an idea. "I might have some Hystoria that could help," he said.

"What would I need that for?" She gave him a funny look. "My time's long gone."

"It's good for all kind of complaints, not just women's." He'd slowly been restocking some of the items he'd thrown out. It was hard to argue with customers—was it, after all, wrong that their faith gave the medicine its power?

"I'll try it, then," she rejoined, still looking at him skeptically.

Two spoonfuls a day of the vegetable compound did a miraculous job of restoring Susan Elizabeth to full health, which was a good thing, as Ila needed the mothering care that only she could provide. Cicero had begun to feel assailed on every front. His father-in-law's affairs had become entangled in outrageous investment schemes— all efforts to become fantastically rich, when what he needed to do was sell half his property just to keep his house. Crabtree would never be able to help, and his other son, Cincinnatus, was struggling to provide for his own family by running a little store in Fuquay-Varina. It would be up to Cicero to provide for his wife's parents. But he had his own concerns, and he had no interest in spending what little he'd saved to bail Captain Billie out of foolishness. He'd wanted to study law, but he'd waited too long for that; he'd tried writing poetry and found it devilishly hard. Now he just wanted to see more of the world, so he had a notion he might someday close his shop and travel around, selling things from town to town, just like the men who sold him nostrums and household wares.

On the day in May that she was to have been married, Ila asked her mother to read to her from Keats and Wordsworth. The poems soothed her, especially coming from her mother's lips. Susan Elizabeth was a good reader, even of things she professed were trivial in comparison with scripture. Mary Bet came in and lay on the floor, as she had during Annie's illness, listening to the restorative words, then stood by her sister's pillow combing her hair.

That night Ila died. In the morning Cicero went out back to the icehouse, and he put his head into the darkness and howled. He tore at his beard and slapped his face, and he went down on his knees and moaned in such a pitiful way that his wife came out and knelt beside him. She put her arm around him and said the Lord's Prayer, until he was mumbling it along with her.

"Why?" he said. "Why am I afflicted so?" Susan Elizabeth could only shake her head and stifle a sob. "Why is misfortune and sadness my perpetual lot? My firstborn daughter before her own wedding to be carried off, and us visited with sorrow again? There is no God."

Mary Bet, O'Nora, and Myrtle Emma were also kneeling together, in the bedroom they shared, looking down through the open window onto their parents, while in the room across the hall their sister lay unmoving, her face not yet covered. They'd gone in there together and peeked because no one had told them not to, and their father had cast out the doctor from the house and the undertaker had not yet arrived.

"We should go sit with Ila," Myrtle Emma said.

But O'Nora didn't want to move; she was curious about things and how they worked. She once watched in fascination as a snake slithered up a holly tree to take the eggs in a bird's nest, while Myrtle Emma turned away in disgust. Now they watched their mother go over to the well to pump water into a basin, and they heard their father say, "Why am I to be tested so? Why must you torment my family? Have I done something to displease you?"

Susan Elizabeth came back carrying the basin with some difficulty, because it was large enough to bathe a small child in, and she poured the water over her husband's head. He wiped the water from his face and said something the girls couldn't hear, and his wife helped him to his feet. They stood there holding each other like clasped hands, their faces not visible.

"Let's go sit with Ila," Myrtle Emma insisted.

Mary Bet didn't want to go back in the dead room, but she didn't want to be alone either, so she went in with her sisters. They all took another glance at Ila, who looked only as if she were asleep, and then Mary Bet went over and kissed her on the cheek, half hoping she would wake up. Her sisters did the same.

They sat on the floor, Mary Bet feeling proud of doing something that her sisters wanted to copy. But she was worried about what her father had just said. She wanted to tell them what she had seen that time—how he had yelled at himself in the mirror and thrown the glass—but she thought she'd best keep it to herself. "Do you think Daddy's going to hell?"

"No," Myrtle Emma said quickly. "He didn't mean it. He knows there's a God. Ila's with him now."

"What's heaven like?" she said.

Both her sisters were quiet for a moment. Then Myrtle Emma said, "Oh, it's beautiful. I've seen it in a dream."

"You can't see heaven in any dream," O'Nora corrected her older sister. "You can't see the real heaven until you get there."

"And when we get there we'll see Ila," Mary Bet said, "and Willie and Annie. And Siler."

"But not for a long time," Myrtle Emma said. She smiled in a sad way that made Mary Bet feel suddenly cold; she huddled next to her sister and with her other hand tried to pull O'Nora closer, as though her sisters were covers. She wanted to stay like this, between her sisters, and never have to go to any more funerals. She closed her eyes. "I promise to be an old maid all my life," she prayed to herself, "and read the whole Bible, if you don't take any more of us."

Later, when she was alone, she squatted down in front of the little fireplace in the bedroom so that she could see her guardian angels, embossed on the iron fireback. Just the barest outlines of a face and halo and wings, but they were her secret angels. "Did you hear what I prayed?" she whispered. She nodded, knowing they'd heard and would protect her.

That night she dreamed of rabbits leaping over each other in a strange dance and beating their strong hind legs on the ground and baring their teeth. She woke up afraid and called out for Myrtle Emma. But everything was quiet, and she would be brave and go back to sleep and try not to think about her dream.

~◡ CHAPTER 4 ◠~

1895–1897

B Y LATE SPRING Captain Billie's speculations had made him
rich in paper certificates and so poor in real money that he was
two months behind on his property taxes. A county tax collector paid a visit to the Murchison house to see what could be done.
He found that the owner, William Murchison, contrary to what
he had been told, was not at all a drink-besotted, short-tempered,
untucked, unshaven old man. He was in fact a jolly, portly, be-
spectacled gentleman, who greeted him at the door wearing a tie
and suspenders, and invited him into the parlor for coffee. After a
few polite words, during which Captain Billie assured the short,
bald man from Durham that, yes, his family was fine and, no, he
needn't worry about the taxes, Captain Billie asked, "Aren't there
enough people up in Durham delinquent on their taxes to bother?"

"Yessir, there are plenty," the man said, "but I cover six counties." Sitting on the edge of the brown plush sofa, he opened up a new-looking
leather briefcase and pulled out some papers and began to speak.

"Before you begin," Billie interrupted, "I need to ask you an important question." The man raised his eyebrows. "Have you read this book?" Holding up his Bible.

The tax collector nodded slowly, confused at first. Something of the old fire returned to the Captain's eyes, as though he were about to burst into a tirade. He checked himself and smiled, gripping the arms of his wingback chair and leaning forward so that his tie dangled. "It's not a hard question, Mr. Throckmorton," he said. "Do you know Matthew six?"

"I'm not sure—"

"No man can serve two masters," Captain Billie recited, "for he will hate the one, and love the other. Therefore take no thought for your life, what ye shall eat, or what ye shall drink, nor yet for your body, what ye shall put on."

"I understand, Mr. Murchison. But to get back for a moment to the unpaid balance on your bill." He looked sadly at the piece of paper in his hand, as if there might be some script there he could follow in such a case as this. "The county would hate to have to assess a penalty, and unless we can get a guarantee from your bank—"

"Mr. Throckmorton, I don't think you're following me here. I ask you to consider the lilies of the field, how they grow. They toil not, neither do they spin. Isn't that a beautiful sentiment?"

"Yes, sir, it is," Throckmorton said, leaning back with a sigh. He took another sip of coffee and hunched his shoulders.

"I can see I've got your attention now, and I'm almost to the end: Therefore take no thought of what you shall eat or drink, but seek ye first the kingdom of God and his righteousness, Mr. Throckmorton. Take no thought for the morrow, for sufficient unto the day is the evil thereof. Which I take to mean worldly things, like that paper you're holding there. I can't very well serve two masters. That's why I gave up drinking and cards and such. You might say, Well, Captain Billie, you're an old man, about to meet your maker.

That's easy for you, but not so easy for a younger man. Huh?" He stared hard at Throckmorton.

The agent shook his head and tried to smile. "I didn't say anything."

"Judge not, that ye be not judged, Mr. Throckmorton. Those aren't my words. I'm just telling you what's in the Bible, right out of Jesus's mouth."

"So are you going to work with me on this, Mr. Murchison? Because, if not, there will be a penalty." Throckmorton sat up, an idea illuminating his dull features. "And you know what comes after that. A man like you doesn't want to have to go to court."

"I would urge you, son, with everything in my soul, to go home right now. Just drop everything you're doing, and pick up your Bible. Do you have one?"

"Yes, sir."

"Good, go on now and do what I say. Start in reading anywhere, and pray, and go to church. And for godsakes, don't slouch."

The agent smiled tolerantly as he stood, folded the bill and shoved it back in his pocket; he then let Captain Billie usher him out to the front porch. After he put his hat on, he stood a moment as though he wanted to say something else. "Doesn't Jesus say," he began, "that you should render unto Caesar the things that are Caesar's? So if there's money belonging to the government, he says it's all right to pay it."

"You're very wise, Mr. Throckmorton, for somebody who's spent so much time studying on commerce. And you might have a point, but for one thing." And now Billie locked eyes with Throckmorton. "I don't have the money. So Caesar must already have it. Look around and ask yourself if you're in the home of a rich man who ought to pay money to the government, when that same government saw fit to run a train up yonder and leave me high and dry. And now the state is paying veteran's benefits, but not a nickel have

I seen of that. Why? I'll tell you why. Because I was too old to get out and fight, though I did my share of training up a whole regiment's worth of young men to fight, and I kept law and order here when they were gone off. Now I ask you, isn't that worth a few coins?"

Throckmorton started to speak again, then, thinking better of it, he shook Captain Billie's hand and said an impassive, "Good-bye, Mr. Murchison."

"I'll see what I can do about rendering unto Caesar," Billie told him. "We've hit a rough patch, but with God's help we'll weather it." Throckmorton was already on the walkway when Billie called after him that he would find the money and pay, sell off his last horse if he had to, but first he had to have a sign. Then he told Margaret he was unwell and he went upstairs to his bed.

Mary Bet learned of her grandfather's newfound religion during an extended stay there that summer, this time because her mother had become gravely ill with typhoid. "Your mama will not beat me to the grave," Captain Billie told her. The words gave her no comfort, coming from a man whose eyes drooped like teardrops and who walked now with a cane, when he walked at all. She spent a good part of the summer memorizing long passages from the Bible. When she wanted relief from this work, she went out to help Aunt Scilla, the cook, make chocolate layer cakes, which Captain Billie ate every day. She did not question why O'Nora and Myrtle Emma were allowed to stay at home and wait on their mother. Two girls were enough, she reasoned, and at eight years old she was more susceptible, though she would have preferred waking up in bed with O'Nora.

Death had become as much a part of Mary Bet's life as going to church and school, or feeding her grandparents' fowl, or sweeping their back stoop, or helping Uncle Crabtree milk the cow. Death was an unwelcome cousin from another state who had taken up residence. And death was a secret between herself and her imaginary friend, Netty, and Netty knew far more about death than anybody—she knew what lay beyond the sundown world of the forest west of town. She would take Mary Bet's hand as they lay in bed and offer to fly her there, but Mary Bet would find excuses. Not this time, she would say—I can't go out in the night air in my nightie. Not just yet, I didn't finish my prayers. No, I'm not ready.

In the mornings she would pretend not to notice Netty; she would dress in a hurry and rush downstairs to help Mama Margaret turn the bacon. Aunt Scilla came only three days a week now, and it was very quiet in the mornings in her grandparents' house. Her uncle got up early to go down to the livery; her grandfather woke only to eat breakfast with his son, then went back to bed and slept until nearly noon. He spent the rest of the day reading his Bible, moving his lips and sometimes whispering the words. Mama Margaret had made him quit reading aloud, saying it was bad for his blood pressure, but she confided to Mary Bet that it was too much like being in church all day.

Mary Bet thought she was too old for Netty, so she didn't tell anybody about her. Not even her little cousins, who sometimes came over. Mary Bet didn't care much for these cousins—they only wanted to go dig worms and make mud pies down in the creek—but she would tend them for a nickel, sometimes pulling them around in a red wagon all afternoon.

Best of all was when she and Mama Margaret would sit in the parlor sewing—mending tears, hemming dresses, making clothes for her two dolls. Sometimes her grandmother would hide her thimble in plain sight, and Mary Bet would have to find it; then she would beg her grandmother to hide it again while she closed her eyes.

Her mother died on a Sunday morning in late July, and she knew it as soon as she opened her eyes. She would not get out of bed, though Netty told her it was time to get up. "Sshhh!" Mary Bet scolded, "you leave me alone now."

After church, her grandmother came in and sat beside her and put an arm around her. "It's all right, honey, it's all right. Your mother's in heaven and she loves you."

Mary Bet thought way back to one of her earliest memories, of standing at the edge of Annie's grave, holding Ila's hand. Then Ila herself had died, because life was fragile, a gift, not something you could ever take for granted—the Lord could redeem it back, suddenly, suddenly. And she recalled how after Ila died her mother had less love to give away, and how she had scolded Cicero and wouldn't speak to him for days after he broke her grandmother's milk pitcher; and Mary Bet had thought, "I will never be like that." Her mother would sit stiff and stern in church, hands folded in her lap, tolerating no whispering or movement of any kind. She used to kneel beside Mary Bet at her nightly prayers, listening as Mary Bet prayed aloud. And on Saturday night, she let Mary Bet rinse out her long black hair as she knelt over the washbasin, her eyes closed, her large bosom wrapped in towels. She was kind to the animals, making sure they were fed before anyone else, and nursing the sick ones with more care and devotion, Mary Bet had sometimes thought, than she gave her own children. Still, Mary Bet had never felt any cruelty from her mother, and though her mother's love was not as abundant and generous as her father's, it was yet love.

For weeks no one could coax a word from Mary Bet. She was afraid to speak, afraid that the Devil would come and take her away if she opened her mouth to say anything. It seemed there were crows everywhere that summer—squawking somewhere in the distance, flapping their black capes up to roosts on high dead limbs, perched in the trees outside her window, clicking and jabbering like crazy people, watching her and waiting. She talked mostly with Siler, using her hands in the way he and her mother had taught her. "Make it go away with your slingshot," she told him. But he only laughed and patted her head, telling her it was bad luck to shoot a crow.

One morning Cicero asked her, "Would you like to go back and stay with your grandparents for a time?"

Mary Bet shook her head. "No," she said, "I want to stay here."

Cicero nodded. "Well, child," he said. "I'm glad to hear your tongue still works."

She talked incessantly after that, to anyone who would listen, including a stray puppy she found behind a neighbor's house and gave to Siler. She talked about the weather and her sewing and the book she was reading that featured a girl who lost a silver dollar her mother gave her and had the hardest time finding it. There was nothing she wouldn't talk about if you got her going, until Cicero wondered if she wasn't talking so she wouldn't have anything else in her mind to trouble her. Perhaps that was a good thing.

The next spring, her oldest brother, Tom, got married; Captain Billie rapidly declined; and Cicero expanded his store to the rear. For now that his wife was dead he could not simply abandon his children and go rambling around the countryside.

Captain Billie no longer got out of bed at all. He would sit up and shout orders as though he were drilling the Haw Boys on the front lawn. Margaret hobbled up the stairs three times a day with a tray of food. In his final week he said he craved nothing so much as a final taste of Tennessee sour mash whiskey, which Margaret refused to supply him.

Finally, she broke down and went to Cicero's store and asked him for a small bottle. Nobody but moonshiners sold liquor in Hartsoe City, but Cicero had a few bottles he kept hidden in the back of his store—gifts from customers who were cash poor. He gave her one as a present. She got home with her package and slipped the little flat bottle from its paper sack, the label with its wicked handwritten script spelling out ruination in honeyed words.

She twisted off the top, breaking the seal and releasing the sharp yeasty sweet smell of the whiskey. She wrinkled up her nose in disgust, pouring a small glassful, for she had no idea how much constituted a proper drink. Thinking she'd put in too much, she considered returning some to the bottle. It would be easier to pour it out, but that would be a waste. She put the glass to her lips and tasted it. Sherry wine on special occasions was the strongest stuff she'd ever had, and since banning all liquor from her house she had not even touched fruitcake moistened with rum.

The whiskey was warming at the first sip, sliding down her throat like a golden spike. She smacked her lips and took another sip—the taste of men and drunken revelry filled her with a satisfying revulsion. She understood at last why men drank it so greedily, but as to why they became slaves to it (and some women too), she could not fathom. It seemed such a pointless thing to devote one's life to. She held it up to the window so that it caught the late afternoon light like water and took one more little gulp, shivered, and carried the rest up to her husband.

Captain Billie, propped up like a grimacing mummy with bristly gray eyebrows and beard, reached a feeble, shaking hand out for the elixir. His once-bulging midsection was deflated now to a shriveled pouch. Margaret had to wrap her hand around his as he drew the glass to his lips. Then he shook his head and pushed her hand away with murmured protest. He touched the liquid to his lips, then stopped. "Get thee away," he said, and tossed the glass down on his quilt that his mother had made for them as a wedding gift. The stain spread quickly over the green-and-yellow-check pattern.

He died that night with Margaret sitting beside him in the bed, the quilt drying over the end of the footboard. She sat beside him until he no longer felt warm, and then she went and roused Crab-tree. It was just after one in the morning.

Margaret no longer wanted to stay in the house, so she sold it, paid off the back taxes and penalties that her husband had made a religion of ignoring, and went to live with Cincinnatus's wife and children in Fuquay-Varina, where nobody knew that he had never enlisted in the war because he didn't believe in fighting. Crabtree moved away to Slocum, and a family from Elizabethtown bought the old house and painted it and fixed it up so that it was hardly recognizable anymore as the old Murchison place. But Mary Bet would remember it all her life.

Her brother Tom got pneumonia early the next year and died, just before their grandmother Margaret, who did not survive her husband by so much as a year. All that were left now were Cicero and his youngest son, Siler, and his three youngest girls.

Cicero let his beard grow long, though it was no longer the fashion, so long that he tucked it into his shirt front. He went to work every morning except Sunday and came home, feeling older and more bent over nearly every day. His friends told him to take another wife. "Don't know one that'll have me," was his response. "Not with my luck."

Her family was diminished, but even so, the next three years were among the happiest in Mary Bet's life, and it seemed as though they could go on living that way for a long time.

1897–1899

A S THOUGH AFRAID their baby sister might die young, Myrtle Emma and O'Nora doted on Mary Bet as they would a cherished plaything, dressing her up in their old Sunday clothes, or taking her temperature if she had the slightest bit of flush to her face. Sometimes Myrt gave her a plaster of camphor left over from Ila's illness. She would smear the fragrant oily paste on Mary Bet's bare chest, then drape a fresh sheet lightly over her, and Mary Bet would lie on her pillow inhaling the nasal-clearing, hot, piney scent and feel as if she were floating in the clouds. Her sisters would wait on her until she grew so restless she got up and ran downstairs and out into the fresh air.

"Mary Bet," Myrtle Emma said, for she was now the oldest at seventeen, "you get back in the bed until I say."

"You're not my mother," Mary Bet replied.

"But you're not well enough to be out. You're sensitive."

Mary Bet smiled prettily at her sister, because she didn't like to contradict her, but really Myrt had nothing to worry about and she ought to know better since she was almost a grown woman. Mary Bet felt her own forehead. "I'm fine," she said.

"But you'll get your dress dirty."

"It's O'Nora's, and she doesn't mind." It was the smallest possible lie—Mary Bet couldn't remember any such permission, but it sounded like something O'Nora would grant. O'Nora was a tomboy who still climbed trees at thirteen.

"It's yours now, Mary Bet. You have to learn to take care of your things." Myrt was quoting their mother and talking in a bossy way—both habits that annoyed Mary Bet.

"I don't need anything nice," Mary Bet said. She shook her head so that the coiled braids Myrt had fixed for her swished against her neck.

"Don't say that, dearest. Don't ever. Everybody needs nice things." Mary Bet looked up and saw that her sister's eyes were glistening; it made her own eyes water. Pretty soon they were both laughing at their foolishness and swinging each other around and around, hand in hand, and Mary Bet wondered if she would ever be as tall and lovely as Myrtle Emma, who could play the piano as if she were playing a harp, her long slender hands flowing gracefully over the keys. She had a narrow waist and a pronounced bustline, and though she claimed her eyes were bug eyes, Mary Bet thought her face was beautiful. Mary Bet had often admired her when she was dressing, and Myrtle Emma said, "You're going to have a right smart figure. I can tell." Which made Mary Bet giggle—but she thought that Myrt must be telling the truth, for why would she fib about that? O'Nora could only look from one to the other of her sisters, shake her head, and say, "I'd rather be strong than pretty." The irony was that she was the most naturally beautiful of all Cicero's children, with snapping blue eyes, sharply defined cheekbones, perfect skin, and dark reddish hair that she kept bobbed and unadorned.

O'Nora liked to go out hunting with Cicero and Siler. She rode horseback with them, wearing a baggy pair of Tom's old riding britches she'd altered and not minding the looks she got from neighbors and farmers. In an old hunting jacket and with her hair tucked beneath a slouch hat, she sometimes went unnoticed out to the cut fields, where she used her father's sixteen-gauge over-and-under to bring down doves and quail. She was a better shot than her father, nearly as good as Siler, which kept him in a nervous state of concentration during their outings.

Mary Bet wanted to be like both of her sisters. But she was afraid of horses and guns, and she thought she would never play as beautifully and look as elegant as Myrtle Emma. She didn't know what she was good at. Siler was good with sums and good with his hands, which everybody thought was wonderful since he was not likely to succeed as a professional man. He could mend tables and chairs and he had made a three-legged stool with tools his father had bought from old man Hartsoe. Mary Bet admired what her brother and sisters could do, and she thought that when the time came she would prove good at whatever needed doing. Her mother had taught her to sew, but though she was the best in the family at mending she did not feel particularly proud of such a talent.

"I'll never be as good as you and Myrt," Mary Bet said to O'Nora one day after O'Nora had told her she was planning on going to South Dakota to become a missionary to the Sioux Indians. "I'm not brave like you, nor pretty like Myrt." They were sitting together in the parlor after Sunday dinner listening to Myrtle Emma play and sing from a book of sacred songs; the windows were open to the sighing of trees and the twittering of birds in their early summer nesting frenzy. Cicero was leaning back in his leather armchair—the only thing he'd bought for himself since he'd started a family—asleep with his mouth open. Siler was out hammering something in the work shed.

"You're pretty aplenty," O'Nora told her, and Mary Bet was grateful she hadn't just laughed. "And you're brave enough. What do you need to be brave for?"

"So I can go work with the Indians."

O'Nora appraised her sister, a skeptical look on her face. "Is that what you want to do?" Mary Bet nodded. "You want to go out to a reservation where it's hot and dusty in the summer and so cold in the winter you can't feel your toes? And there're Indians everywhere?"

"I'll go if you're going. You oughten to be alone."

Now O'Nora gave a little laugh. "I won't be alone, silly. Who's going to take care of Daddy if we both go?"

"Myrt and Siler, I reckon," Mary Bet said. She could feel a sly smile cross her face—the whole thing sounded absurd. Surely O'Nora would never go clear across the country to South Dakota.

"Suppose they get married and move out?"

Mary Bet shook her head and turned away, and when O'Nora realized her little sister was upset she took her hand and turned it over and, studying the lines on her palm, told her she was going to have a long life and two love affairs and three children.

"Do you think Myrt'll get married and move away sure enough?" Mary Bet asked.

"Myrt's a flirt," O'Nora said, loudly enough that Myrtle Emma looked up from her music to where her sisters were giggling on the sofa. But whether or not she'd heard, she was still in the world of her song and Mary Bet knew she wouldn't stop until it was over.

Mary Bet wanted to ask O'Nora, "Will I ever be good at anything?" but it was vain to worry so about oneself. Just be good, she told herself. Just try to be good at being good, and, as Captain Granddaddy said, God will take care of the rest. "I think I'll be the nicest," she said out loud. But O'Nora was reading a book now and was too gone in the story to hear anything.

Being nice was something Mary Bet thought she could be very good at, yet she did not always feel nice. Her brother, who was between Myrt and O'Nora in age, had a way of aggravating her without his trying. Siler was different from anybody in her family living or dead, and not just because he was deaf. He was alert and sensitive to everything around him to such a degree that if anything was amiss, he was the first to know of it. If Myrt and O'Nora had been arguing with each other privately, he would know right away, and he would sulk off by himself until they had made up and come and found him, holding hands to show that they were no longer fighting. He was relentless until the things of his world were back in their proper place. "It's his way of keeping himself from grief," Cicero explained. Myrtle Emma liked that Siler would put his hand on the side of the piano and watch her, and she thought that he might've been a great musician. It seemed tragic to her, watching him trying to understand something that was in the air all around, yet as hidden and mysterious as signals running through telegraph wires, or the voices of ghosts who were not yet angels.

There were things that Siler seemed not to understand. Words that had more than one meaning were particularly hard for him to grasp, so Mary Bet would talk to him in the most basic way she could. You couldn't say "make haste," because there was nothing to make; you just said "hurry." It was silly to pick a crow with Siler—he would only laugh. Yet he knew distances "as the crow flies," and was delighted when some expression like that made sense.

It irritated her that he knew more about her and her secrets than did her sisters. He could tell when someone was coming up the stairs; he knew by feel who it was. And he knew about the crow. When she was out in the chicken yard once gathering eggs in a basket and he was pouring water into the trough, he gave her a stern, meaningful look. He was like a watchful spirit; he seemed to know everything about everybody. And he told her one time that Netty was not real, not even a ghost, and that she should stop talking to her. "Who do you mean?" she asked. Not bothering to use his hands, he said, "Yah Nadda." Then he mimed patting a little girl on the head, exactly as Mary Bet had done earlier in the day. When his back was turned she said, "You're stupid."

She felt bad, so she went off to find a place where he could never follow her; she walked up to the First Baptist Church and around back to the cemetery where the new graves belonged to people other than her family. It was cool on the grass at the edge of the little graveyard under the shade trees, and she thought it was all right to sit there in her skirt on a warm summer day. One newly cut stone was that of a four-year-old boy, who had died from pneumonia—she'd heard her sisters talking about him. She said a prayer for him, ending with, "If you're in heaven, see if Annie's all right." She made a cross in the air with her joined palms, a ritual she'd invented after her mother died. When she wanted the prayer to have special weight—if someone was sick, or late coming home—she washed her hands before praying. She would also touch her fingertips to her chin three times while praying and whisper the words.

"You stay here, Netty," she whispered, as though still praying. When she opened her eyes, she looked around and realized that her friend was gone. But she knew that she could find her here if she ever needed to.

Later in the summer, Siler was afflicted with glossalalia. It happened in the middle of a tent revival out at Calvin Grove. He stood up when the preacher asked if there were any souls ready to be washed in the spirit. It was as though he'd actually heard the preacher speak. He raised his hands in the air, and began talking in words that came from much farther back in his throat than ever before. The words seemed to issue from down in his belly, from deep in the earth, and he a faucet of indecipherable language that had not been heard since man first named the beasts of the field. It lasted less than a minute—a period of time that felt stretched into the edges of the day—and left on his face an expression of joy and satisfaction.

That evening Siler told his father that he thought he might like to go spend a year at the institution in Morganton after all. He could make friends and get a job as a carpenter and maybe even learn to minister in some way to the deaf. He'd had tutors over the years, and spent weeks at a time in Raleigh, but he'd always grown too homesick to stay for very long. His parents had relented and let him come home. "I believe our boy is growing up," Cicero announced to his family at supper, Siler grinning self-consciously. He patted his little sister's shoulders, and Mary Bet felt a warmth spreading through her body. Siler was never affectionate with her, had never hugged or kissed her that she could remember, and now he suddenly seemed different.

THE CENTURY WAS on the point of turning, Mary Bet not yet twelve years old, when O'Nora fell off her horse jumping a stone fence.

By this time Haw County had shaken off its postwar depression and was shambling toward a modern agrarian future, with Hartsoe City as its boomtown. The Silers and Murchisons and other pioneers were no longer the most prominent families. Newcomers seeing opportunity in the forest and the railroad bought up acreage and built mills to turn trees into lumber, sometimes without even moving from Richmond and Raleigh and wherever else they lived. The village had become a town with a handful of little stores, a tobacco warehouse, two saw and planing mills, an agricultural machinery plant that also made window sashes and blinds, three boardinghouses, and some thirty-five houses clustered around the old Murchison place. There was a farmers' alliance and a weekly newspaper that advocated for farmers' rights over those of business-men. A black entrepreneur named J. T. McAdo opened a barber-shop, and then a photographic studio and a jewelry store. And still more things were coming—there was talk of a furniture company and a telephone line to connect Hartsoe City to Williamsboro. Out in the county, the cotton mill up on the Haw River in London was the biggest cash concern.

For all the changes, though, Haw was rural to its dirt-road, pine-strewn, silage-scented core. A couple of thousand farms large and small—and nearly that many tenant farmers—raised crops and livestock. And the new things, when you stumbled upon them, took you by surprise.

Old Hartsoe's gristmill had been eclipsed by others—bigger mills with better equipment, some of them running two stone sets at a time. Now an old man, Hartsoe still had a ferocious energy, which he channeled into an obsession that had been steadily con-suming him for the past several years—the creation of a perpetual-motion machine. O'Nora was on her way to see her grandfather, his mill an hour south of town. She had talked Mary Bet into coming with her, riding behind her in the saddle, on the promise that they wouldn't go faster than a trot. There were three things that Mary Bet feared most, and they were germs, horses, and her grandfather Samuel. He had a stern, unyielding way with children—what little he said was in a nearly incomprehensible German accent that made him seem as distant as the prophets.

O'Nora wanted to do something for her father, and at sixteen she also wanted to prove her independence. She offered to deliver some swamp-root tonic to their grandfather—really in the way of a peace offering from Cicero to his father, after Cicero had neglected to send for his weekly supply of flour and feed. To Samuel this could only mean disloyalty, never mind the fact that there were closer mills for his son to do business with.

So O'Nora loaded her saddlebag with two bottles of tonic and a dozen big yellow onions—the kind her father ate raw for his health, as he had since the war. "Don't be scared of Grandpa Samuel," O'Nora told her little sister. "He won't bite you."

Mary Bet pictured her grandfather baring his teeth at her, then thought of the big dapple-gray horse doing the same. She stood on the mounting box in the barn and let Siler help her into the saddle behind her sister, and off they went. It was a beautiful May morning, wild jonquils and sweet yellow jasmine blooming along the roadside. After a mile, O'Nora announced that there was a shortcut through the woods that Siler had showed her and she wanted to try it.

"Maybe we should stick with the road," Mary Bet said. She felt less confident of O'Nora than of Siler and Myrt, and not simply because they were older. O'Nora was apt to try something just for the sake of trying it, and then later find that it was not a good thing to do.

"If it doesn't work, we'll come back," O'Nora said. "It might be easy as pie, so what's the harm?" At her command, Jackson stepped across the culvert on the left and up the little embankment and into a shadowy copse of trees, the white-flowering hawthorn and red-tinged crab apple as pretty as candy. Soon the woods gave way to a clearing of low weeds and stumps ringed by shreds of morning fog. A bluebird flitted from a hickory stump at their approach. It was quiet. "I don't remember this," O'Nora said. "This is new. But the trail must go on into those woods yonder."

"Don't you think we should go back?"

"Let's go a little farther." The horse continued, picking his way between log skids and plow clods, the torn land unreadable. After several minutes they came to the woods' edge, but the trail had disappeared. O'Nora slid from the horse, smoothed out her skirt, and began studying the ground in all directions. Before them lay a dappled wood, carpeted with mandrakes, a fairy forest of little green umbrellas. Mary Bet knew it was no use to argue with her sister. "I maybe took the wrong turning," O'Nora finally said. "We'll cut through these woods and find it farther on."

Mary Bet gave her a hand up and after a while they were through the woods and out to a meadow. O'Nora looked all around.

"Maybe we should go back," Mary Bet said.

"No, this is right. I remember that tree with the pitchfork-like." O'Nora clicked her tongue and began posting, pushing Jackson into his fastest trot.

Mary Bet kept quiet so as not to be thought timid. She wrapped her arms so tightly around her sister she felt she must be squeezing the air out. She pressed her cheek into the velvet of O'Nora's riding jacket and she could hear her heart thumping along with the horse's hooves. The thickets and deep woods flashed by as they jounced along, now so fast that her bottom no longer hurt—they went bounce, bounce, bounce in the saddle, and the woods moved as they veered left or right, sometimes downhill, then slowing to step through a creek, then back up again. A strand of O'Nora's hair came loose and flew across Mary Bet's face so that the green world smelled like her sister's warm red-brown hair.

Out into a field of switchgrass and meadow grass they went. There were doves calling off somewhere; Mary Bet remembered this distinctly, because she had always thought that doves sang only in the late afternoon, mourning the end of day. They were cantering through a field, the grassy ground moving under them faster and faster as they plunged down through a thicket, and O'Nora said, "Hold on!" as the horse leaped a stone fence. The wind felt sharp in their faces. O'Nora hooted a laugh and made Jackson go even faster, until they were bounding over the ground. O'Nora hated riding sidesaddle because you could never go this fast—she liked bareback best of all because, she said, "you can really feel the horse." But she only did it when her father was not around.

There was another dip and then a rise and then a sudden dip, and a fence that Mary Bet saw just as they started down. There was something about the gait that seemed wrong—they were going too fast, then they slowed way up as O'Nora tried to veer off to the side. At the last second she went ahead and made Jackson jump. Mary Bet clung to her sister, and she heard hooves strike the top stones as her insides rose and fell. And yet they were still sailing over the fence.

When they landed on the other side, Mary Bet at first wondered why the trees were so high and moving in a circle instead of rushing by. She was still touching her sister, though only with one hand. Then she saw a horse standing a little ways off, shaking and snorting. It looked like Jackson, yet he was riderless. "It's Jackson," she said, laughing, as she pulled a little pinecone out of her hair. She realized that her back was sore because she was lying on a pinecone in a soft pile of needles.

The sun angled through the skinny limbs overhead. Beyond them was blue sky. A bobwhite called far off in the woods, and the wind disappeared in Mary Bet's ears. O'Nora's ankle crossed Mary Bet's, and when Mary Bet sat up she saw her sister lying faceup, her arms out as if she were flying. Her head was turned away. Mary Bet crawled around and saw that her sister's face was still, the eyes closed, the jaw slack. She kissed her forehead. "Wake up, O'Nora," she said, "please." Not a whisper of breath came from her sister, nor a ripple of movement, nor was there any sound but the sighing of wind in the trees. It blew a loose lock of hair across O'Nora's rosy cheek.

Mary Bet began crying. But she angrily wiped the tears off her face and stood up and started calling "Help!" After a while she began walking. She finally came to a road, and after a few minutes an old Negro cart driver came along and went with her back across the fields, his cart bumping slowly lest a wheel break in a burrow. "No use in hurryin' just to be late," he said.

It took a lifetime.

All the way home, the man tried to comfort her, telling her of his wife's many sorrows and saying, "It's just a cryin' shame, missy, a sweet girl like that." Jackson plodded along with the driver's mule, and all Mary Bet could do was stare at the driver's bare toes sticking out through his shoes and wonder why one of his big toes had a cracked yellow toenail that angled off his toe while the others looked fine. She wondered if it hurt, and she wondered why Negroes had brown nails. She wished she could have cracked yellow toenails if it would make O'Nora well. And when she thought of O'Nora and glanced back into the cart and saw her curled up between burlap sacks, she prayed that she would wake up by the time they got home.

When they arrived, Mary Bet and the black man were praying aloud together, and she couldn't remember who had started it. Yet when she saw her house she realized that her own grief was not what frightened her the most nor held her in the most suspense. She thought she could not bear to tell her father.

Siler was the first person she found. She pulled his hand because she did not want to make the word for "dead." She would show him and let him decide what to do.

Mary Bet held Siler's hand through the whole funeral, and it felt to her as though she could never let go. Cicero got the stonecutter to carve a bas-relief hand in the stone, with a finger pointing the way to heaven. The stonecutter had a number of new sayings. None of them seemed just right for O'Nora, but Cicero picked out, "None knew thee but to love thee," engraved in cursive. He decided it was after all perfect. After the service he had Essie strip O'Nora's bed and bring him the sheets. "These is good sheets," she said, shaking her head at the waste, and at her employer's impulsive, erratic grief.

"Let the day perish that I was born," Cicero said, taking the bundled bedding. "Let the stars of the twilight be dark." He took the sheets out into the backyard and tore them into strips, then placed them on the fireplace where Essie boiled the laundry, shoved the cauldron to the side, and burned them. Then he ordered Essie to scrub the floor of the girls' room.

The gray-haired servant got on her swollen knees and scrubbed the floorboards to wipe away the curse. "At least he didn' tear his own close," she said, hoping Mary Bet would hear. "Ought to be grateful for the livin'," she said, eyeing Mary Bet and pitying the motherless girl. She shook her head and continued with her work, pausing every so often to glance up to Mary Bet. Essie's lower lip nearly covered the upper, the way it curled over, hiding an almost bare gum—her ponderous slowness reminded Mary Bet of a large turtle. She liked the comforting slowness of Essie and her heavy smell of laundry and cooking and sweat; besides Myrtle, Essie was the only woman in the house now, with any regularity. She was tall and had heavy eyebrows that knitted together when she was serious and opened out when she was making a joke. Mary Bet could talk to her and not have to think about O'Nora, and the thrown glass, and the soft rabbit that loped through her dreams and followed her in daylight shadows.

Though she was too old for imaginary friends or guardian angels, she knelt before the small fireplace in her bedroom that evening, the low-banked fire making the angels glow and seem to move upon the black iron. There were two of them—surely enough to watch over herself and Myrtle Emma. You couldn't pray to graven idols, but you could pray in front of them and so she said her prayers right there on the hearth bricks.

Cicero aired the room out, as he had done after the other deaths. And he went back to work, his family now down to four.

∽ CHAPTER 6 ᴄ

1900

IT WAS JUST before Siler was to go off to Morganton that he and Mary Bet became at last good friends. She had school friends, but she had always preferred her own family. Now with O'Nora gone, she and Siler, five years apart, were the youngest. Siler would've had trouble making friends in the village even if he were outgoing, which he was not particularly. At home he would do and say funny things that made Mary Bet laugh, yet in public he behaved like a trim little soldier, his watchful, deep-set eyes ever alert and his thrust-out chin daring anyone to make fun. He wore a boater tilted back on his head in the cocky way the baseball players did. He tried out for the Hartsoe City team and made right field, his strong arm cutting down many a would-be run. He was considered friendly and handsome, but, above all, quiet, deaf, and a loner. Mary Bet noticed him more now that he was leaving.

They went together to the Fourth of July celebration. The Hartsoe City Concert Band was marching by, the trombones and drums pounding excitement into the chests of the bystanders, the dignitaries' carriages draped in bunting, the flags, dipping and rising, carried by the Masonic Lodge members, stiff in their starched white shirts and dark ties, stepping proudly along. A midget named Gus Hightower marched by holding a large flag, beside six-foot-five-inch farmer Richard Wren, who waved a small flag. Then came the veterans, some in uniform, some on horseback, with swords strapped to their waists, and as the crowd cheered Mary Bet felt a strange sadness that had been with her for days now. She had been feeling out of sorts in a way that was new and disturbing. And then she decided to go home, and she wished she had brought a friend other than Siler. She made her way out of the crowd of mustached men in linen suits and bow ties, women in flower-pile hats and long-sleeved white blouses, then hurried back to her house.

It felt as if she had sat on a wet chair—why did she have to wear white today? Well, there was nothing she could do about it now. Myrt had showed her what to do with the sanitary napkins, so she was not unprepared. She washed her hands, letting the water trickle down past her wrists, the way the Hebrews did long ago. She laughed at herself in the mirror—it's just me, she thought. No more a woman than I was yesterday. Her breasts were growing, her hips taking shape, yet she was still short, still unsure of herself. No one at school thought so, of course—at the new public school, divided into two rooms and attended by fifteen children, she was a smart aleck, always quicker to answer than anybody and reading books that the others could not understand. They thought her strange. One teacher told her not to be so proud of herself, and for the rest of the year she quit raising her hand until, her mind wandering during class to the characters in her book, she was thought as dull as the others.

When her father heard about it, he came in and spoke with the teacher, who told him that his daughter was of average intelligence.

Cicero said nothing. He went home and told Mary Bet to answer up loud and clear in school. "I shouldn't be proud," she said. "Not if you don't have anything to be proud of," he replied.

She wanted to tell someone about what had just happened to her. She wanted to open the window and shout, "My monthly started!" She looked at herself again, tucked a loose piece of hair, readjusted a clasp on the back of her head, and thought, "I'm not bad-looking." She shook her head at her vanity, staring into her own black, impenetrable eyes. "Not pretty," she whispered, "just not bad to look at." .

The next week was sweltering hot, a hundred degrees, and there was talk of a group going down to Hackett's Mill on the Rocky River for a picnic and swim, but then somebody suggested they go to Hartsoe's. Mary Bet and Siler were against this plan, but Myrtle Emma said she wanted to go see her grandfather. After all, he was their last grandparent alive. That he had lately become obsessed with perpetual motion should not prevent them from making a visit.

Myrt and a friend named Sallie Wood were going in the Woods' surrey, with room for four more. Mary Bet was not much on swimming in places where there might be snakes, but she was not about to be left out. Myrt was going away to Wilkesboro to teach at the end of the summer—a prospect that, along with her brother's imminent departure, scared Mary Bet more than snakes. Now twenty, Myrt told her father she needed to go out in the world and do some good and make a living. Cicero could only shrug mutely at the diminishment of his family, vowing silently that Mary Bet would never leave him.

Mary Bet and Siler squeezed in on the two seats, along with Sallie, Myrt, and Sallie's two cousins, visiting from Rocky Mount. The mill was a journey of about an hour, during which Mary Bet discovered that Sallie Wood's cousins, a boy and a girl—straddling her in age—were unimpressed with anything they had seen in Haw

County. They and Mary Bet were on the backseat, and Mary Bet pointed out some daisies growing next to a patch of little sunflowers. She said, "That looks like eggs and suns. It looks like pastries you could eat nearly."

The boy sniffed, and the girl, sitting in the middle, didn't change her sullen expression. Mary Bet wished she was up front with the others. "I can drive a horse and buggy," she said.

"Who can't?" the boy asked. Siler turned around and glanced from one person to the other, Mary Bet smiling at him with eyes that she knew he could interpret. He shot a stern look at the boy and girl, but they seemed not to notice.

"I can ride sidesaddle and astride," Mary Bet said.

"I could ride bareback when I was four years old," the boy answered, kicking the seat in front of him.

"Well, I can wring a chicken's neck," Mary Bet retorted. "I like doing it too."

The boy was quiet a moment. "I don't even like chickens," he said. The girl laughed quietly at her own thoughts. Another mile rolled by, the two young women talking in the front seat and the shadows of pines across the rutted road alternating with the clear spaces where there were green-and-gold fields of knee-high tobacco and corn and wheat and hay and sometimes cotton, not yet flowered.

The boy pulled a tin from his pocket, took a pinch of snuff, and sniffed it into his nose. He offered some to his sister, but she shook her head. Then he held it over to Mary Bet. She too shook her head. "Go on and try it," he said. "It clears your head right up."

Sallie Wood turned around. "Leave her alone, Jacob," she said.

But Mary Bet reached into the tin and took a big pinch like she'd seen the old men doing down at her father's store. She held it to her nose and smelled the sweet dank foresty odor, and then she breathed some in. It tickled her nose so that she sneezed. But Jacob had been right—it felt as though cool air filled her entire head. Siler turned and gave Mary Bet the same stern look he'd given the other children, but he took some snuff himself. The young women politely refused. "Not too much," Myrt warned her sister. "It'll make you sick."

When they got there they saw no one about, except Samuel's last remaining black man, whose name was Ezekiel Hallelujah Monday. He was known as Zeke, and he had once been Samuel's property. The other handful of slaves had drifted away as soon as the war was over, including Zeke's own mother. Zeke was older than Samuel, which put him somewhere over ninety. Still, he came out of the barn when the carriage pulled up and greeted the arrivals with a toothless smile, or what appeared to be. He was wearing a shirt of blue homespun, butternut trousers, and a straw hat. He unhitched the horse and led him to a tree, where he watered him, then curried and brushed and rubbed him down.

It was a sweltering, hazy July day, but Mary Bet had not brought her bathing costume because she wasn't sure the bleeding was finished. She might wade in up to her knees, but that would be enough cooling off. They went around the barn and down to the mill house. The wheel was turning, while behind it in the pond ducks dabbled among the lilies and cattails. The miller waved to them from the window of the two-story whitewashed building. He was a new man, Samuel going through a miller every couple of years because he always thought he was being taken advantage of.

Jacob and his sister took off their shoes and went to dip their feet in the pond, and Jacob found rocks to throw at the ducks. Mary Bet and Siler stayed up under the shade of a willow and helped Myrt and Sallie spread out the picnic.

They had laid everything out, when they heard, from the direction of the main house, a man speaking. It was Zeke, saying something incomprehensible. Then they saw him, his nearly bald head glistening in the sun, walking alongside Grandpa Samuel, fanning

him with his straw hat, and it was hard to say who was support-
ing whom. Samuel wore a gleaming white suit and a boater with a
baby-blue ribbon. "The vheel," he said, pointing it out with his long
beak of a nose, "it never stops. It just goes around and around and
around." He refused a cane because Captain Billie had used one.
He stood there seeming to teeter forward, then backward, Zeke
catching him as best he could.

Myrt sprang up and went to her grandfather. "Grandpa Samuel,"
she said. "We were going to come in and say hello. How are you?"

He nodded, looking at her through filmy, rheum-swollen eyes.
"Just fine, dear," he said. "And how is your mother?"

Myrt glanced at the others. "It's me, Myrtle Emma, Grandpa.
Cicero's daughter. Mama died three years ago."

"That's right, she did. I'm sorry to hear it." He looked away from
the group to the mill wheel, its paddles appearing to endlessly
channel water down the race. "I've finally done it," he said.

"Done what?" asked Myrt.

"Achieved perpetual motion. You see, it vas the vay the Archimedes' screw ran through the gear that vas the trouble. If you'll
follow me, I'll show you."

They got up and moved slowly along with him to the mill house,
the smell of ground corn hitting them as soon as they entered. The
building hummed and throbbed, the heavy stones churning away
upstairs and conveyor belts carrying the meal to the sifting platform. A floury dust covered everything. "I've had Roberts build the
model, according to my diagrams," Samuel said. He pointed a bony
finger to the upper level. "I've already sent the papers off to the
patent office in Vashington. Now they vant to see a vorking model,
vhich suggests to me that they like vhat they've seen. Roberts can't
claim it as his, yah, because I'm one step ahead." On a workbench
along the wall of the stone-floored room stood a model mill wheel.
Around it and on the floor beneath were odd pieces of wood, bits of

metal tubing (some still wedged in a vise), screws, nails, hammers, tin snips, levels, rulers, and a blowpipe.

Samuel took a ceramic pitcher of water and emptied it into the miniature millrace. The water trickled through the sluice, then down into a twelve-inch-diameter wheel mounted into a vertical framework. The wheel turned, splashing water into a tin basin. A long wooden shaft with spiraled metal piping rose at an angle from the basin and ran up to the end of the millrace where the water had first entered. Samuel gave the shaft a twist. He banged his elbow into Siler, who had been leaning over studying the device with fascination. Only then did Samuel take notice of his grandson, but it was just a vague recognition of a person, like the others there, connected to him in some way.

He stood back and glared at his invention, daring it not to work. The gears cranked and the water began pouring out the top of the Archimedes' screw into a little collecting pan, then flowing back down the millrace, through the wheel again, into the basin, and up the screw. "It vorks!" Samuel shouted. "It vorks better than ever! I knew it just needed to settle in."

"Cose it did," said Zeke.

Samuel stood admiring it, Zeke steadying him. "Now it's turning nothing but an arm, but ve'll attach a gear here, and some millstones. And I'll tell you a secret." Here he quieted down and looked all around, the others leaning in to hear him over the incessant noise. "I'm not going to send them the model. Vhat if somebody should steal it on the vay? I'm going to build the whole thing here, full-size, and invite the director of the patent office down to see it for himself."

The wheel stopped turning, the gears creaked over and were silent. Samuel gave another twist to the shaft, but nothing more happened. He shook his head. "Thass alright, Mr. Sam'l," Ezekiel said, "we looks to it after while. It's time for dinnah now."

"No," Samuel said, "it has to be the tubing. I knew I needed copper! And the coils should be looser. Roberts knew it all along. If he thinks he can get a jump on me, he's dead wrong. Roberts!" he yelled. "Get down here this instant."

It took some time for Roberts to come downstairs—he'd lost much of his hearing over his years as a miller. He was a burly, sad-looking man of middle years with a soft face; he wiped his floury hands on his apron and looked around at everybody. He listened to Samuel's accusations. "Well, vhat can you say for yourself?" Samuel demanded, then spat on the floor.

"I wouldn't do that to you, sir. I don't know a thing about per-petual motion. I told you I don't think it works."

"Haaagh," Samuel raged, spitting again. "I should fire you for impudence, you young rascal. I'd better not find out you've been stealing my idea. I'll sue. Vatch and see if I don't. You can go, Mr. Roberts, 'fore those stones up yonder catch fire."

Myrtle Emma said, "I think we'd better go back to our picnic, before the ants get it." She took her friend's hand and led the way. Mary Bet started to follow, then grabbed Siler's arm and pulled. He shook his head. Myrtle Emma's translation of their grandfa-ther's scheme had been inadequate—he wanted more details.

Myrtle Emma and Sallie were already out the door. Siler was trying to say something to both Samuel and Mary Bet, desperate that one of them would understand. "Baamb hah," he said, spell-ing furiously with his right hand. He went over and touched the Archimedes' screw portion of the model, then pointed out a place above the collecting pan.

"He's the one that's deaf, ain't he?" Samuel said, to nobody in particular. "Vhat is it you're saying, boy? I can't understand that gibberish." Then louder, "Vhat are you trying to tell me?"

"I think," said Mary Bet, "he's saying something about the pump being too high, or not high enough."

Now Siler wrote with his hands so fast that he seemed to be conducting a band at a runaway tempo. Suddenly he stopped, his eyes going back to their deep, mystifying look, as though he'd either given up trying to explain to idiots, or he'd reconsidered. It was a look he often put on in public when he wanted to act as though he didn't understand. He shrugged, then knocked his fist against his forehead: "Dumb." Only Mary Bet knew that he was saying both *I'm dumb* and *You're dumb*.

"Vhy would he say it was too high?" Samuel asked.

Mary Bet smiled, wishing she were anywhere but here, under the fierce stare of her grandfather, in this building that hummed and shook as though it would fall apart. His white eyebrows twitched and fluttered at her, demanding she behave herself and say the right thing. "I don't know," she said.

"He's the one that makes things?"

"Sir?"

"Makes things vith his hands!" Samuel thundered. "Who's the deaf one here?"

Mary Bet froze. She opened her mouth to say something, but no words came out. She nodded.

Samuel looked suspiciously at his grandson, but Siler only shrugged again and so Samuel returned his attention to the miniature water mill. He uttered a low grumbling noise. "Thinks he knows more than Archimedes," he said to himself. "Ve'll just have to see about that. Ve'll just have to see."

Now it was Siler who led the way, pushing past the heavy door and leaving Mary Bet to follow. Zeke called after them to mind that they didn't go in the water over their heads. "Mr. Sam'l don't 'low no drowndin' 'round heah."

When they got outside, Siler signed to Mary Bet, "Grandfather crazy," his finger swirling around his temple. She liked that he raised his eyebrows, wanting to know if she agreed. She shrugged

her shoulders, lifted her palms. They went over to the picnic blanket and joined Myrt and Sallie. There were deviled eggs wrapped in
waxed paper, roast beef sandwiches with mayonnaise and pickled
cucumbers, ham sandwiches with thick slices of cheese, an apple
pie Myrt had made the night before, mason jars of sweetened ice
tea, and a small watermelon. They sat and ate and watched the mill-
wheel turn, and Jacob said he'd heard of such a wheel that could
carry people around and around. Mary Bet didn't know whether to
believe him or not, but when she translated for her brother he said
that it was true. "What's it for?" she asked.

"For fun," Jacob answered.

"Looks like you'd get mighty wet," she observed.

"There's no water to it."

"Then what makes it turn?" Myrt asked, as skeptical as her sister.

"I don't know," Jacob replied. "Mules, I guess."

Siler shook his head and signed. "An engine," he said, "powered
by steam, or gasoline."

Since nobody could debate that, they went back to their eating.
But it was too hot to eat much, and Jacob got up and announced
that he was tired of sitting and doing nothing. He took off his shirt
and shoes and went over to the pond, but then he just stood there,
not willing to be the first in. Siler pointed at him and laughed.
Jacob's little sister poked her lips out at Siler when she thought no
one was looking, but Mary Bet saw. She couldn't help admiring
the girl for siding with her brother, yet she felt sure that the girl
didn't like Siler because he was deaf and smart. The girl went running toward the pond, her pigtails flopping along her back. Her
brother reached up and pulled her in with him, and she splashed
and squealed, her white pinafore clinging to her chubby body.

"Your shoes!" Sallie called out.

After a while, Siler got up and headed the ten rods or so down
toward the river, a branch of the Rocky that had, in addition to a

generous supply of shin-barking boulders, a few holes deep enough for bathing. Mary Bet saw that Jacob and his sister were getting out, as though trying to decide whether to follow Siler. She went on and caught up with her brother and took his hand.

They walked down to the edge of the river, where the ground was veined with the roots of tall sycamores and locust trees. Crickets rasped loud in the midday heat, and overhead the sky was the faded blue of old china. The river swashed around boulders that were slung at random up and down the streambed. In the air, the smell of growth and decay hung heavy in the bracken just off the river, and as Mary Bet stood there with her brother looking at the river she felt its downward pull as something elemental in life, a force that had to be struggled against. She squeezed Siler's hand and looked up to his face, but he was intent on watching something beneath the surface—he freed his hand and pointed to a fish, but Mary Bet couldn't see it.

He took off his shirt and shoes and began wading in, beckoning for her to follow. She didn't like the idea of shivering in cold wet clothes that would have to dry while she wore them. No, that wasn't it—she was just afraid. Siler, up to his waist, sucked in his pale flat abdomen until his ribs jutted out and his suspenders hung loose, and signed that she was a weak sister. He splashed water toward her and made a cradling motion with his arms.

She bent and unlaced her shoes and then stepped carefully over the mossy stones at the water's edge. The rocks underwater were slick to her feet, but she found a place on the muddy bottom to stand, and she lifted the hem of her skirt and began wading out into the current, toward her brother. She wished she'd brought her bathing costume—a navy knee-length dress and pantaloons.

When she was up to her knees, she twisted her hem so that she could hold it with one hand, lifting it as high as she dared, and wading in a little farther. By now the other children, boisterous from being already soaking wet, were picking their way over the stones at the river's edge. Jacob plunged in on his belly, splashing Mary Bet so that she leaned away and lost her footing. She came up with her hair dripping, hanging like weeds about her face and neck. Jacob took up a mouthful of water and fountained it out toward her. Siler was floating up to his neck, staring at Jacob with the same intense expression he had when he was standing at bat, or hunting.

Mary Bet didn't want to be the cause of any ill will, so she began laughing and paddling over to her brother. She looked back and saw that Jacob's sister was still sitting at the edge, elbows on knees, hands cupping her chin, with a bored expression. *I can swim!* Mary Bet thought, treading so that her toes would not have to touch the slimy bottom, *and I'm not afraid of the river.* She caught hold of her brother's shoulders and clung to him like a possum baby. His wet skin smelled like cold slabs of bacon. He rose up and shook her off and swam to the other side, and he sat there with just the top half of his head above the tea-colored water, surveying her like some ancient reptile. She laughed out loud and splashed, until finally he broke into a smile. She admired how lithe and handsome her brother was; she thought him about as handsome as any young man she knew, and she imagined that if he were not her brother she might have feelings for him. It was wrong to even have such a thought in her head, she knew, and she took her eyes away from him and stared at the ripples around her wrists. Could he possibly think of her in the same way?

Siler stood, preparing to dive into a pool. She tried not to look at his bare chest, his strong arms and legs. He was better formed than she would ever be, she thought—it wasn't fair that a boy would be so good-looking. Half afraid he could read her mind, she turned away and headed back to the stream bank, then hurried through the bracken, her wet skirt dragging over gap-toothed cogwheel daisies and maidenhair ferns. She wanted to ask Myrt if she thought calico would work for a bonnet—a sturdy slat bonnet for colder weather.

In the weeks before Siler was to leave for Morganton, he and Mary Bet took long walks together, sometimes out to the cemetery at Love's Creek to put fresh flowers on the graves of their brothers and sisters and grandparents and their mother—ten in all. An epidemic of diphtheria swept through the eastern part of the state, and there was fear of it spreading their way. It never came, but Mary Bet began writing a diary, thinking to hand something of her life down to posterity. She also started a keepsake book, with things that O'Nora had liked—pressed fall leaves, jack-in-the-pulpits and other wildflowers, a tiny wreath made of Myrt's and O'Nora's hair twisted together, photographs, bits of poetry O'Nora had liked, letters she'd received.

One Sunday afternoon Cicero went down to the mill for the afternoon, having received word that his father was ailing. Myrtle Emma was at Sallie Wood's. It was a balmy afternoon, the open windows drawing a faint breeze through the house. Mary Bet was half-reclining on the sofa, adding a photograph of herself to the scrapbook—a picture of her sitting horseback in a sidesaddle, the flounces of her petticoat showing above the tops of her boots. Siler came in from the backyard and hung over her shoulder looking at what she was doing. His warm breath made her neck tingle, and the sound of him moistening his mouth was oddly comforting— soon all his strange little noises would be gone. He pointed at the picture and signed, "O'Nora laughs in heaven." Yes, Mary Bet thought, O'Nora would think her funny looking, perched on the sidesaddle.

Siler came around and sat beside her, the dried rivulets of sweat on his ropy arms and the close smell of him making her heart beat a little quicker. He had such a familiar, comforting smell—like the outdoor hearth, fresh-cut logs, home. She had a headache, not a terrible sick one, and there was no one to ask whether it was from her monthly and whether she should take willow tea or aspirin powder. She took his hand and placed it on her forehead—it was like a warm animal covering her face. Now he gave her a funny, sad, longing look that made her feel weak, low in the pit of her body, and he put his arm around her and smelled her hair. He held her close like that and murmured something she could not understand, and yet she knew what he meant. He kissed her cheek, and she kissed him back on the lips. And then he held her face in his hands and looked deep into her eyes. She could see herself mirrored in his black irises, and she knew that he could see himself in hers. She waited for him to kiss her again, to do anything, anything at all—they could burn in hell together and never, ever be alone. His hands trembled on her face as his eyes moved down her bare neck to her shoulders and her chest. Then he kissed her forehead and stood abruptly and went back out.

It's not incest, she told herself. *Forgive me, Lord, and forgive Siler too. I will never let it happen again.* She pictured coming to him in his bed some night and giving herself to him, letting him do whatever he wanted with her. She shook her head and mumbled, *No, I won't.* She found herself wishing that Myrtle Emma had her own room so that Siler could come to her if he wanted to, and immediately she thought how lucky it was that she and Myrt shared a room.

For what seemed hours, she lay there, the windows open to the noise of Siler sawing and the songs of birds and, behind everything, the chirr of cicadas, as incessant as the heat itself. She felt as though she could not move. When would God choose to strike her dead? Siler was still alive and able to work—the *sizz whoo sizz whoo* of his saw like breathing. And here she was lying on the sofa as if she were unable to move because of a little headache. She jumped up and went over to the bookshelf behind the piano and took down her Bible with the family tree in the front pages. She studied the limbs of the tree, the strange German and Irish names going back a hundred years and more, and then saw how the branches led out to her own family, and her very name, inscribed by her mother. She flipped over to Proverbs and read, "Be not wise in thine own eyes: fear the Lord, and depart from evil." She nodded and closed the book, *I* will *depart from evil*, she thought, *I will I will I will. I must.*

∽ CHAPTER 7 ↺

1900

OR SOME DAYS she could not shake off a sense of impending doom. She and Siler avoided each other, speaking to the other only when they had to. He went off to school and his short, weekly letters, ungrammatical and misspelled, were the only news they had of him for some time. Then came word that Grandfather Samuel was on his deathbed, and Cicero and Mary Bet traveled down to Hartsoe's Mill to bid him good-bye.

This time Zeke did not come out to greet them and unhitch the horse from their buggy. A stillness hung over the place, and as they alighted and began to walk toward the house, something caught Mary Bet's attention. It was peeking out from beside the barn—a curved piece of wood that looked out of place. They walked around to the back of the barn and beheld the strangest contraption they had ever seen. Mary Bet knew right away that it was the remains of a full-size version of the model she had seen months ago in the mill house. A wheel mounted to the side of the barn sat suspended above a wooden basin lined with clay and sand, in the bottom of which stood a few inches of murky, putrid water. A long, hollowed-out pole teetered on the edge of the basin and ran along the ground to a pile of timbers that suggested perhaps a scaffolding system that had given way and tumbled over, taking with it the pole and its complicated gears and helical piping. A long trough lay at the farthest reach of the destruction, the millrace that, but for gravity, might have channeled an unceasing circuit of water. Off to one side were the crude beginnings of a millstone apparatus. Lying spread on the ground, recumbent as a dreamer, the whole thing bore a kind of grand abstract logic that it was apparently unable to achieve standing up.

"What in God's name?" Cicero said.

"Perpetual motion," Mary Bet replied.

They stood gazing at the fallen pile of timber and metal, grass and jimsonweeds sprouting up through the heap, as at the ruins of a stone colossus in the desert. "Perpetual motion," Cicero echoed quietly.

They went inside. Mary Bet had been in her Hartsoe grandparents' house only once, and that had been so briefly and so long ago she could barely recall it. Now strips of whitewash hung from the clapboards, and bees flew in and out of a chimney.

They let themselves in the dust-rimed front door. The first thing that Mary Bet noticed was the smell. It was as though she had entered a tomb that had been anointed with camphor and sealed up for a thousand years. The odor was so sharp she had a hard time inhaling, yet in a few moments she adjusted to the predominant smell and noticed complicated hints of mold and overcooked greens and chicken grease. The furniture was draped with heavy cloths bearing a gray film that turned out to be thick, coagulating dust. Cobwebs festooned the walls and stretched from the corners down to the cracked ridges of ancient china cabinets and the latticework on an old secretary. Shawls of cheesecloth soaked in moth-proofing camphor were draped on floor lamps and chandeliers and even doorknobs, like hexes to keep out the Devil.

It was so hot and musty they were sweating just walking around the first floor, looking for a window to open that wasn't nailed shut. They headed upstairs and then along the dingy corridor that overlooked the vestibule, the bare floor canted dangerously toward the rail and balusters, which themselves looked less than sturdy. Outside the closed bedroom door of his father, Cicero paused. He tapped lightly with a fist. "Father?" he said. "It me, Rezin Cicero."

For a moment the house was as quiet as the wreckage outside; then they heard a shuffling from within, and a strange, soft jabbering. They entered the room. Zeke, dressed in a patched-up butler's uniform, with tails and white gloves, was just coming to the door. He raised his grizzled head, sunk beneath bony shoulders, and said, "Won't y'all come in?" He gestured vaguely toward the opposite wall, but there was nowhere to sit, other than the broken split-bottom chair that was apparently Zeke's final post in the house. Samuel lay propped on feather pillows, his long nose angled not quite heavenward and his right hand gripping the edge of the sheet up at his chest as though afraid someone might try to pull it away. His left arm was crooked around a leather bag that lay half on the bed, half in his lap. The bed was littered with open books, trays of food-encrusted dishes, and papers filled with diagrams and writing in Samuel's precise, minuscule cursive.

Zeke picked up a flyswatter and leaned over to where he could fan Samuel, who lay there quietly mouthing strings of words. "Damn Flood and his Rosicrucians." "A *closed* cycle, a *closed* cycle." "Around and around and around." "Vhat did Newton say about it? Not a thing, not a damn thing."

"He just keep goin' like dat," Zeke said. "Sometime for a hour. Den he shake de bag, and I undo de drawstring so he can see what's in it."

"What is in it?" Cicero asked.

Zeke looked at Samuel, who at that moment opened his eyes and shot a searing look back, then closed them and said, "Around and around. Sie sind der Teufel."

Zeke said, "I'm not s'pose to know, but it's gold coins, mostly, and some silver. 'Long with some Confed'rate money that ain't worth burnin'."

"How long has he been like this?"

"I'd say about two, th'ee weeks. But he took a turn for the worse on Friday. That's why I sent word."

"Does he eat and drink regularly?"

"Won't touch nothin' but graham crackahs and chicken brof, chicken brof and graham crackahs. I don't have the strent in my legs hardly to keep bringin' it up and down the stairs."

Samuel opened his eyes again and tilted his head so that he could see his son and granddaughter. He seemed to look beyond them, and Mary Bet thought she had never seen a head that so nearly resembled a skull, the skin the merest gauze over the bones. He mumbled, "Have you read your book? Your book?"

"Yes, Grandpa," Mary Bet said, "I have."

"Don't be proud, proud."

"I won't be," she said.

Cicero looked back and forth from his father to his daughter. "Daddy," he said, "it's me, your son."

Samuel made a faint gravelly sound and closed his eyes. "I know who 'tis," he breathed. "Vhat do you vant?" He clutched the bag closer onto his lap.

"Just to see how you were getting along."

"Huh," Samuel noised, his chest rising and falling with the effort of showing amusement, or disgust, or something else—Cicero could not tell what.

Zeke held two long leather straps that looked as though they'd been cut from bridle reins. "I had to tie his arms to de bed so he wouldn't bite his toes. Twiced I did dat." He shook his head, its gray fringes thin and straight as a white man's. "I din think a old man could do dat. But wif his hands tied, he cain't pull his feet up close enough to his mouf. I come in once wif a tray and he had his toe in his mouf, bitin' till de blood come. I say, Mr. Sam'l, no need for dat, I got sumpn to eat right heah."

Mary Bet stared at her grandfather, trying to picture him devouring his toes, but he seemed peaceful now, his breaths coming in little puffs from his half-opened mouth.

"I don't want your money, Daddy," Cicero said. He stood there in his rolled-up sleeves, arms crossed over his chest, staring at his father. "I never did."

But Samuel lay unmoving and unheeding, and Mary Bet took her father's hand and said, "We should go downstairs and let him rest."

Cicero scratched his beard and nodded. "Well. I 'spect you're right. Ezekiel, I appreciate all the trouble you've gone to. I'll make sure you're paid for it."

"Mr. Sam'l say he done laid sump by for me. I reckon I be all right."

"You know whereabouts he laid it by?" Cicero gave Zeke a friendly, conspiratorial little smile, the look, Mary Bet thought, mixed with a just a hint of skepticism, as his glance shifted over to the bag of money and back.

"Yes, suh, I do know."

Cicero nodded. "Good then. We'll just go on downstairs and make ourselves at home. Call down if he needs anything."

Samuel stirred and muttered something. Then, "I don't need that house. I'll build my own." A few garbled sounds followed, then silence.

Throughout the day and into the night Mary Bet went up and down the stairs checking on her grandfather. Finally, just as dawn was breaking, Cicero said they might as well go on home. "He could last like this for another week." They went up a final time to say good-bye to Zeke, and found him curled up on a pallet of blankets beside the bed. Cicero leaned down to his father and said, "We're going home, Daddy. We'll be back soon." He touched the old man's shoulder and looked closely at him. The leather bag lay enfolded in Samuel's embrace, his other hand clutching a piece of rolled-up foolscap. "I don't think he's breathing," Cicero said. "Daddy?" He removed the paper from his father's grasp and unfurled it. Covering every square inch, front and back, were drawings of wheels and inclined cylinders and sluiceways, their lengths and other specifications indicated with arrows and notes.

It was impossible to tell when he had done these drawings. One doubly underscored note read: "radius must be exactly ¼ the screw's length!" Another: "as it were a wheel in the middle of a wheel." He handed the paper to Mary Bet and she read aloud, "To grasp the total process of redistribution of matter and motion as to see simultaneously its several necessary results in their actual interdependence . . ." She left off and put the paper back on the bed.

Mary Bet thought that if she didn't ask now, she might never have another chance. "Why didn't you and Grandpa Samuel get along?" she asked.

Cicero shook his head. "I don't know," he said, staring at his father's lifeless face. Then, "He thought I was weak." He stopped, his mouth open to words that would not form themselves—in his mind or on his tongue, his daughter could not tell which. He said, "I had a dog. He used to beat it, and then he laughed if I cried. To make me tough, I reckon . . . I didn't care for how he treated the servants either—he had a different idea about things."

"What did he—" Mary Bet started. She didn't know what she wanted to ask.

Her father smiled, but his eyes were far away. Then, so quietly she could hardly hear him, he said, "There was something his father did that affected him . . ." Mary Bet looked from her father to her grandfather and back, waiting for more. "He did the best he could," he finally said.

She wanted some explanation—no, he hadn't done the best he could, she wanted to say. He was mean and miserly, as mean as Satan her mother had said. But her father had gone mute, and would say nothing more about what had happened long ago. He reached into the leather bag, forcing his father's dead arm out of the way, and pulled out a handful of coins. "Here," he said, offering a few to Mary Bet, "here's your inheritance."

Mary Bet looked at them and shook her head. "It's too much."

"Just take it. Zeke won't know what to do with all that." He grabbed her hand and gave her two five-dollar and two ten-dollar gold pieces. "I'll give the rest to Myrtle Emma and Siler." She looked at the money, still shaking her head, then regarded her grandfather. It seemed wrong to rob him like a vulture while he was lying on his deathbed. But perhaps her father was right, and she thought with greed of all the rest of the money still in the bag.

The funeral at Love's Creek was sparsely attended, most of those who knew Samuel Hartsoe having long preceded him to the grave, and the others not particularly moved to see him off. Some friends of Cicero's came and a few distant Hartsoe relatives. Zeke was the only black person in attendance, and after the burial he shook hands with Cicero and his children and, with a forlorn look, said he didn't know what he was going to do with himself. He came to live with the Hartsoes, occupying a little storage room in the summer kitchen. Cicero told him it would be too cold out there in the winter but that they would figure something out; Zeke said he didn't mind the cold at all, that the stove on the other side of the wall would make the room warm as toast. In the end it didn't matter, because he died a week after Thanksgiving. It was unclear what became of the money bag, or exactly how much was in it.

When they got home the reception had already begun, the house no longer their own. Women from church had laid the dining room table with platters of fried chicken and roast beef, kettles of rabbit stew, pies and layer cakes, casseroles and other dishes that this time would actually be eaten. "R.C.," one old man said to Cicero, "I'm sorry about your daddy."

"I am too," Cicero said, shaking his hand.

When she could slip away, Mary Bet went out to meet her brother, who was making his way on a path between the fields at the edge of town. She knew that he would come this way rather than taking the road, where people would offer him rides that he would have to politely refuse. They met up in a grove of tall trees and didn't say anything at first, just walked back toward their house. After a while Mary Bet said it was sad about their grandfather.

"He was a mean old man," Siler said. "He never spoke to me."

"He told me to read my book, and not be proud." They walked on a ways, into a glade with shafts of sunlight pouring in like the foundations of heaven. "I saw him playing cards once with Captain Granddaddy. He was scary."

"He was the Devil."

Mary Bet grasped her brother's wrist, and put a finger to her lips. "Hush, Siler. God can hear you."

"God can't hear anything," Siler told her, scowling at the ground as he walked. Then he brightened suddenly and looked up into a shaft of sunlight and raised a fist and uttered something loud and incomprehensible.

"Are you talking in tongues again?" Mary Bet asked.

Siler shook his head.

"Then what did you say?"

"I said, 'If you can hear this, strike me dead.'"

Mary Bet breathed in sharply. Of all people, she thought, her own brother, who had sinned with her, should not test God so, and yet she could not bring herself to chastise him. "You don't think God punishes us for our sins?"

"He punishes the righteous, and exalts the sinner. Ask Daddy."

"Daddy says things because of all his sadness. But he knows it's not true. Not in heaven."

"I don't care about heaven."

"Well, you should."

Siler nodded and glanced at his sister. "Maybe you're right," he said, smiling his half-smile.

WHEN SILER WENT back up to Morganton, Mary Bet felt a measure of relief. But then Myrtle Emma headed west to her teaching job, and the house seemed forlorn. The night before she was to leave, Myrt saw her sister's tears and said, "I've made up my mind. I'm just not going to go. I'll find something here."

Mary Bet put her arms around her sister, as much to hide her face as anything, and said what she knew Myrt wanted to hear. "Don't be foolish. There's nothing for you around here. You go on, we'll be fine."

And then she was gone and like that they were down to two people, the youngest and the oldest. There was something about the community of three people that was lacking with two—with three nobody had the responsibility for keeping a conversation going at meal times. Now the family was like a two-legged stool. Whatever was she to say to her father, who seemed more remote and older than ever? Was he going to end up as austere as his father? They would pass each other in the house and glance shyly at the other, as if to say, "I see you, I know you're here." Every creak on the floorboards, every cough and scraped chair could only be coming from him, and she wondered if the little sounds she made were as obvious. Did she bother him? Was he just being polite around her for the sake of a harmonious household? She would linger in her room if she heard him on the stairs. During the day she would make sure she knew where he was before she attempted the outhouse.

He let her bring in one of the barn cats for company, and she invited friends over for dinner, and sometimes in the evening as well. He went to his Columbus Club and his church committee meetings and his county road commission meetings. But as the weeks went by, it was mostly Mary Bet and her father, and they settled into a routine that, if not perfectly happy, was not exactly unhappy.

One night, after Mary Bet had brought her father his evening cup of tea—always with honey and a curl of sassafras—and was sitting down to mend his shirt while he read his newspaper and biography and Bible, in that order, he said, "I'm not feeling too good, Mary. I think I'll go on to bed."

She glanced at him, thought of how peaceful it would be in the parlor without his rustling and belching and reading aloud passages about Hannibal or Jefferson, which was like coming into the middle of a story for one minute and then leaving, and then she thought how quiet and lonely it would be without his voice on such a cold, windy autumn night. Then she felt a panic of guilt and terror. "What is it, Daddy?" she said, trying to keep the urgency out of her voice.

"Just feeling a little poorly, a little sore in my bones. Rest'll cure me up." He rose with a groan, smiled at her, and made his way to the stairs. She noticed age spots she had not seen before, and his hair, what little was left, seemed as white and sparse as dust.

"You're losing weight," she said.

He straightened to his full five feet eight inches and patted his belly. "Well, I could stand to."

"I'll get you some more tea," she said. "I'll bring it up, and your oatmeal."

"Thank you, baby girl," he said. "Put a thimble of brandy in the tea if you don't mind."

She looked at him, then down. He knew how she felt about drinking, how her grandparents had preached the evils of liquor until she couldn't stand the sight of it. She was allowed her moral high horse as a kind of eccentricity, and Cicero's own modest indulgence went on unobtrusively, the bottles secreted on a high shelf. That he would ask her to dose his tea must mean he was very sick indeed.

In the morning, he told her to stop in at the store on her way to school and report that he was feeling unwell and likely would not be in. He had never missed a day from illness that she could remember. "I'm going to get Dr. Slocum directly," she said.

Cicero raised himself on his elbows and said, "I won't have that man in this house. Not on my account. You hear me?" Then he sank back and made such a rattling cough he had to roll onto his side to clear his throat.

Mary Bet fetched a pink-and-red afghan she'd knitted, and draped it over him. He was shivering and she felt his forehead and found him clammy and warm. "I'll stay home today, Daddy," she said. "I'll make you chicken soup and soft-boiled eggs on toast."

"No, you don't. Essie'll tend to me."

"She's afraid of sickness. I'm not," Mary Bet said.

"You run along," he managed, then lay there, his eyes closed, his mouth open so he could breathe.

She went down to the pantry and found an old bottle of swamp-root tonic and poured a spoonful in a teacup. To this, she added a spoonful of Valentine's meat juice. She put the kettle on the stove. Then Essie began lumbering up the back steps. "What is it, child?" Essie said, letting herself into the kitchen. "Why you not at school?"

"Daddy's taken sick."

"Law. Is it the typhoid?" Essie's veiny eyes opened wide, lighting up her sagging face.

"I don't think so," Mary Bet said, calming herself in the process.

"You bednot go up there," Essie replied, her brows relaxing. "We better call the doctor."

"He doesn't want the doctor. Maybe some ox gelatin." Mary Bet was pleased with herself when Essie agreed.

When the tea was ready, Mary Bet took it up to her father and sat at his bedside for three-quarters of an hour until he began stirring. She went back down and reheated the tea, then came and woke him and helped prop him up on pillows so that he could drink. He wrinkled his face. "That doesn't taste right," he said.

"I added some meat juice to give you strength," she told him. She didn't mention the tonic, and she watched him until he had drunk the whole cup.

The next day he was worse. Though he would not want to see the doctor and she was only thirteen, she had to do something. She decided that her father wouldn't even know whether or not Dr. Slocum was there, so she sent a neighborhood boy to fetch him. Dr. Slocum arrived, dressed in his suit and overcoat and carrying his black medical bag.

After his examination, Dr. Slocum announced, "Bad case of influenza. He needs plenty of rest and liquids. A cup of water alternating with a cup of broth every hour." How could he rest with all that drinking? Mary Bet wondered. But for the next five days she arranged for both Essie and her sister Elma to tend to her father while she was at school, then in the afternoons she took over the job herself. She wrote letters to Siler and Myrtle Emma and wondered if the matter were urgent enough for a telegram. Dr. Slocum said not, and the nearest neighbors—the Dorsetts, who lived across the road and down near the creek—agreed that the flu was not usually a matter of grave concern, but they were new in town and didn't know her family history.

The oldest Dorsett boy, named Joseph, began coming over with gifts of food from his family. They were from Salisbury and they were fond of canning. They sent over cucumbers in brine, jars of green beans and kraut, apple jelly, pear and strawberry preserves, and dried peaches. Their new garden and orchard promised to be just as fruitful as the one in Salisbury, while Cicero's garden was going to weeds now that Siler was away. Joseph was fifteen and he told Mary Bet he hired out at fifteen cents an hour and would happily do whatever needed doing, including putting in a new garden in the spring.

"We don't need any help," Mary Bet told him, annoyed with this new boy's impudence. She didn't like the way he regarded her with half-closed eyes, as though sizing her up and finding her lacking. He was red-haired and freckled, and stood with his hands on his hips like a grown-up, but what she disliked most was the defiant way he tilted his head back, his chin out. It was uncannily like Siler, yet he was loud and broad-chested, light-haired and short— an anti-Siler if ever there was one.

"I'm plucky," he told her.

"Is that so?" she said.

"Yep, everybody says so." He handed her the jar of damson preserves his mother had sent. "This is good for colds, and hiccups." She took it and thanked him, and as she was closing the door on him, he asked, "How is your father?"

"Better, thanks," she said.

But just as he seemed to be recovering from influenza, Cicero came down with something that at first seemed to be a relapse. He went to bed in the middle of the day with a high fever and woke up after midnight, his sheets soaked and his head "swimmy." He called out for Susan Elizabeth, and Mary Bet awoke and came into his room and stood by the old four-poster bed where she and her siblings had been born and where her mother had died, the bed that Captain Billie had provided as a wedding present. "Susan," he said, "is that you?"

"No, Daddy, it's me, Mary Bet." She stood holding onto one of the turned wooden posts at the foot, afraid to look him in the eyes. The post was loose from when her father had twisted it, anguished over his dying wife and his inability to help.

"Mary Bet? I can't see you."

She came around and felt her father's face and held her kerosene lantern up to where she could see him. He stopped turning his head side to side and stared up at her with wide, terrified eyes. "It's just me," she said, quietly, trying to keep the fear out of her voice. *What was he seeing?*

"It's my leg," he said. "Take it off, for God's sake." He lay back. After a while he sat up and said, "They're coming over that rise yonder."

She had the thought that if he just went ahead and died she could bear it better, and then she felt so ashamed she thought she might faint right there. She set the lantern on his bedside table and went to pour him a glass of water. Somehow he had gotten himself out of bed to use the slop jar, which she took as a good sign. She watched as he drank the water—his eyes were red, the lids swollen; and when he sank back onto his pillow he was racked with a coughing fit that bent him double and had him clutching his ribs and then his throat, inarticulate with pain and delirium. She didn't think she could stand to see him like this, nor to wait all night before summoning the doctor.

Her father kept no chairs in his room, except the toilet chair, so she went and sat on her mother's cherrywood quilt chest, determined to stay there until morning's first light. As soon as she sat down, her father roused himself from his layers of fevered half-dreaming and said, "I'm sorry, Susan. I never meant any harm."

"It's all right, Daddy," Mary Bet said.

"You're a good wife," he said, then lay back, breathing heavily and coughing to clear his throat. He drifted back into a restless sleep, and after a few minutes Mary Bet got up, took a quilt out of the chest, and curled up on the floor to wait until morning.

~ CHAPTER 8 ~

1900

ICERO DEVELOPED A case of measles, then pneumonia, and he had Mary Bet wire her aunt Cattie Jordan in Williamsboro to come help out for a week or so. He didn't want to bother Myrt way off in the mountains at a new job. Mary Bet knew her aunt to be more than a little bossy, but she could not convince her father that she needed no extra help. Arguing with him only seemed to agitate him the more. She imagined that if he were just a little sicker she would take charge completely. Cattie Jordan was not Mary Bet's favorite, but the other two aunts had moved out of the state and there was no one else to call on, except Cincinnatus's wife—and she had a large brood to take care of. Anyway, she thought, with another person in the house she would not feel so alone.

She wondered if this turn of her father's meant the end of his life. Or if it could trigger the mind sickness inherited from Grandpa Samuel. The sickness went back at least as far as Samuel's father, though Cicero never talked about his grandfather. Mary Bet remembered her grandma Margaret telling her stories about John Hartsoe, the same who had built the house that Margaret and Captain Billie had owned. Not long after selling the house, he had moved in with a daughter who lived on a farm up near Silkton. There he had given way to dementia, and as there was no hospital then for the insane, they had resorted to tethering him to a China tree during the day and to his bed at night to prevent his running off—as he'd done on several occasions—or trying to hurt himself. One time he attempted to put his hand in a meat grinder while turning the handle, and once he sat on the stove until a servant smelled the peculiar mixed odor of singed wool and flesh. He developed the notion that he was responsible for keeping the China tree standing, and he got to where he refused to come in. He ate the tree's poisonous yellow berries, claiming they gave him the strength of Samson. They built a lean-to for him to shelter in, but in the winter they had to drag him inside, where he developed a case of pneumonia and died.

Except for the time he talked to himself in the mirror, Cicero had never shown any sign of mental instability other than an occasional burst of temper when something didn't suit him just right, and an equally occasional outpouring of what his wife used to call "the joys" when he was happy. The former caused him to rush outside and start splitting wood (a therapy his mother had suggested); the latter made him practically vibrate with excitement—his eyes would light up, and with gritted teeth he would grab the nearest person and dance around the room. It was an almost terrifying, mad overjoy that took possession of his entire body, sometimes for no apparent reason other than that he was happy. And then it would as suddenly disappear and he would return to his usual quiet, self-effacing demeanor, and it could be months before such an outburst would recur.

Now that her father was sick with something in his body that the doctor could label and give medicine for, Mary Bet thought that she would have to do as he wished, as long as he had the strength to speak. Two days later, Cattie Jordan arrived in a canopied carriage pulled by two fine black horses and driven by a young Negro wearing a sable suit and silk top hat. Her husband ran his hotel so profitably that he'd added seven rooms to the original ten, and they had started going to Wrightsville Beach for a week every August.

Cattie Jordan was short and stout and though many people had observed how much Mary Bet favored this aunt, Mary Bet would look in the mirror and be relieved when she saw no resemblance. Cattie Jordan was even quicker to deny the likeness, saying, "I don't see it atall," and adding, with what seemed to Mary Bet a disingenuous tone, "Mary Elizabeth is much the prettier." Cattie Jordan's hair was lighter, her eyes brown instead of black, her facial expressions of a more limited palette, ranging from placid to mild. But there was that same square Murchison chin that Mary Bet wished for the world she didn't have, and her mother's narrow upper lip that only accentuated the nose—though on Cattie Jordan, the effect was exotic, even pretty. Cattie Jordan had the flared nose of the Murchisons, instead of the Hartsoe beak.

Cattie alighted with her driver's help, and was pulling off her gloves so that she could take her niece's hands and offer a cheek to be kissed. She looked around as though for a greater welcoming party. "It's just me and Essie," Mary Bet explained. "We don't need a houseboy but three days now."

"Essie and I," Cattie Jordan said, then, "you might have arranged for this to be one of the three days. But I know you've been terribly upset with your father's illness." She motioned for the driver to get her luggage, then she gathered the hem of her skirts and climbed the steps to the porch, her wide felt hat blocking the sun. Mary Bet stared at the imposing figure of her aunt. Cattie Jordan kept up with the latest styles, which in her case meant that she might add a mauve ribbon round her hat and wear jackets—always brown or navy—with a bit of rise in the shoulders. The sleeves were tight, the skirt long, with flounces showing at the bottom. She kept her hair in the old style, wound up on the back of her head, and her collars revealed only a sliver of neck.

After she had settled herself in Ila's old room and taken a nap, she called for Mary Bet and told her that they should sit down in the parlor to discuss her father's situation. "A pot of tea goes well with talks like these, don't you agree?" she said, her rouged face lifting into as much of a smile as it ever dared. Mary Bet agreed, though she could not understand what tea had to do with her father's illness.

They sat in the two formal wing chairs, Mary Bet unsure of herself in her own home. "I see mother's china has been kept in good repair," her aunt said. "You don't use it for everyday, do you?"

"No, ma'am," Mary Bet replied, wondering whose mother Cattie Jordan had meant, because the china had, now she thought about it, come down through the Murchisons. Her aunt was looking around the parlor in an appraising way—at the little ormolu clock, the brass andirons, her father's encyclopedias and leather-bound volumes of ancient history and philosophy, the love seat, the straight-back chairs, the square piano that only Myrt ever seemed able to coax music out of, the fold-up secretary in the corner with its vase of dried flowers, the red oriental rug at their feet—worn thin over the years and not likely now to ever be replaced.

Mary Bet got up and added another log to the fire—there was still an early spring chill to the parlor that wouldn't go away for at least a month. And somehow it felt even colder than when she was sitting alone with her needlework.

"As I see it," Cattie Jordan said, her eyes tarrying over the piano, "your father is going to need all the help he can get for the next fortnight, at least." She paused to sip her tea, then glanced at Mary Bet, not for an answer so much as to register her presence. Mary Bet had never heard anyone use the word "fortnight" before, and it sounded ominous, for it meant her aunt would be here for some time.

"He's a gravely ill man," Cattie Jordan went on, "and the house must be kept quiet and clean." Now she looked at her niece and gave her a conspiratorial wink that felt to Mary Bet like a little stab in the heart.

But Mary Bet nodded and said, "I like it clean too—Essie and Elma and I manage with that, and it's quiet except for when I have friends come over. And when Joe Dorsett brings preserves or something, I talk to him on the porch."

Cattie Jordan listened to all this with her head resting on the tips of her fingers as though she had a headache, her eyebrows rising higher at every word from Mary Bet's mouth. "Joe Dorsett?" A slight shake of her head.

"The boy across the street. They moved in last fall. They're from Salisbury. His father is assistant manager at the bending and chair factory."

Again, Cattie Jordan slightly shook her head, as if shooing away a fly. "Your father is going to need absolute quiet. The friends will have to take a hiatus, I'm sure you understand, honey."

Mary Bet nodded, trying to be agreeable, "We can meet over at Clara's for a while. She likes to play our piano. She just has a spinet, but it works fine."

"Mary Elizabeth, I'm afraid I'm going to need all the help I can get. If you go traipsing all over town to parties and jamborees, where does that leave me? Now is not the time to think of our own needs and comforts. It's time you learned that life is not just about having fun. Your mother was the baby of the family, just like you, and it's a hard lesson for the youngest to learn. Now, as for entertaining boys over here by yourself—it's strictly forbidden. I don't know what your father allowed when he was well, and frankly I don't care. I can't be up and down the stairs, worrying about your sick father and you down here with some neighbor boy."

"Yes, ma'am." Mary Bet saw the fortnight now stretching out like the longest train at the crossing, boxcar after boxcar after boxcar.

"Don't look so blue," Cattie Jordan said. "We'll have us some fun. I brought my dominoes. I just love dominoes, don't you? And there's not a word in the Bible against them—not that I've found." She made another wink, as if she had just sold a wagonload of bootleg whiskey to a preacher, and said, "And we can tell stories."

"Stories?" Mary Bet asked.

"I could tell you things to make your hair stand right on end." She seemed to enjoy the thrill this produced, the nervous excitement in Mary Bet's eyes now that she had her full attention, and Mary Bet was not at all sure she wanted to have her hair stand on end.

The doctor came by in the morning. It had been a long night, Mary Bet spending most of it by her father's bed and not saying a word about it in the morning when Cattie Jordan awoke with the sun and found her niece asleep. "Am I to wake you, Mary Elizabeth?"

"No, ma'am," Mary Bet said, getting up in a hurry.

With Dr. Slocum there and attending the patient, Cattie Jordan looked more relaxed. "It's the Lord's will, honey," she said, "and if your father were taken today, we should be happy that he's in a better place. Isn't that right, doctor?" She smiled so that the rouge fissured along the wrinkles in her face.

"Yes, well," Dr. Slocum said, looking from the aunt to the niece, uncertain whom to address, "this is a very serious business, coming right after the flu and the measles. He'll need constant vigilance for the next few days. An elderly man doesn't have but so much fight in him."

Cattie nodded and smiled, as if certain that the vigilance was only for the sake of his not dying alone. "We'll read to him, and pray to him," she said. The doctor said that would be fine, and he gave her a list of medications and instructions and said that he would stop by in the evening.

When he was gone, Mary Bet went right back up to her father's room, where he lay asleep, his mouth half open, his face so gray and closed upon itself he seemed gone already. She sat on the chest trying to figure the right prayer to say. While she was sitting there with her head bowed, Cattie Jordan tiptoed in.

"We should let him rest," Cattie said. Mary Bet nodded, then yawned. "Cover your mouth when you yawn, honey," Cattie told her. "It's unladylike."

At dinner Cattie, sitting in Cicero's place, helped herself to the fried chicken breast, then passed the platter over to her niece. Mary Bet didn't care for wings or drumsticks—with their rubbery bits and tiny bones, it was like eating fried rabbit. She selected a second joint and was on the point of reaching for the bowl of succotash, when Cattie picked it up and scooped the top layer, where the butter had just melted. Mary Bet started to eat her chicken.

"Wait for the hostess," Cattie said, a faint, condescending smile on her lips. When her plate was finally piled with cucumbers and tomatoes, mashed potatoes, and biscuits, she carefully placed her napkin in her lap and then began eating. "I'm surprised you haven't learned some etiquette in school."

"It's a public school," Mary Bet said.

"That explains it. Well," she said with a gay laugh, as if they were having a merry time, "we have quite some work to do. And just in the nick, with you going on fourteen. Just in the nick." Then she continued eating, licking her lips between bites, and her features relaxed into more natural contours and she became again the cheerful, if somewhat greedy, aunt that Mary Bet knew from family reunions.

She studied the contents of her plate with the happy concentration of a shopkeeper counting his money after a good day; she chewed thoughtfully, serenely, her eyes closing each time she swallowed.

But as the food dwindled on her plate, her eyes took on a worried, harrowed look. Mary Bet was on the point of helping herself to a mean-looking wing, but Aunt Cattie lifted the platter and called for Essie. "We mustn't indulge ourselves," she said.

"I'll take it out," Mary Bet told her. "Essie's eating her own dinner."

Cattie's jaw dropped, the platter lowering to the table. "You, waiting on the servants? Mary Elizabeth, what would your mother say?" She shook her head, denying what she'd just heard.

"Mother taught us to clear the table ourselves."

"When a servant was in the very next room? I can't believe it." Essie came, wiping her mouth with the hem of her apron. Cattie simply gestured to the dishes and Essie, with a half-amused glance at Mary Bet and a little shake of her head, began clearing. Mary Bet stared darkly back at the servant, upset at both these women— at her aunt for turning things upside down and at Essie for being unable to do anything about it.

For the next few days, Mary Bet did her best to avoid her aunt. Mealtimes were the only occasions Cattie Jordan required, or seemed to want, her niece's presence, and then only for decorum's sake. Mary Bet imagined that her aunt would have been perfectly content to sit in solitude as she chewed contentedly and fixed her gaze in the middle of the table. Mary Bet recited the events of her day, careful to make them sound as uneventful as possible. She'd learned that her aunt at mealtimes wanted to hear nothing that would upset her or call for her attention in any way. This nonnews, though, could include gossip about other children—to this, Cattie was happy to listen and add tidbits from her own storehouse of gossip going all the way back to her own schooldays. Mary Bet almost came to enjoy these little gab sessions, though she thought it wrong to tell so many stories about people she hardly knew.

Sometimes her aunt's stories were about people who had ruined themselves with drink, or suffered a financial setback, which was always traceable to some character flaw or personal failing. "Everything happens for a reason." She would say this with a faraway gleam in her eye, as though she had been blessed with a privileged vision into the Lord's plan. Cattie Jordan's inside track to God seemed to put her out of patience with grieving, so that Mary Bet was afraid to show any fear.

Cicero spent the next seven days slipping in and out of consciousness. He slept nearly twenty hours a day and he lost so much weight that his nightshirt hung on him like a sheet over a broom. Every day, Mary Bet came home from school at dinnertime and ran, then—because of Cattie's scolding—walked, up to her father's room.

At dinner, Cattie was always dressed as if for church, a silver or pearl brooch pinned to the front of a dark brown or blue dress that had puffed sleeves and a tight, boned bodice that still attempted to show a waist, with a scarf around her neck—the one bit of color she indulged. "You never know when your time is coming," she said. "You want to look your best." She didn't insist that Mary Bet follow suit, for which Mary Bet was grateful, until she realized that her aunt simply did not trust her not to dirty her nice things. Every day Mary Bet would ask if they shouldn't wire Siler and Myrtle Emma, and Cattie Jordan would always assure her there was no need for them to come.

One afternoon, as Cattie was lingering over the last two bites of chess pie on her plate, eyeing them as she would friends embarking on a long journey, she said, "Mary Bet, you know we'd be happy to take you on should the worst happen." Mary Bet nodded, her lower lip tucking under, waiting for what her aunt wanted to say. "Do you know what your father had, has, in mind for you?"

"Ma'am?"

"For you to take with you. He must've said something about so-and-so is intended for Myrtle Emma, such-and-such for your brother, and the like for yourself." She glanced over at the sturdy sideboard and the corner cupboard, its panes revealing Murchison china that had gone to the youngest daughter, Mary Bet's mother. As a middle daughter, Cattie Jordan had received very little from her parents, though Mary Bet did not know this. Mary Bet thought of everything they owned—the two horses, one nearly blind (though Cicero didn't have the heart to sell it to the boneyard), the goat, the pig she had to slop every morning, the clutch of scrawny chickens, the house and land and furniture, the clock on the mantelpiece— what was it all worth? How would it be divided? What about Essie? Where would she go?

"I don't know," she said.

Her aunt smiled at her, a smile that reached out and patted her head. "Well, I'm sure there's a will." She sighed, an effort to be sturdy and patient in the face of trying times. Mary Bet did know that Cattie's husband, Uncle John, owned a good bit of land, and that their three children were grown. "I expect Myrtle Emma will want your mother's good things. Though you *have* been the one who stayed with your father," she said, winking at her niece. "If there's anything you especially like, you might ask him sometime when he's awake. And you needn't feel at all ashamed. I know he would want you to have some nice things."

Mary Bet did not know how to respond to this suggestion, so she nodded and quickly finished eating. She asked to be excused.

"Yes, you may be excused," Cattie Jordan said, seeming relieved. She smiled in a way that Mary Bet took to be genuine, even heart-felt. Then she sighed. "Mary Bet," she said, "you should start looking to your appearance a little more. You have a nice figure coming along, a fair complexion. You have the Hartsoe nose, and there's nothing to be done about it. But young men won't mind, as long as you carry yourself with pride and have a strong bosom, and I think you will. Go look in your room. I brought you some clothes. You don't have to wear your sisters' things."

"I'm never getting married," Mary Bet said. She regretted it immediately. Cattie looked as if she'd been slapped. She'd clearly been expecting her niece to be speechless with thanks, maybe even throw her arms around her, and here Mary Bet had said the first words that came into her head. "I mean I don't think any boy would ever ask me," she said, trying to reverse the pink flush in her aunt's face. Cattie's expression relented a little, softening back to her neutral, controlled smile. How simple it was, Mary Bet thought, to fool a grown-up who was not very smart—she didn't like doing it, but she didn't like Cattie trying to marry her off. "Thank you, Aunt Cattie," she said, with a little curtsy. "I'll go try them on directly."

"You're welcome," Cattie said. "I'll be up to help if you need it."

Mary Bet almost said she needed no help, but she held her tongue; anyway, Cattie had already returned her attention to her pie. Mary Bet hurried upstairs to her room and saw spread across her bed several things, including a grown-up corset, the kind that hooked in back and laced in front and had button garters hanging from the bottom. She knew from watching her sisters how it was worn. She picked it up and slid one of the stays from its sleeve, a translucent sliver of whalebone you could cut someone with if you had a mind to. She pictured Joe Dorsett trying to kiss her—why, she'd reach into her corset and pull out a stay and hold it to his chin. She laughed, her skin tingling, and wondered why in the world she would have such thoughts.

She decided to try on the corset so she could tell her aunt she had. It was like an ivory-colored shell, going all the way from the top of her bust to below her hips. She had to cinch it almost all the way for a snug fit. She stood away from the oval mirror above the dresser so that she could see the whole thing. Standing so, she could not see her own face, but she could not help smiling at what she saw—a young lady, her black hair draping over the top of the corset. She put a hand on her hip and cocked it in a saucy way, then leaned down so she could see her expression. The smile disappeared. *Lord, why did you give me this nose?* Everything was fine, maybe even pretty (lots of people said so)—but the nose . . . *So you won't be vain*, she heard herself saying.

The voice that had started sounding in her head, as if she were becoming twins, was a nuisance and a disturbing thing that she wished she could talk to Myrt about. You couldn't explain in a letter that you were always arguing with yourself, or talking to God, or hearing yourself tell yourself how foolish you were—no one would understand. She remembered her father yelling at himself in the mirror and wondered if she was doomed to live with a double self that would grow ever more unpredictable and troublesome. She flopped back on the bed and lay there until she heard footsteps on the stairs. She jumped up and stood in front of the mirror, brushing her hair and singing "Jesus Calls Us."

Her aunt came and stood behind her for a moment, until Mary Bet remembered that Cattie didn't like singing unless it was in church. "It fits nicely," she said, turning around.

Cattie stood there a moment, studying her niece as if she were sizing up a pig for slaughter. She frowned, then came over and relaced the corset until Mary Bet couldn't breathe. She realized too late she should've taken a breath like the horses tried to do before you cinched their girths. She felt her ribs would crack if she took more than just a sip of air, and she wondered if she might faint.

"There," Cattie said, standing back to admire. "That's perfect. Lots of boys will be interested in you, young lady. Just wait." She winked, a hint of chastisement in her eyes, and Mary Bet smiled back, but she wished more than anything that her aunt would leave so that she could take the contraption off. It would not hurt Cattie's feelings, because Cattie was too vain to let herself be hurt. There was a way in which she admired Aunt Cattie, even while wishing she would leave and never come back.

Cicero in the meantime grew incrementally worse, until there came an evening when he was balanced like a beam scale between life and death. The smallest thing could tip him over, a breath of wind on a candle flame. Dr. Slocum called in, with the intention of spending the night, if necessary, and checked his pulse hourly, changed the poultices, and forced some tonic-laced broth, Cicero all the while so far out on the borderland of existence that his few incoherent mumblings were as faint as a distant train. Mary Bet brought in two rattan chairs so that she and her aunt could take turns sitting up with the doctor. She wanted to stay there the whole time, but Cattie told her she should get some rest.

She went back into her room and lay on the bedspread in her clothes, staring at the dark ceiling. She wished Myrt were there, but the doctor said there was no point now in sending a telegram—the next twenty-four hours would decide everything. At a little before eleven, she heard her father saying something that sounded like actual words. She jumped up and rushed into his room.

"It's all right, Daddy," Mary Bet said, tears glazing her vision. She took one of his hands.

"They shall not awake," Cicero murmured, "nor be raised out of their sleep." Mary Bet sat on the edge of the bed, holding her father's hand to her lips. "Daddy," she whispered, "you must get well. God, don't take him. Please make him well. Please, God."

Cattie came over and stood just behind Mary Bet so that she could not see Cicero's face. "Lord," she said, "let us be obedient to thy will. In thy holy name we pray. Amen." She placed her hand on Mary Bet's shoulder, and for a moment the only sound was Cicero's breathing and the doctor's pocket watch, dangling by its gold chain from his hand as he stood, head bowed, waiting for the prayers to end. He glanced up, then went ahead and took Cicero's pulse, his stethoscope on the patient's wrist.

The doctor was portly and florid-faced, his hair mostly gone to gray, but he had a way in times like these of making a desperate situation seem bearable—there was a pride and competence about him that could verge on arrogance and testiness, then soften into compassion when he had done all that he could, and the contrast made him seem almost more than human. "Weaker," he said, "but still steady. He has a strong heart, your father. A strong will to live."

Mary Bet nodded, and now Cattie patted her shoulder and said, "Or a healthy fear of dying. We should let him rest, shouldn't we, doctor?"

Dr. Slocum hesitated, his nose and mustache bunching as he inhaled, and considered. "I don't know as it makes any—"

"We'll just go out awhile and let you do what you have to."

Mary Bet shook her head and said, "I'm not going out, Aunt Cattie. You go lie down if you want to." She regarded her father's face in the flickering shadows of candlelight and firelight. She felt a chill around her ankles, while the rest of her was burning hot from the high-banked fire the doctor had ordered. The smell of camphor poultice and stale breath was strong in the stuffy air. After several minutes the odor of ammonia cut through, and Dr. Slocum said he was going to need some help changing the sheets.

"I'll send out for Essie," Cattie said. "Mary, you'll have to get the Dorsett boy to fetch her."

"No," Mary Bet said, "I can help do it."

"But whatever for? You needn't do such a thing. Should she, doctor?" Her whole face showed dismay and repulsion at the very idea of changing a man's soiled sheets.

"I just need a person who's strong and willing," Dr. Slocum said. "Doesn't matter much who 'tis." He motioned for Mary Bet to go around to the other side of the bed, and as she did so she saw her shadow, cast by fireplace-glow, ride up the wall like her own ghost moving to keep her father's from leaving the house. She peeled back the sheets on her side and helped the doctor pull her father over to the edge. Then she held her body against his so he wouldn't tumble to the floor while the doctor slid the sheets out, Cattie now helping.

Cattie took the wet sheets downstairs, and Mary Bet went over and dipped a washrag into the ceramic basin on the dresser. She began wiping her father clean, while Dr. Slocum spread fresh sheets on the empty side of the bed. She finished toweling and powdering her father and helping dress him in a fresh nightshirt. He was comatose, his broad nose pointing up, taking in perhaps his last breaths, and she wondered if the family was coming to an end. All the generations in the family Bible—leading up to and ending with her. Unless Siler and Myrt came back to live here, she would be the last. What she would do if her father died she could not imagine. *I'll never go live with Aunt Cattie*, she told herself, *never ever*.

On the stairs she had to flatten herself against the wall to let Cattie by. "Excuse me," she said.

Cattie held her candle up so that she and her niece could see each other clearly. "How is he?" she demanded. For answer, it began to rain, drumming on the cedar shingles, making the house sound hollow.

"The same," Mary Bet answered. She felt her heart beating at a faster tempo as the rain increased, as though God were directing her to say something to Cattie that would make her understand that her own precious father was upstairs dying and she could hardly stand it. "It's raining hard," Mary Bet said.

"Raining, you say? I'm the one went out there and got soaking wet." Cattie Jordan looked as if she wanted to say more but was restraining herself. "I'll take that." Mary Bet handed over the nightshirt.

"You don't have to take it outside," Mary Bet said, as her aunt was turning away. "You can leave it in the basket by the door." Too late she realized it had sounded like an order to a servant. Cattie turned and glared up at her niece.

Before her aunt came back up, Mary Bet told Dr. Slocum she was feeling tired and asked him to please come rouse her if her father got worse. She and Cattie spent the rest of that long night taking turns standing vigil. Mary Bet would lie in her room for an hour, listening to the rain pelt the roof, then lighten to gentle tapping, then pour again in percussive welts. And then she would get up and relieve Cattie. They spoke to the doctor instead of to each other.

CHAPTER 9

1900–1901

S HE WOKE UP to the rusty-gate cry of the rooster and the smell of frying bacon, and when she looked out her curtainless window she saw mist rising from the ground and the trees into a thin blanket of clouds, the sun trying to burn through. Essie was here, thank the Lord. She prayed, "God, if he's alive, I'll devote my life to your service. I'll deprive myself. I'll never marry. I won't ask for anything fancy. Ever." She recalled making the same promise to God if He wouldn't take any more of her family, but it hadn't stopped Him from taking O'Nora. She sprang up and hurried to her father's room. Dr. Slocum was putting his things back into his bag, and Cattie was nowhere in sight. So it was over and she had missed being by her father's side at the very end.

She threw herself now on his bed, and he said, "Careful, baby girl, you'll knock me off."

"He's a little dizzy," Dr. Slocum explained.

Mary Bet tried to blink back the tears, but they came anyway. She got up and came around to kiss her father's bearded cheek. "Daddy," she said.

Cicero watched the doctor buttoning up his shirtsleeves and putting on his jacket, and he said, "They brought you here against my orders." His chest bounced as he tried to speak. "But I don't know as you did me any harm."

Three days into Cicero's recovery, Joe Dorsett came over with a strawberry rhubarb pie and a jar of apple jelly. Mary Bet stood on the front porch talking to him, wanting to invite him in simply to have another presence in the house for a while besides her aunt's. "And I brought this just for you," Joe said, handing her a little tin of Pendergrass snuff, made with tobacco and sneezeweed. "I don't know if you care for it or not."

"My aunt doesn't allow it," Mary Bet told him, glancing back into the house. But she took the tin and slipped it into the pocket of her strapped frock. "Why don't you come in and visit for a minute."

"I can't—" Joe started, then, surprised by the invitation, said, "okay, just for a minute then." He'd never been inside their house and he entered the vestibule and looked around as though he were in a bejeweled cavern. "I didn't know you had all these things. A piano—does it play?"

"Not by itself. My sister can play. I can play one thing she taught me."

"Play it."

"No, I better not." She glanced over her shoulder toward the stairs.

"Where'd you get all these books?"

"They're my father's. He reads a lot. Sometimes I read to him." She felt suddenly self-conscious, and her hand went to her hair; it was as if she were seeing the living room for the first time. How ridiculous, she told herself—it's just bragging old Joe Dorsett. But he wasn't bragging now; he was actually being polite, and he was glancing at her kind of shyly, as though they'd never met. She wondered if they should take seats in the wing chairs, but that seemed even more ridiculous.

"We have peacocks," Joe told her. "You've probably heard them." He made a funny little trumpeting sound that was more like a goose than a peacock, and Mary Bet was sure that her aunt would appear any second now. "I'll bring you a feather. They're right pretty, with a big black eye in the middle. They'll ward off the evil eye."

"I don't believe in that," Mary Bet said. What she'd heard was that a peacock feather in the house was a harbinger of death. "I like to see them outside," she said. And then Joe stood there looking at her eyes and her mouth with a serious, almost frightened expression, as though he wanted to come over and kiss her. Then, as if she'd been waiting for just this moment, Cattie appeared from the vestibule. She had not been on the stairs, for surely Mary Bet would've heard the treads creaking—she had simply materialized out of the air.

"Look, Aunt Cattie," Mary Bet blurted, "Mrs. Dorsett sent us some strawberry pie and apple jelly."

She regarded Joe, and in a tight voice, said, "Hello, I'm Cattie Jordan Teague, Mary Elizabeth's aunt from Williamsboro. You must tell your mother how much we appreciate her thoughtfulness." Before he could think of a reply she turned back to Mary Bet. "I've been lying down with a headache." She paused to see what effect those words would have.

"Yes, ma'am," Mary Bet said. "I'm sorry." Then, in a quieter voice, she told Joe, "I have to go now."

Joe showed himself out, and when he was gone, Cattie turned to Mary Bet and said, "What did he want?"

"He just wanted to bring us these things," Mary Bet replied, feeling the complaint in her voice, the edge of indignation.

Cattie's eyes surveyed Mary Bet, passing over her frock, where the tin of snuff was secreted, then down her legs and back up to her face, trying to ferret out every hidden secret and thought. "Is that all?"

"Is that all what?" She hadn't said it in an impertinent way—she simply didn't know what her aunt was driving at.

"Don't you get smart with me, young lady."

"I wasn't being smart," Mary Bet snapped back, tossing her head, because she had had enough. "If I was smart I'd've known what you were getting at, but I still don't." She felt blood rushing to her face, then draining, as she waited for her aunt to come over and slap her, or yell at her, or send her off to her room—something, anything, to relieve the tension. She closed her eyes, then opened them, her hands hanging limp at her sides. There was something about her aunt that suddenly seemed simple and pathetic, standing there in her plain brown dress, almost the exact match of half a dozen others, her little pearl-ringed brooch at her bosom, her solid arms and legs ready for daily battle with forces beyond her control that would want to interrupt and vex her. She was no longer even facing her niece, but looking off toward the vestibule, as if she wanted to leave.

"Honestly," Cattie said, as though talking to an invisible person, "I don't know how my poor sister stood it. With the typhoid, a deaf mute, a husband who spoils his children, and a willful little girl."

"I'm not a little girl," Mary Bet said quietly.

Cattie nodded and sniffled. "We've all been strained to the breaking point," she murmured. Mary Bet could see that her aunt was crying, and she felt more wicked than she had in a long time. Cattie Jordan took a handkerchief out of her bosom and blew her nose, and after a moment or two Mary Bet went quietly up the steps to her room.

She managed to keep out of her aunt's way for the rest of the fortnight. She brewed her father a Dorsett family recipe of sassafras tea with cinnamon and licorice root, and, when Cattie Jordan was not around, she reached up to the flour tin behind the canned beets on the top shelf of the pantry for an unlabeled jar of moonshine whiskey and added two or three thimbles to a hot toddy of lemon and honey. On Essie's days off, she found relaxation in going out to the backyard to churn butter or stir a steaming vat of laundry and bluing with a long-handled, triple-pronged agitator while staring meditatively off into the woods. She would imagine her grandmother's grandmother Sally, a Tory who married an Indian named Rufus Cheek and moved west from the fall line until they found this hilly fertile land and its patchwork of land grant farms owned by English pioneers, who then intermarried with Scotch-Irish and German pioneers down from Virginia. Her grandmother had told her that Tories and Regulators, or Patriots, as they came to be called, did unspeakable things to each other. There was something called spigoting that she never explained, but the word was itself enough to send shivers down Mary Bet's spine.

One evening shortly before her aunt was to go, Mary Bet asked Cattie Jordan if she knew how Captain Billie and Grandma Margaret met.

"They met at church," Cattie said. "Daddy had just bought the house we used to live in. He said all he needed now was a wife. It was a shame Mama had to let that house go. You know he bought it from your father's grandfather, John Hartsoe?"

"Yes, ma'am." Mary Bet vaguely knew the overlapping family history.

"They used to keep your father's grandfather chained in the barn up there."

"I thought he was roped to a tree," Mary Bet said, wondering why her aunt had chosen to tell her something from the Hartsoe closet instead of her own.

"A tree? Where did you hear that? No, indeed. It was the barn and a chain. I could show you where 'twas. Aunt Scilla, the nigger cook we used to have, showed me. He'd lost his mind and there was nowhere else to put him. Aunt Scilla said her father got himself put in charge of John Hartsoe and he would whip him if he soiled himself—that was to get him back for all the times he'd been beaten himself and, a worse disgrace, for making him stand out in the rain until his shoes were nothing but mud. Can you imagine? A slave in charge of his owner? Scilla would hear them out there yelling at each other and she and the other black folks would sing so nobody could hear them. But the funny thing was that after years of beating that poor old lunatic, and getting away with it, he felt sorry for him, and he started taking the old man out on walks, with a rope tied around his waist like he was leading a horse. And when John Hartsoe died, Scilla's father went out and sat on the grave all night crying and begging forgiveness. Isn't that the strangest thing? I've often wondered if Aunt Scilla didn't make it up to scare us children into behaving."

She paused and looked at Mary Bet with a gleam in her eye, trying to judge the effect of her story. Mary Bet did feel the hairs standing up on her back, and her palms felt cold and sweaty, because her aunt had brought to life some long buried people Mary Bet knew only vaguely, and it seemed as if they were walking around the parlor when they should be resting quietly in their graves. And something else—there was more to this story, the part her father had withheld at Grandpa Samuel's deathbed. She felt a leaden weight of gloom tugging her, a mind sickness that she thought might haunt her entire life. And then an image of splintering fragments, as though her memory, and her family's memory, were pulling apart, breaking into shards of light. It was the queerest sensation.

"What did he do besides beat Scilla's father?" Mary Bet asked, though she didn't want there to be an answer.

"Lord, child, I don't have any idea. Those things are long gone, and Scilla's dead now so you can't ask her, though I don't know why you'd want to. The sins of the fathers, they say, are visited upon the sons. I don't know why your father has suffered so much tragedy. It seems to me as if those sins were paid for at the time. If losing your mind and having your servant beat you isn't payment I don't know what is. But then I'm not one to judge."

Finally the day came when Cattie Jordan's packed bags were sitting at the top of the steps, waiting for someone to haul them out to the carriage she'd hired for the ride back to Williamsboro. This not being the houseboy's day, Mary Bet happily volunteered for the job. At the carriage, Cattie leaned over, and briefly held her niece. "Take good care of your father, now," she said, "you know he counts on you." Mary Bet said she would, and then she was waving to the black carriage, the dried flowers of her aunt's hat just visible over the seat back.

CHRISTMAS CAME AND the family was back together again for one brief week. Siler cut down a cedar in the woods south of town, and they decorated it with strings of cranberries and popcorn, chains of paper angels, and candles on wire fasteners, with paper doilies to catch the drips. When the candles were lit, Mary Bet was in charge of making sure the tree didn't catch fire.

Siler told them that he had a special friend, a girl from Wilmington whose father was in the railroad business. He seemed more outgoing, less brooding than before, but Mary Bet could never seem to find him alone to talk as they used to. He had started smoking cigarettes, and he came in late at night and stumbled up the stairs—no one knew where he'd been or what he'd been doing.

Myrt was faring well with her students up in the mountains—she was also playing piano in the Baptist church out there, volunteering twice a week at the colored school, and had joined the Women's Auxiliary Charitable Committee which put her in charge of distributing food and clothing to the needy families of Watauga County. "And there are a lot of needy families, I can tell you," she said, her eyes popping wide.

Just when they had begun to seem more like family than visitors, it was time for them to leave, and Mary Bet and Cicero were alone again in a house that seemed even emptier than before. Another term at school went by, Mary Bet going to the four-month public school, then switching in the spring to the Thomas Academy. She had just turned fourteen when they got an important letter from Boone. Myrt wrote to say that she was doing well, and that she had made a good friend at church and they went on long walks together, sometimes taking a picnic up to a waterfall with gentlemen friends. She had decided to stay on for most of the summer because of her church job, but would be home for all of August. "P.S. I got kicked milking the cow here at Mrs. Henderson's. It cut my leg pretty badly, but the doctor says I'll be fine in no time."

Her letter the next week began by saying that her leg was better but that she felt stiff and sore, "especially in my neck. I hope I'm not coming down with the flu." Four days later another letter arrived: "Dear Daddy and Mary Bet, I hate to have to tell you this, but my condition has not improved. I'm stiff all over. I can't chew good, so I have to drink soup through a straw. The doctor here said it could be lockjaw and that I should write you to come up, if you can. I'm feeling out of sorts and I hate to bother you. I don't think it's serious, but I am rather blue and my arms are awful sore and they've begun twitching and my neck is worse, like my collar is too tight, even when I'm not wearing one. Please pray for me and come if you can. The weather here is real nice. Mrs. Henderson brought me a bouquet of daylilies to cheer me up. I'm too tired to write more. Love, Myrt."

Mary Bet wanted to travel up to the mountains with her father, but he told her she should stay at home and take care of the animals. She said, "I'm not afraid of seeing Myrt, Daddy. I'd a sight rather see her like that than in a box."

Cicero looked at his youngest child, nearly a young woman now, and he could not bear to see her unhappy. She had never ridden on a train, nor been anywhere beyond Raleigh—to see the Reverend Billy Sunday preaching on the sins of pride and anger—and he supposed he had neglected to attend to her broader education. He prided himself on being fair-minded.

They were waiting at the depot at sunrise when the telegram came from Boone: "Mr. R. C. Hartsoe, Hartsoe City, N.C., I regret to tell you your daughter Myrtle Emma died this morning at 3:30. Please advise us your wishes in regards to arrangements. Yours in sympathy, Mrs. Eulalia Henderson."

Cicero stood in the station agent's office, staring at the cruel little device that had received this coded message and the typewriter upon which the agent had written it. The agent, a short man with a bristly mustache, said he hated getting messages like that. Cicero nodded and said, "I thank you. It's my cross to bear, and I don't complain." He went out, the telegram dangling from his hand, looking up and down the platform and seeing nothing.

"Daddy, I'm right here," Mary Bet said, waving. "What are you looking for?" She saw the distance in his eyes, the piece of paper he was holding, and she knew.

He looked so small and lost in his hopeful blue seersucker suit and boater—they were supposed to be on an errand of mercy, of cheering-up. He came and put his arms around her, holding her for what seemed could never be long enough. She buried her face in the warm, cigar smell of his jacket, gripping his wide middle, the end of his gray beard entangling with her dark hair, and the world ceased and there was no sound but her breathing. The pain she felt was for him—there would be time later for her own private pain.

She glanced at the WESTERN UNION headline, an epitaph to the typing below. "Will we go to get her?" she asked.

He shook his head and said, "I don't know. What should we do?" He looked around. Presently, people began coming over and shaking his hand and telling him how sorry they were, and they said the same to Mary Bet: "I just can't believe the tragedy yall've endured," one lady said. "The Lord must need your people something terrible." Another, older lady said Myrtle Emma was an angel who was too perfect to stay in this world for long. But most just said they were shocked and sorry, and a few of them kept standing there as though protecting Mary Bet and her father from the grief that was stalking them.

"I think we should send a telegram back," Mary Bet told her father.

Alson Thomas, the same who had played cards with her grandfather, happened to be standing there and agreed. "I'll send it," he offered. "Shall I tell them you're on the way?"

Mary Bet looked up at her father, but he stood mute and immovable, a breeze lifting the ends of his sparse hair and beard. "Yes," she said, "the train's due any minute. Could you tell Mrs. Henderson we'll be there by suppertime, as we'd planned?" She took the telegram from her father and handed it to Mr. Thomas. He glanced at Cicero for confirmation, and then came the rumbling of the train from far down the track, tremoring up from the ground into the concrete platform. And Mary Bet heard the rattling of the wheels and the huffing of the steam before the engine came into view.

"Daddy?" she said, tugging at his hand. "Mr. Thomas is going to telegram we're on our way." Two whistle blasts tore the air, and the *huff*-chug-*huff*-chug began to slow as the engine showed itself at the end of the track, its plume of steam and coal smoke trailing. She suddenly did not want to go, did not want to ride the train as if it were a hearse. The harsh smell of burned coal filled the air and she said, "Daddy, I don't want to go off up to the mountains. Let's stay here."

"I'll wire them up there if you want," Mr. Thomas offered. "Make arrangements to have her sent home." He stood there in his old Confederate slouch hat and farmer's worn boots, looking from Mary Bet to her father. He and Cicero were fast becoming the old generation; the new world with its factory towers and whistle blasts and telephone wires was wiping away the old-timers' world. The war had once been their common bond and brotherhood, and now, a generation later, it didn't so much matter—what mattered was how good you were at spotting an opportunity and taking advantage of it. The newcomers seemed to be the ones making the money in Haw County, while men like Cicero and Alson—one in the town, the other in the country—saw their day slipping past, no longer heralded nor much regarded.

"What say you, R.C.?" Alson asked, a sympathetic smile creasing his sun-leathered face.

Cicero took hold of Alson's hand and shook it. "Much obliged," he said. "I don't seem able to think clearly." He'd once looked down on these farmers his father-in-law had gambled with in his declining years, yet he saw now that Murchison as a drunk was no different from himself—furious about the railroad and the change of fortune it brought. How was Captain Billie any different from men like himself who thought the new stores and hotels and mills were too much too fast? Hadn't he himself just this week cursed a buggy driver for nearly running him down, and he didn't even know whom he was cursing? He felt his daughter pulling him along the crowd gathering for the morning train. But he and Mary Bet were going the opposite direction, following Alson Thomas to the station agent's office. He helped Alson compose the message, paid the agent, then shook Alson's hand again, and he and his only daughter took a hired buggy back home. "I think if I didn't have your hand to hold on to," he said, then stopped himself. They rode on in silence.

"It's all right, Daddy," Mary Bet said. There would be time later for crying. She pictured the mountains and how beautiful they must be this time of year. From Myrt's letters she knew they rolled like giant blue waves off into the sunrise and the sunset, and that there were pink and white dogwoods in bloom and mountain laurel. She had a favorite picnic spot "with a tumbling waterfall and a symphony of soft colors and the mountains all behind like the voice of God." Myrt had a way with words, and someday, Mary Bet told herself, she'd see what her sister had been talking about.

They got halfway home before Mary Bet said, "Daddy, shouldn't we wire Siler's school and let him know?" So back they went to the depot, her father still clutching her hand.

Then they were headed home again, and morning sunlight was flickering through the trees and the smells of breakfast made Mary Bet's stomach rumble. They'd had a cold breakfast before they left the house at dark earlier in the morning, thinking they'd get something hot on the train. That was when they still had Myrt. But hadn't they known all along? By then, of course, Myrt was already dead. Mary Bet wanted to tell her father this, but he was sitting quietly beside her, no longer holding her hand, lost in his own thoughts as the buggy jostled down the muddied ruts of the Raleigh Road.

He said, "I've tried to live an honest life, and yet I've made my bed in the darkness. I've—" He stopped talking and looked at his daughter. "Myrtle Emma was—she was the most considerate child I've ever seen. She never thought of herself, only of how she could help other people. I didn't have anything to do with that—that's just how she was. God didn't have any need for her in heaven. I'm sorry if that's a blasphemy, but it's what I believe." They rolled past the old Murchison house, still prominent among the newer dwellings.

"She took care of me when I was sick," Mary Bet said, picturing her sister getting in the bed with her when she had chills. Cicero nodded, but he seemed preoccupied by his quarrel with God.

"What an utter waste," he said. "What was the point of all her reading and practicing?" The carriage wheels rolled on. "Life's hard, Mary Bet. You either work hard, or you feel guilty for not. There's no real rest. Until the end."

"And then we rest in heaven."

Cicero shook his head. "I don't know. I think maybe our cells just decompose, and that's it."

"Don't say that, Daddy. Of course there's a heaven. And everybody'll be there, and it'll be nice."

"Don't be a fool!" he snapped.

They rode the rest of the way in silence. But when the driver pulled the buggy up at their gate, Cicero said, his voice catching, "I'm a fool, baby girl. The biggest of all."

"No, Daddy," she said. And she helped him down and paid the driver, and they went back inside.

~◡ CHAPTER 10 ◠~

1901–1902

MARY BET'S MOTHER had not been much on jewelry, or
finery of any sort. There were a half dozen pieces worth
something, most of them inherited from her own mother.
She'd left them all to Myrtle Emma, her oldest surviving daughter. O'Nora hadn't cared, or at least said she hadn't. It had seemed
thoughtless to Mary Bet that her mother's last will would give
Myrtle Emma the jewels, O'Nora the monogrammed silver, and
Mary Bet the family Bible, as though she'd decided that Myrtle
was the beauty, O'Nora the ambitious one, and Mary Bet (nine at
the time) the keeper of family history. She'd said nothing about her
clothes or anything else, and O'Nora—her mother's same size—
had helped herself to a few dresses.

When Mary Bet was no more than six years old, she'd found
her mother's jewels, hidden beneath the lift-out tray in the leather
sewing box. There on red velvet lay the pearl earrings, the diamond
necklace, the sapphire pin, the opal ring, and the cameos. Sitting

at her mother's dressing table, her feet not touching the floor, she took out the opal ring and tried it on her finger, admiring the rainbow colors in the light that streamed across the table. Her mother came in and quickly removed the ring from her finger and told her she had no business snooping in grown-ups' things. Mary Bet had come to think that her mother was ashamed of laying up any treasures on earth.

Myrtle Emma had insisted that her sisters each select something. O'Nora had taken the necklace, but Mary Bet said she didn't want anything. It seemed wrong for O'Nora to take jewelry without offering some of her silverware, and she told Myrt so. Myrt explained that the silverware would stay in the family until O'Nora left, and anyway you couldn't break up a set of silver.

Now Mary Bet looked at Myrtle Emma's jewelry—she thought of it as Myrt's, even though it was hers now—in the same leather box with the false tray. She tried on the opal ring again and felt no pleasure in its shifting colors. She wondered how her mother had come by it, but thought her father would either not know or not want to think about his departed wife. When her mother caught her trying on the ring, it wasn't just shame and anger, but covetousness too; her mother had secretly loved her jewels and hadn't wanted to share them.

Why was there a curse over her family? Was there any holy way to undo it? She prayed on it daily. She decided that it couldn't be her fault, not entirely, since the first Siler had died before she was born. She wanted to ask her brother what he thought, but he had become so distant with her she was afraid to say anything more to him than "your pants are hemmed" or "Daddy wants you to chop some wood" or "supper's ready" or "will you be home for supper?" He had been morose since Myrt's funeral, an event that had seemed unreal, a joke being played on their family.

And then it was September and Siler would be going back to Morganton soon, and Mary Bet would start up school again. Then the President was shot, and every night for a week Cicero said, after the blessing, "And, Lord, please help our President in his time of need." Once, he added, "He has already suffered enough—," paused, and said, "He's had such tragedy in his life. Amen." It seemed to Mary Bet that the suffering of the President—his little girls dying, his wife becoming an invalid—must be of a greater magnitude than their own. If he could prevail over such hardship, then of course they could too. Yet to lose so many—eight of her ten family members, and all her grandparents—was there not some reason for it?

"Daddy," she asked, looking from her father to Siler and back, "do you believe in curses?" She signed, but Siler just shook his head, a scowl darkening his handsome features. Her father looked at her as if he hadn't understood, and he speared another bite of pork chop with his fork. "I mean could a family be under a curse for some—"

"I understand your meaning," he said, then inserted the bite and began chewing, and Mary Bet thought perhaps her father was dismissing the idea as foolish, the way Siler was. After a moment, Cicero said, "I don't believe the President is cursed."

"But anybody—"

And Siler put his fork down and began gesticulating rapidly and noising words that sounded almost like glossalalia again. "She means *us*," he said, his raised finger sweeping around the table. "Are *we* cursed. It's nonsense." He waved his hand in front of his face. "God can't curse anybody, because there isn't any God! People get sick and die because of germs, and it's just bad luck." His dark eyes gleamed in rage as he leaned forward, his hands tensing after they'd pulled words from the air, as though seeking something to throw.

"That's enough, son," Cicero said. He'd never learned the signs the way everybody else had, but Siler understood him well enough.

"There is too a God," Mary Bet said, feeling her face flush. She felt sorry for her brother and afraid of him, as though the Devil might jump out of him and get her.

"Of course there is," Cicero told her, "and he loves us and watches out for us, and we can't question why he does what he does. We just can't understand it."

She smiled through glazed eyes at her father, then glanced at Siler, who was intent only on finishing his food. Her father smiled back at her, his cheeks sagging and his once-clear gray-blue eyes now murky, and he looked as though there were more he might say on the subject. But he too returned his attention to his plate and Mary Bet felt suspended over a void with no ceiling or floor—what if they were to die too? Her father was sixty, and had come back from the edge of death already.

Then, a week after he was shot, the President died, and at the dinner table Cicero said the blessing and added, "And, Lord, we pray for the soul of the President to rest in peace, and we pray that you protect the new President. Amen." Mary Bet translated for her brother. Siler flashed his dark eyes and said nothing.

"That's three killed," Cicero said. "All in my lifetime. The world is not what it was." He looked at his children. "But I will not complain. I lay at the gate of heaven and was spared." Mary Bet signed this as, "Daddy isn't complaining," but Siler, watching his father's lips, had drawn his own meaning and scoffed audibly. Since his son was to leave in two days, Cicero let it go.

After Siler went back to school, it seemed that the house itself was grieving. Mary Bet began having more people over for dinner and supper, and she started holding tea parties and regular musical gatherings. She formed a sewing circle that met every Wednesday evening when Cicero was out at his lodge meetings. Her mother had never looked on entertaining as more than an obligation: dining at other people's houses meant acquiring social debt. So there was not much pattern for Mary Bet to draw on, other than her sisters' occasional informal gatherings.

One of her school friends, a tall, fair-skinned girl named Clara Edwards, played the piano well enough to read through Myrt's old songbooks, and while she played the other girls gathered around and did their best to read the words and pick up the tune. Though Mary Bet had little of her sister's ear for music, she liked blending her voice in with others.

Sometimes they would have boys over, as long as Cicero knew them and as long as there was no dancing. "Of course not, Daddy," Mary Bet said, though she didn't know why no dancing was allowed, and it was some time later that her father mentioned her mother's disapproval of dancing. There were formal dances with chaperones, and Mary Bet took part in these, though without any great enthusiasm, for she felt ungraceful, and she decided that dancing was, after all, a silly pastime—yet, she did enjoy watching it. She assumed the role of eccentric among her friends: at her house they could play checkers and charades, but not cards; they could dip snuff and talk about having babies, as long as no boys were present, but if somebody said "I swear" or told a funny story about a drunk person, Mary Bet informed the speaker she didn't think it was funny at all. She didn't care what the social consequences were, though the usual consequence was that the new person either reformed or dropped out of Mary Bet's circle. Her friends also talked about sex and what it would be like—the most any of them had done, or admitted to doing, was kissing a boy on the lips—and though these discussions always embarrassed her she was too curious to try to stop them.

One day after church Joe Dorsett came calling with a posy of wildflowers, ones she'd mentioned she needed for her scrapbook.

She showed him the book, its red leather cover embossed with a flower wreath and the word "Remember," and then the blank brownish-white pages, some of them holding keepsakes. He was respectful as she turned the leaves and explained why there was a tuft of horsehair for O'Nora, the rider, or an orange maple leaf for Myrt, who loved the fall. It was nice having a boy in the house, with his heavy boyish smell and breath and his smooth girlish cheeks. She liked the spray of freckles across his upturned nose and his fuzzy upper lip.

"I know a way to talk to spirits," he said. Then, seeing the skeptical, disappointed look in Mary Bet's eyes, he added, "I'm not sure if it really works. A colored woman told my sister, and she told me. But she said it wasn't safe because it was unholy. You have to get in a circle and hold crossed hands with a candle in the middle and something that belonged to the dead person."

"I don't believe in séances," Mary Bet said. "Nor transmigration of souls. I don't think we should try to speak to the dead, or fly around at night. What if we couldn't get back into our bodies?"

"We'd die, I reckon," Joe said. They were sitting on the sofa together in the living room, Cicero out reading in his smoking room. Joe leaned over and kissed Mary Bet on the cheek. The suddenness of it annoyed her more than the kiss itself, and she instinctively wiped it away. Yet she enjoyed the attention; she couldn't help giving him a coy smile. "When they get the telephone line in," Joe said, "my daddy says we're going to get our own telephone."

"I don't believe it," Mary Bet said.

Joe looked at her, started to protest, then said, "I don't either. He says things that don't always turn out to be true."

Mary Bet shook her head and smiled. She liked the way his eyes danced when he was thinking of something, and she had the sudden desire to run her hand over his spiky brown hair with its whorling cowlick—she thought it would feel as stiff as a shoe brush.

She went over to his house one evening for supper. She knew his brothers and sisters, but she'd never met the old man they called "Daddy Roderick," a wizened little man with skin so tight around his skull you could see the blood vessels keeping him alive. He sat at the table with a red crochet shawl around his shoulders, while Joe's mother cut up his food and fed him. "Daddy Roderick just celebrated his hundred and third birthday," Mrs. Dorsett told Mary Bet. "He fought in the War of 1812."

The old man coughed, sounding as if he were strangling. Mrs. Dorsett gave him a sip of warm water. "I never did," he said, his voice like dry leaves scraping across a porch.

"You said you did," Mrs. Dorsett rejoined.

"Well, then I was tellin' a tale. I met the president Jackson." His thin, cracked lips curled at the edges. "And I won the rabbit contest wonst." He said nothing more the rest of the meal, but sat quietly eating the spoonfuls of chopped ham mashed into buttery sweet potato that Mrs. Dorsett fed him. Joe later told Mary Bet that he thought Daddy Roderick was his great-grandfather, but he might've been his great-great-grandfather. He didn't know for sure.

He started coming over regularly, asking Cicero if he and Mary Bet could go out walking together. They walked all over town, up to Stroud's feed mill on the Greensboro Road, out past the brickyard and lumber yards to the east, and in the west they'd pass the yarn factory and then the washboard factory. Beyond the washboard factory there was a big farm owned by a New Yorker who came there just to hunt, and there was a copse of huge, ancient hemlocks where they would stand and listen to the birds that sheltered there in the evening. And Mary Bet would let Joe kiss her on the mouth, and she kissed him back and held his arms. He told her he aimed to marry her when he was old enough. He would be eighteen in two years, and he thought they could get married then. Mary Bet only nodded, though in her heart she knew she would not leave her father to marry Joe Dorsett when she was seventeen.

ONE OF CICERO'S two horses grew thinner and was weakened by ringbone and glanders, and by the summer it was clear he was not going to recover. The day finally came when Cicero knew what he had to do. Because there was no point in paying the boneyard man to kill an animal that had no meat on him, and because he didn't want to wait until he had to take a twelve-hundred-pound animal out of his stall in parts, he went out to his wooded lot and dug a big hole. But after leading the horse out there with his Winchester lever-action, he unchambered the cartridges and guided the horse back to the pasture, then went inside and told Mary Bet he thought he would call on the boneyard man. "Might be worth a dollar after all."

"Do you want me to do it for you, Daddy?" Mary Bet asked.

"No, I'll see to it this afternoon."

"I mean do you want me to shoot George?"

"Why would I want that?"

"It won't bother me the way it bothers you. You've had him longer than you've had me."

"I couldn't ask you to do that."

"You're not asking. I'm telling you I'll do it. I'm as strong as O'Nora ever was, and not afraid."

He considered. "All right, then," he said. "You go out there and see if you fare any better than me." He looked at her as though expecting her to change her mind, but she got up and went over to the corner where he'd leaned the rifle. "Mind yourself now," he said.

She opened her hand for the cartridges, which she tucked into the pocket of her skirt. Then she went out to the porch to put on her riding boots. Now she wished she hadn't made any such offer.

She was just as scared of failing her father as of shooting the horse. And what if she were to miss, or just wound him?

She moved quickly, worried that if she paused to think for even a moment she would lose her courage. She led the horse out of the fenced part of the yard and down to the woods. If only Siler were here to do this thing for her father—why did she have to be left alone to take care of him? The air was heavy with the summer smells of honeysuckle and fungus, things growing and dying. They headed out toward the woods, the horse chuffing along at her shoulder. He nuzzled her hair, the rubbery lips seeking something sweet in the smell of her hair soap. She reached into her pocket and pulled out half a carrot and gave it to the horse. She tightened her mouth and kept on moving, the horse crunching the carrot beside her.

The hole was ready, the fill-dirt piled high beside it, a shovel stuck in the ground at the edge. She stood George on the upper lip. He backed up a few steps and she had to haul him forward into place again. She imagined herself as Siler—he would only want to do the job right and quickly. He would think, "The horse doesn't know, it's just impatient." She levered one cartridge into place and slid another behind it, though she was sure it wouldn't be needed. It was strange how calm she felt. She dug her feet in, studying the ground behind in case the kick should knock her back.

"Good George," she said quietly, stroking across his cheek down to his throatlatch, picking out the spot beside his eye where she would rest the muzzle of the gun. She stood on a rise just higher than the horse so that there was not much angle to the barrel as she brought it into place. She clicked off the safety. At the last moment she closed her eyes.

She heard the echoing report as though it had come from some-where deeper in the woods. The horse was gone. She leaned over and saw a crumpled mass of spindly legs. She squatted and reached the gun barrel into the pit and pushed it against George's side. He was stone dead. When she realized she was not going to cry, she stood and unchambered the other cartridge. Then she shoveled some dirt over the carcass so her father wouldn't have to see it.

Other than her father, the only person whom she told was Joe Dorsett. They were out in their coppice on the western edge of town, sitting on pine needles, their backs against a towering pine. Mary Bet had lifted off her sun hat and was smoothing her skirt over her pressed-together knees. She had taken to wearing blouses with low collars like the other girls—it was much cooler in the summer. She had decided she wanted to be as unlike her aunt Cattie Jordan as she could, so she did not wear jewelry except on special occasions, nor did she pluck her thick eyebrows. The only cosmetics she used were lipstick when her lips were dry and a little powder on her cheeks and nose, and on days like today she sprinkled a few drops of rose perfume on her wrists and rubbed them against her neck.

"It wasn't as hard as I thought it would be," she said. Joe studied her face, waiting for her to go on. "Is that bad of me? That I killed a horse and didn't even cry?"

"Weren't you just a teeny bit sorry for it?"

"Of course I was, Joe. What kind of question is that? But I was more sorry for my father."

"That's all right, then." Joe took hold of her hand. Then he tried to put his arm around her, but she took it off. She wished that Siler could be here so she could explain it to him—he was the only one who would understand and there would be no need for words, or signs either. Just his presence, and his deep, knowing eyes, looking for something long gone.

"I just want to sit today and watch for jackrabbits," she said. Joe sat quietly, his hands in his lap, and she knew he would soon be bored of this and want to kiss her. She wondered if she would ever be able to marry and have children—maybe she would stay an old maid, living by herself or with some old-maid companion. She had practically told God she would, hadn't she? She tried to remember the exact wording of her vow. Anyway, if God meant for her to marry, he would give her a sign.

A large rabbit loped from the woods to the edge of a meadow, put its ears up, then began nibbling at the grass and clover. "If I had my gun," Joe said, "I could shoot that thing."

"I don't want to talk about shooting," Mary Bet replied.

He took her hand and she let him hold it. "What do you want to do when you grow up?" he asked.

Mary Bet thought about her uncle Cincinnatus and his wife, Nancy, and all their children that they had to take care of and worry over. Then there was Aunt Mary, who had died giving birth. And Aunt Emily, who had married young and moved to Indiana—she hardly ever wrote. And Cattie Jordan. "I want to be like my sister Myrt. I want to have lots of friends around me all the time."

"That's all?"

"I reckon I'd like to see the mountains where Myrt was, and the seashore."

"I've seen the mountains. They're right nice. What else?"

Mary Bet thought about the new houses going up in town. One of them, owned by the chair factory manager, was going to be a mansion—a castle with turrets and bay windows and who knew what else. It would be nice to have a brougham carriage like they had. Clara's family had a tall-case clock with a stained-glass panel. "I'd like a new sewing machine. The bobbin on mine's loose and it's hard to keep the stitching straight, but it still works. It'd be wasteful to get a new one. I could use some more dress patterns, though," she said.

She suddenly stopped. She found that she couldn't help the tears from coming, and she turned away. Joe put his arm around her and asked her what was the matter. She shook her head. "I was thinking of Myrt and how she used to tell me that I was sensitive, and she always took my part for me when O'Nora was pestering me."

They listened to the birds lamenting the end of day, and after a while Joe said, "I'll buy you a sewing machine. I'm going to own a factory someday and a big house and an automobile."

Mary Bet laughed so loud she covered her mouth in embarrassment. "Whoever heard of such a thing," she said.

Joe stood up and spread his arms out as though to grab the entire forest. "I'm going to work in a factory, just like my daddy. I'm going to become assistant manager like him, then manager, then owner."

"Then you can give me all the yarn I need."

"Of course I will," Joe said, almost shouting now. Mary Bet was moved by the power in his voice—she wanted to believe him, but there was something crazy about him, a gleam of the fantastical in his eye, as though he were telling a story and it was all make-believe, not something he would really do. "But I might not make just yarn," Joe went on, "I might make other things."

"Like what?" Mary Bet asked, because she genuinely wanted to know if he had anything in mind at all.

He thought a moment, then opened his hands like a preacher. "I might make steel like Andrew Carnegie, and trains. And I might make guns. And bicycles. And I'd have a telephone in my house. I'd have one in every room, just like Vanderbilt."

"You would, huh?"

"Yes, I'll own this tree right here," he said, slapping the bole of the pine. "I'll buy this farm out from under the Yankee who moved in here, and I'll chop this tree down if I want to. I'll chop it into little pieces and have matches made out of 'em. And I'll use the matches to light my cigars."

Mary Bet just shook her head, delighted but at the same time afraid of his giddiness. "I don't care for cigars," she told him. He leaned against the tree, still standing, and they were quiet for a while, watching the dark of evening steal in among the naked trunks of the trees, as though clothing them. It was so quiet there was no sound at all, not even a breeze overhead.

Then from far away came the seven o'clock bell of the Methodist church. "I have to go," she said.

She took his hand as she stood, and when he bent his head to hers she kissed him on the lips. He kissed her face, then down to her neck, and she pulled back. "That's enough, Joe, for now," she said.

"Will you marry me someday?" he asked. He was holding her by the shoulders the way he liked to do, and looking down into her face, trying to see her eyes in the fading light.

She nodded. "I'll think on it. You sure you want to take on the Hartsoe curse?" She'd only wanted to see what it sounded like to say it to a friend, and now she realized she was serious.

"I don't think you're under a curse. If you were, you wouldn't be here now with me on this evening. You're going to live a long and happy life."

She felt warmed by his words and smiled up at him, but she could not see his eyes because he had pulled her tight to himself and was stroking the strand of hair that she'd let down the back of her neck the way he liked.

~つ CHAPTER II C〜

1902

SILER WAS STRANGELY quiet when he came home that summer. He was moody in ways that Mary Bet had never seen before. He would stand in front of the parlor window, smoking and staring out across the yard in a thick, concentrated way, and if Mary Bet came up in a gay humor and tapped him on the shoulder he would turn suddenly with a scowl that made her shrink away.

They went walking one evening and he told her in a sudden burst of his hands that he had a new girlfriend, Rebecca Savage from Raleigh. She was Jewish and he was afraid to tell their father about her, but he was even more afraid that she could not tell her parents about him. Mary Bet asked about the girl from Wilmington, but Siler dismissed the thought with a quick wave, as though backhanding a fly. Rebecca was all he could think of, how beautiful and sweet she was and how they wanted to run off together, but they didn't know where. While he talked, Mary Bet wondered whether marrying a Jewess (in his language, a bearded girl) would be the same as giving up his own religion. The thought made her almost queasy—he might be buried in a Jewish cemetery, he might even spend eternity in some different heaven, if the Jews had a heaven. "What about Jesus?" she asked. "Does this mean you don't believe in Jesus anymore?"

"Of course not," he vocalized, snapping his fingers. "She doesn't care what I believe."

Mary Bet pulled back, afraid to ask what he meant. Her brother scanned the tobacco field they had wandered to the edge of, its leafy green plants thigh-high and ready for picking. He appeared to be seeing nothing but what was in his mind, far away.

"She has straight black hair, like yours," he told her, "but shorter. And she types faster than anybody in class. She calls me Silo." He made the sign. "Because of my name and because I'm tall and thin."

"What about her family?"

"She has a sister and two brothers, and she's the youngest." He started to go on, then stopped. "Her father works in a brickyard. She goes to a synagogue. I went with her once."

"Was it strange?"

"Yes, but not much stranger than church. I didn't understand anything. She explained it later." The road now passed between two long fields of corn, the stalks so high they were like walls of green and yellow; overhead, birds perched on the telegraph wire that ran from one pole to the next.

"What do you think Daddy would say about it?" he asked.

She was going to say "About what?" to give herself time to think, but she knew what he meant and she wanted him to feel connected to her in their old way, so she said, "He will say fine, if she is pretty and will have pretty children."

"But he wouldn't like it. Mama wouldn't have allowed it."

"That's the only reason he wouldn't like it," she said, and was immediately sorry she'd agreed with him. "But he's different from her." She decided to change the subject. "Clara told me her aunt heard of a white woman in Lumberton that married a black man."

"I don't believe that," Siler said. "It's against the law. How black was he?"

"I don't know. Clara's aunt said it was the most horrible thing she'd ever heard of." Then, realizing this was not the kind of gossip that would help her brother, she said, "I don't see what would be wrong about marrying a Jewish girl, if you loved her and it wasn't against the law." But she *did* think that it would be better if she weren't Jewish—why couldn't Rebecca Savage be Episcopalian, or at least Catholic? She might as well be black—it would be better if she were, then Siler wouldn't think of marrying her.

They crossed the road over toward Love's Creek Church. They walked along the edge of the cemetery picking daisies and touch-me-nots and whatever else they could find to decorate the graves of their family. No one had come out the past few weeks and the flowers on the stones were wilted and sad. Mary Bet liked putting fresh flowers on all the stones—so many of them now—though she didn't think that her dead brothers and sisters minded if the flowers got old.

She saved the largest and prettiest bunch for Myrt. It was a small arched stone with her name and dates and the inscription, "Weep not for me. I am waiting in glory for thee." An engraved olive branch curled along the top. Mary Bet got on her knees and placed the flowers on the grass at the foot of the stone. She closed her eyes and tried to recall Myrt's voice when she was telling a funny story, but she couldn't bring her voice to mind at all. It had only been a year—in another year what would she have forgotten? She would never forget the feel of Myrt's hand on her forehead, or the warm scent of her hair, or the way her cheek dimpled when she smiled, tucking the corners of her mouth back just so, or how her fingers looked like spiders on the keyboard, or a million other things. How could they just disappear and never come back?

She came over and stood beside her brother. She shook his arm to make him watch her signing. "I had to shoot George," she said.

"I know," he cut in. He pointed down to the river, past the confluence with Love's Creek, where the water glinted in the last rays of sunlight. There were no signs of life but a vine of smoke from an outdoor fireplace across the river and the barking of a dog.

"Siler," she said, "you know I killed that crow." And now she was crying and trying to catch her breath.

"What crow?" he asked. He gave her a puzzled look, tilting his head, biting his lower lip the way he did when he was thinking hard. There was not enough light left to the day now for her to see into his deep-set eyes—we're all just skulls with skin, she thought. Across the river she could no longer make out the smoke, or the chimney, and the opposite bank was indistinguishable from the darkening water.

"You know that crow that belonged to Willie and I was supposed to take care of it, and I forgot to give it water—well, I didn't give it water because I was afraid of it, and then I thought it was going to die and I prayed for it to die quickly, but it didn't. And when it did die I thought I was going to be taken by the Devil that very night, and I tried to stay awake all night. And in the morning when I wasn't gone, I thought he was coming for me, and was going to surprise me. I don't know but he's not coming someday." She wanted to tell him more, but she just couldn't.

Siler shook his head at all this. It was becoming hard to see, and her signing was imperfect anyway. What she was trying to tell him seemed crazy, but she was upset.

"And you knew about it, didn't you?" she asked. "I thought you knew. Don't you remember?"

"No," he said. "I don't remember. Let's go home." He took her hand and walked with her back up to the cemetery. Now the dusk had faded to night and the evening star was out in the western sky.

"I've done worse things," she whispered. But he had not seen her lips. "I killed a living thing, on purpose." She thought, I don't believe in the Devil anymore, but I saw him there with Daddy, *I know I saw him in the broken glass.*

At supper that evening, she was again left to start the conservation, if there was to be any at all. "Daddy," she said, "who was that down at the store today, the old man with his dogcart?"

"Nobody," he said, shoveling his peas toward a piece of cornbread. "Just a Jew peddler named Gubbs that comes by every now and again, selling goose grease and string and such. Got a swayback pony so he doesn't have to haul the cart himself."

She glanced at Siler to see if he was attending to the talk, but he was paying no attention and she didn't bother to translate. She told Cicero that Siler had a new girl named Rebecca, and as soon as the words were out of her mouth Siler glared at her. He shook his head curtly and she signed, "What's wrong with telling him that?"

"I told you in confidence," he said, squeezing his fists. He pushed back from the table and cleared his plate.

"What's the matter with him?" Cicero asked.

Mary Bet shook her head, tears coming to her eyes. "He can't talk about it."

"I know that," Cicero humphed, "but why—"

"Daddy, he's just eaten up from the inside, he doesn't know why, and I think he suffers worse than any of us, because he's more sensitive. He always has been."

"I didn't say anything—"

"No, it's not your fault. It's just—he's going with a Jewish girl. There, I shouldn't have told you, but I did. Please don't say a word to Siler about this." She studied her father, but he betrayed nothing, just continued to mop up the molasses on his plate with his last bite of cornbread. What was he thinking, and why would he not say a word? "Well, Daddy?"

"Well, what?"

"Why don't you say anything?"

"You told me not to."

"You can talk to me."

"There's nothing to talk about. He's a grown man, he can do as he pleases. I don't know what they do out there at that school. I know they go to church, and the Jewish people have their own church, or synagogue, or what have you. I don't know what your mother would say."

"It doesn't matter what mother would say. What do you say, Daddy? Why don't you go out there and talk to him, he's eaten up inside about it because he's afraid you won't approve." The front door opened, then closed again. "All right, just go after him, I don't know what he's liable to do in this state."

"What do you think he'll do? I'm just sitting here a-wondering what the girl's parents are thinking. You know, Jewish folk don't cotton to marrying gentiles anymore than the other way around."

"That's good that you're seeing things from that angle, Daddy, but who's talking about marriage?"

"If we're not talking about marriage, what's the problem? Unless he's dallying with her." Cicero slowly got to his feet, a hand going to his back as he straightened up and arched. "I won't catch up with him, you know. And by the time he gets home, I'll be asleep."

"Then speak to him in the morning."

"He's always up and doing his deliveries before I'm hardly awake," Cicero said. Then, "I'll speak to him tomorrow," raising his voice just enough to make her back down. "Now I'm going to my study where I don't want to be interrupted for the next hour solid, not unless the house is afire, and then only if you can't handle it yourself." He trundled off, leaving her to clear the table and take the dishes out back to the washstand, where she worked until the light had turned grainy and the lightning bugs winked like watchful little eyes in the warm, still air.

She waited for Siler to say something to her the next day, but he acted as if nothing unusual had happened. Her father was short with her, and so she assumed he'd not had a pleasant day and was not disposed to conversation. The next day he was at his lodge meeting, and it was not until the day after that she had a chance to ask if he'd talked with Siler. Cicero shook his head as if hardly remembering. "I've been so busy, I haven't had time. It slipped my mind. I'm not sure why it's so important to you. You could speak to him yourself."

"Daddy, you don't—" She'd started to say "understand," but that would be rude, and not quite accurate—he understood.

There was never a good time to bring the matter up again, to either Siler or her father. When they saw Siler off at the train station, he seemed happy, probably, she thought, to be leaving and heading back to what he considered his real home now. He looked so serious and grown-up standing there in his gray pinstripe suit, his raincoat draped over his arm, his fedora cocked to one side. She felt an upwelling of love for him that she was afraid of—she wanted to embrace him there and tell him that she loved him and would always love him, and that they should forgive each other for what had happened that dreamy afternoon years ago. But the train was coming, its scolding whistle shrill and certain as it cut the morning air. There was still time to kiss him . . . all her life, she thought, looking back on this place, she would regret that she hadn't.

But in the bustle of bags and last-minute questions about tickets and his lunch sack and reminders to write every week, there was no chance even for another hug. Siler shook hands with his father. "I'll be home Christmas," he vocalized. He winked at Mary Bet. "Be good," he said.

At the "All aboard!" he was swallowed in the gathering of passengers, and he never looked back.

ON THE EIGHTH day of November the Western Union telegram came. Siler had been making his way along a train track outside of Morganton, where the roads were too muddy for walking. The conductor had blown his whistle in plenty of time, he said, and had put on his brakes. He couldn't understand why the young man wouldn't get out of the way, but he never even turned around. When Mary Bet later had time to think about it, what she could not understand was how Siler was unable to feel the train coming. She could feel it herself down at the platform—you didn't have to see it or hear it. "He couldn't hear it," Cicero said, "that's all there is to it. He had no business walking along the tracks like that."

"The girl—" Mary Bet tried to tell him. But when she saw the pain in her father's eyes, she couldn't go on. She wanted to tell him what was on her mind, that perhaps Siler had had a falling out with Rebecca, that they were afraid of what their parents would say if they were to become engaged.

Cicero shook his head. "He couldn't always feel vibrations. I could walk up right behind him sometimes and he wouldn't know I was there."

He always knew, Mary Bet thought. He just didn't always turn around. But he always knew; he knew even better than people who could hear. *He chose to stay on that track, and he left us no reason why.*

After the funeral, Mary Bet went into her father's study and sat with her toes just touching the carpet, the way she used to as a little girl. He was in his easy chair, a book on his lap, his glasses midway down his nose, and it was hard to tell if he was reading or just staring at the book.

"What is it, Daddy?" she said.

He shook his head. "I'm not sure if we shouldn't've asked more questions."

"Questions?"

"Of the sheriff out there last week. Why did they not take him to the hospital, or a doctor?"

"I'm sure it was too late for that, Daddy."

"But why to the sheriff's office, then, and not straight to the coroner's? Why do him that a-way? If he was dead and hadn't done anything wrong."

"I'm sure there's an explanation for it. We'll wire and find out. Or you can call on your telephone at the store."

Cicero shook his head. "No, I'll write, if I can think what to say. I don't want to trouble anybody, and I'm sure you're right."

It was not for another three weeks that Cicero brought the subject up again. One evening as supper was ending, he reached into his jacket and pulled out a letter and his reading glasses, which he exchanged for his regular pair.

"Letter here from Sheriff Meacham out in Burke." He read,

Dear Mr. Hartsoe,

In response to your inquiry, your son, Siler B. Hartsoe was brought to this office by the Southern Railway Company after the accident on the 8th of November. He was already deceased and had been declared so by Dr. J. Trimble Bone, Burke County Coroner. Since your son was not a local resident, the railway company decided to transport the body to my office rather than an undertaker's to await shipment back to his home and so that I could sign the release form allowing said shipment and provide you with a copy of the death certificate. We have had two similar cases that I recall, one when I first took office nine years ago, and another a

*few years before that time. After the superintendent of the North
Carolina School for the Deaf came and identified your son (veri-
fying the identity card in his wallet), I immediately called the
Hartsoe City sheriff's office and was given your telephone number
at the Alliance Store. The death occurred at approximately 3:15
p.m., and I spoke to you at approximately 5:30 p.m. that same
day. I believe, from the wire I received, that the body of your son
arrived the next morning at approximately 8:45 a.m. I hope this
clears up any questions and concerns, and I want to express my
deepest sympathy for the loss of your son.*

  Yours sincerely, John Meacham, Sheriff

He carefully folded the letter, replaced it in the envelope, and
tucked it back in his pocket. "I reckon that explains it."

Mary Bet nodded, and though she wasn't convinced, she didn't
want her father worrying about it any more. But now the letter
had raised more questions than it had answered, and she could
not help wondering what Siler was doing out there. Was he alone?
Where was he going? And were the reports from the railway and
the coroner and the sheriff one hundred percent accurate? She had
no reason to doubt them, but she wondered how complete they
really were, and if the conductor, for example, had something
more to add than the impersonal statement on record, "male pe-
destrian failed to heed warning whistle." She would like to talk
to the conductor, ask him if Siler turned around at all, shrugged,
gave any sign of awareness. Anything would help put her mind
at ease, because she could not help imagining the worst possible
scenes. If Siler had thrown himself under the wheels, certainly the
conductor would've reported it, but if he'd glanced back, ever so
briefly . . . well, that would be worth knowing, though she couldn't
say exactly why. Maybe it was better to assume that he simply was

lost in his thoughts—but what thoughts? Could his foot have gotten stuck? She looked at her father, tears stinging her eyes, and she didn't bother wiping them away.

"What is it, baby girl?"

She shook her head. "Nothing, Daddy, I just don't want you to worry so." She got up and cleared the dishes.

～つ CHAPTER 12 C～

1903

T HE MONTHS AFTER Siler's death were among the hardest Mary Bet thought she'd ever be able to endure. If there is
more grief to come, she told God, I will not survive, and when
she thought she might not be able to stand waking up and going
to school one more day she pictured her father, more bent now, but
still walking to his work. She thought of him sometimes as a gray
statue carved from a lonely mountain, bearing the wind and the
rain. We go on living because we have no choice, she told herself,
because there is nothing else for us to do.

Several weeks before the monument that was to grace the courthouse grounds arrived in Haw County, the Winnie Davis chapter
of the United Daughters of the Confederacy held a contest to elect
a speaker who would represent Hartsoe City at the unveiling. The
event promised to be the biggest gathering in the county since the
hanging of Shackleford Davies.

"You ought to enter that contest, R.C.," said Oren Bray one morning at the Alliance.

"What contest?" Cicero said, not looking up from the clipboard where his monthly tabulations ran in neat, hand-ruled rows.

"Why, to speak at the unveiling. Looks like you'd want to represent Hartsoe City, with your name and all. Course, they's other Hartsoes could do it, but none with your learning and eloquence." Oren spat into a pewter cup he kept on his lap, then tilted his chair back until it leaned against the wall beside the stove.

"I don't know about that," Cicero said, judging the amount left in the flour bin by shifting its contents until it was level, then pulling back and eyeballing the whole. "I don't know about any contest."

At home Mary Bet said that her teacher had announced the Confederate Monument Oratorical Contest for the unveiling in June. One child and one adult would be invited to deliver an address in Williamsboro. "She told me I should submit an essay."

"Oren Bray told me the very same thing," Cicero said. "Maybe that way we'd both be up there at the podium. Wouldn't that be a sight?" He reached over and touched her arm, and the rare feeling of his hand on her sleeve warmed her. She knew he'd forget about the essay contest, but that it didn't matter. She would write something and show it to him, and then remind him to do the same, and in this way they could work together on a project that was not just for getting through the day but for a loftier purpose, for giving voice to their thoughts and beliefs, even if destined only for the scrapbook that now had three names on its inside cover—O'Nora, Myrtle Emma, and Siler. She would later look back and wish that she had urged her father not to give the contest another thought.

She forgot all about it until some weeks afterwards when Clara told her that she had composed an essay called "The Spirit of Liberty" and wondered if Mary Bet would read it and tell her if it was good enough to send to the D.O.C. organizing committee. Mary Bet read it and said that not only was it good enough to submit to the adult category, but that she couldn't possibly write anything as good so there was no point in trying.

"You're just saying that," Clara told her.

"No, I mean it. I don't have the knack like you for making things sound clever."

"Of course you do. You're just being modest."

Mary Bet smiled at her friend and kissed her on the cheek. They'd walked out to Love's Creek so Mary Bet could put fresh flowers on the graves. "No," Mary Bet said, "I have a gift, I'm sure I do because everybody does. I don't know quite what 'tis yet." At the foot of Siler's grave she placed the last of the hothouse roses she'd bought with the weekly dimes Cicero gave her for her few needs beyond food and clothes. He was not one for appeasing or communing with the dead, though he didn't mind his daughter doing so, provided she spent her own money.

"I should visit my grandmother's grave," Clara said.

"Then take one of Siler's roses," Mary Bet said. "He doesn't need but one."

"No, I couldn't possibly," Clara responded. "My granny won't care. She didn't even like roses. She said they were mean, because they'd prick you." The girls laughed as they made their way between the stones. "I don't much like cemeteries," Clara said.

"They won't hurt you atall," Mary Bet told her. "They're peaceful and green."

"Do you think the people here will rise up someday and go to heaven?"

"You know I don't believe that, Clara. I know it's just their bodies, and their spirits might not be here now. It's a place to come and think about the people you loved. All these people around us—they could laugh and talk and walk just like us."

They stood a moment at the wide polished granite marking Clara's grandmother. "My mother didn't like the idea of sharing a grave," Mary Bet said. "So Daddy'll have his own."

"They didn't want to be side-by-side for all eternity?" Clara asked. She started to laugh, then stopped herself. "I didn't mean disrespect."

Mary Bet clapped a hand to her mouth, then caught her friend's wrist, and they both burst into laughter. "We should stop, we should stop. 'Tisn't right to laugh." They both went silent, then burst out anew in gales of mirth, sucking in breaths as if they were about to expire. Clara fell to her knees at her grandmother's grave, and Mary Bet dropped along beside her and draped an arm around her shoulders. "Should we say a prayer?" Clara nodded, but her shoulders kept heaving up and down, so Mary Bet said, "Maybe we better not right now. I don't think it would take."

That night she wrote an essay; in it she listed all the good traits she could remember about her brothers and sisters, and her mother too. She read it over and decided it was too personal for the contest, so she crumpled it up and threw it in her wicker wastebasket. She retrieved it, flattened it out between her book of English poetry and her cherrywood desk, and then placed it in the scrapbook. Until she could give it to a daughter—that's how long she would hold on to this book; and if she never had a daughter, then until she died.

She asked her father if he'd written anything. He said he hadn't given it much thought, things being kind of busy down at the store.

"Well," said Mary Bet, "don't neglect it too long. Or you're liable to miss out."

He gave her a droll look, but stopped himself from smiling, knowing she might take it amiss. They'd lately drifted into the kind of relationship old couples have. Instead of flaring into resentments and recriminations, they would hide what annoyed them, knowing that their time together was probably limited to a few more years.

Sometimes Cicero raised his voice to Mary Bet when she forgot to pull out the stove dampers on a cold morning, or broke a saucer. "How can you be so careless?" he'd snap. Instead of apologizing, she'd look straight at him with a punished expression, then get down on her hands and knees and pick the shards up. For hours afterwards he'd mope about in a sheepish way until she forgave him. Though he never asked for her forgiveness, she learned that they would both feel better if she offered it. "I'm a stupid old man," he'd say. "You mustn't mind me."

"No, Daddy," she'd reply, coming over and putting an arm around his shoulder. "I *am* clumsy, and I don't know why." And in this way, she would end up entreating him to forgive both her and himself.

She hid things from him. She saw him thumbing wordlessly through her scrapbook one day, so she removed it from the living room and tucked it in the bottom of her trunk. She no longer told him when she was feeling sick, because it only upset him. So she lay in bed at night worrying about herself and hoping she wouldn't die before morning. She'd stopped telling him about her jaunts to the cemetery, for he looked old and sad even when she described the flowers and the beauty of the day. And what about Joe Dorsett—would her father not be angry if he found out she was engaged? Their dinnertime conversations revolved around church and school and the characters that came into Cicero's store and the sewing projects Mary Bet was occupied with and what household items they needed to restock.

Thus it was Mary Bet who was surprised to discover that her father had been hiding things from her. When the winner of the essay competition was announced in school and her teacher read out her father's name along with that of eleven-year-old Clyde Fore, Mary Bet was at first confused. Her classmates came over and congratulated her and asked if she and her father had helped each other—all she could say was no. She took her time walking home at midday, then went up to her room and buried her face in a book about a girl growing up in the mountains. Someday, she thought, she was going to see Grandfather Mountain.

At dinner she sat quietly eating, while her father asked if she'd seen to his britches that needed letting out and when she was planning on boiling the silverware. She told him pants and silverware would be done that very afternoon. She ate some more, glancing up at his face and waiting. Finally, she could stand it no longer. "Well?" she said.

"Well what?"

"Don't you have something to tell me?"

"What about?" He stifled a belch, then picked his teeth with his little finger, a habit that had crept back after the death of his wife.

"Your winning essay."

"Oh, I forgot to tell you." He smoothed his beard with one hand while tonguing up bits of stray food on his lips. "I entered that contest and now I have to read at the unveiling. I wisht I hadn't, though. Fellers I don't even know came up to me in the street a-wantin' to shake my hand. One of them said 'so the good luck'd rub off.' I said, 'I don't want my good luck rubbing off. I don't have that much on me, that I know of.'"

"Daddy, you could've at least told me you were writing something." She could feel tears coming to her eyes, and she couldn't understand why but she was furious at her father and upset with herself. He was a stone visage, he was Grandfather Mountain himself, sitting there eating his canned corn and beans as if she were some mouse that perched at his table nibbling scraps.

He glanced at her, then stopped his chewing. He swallowed. "Baby girl," he said. "What in the world?" For now she had her head turned away, a napkin at her eyes. "I reckon I beat my own daughter in a contest, and I was too foolish to know how much it meant. I'll tell them I'm not interested."

She shook her head, even more angry with him. "No, Daddy. I just—I thought we'd work on it together."

"Oh," he said. "I see." He sat up and looked out in the yard at the swaybacked gray he'd bought to replace George. "I thought I'd surprise you. Then, when I won, I thought I'd really surprise you. I'm ashamed."

"No, Daddy, don't say that."

"Yes, I'm an old fool and I had no business in any such nonsense. I shouldn't have listened to Oren Bray." He stood up and pulled his napkin from his collar.

"No, Daddy, I'm glad you won. Read me what you wrote, please."

He stood a minute, shifting his gaze from the window to his daughter, then down to the green beans still on his plate.

"Please?" she said.

He sat back down and finished the food, feeling a little silly for his theatrics. "I'll read it directly I come home this evening. And you tell me if it's worthy of reading at the courthouse. If not, I won't."

Mary Bet told her father she knew she'd like whatever he'd written and that she'd be as proud of seeing him up there reading in front of all those people as if he were preaching in church. She rapped her knuckles on the underside of the walnut table and touched her joined fingertips to her chin as though she were resting her chin a moment, a habit her father noticed but never commented on. She imagined that, if he gave the matter any consideration, he thought of her as a strange little creature, a child of odd rituals and quixotic temperament. Yet she knew that love did not require complete understanding.

THEY TOOK THE carriage to the unveiling and had to park a half mile away from the courthouse, so many other vehicles were there. They joined with the crowds heading east, everyone turned out in their finest suits and dresses. Cicero tapped the ground with his new, brass-capped hickory walking stick, a birthday gift from his fellow lodge members. His hand kept going to the breast of his jacket, wherein his speech was folded.

They went up to the dignitaries' platform, behind which rose a three-tiered grandstand festooned with red-white-and-blue bunting. The mayors of both Hartsoe City and Williamsboro were there, as were a number of commissioners and postmasters, the county school superintendent, three preachers, eighty-seven-year-old Mexican War veteran Lane Womack, and one-armed Major William London. But the highest-ranking member of the entire assemblage was the chief justice of the state supreme court, who had graciously agreed to deliver the keynote address.

Mary Bet had never seen so many people. There were boys up in trees and on top of buildings all the way up Main Street for two blocks to where downtown ended and the houses began.

A thirteen-piece band from Silkton led the parade, coming up the Raleigh Road, circling three-quarters of the way around the courthouse, then heading north on Main to the edge of town. They were followed by Colonel John Hatch, chief marshal of the parade, on his tremendous black mare, leading a group of carriages occupied by civic leaders from around the county. Then came the Raleigh fife-and-drum corps, composed of Confederate veterans, almost all of them with gray beards, some on horseback, one limping proudly along, a well-worn drum draped around his neck. Just after the Masons, who rode by in gold-trimmed purple robes, came several groups of schoolchildren, including a final group of twenty—one for each company that had served in the war. A group from the Moses P. Archer School for Negroes marched along in smartly pressed homespuns, and a black contingent that had been on the periphery surged forward, watching as the school leaders carried flags of the state, the nation, and the Confederacy.

Sally Lenora Horton, president of the Winnie Davis chapter, told the crowd that she wasn't used to speaking before such a big group, which remark received so many sympathetic chuckles that her next sentence was inaudible, as was most of her speech anyway, though stray bits were relayed through the crowd. She said the monument under the white covering before them honored the county's eighteen hundred and seventy-three veterans. And that was about the same number of letters she and the women of the local chapters had had to write to get the monument built. A big cheer went up. Then she introduced the four winners of the essay contest, two each from Hartsoe City and Williamsboro. Clyde Fore spoke first, reading his speech so quickly and quietly that he was back in his seat before anyone thought to clap. Then came a ten-year-old girl from Williamsboro, who spoke of her grandfather's bravery at Sailor's Creek in Virginia.

Cicero walked up to the podium, his speech in one hand, his other hand adjusting his reading glasses. He glanced out at the crowd and said he had been given three minutes to speak and he wouldn't go on a second longer, especially in view of the fact that he couldn't possibly top what he'd just heard. His voice was strong and Mary Bet could feel it carrying like a stiff breeze up to the rooftops, where young men leaned against chimneys and flagpoles. And then an actual breeze did come along and lift the edge of her father's paper, his scrawled pencil filling every line front and back, as though he'd decided that one piece of paper was sufficient for what he had to say. As he spoke about growing up in Hartsoe City before the war, the page flipped over and skittered across the platform and out over the heads of those closest in the crowd.

There was a collective intake of breath as a thousand eyes shifted from the speaker to the speech, the tension rising as the distance between the two increased. Cicero paused a moment, glanced out as though nothing had happened, and continued: "And now we come to the business at hand. The statue yonder that everybody wants to see. I fought in that war, and I was lucky. Some weren't." His speech, finally arrested in flight, was handed back through the crowd, then offered up to him by an earnest-looking young man. "You can keep that for a souvenir," he said. "If you think it's worth it . . . Some of those veterans weren't as lucky. I didn't so much mind all the marching and drilling. But the food was the worst I've ever seen, and it was miserable cold and wet sometimes and I didn't much care for being shot at. But we all did what we had to, mostly. I wish we hadn't had to, because I lost some good friends. Someday nobody will remember those people. But that statue will still be there and people will know it meant something." He couldn't re-member the ending he'd written, and it seemed as though he should end on something uplifting, so he took off his wide-brimmed hat and held it over his chest. "God bless those brave men that died, and the brave women they left behind."

The crowd cheered as he took his seat. They were still clapping after he sat down, so he waved and smiled, then turned to Mary Bet and whispered, "Was it all right?"

"It was great, Daddy," she said.

Then it was time for the unveiling. A bugler blew a triumphal series of notes, and Colonel Hatch's seven-year-old grandson, John R. Hatch III, surrounded by the nineteen other children from his group, grabbed the silk rope and began to pull the cloth covering away. He had not practiced, because there had been no need for practice—Sally Lenora Horton had witnessed the head carpenter pulling the covering off himself, heard him saying it was a cinch.

The covering was a light, nearly translucent voile that was sup-posed to simply fall away like silk. But it was hung up on some-thing. John R. Hatch III, instead of being flustered, was enjoying the crowd's gaping attention. He tugged to one side, then flipped the rope up and, with a determined set to his face, yanked to the other side. Two other boys now gave him a hand, and more than one person in the crowd wondered if the entire statue might tumble over and crush the children and turn the day into a tragedy. Somebody yelled, "Lift it off!" Another voice called out, "Let the colonel show 'em how!"

It was then discovered that someone had placed bricks on the edges of the covering, presumably to keep it from flapping like a skirt in the breeze, and forgotten to tell anyone. With the bricks removed, the children gave one more mighty pull, and the covering flew off, the children collapsing in a boisterous heap at the foot of the viewing platform. The crowd again pressed forward as though toward a sacred icon, the thing that would make this day memorable and joyous and make them proud of who they were—even those many born after the war. The granite pedestal was higher than a man, but by standing on tiptoe people could touch the feet of the gleaming bronze soldier, as he clutched the barrel of his grounded rifle and faced north.

Mary Bet and her father left the grandstand as soon as the last speech had ended. Cicero seemed quieter than usual as he drove the rockaway, and Mary Bet thought he must be thinking about all that they had seen and done. "Did you see that little boy trying to shin up the flagpole?" she asked.

"No, I didn't," Cicero said.

"He liked to hurt himself falling, but I reckon he was okay." She looked up at her father, sitting beside her with the reins in his hands, but he kept his eyes ahead. A minute later he suddenly said, "Oh!" and touched the side of his face as though something had occurred to him. "Why don't you drive awhile," he told Mary Bet, handing her the reins.

Mary Bet was happy to drive, but it was unusual for her father to ask her to. He stared vacantly at the road ahead, his shoulders slumped, his mouth half open, and he began to blow air out in a random tune, not quite a whistle, nor yet quite a hum. His large, strong hands were grasping the tops of his legs as though to keep them from floating away. Mary Bet looked at him and saw nothing in his eyes but a dead forward stare, the brim of his slouch hat shading his face from the late afternoon light. "Daddy?" she said, "Are you all right?"

He nodded and kept up his mournful little tune. Another mile went by, during which he hummed, clucked his tongue, and tapped his heels, answering in monosyllables to anything Mary Bet said.

They were coming into the homestretch—approaching Love's Creek Church—when Cicero had his episode. He began by scratching his face, which then turned into pulling his beard. He stood up and jumped from the moving buggy, tumbling over into the weeds and thistles in the ditch lining the road.

The crickets shaking in the grass. The clouds neat cutouts against the blue fabric of heaven. The air still as breath. A moment come and gone and her father lying there with burrs and fluff on his jacket and beard. Then him on all fours, looking around as though trying to remember something. He had a new leg and it had come clean off its stump, and she had to wait until he adjusted the straps. She started helping him back into the buggy and he said, "I thought something was trying to get us, and if I jumped out it would only get me and leave you alone."

"Daddy, are you seeing things?" She tried to keep the fear out of her voice, to push it back down her throat. He hadn't been drinking, so what was the problem?

"I'm not sure. But it was as clear as a dream, as clear as day."

"Was it a person? A phantasm? What was it?" She tried to concentrate on the horse's ears, the way they flicked against the flies.

"Yes, I think so. Did you hear something?"

"No, Daddy, I didn't hear a thing."

She looked around now and wished there were other carriages on the road, somebody just to wave hello to, but all she could see was the sun lowering toward the tree line and, down the road, the little church steeple and cows under a wide shade tree on a tussocky hill. Back the way they'd come, the green fields gave way to pines as the road dipped out of sight. A catbird whined somewhere off in the underbrush. "Let's get on home," she said, helping her father up.

The air was redolent of barn smells and fields of new crops, alive with birds and their songs, as the carriage rolled westward toward a sun dropping through a purple sky. "We'll be home soon," she said, clicking her tongue to liven the horse's step. "You'll be better when you're lying down. I'll get you some ginger ale, and some licorice."

Cicero made a noise, but Mary Bet couldn't tell if he was agreeing with her or moaning. She clucked again and slapped the reins, and the horse, surprised at this treatment, rolled his eyes toward the driver, then hastened his step for a while—until he could settle back into his normal gait. Cicero's eyes were closed, his head lolling forward as though he were asleep, or trying to sleep. She suddenly felt so cold that she wished she'd thought to put a blanket in the carriage—but who would've thought to on such a warm day? She felt alone and frightened, as if there were no one in the world but herself and her father. A cart was coming toward them—a Negro on a mule pulling a load of chickens in wicker cages, and an odd assortment of colored bottles, old tools and rags, and rotten lumber. She waved to him and he waved back.

But he rolled on past and then there was no one in view, only the rise and fall of the road and the farms and a long stretch of woods. She wished they had ridden caravan-style, but her father had been in a hurry to get going.

The rest of the way back, he sat quietly, hardly moving at all, and by the time they'd alighted and were in their house he seemed himself again. Perhaps it was the strain of the day, she thought; he was unused to speaking in public, certainly not before such a large gathering. She wondered if she should tell Dr. Slocum, just to be on the safe side; maybe there was some medicine her father should be taking, something to calm him. She decided that the next day she would call on the doctor privately.

She almost forgot that the next day she and Clara were getting together to plan the next musicale and that she had promised to go over to the Dorsetts and help teach the girls how to fix a dropped stitch. And, of course, Joe came home from his job at the furniture factory and wanted to go out walking. So the day got away from her, and the next day as well, and anyway her father seemed completely back to normal. But once she had thought of the idea of bringing sugar cookies to Dr. Slocum, she couldn't very well not do it. That would be like breaking a promise. She finally went over, five days after she'd intended to, and after his wife took the tin and told Mary Bet she would pass along her thanks, she said, "Was there something else, honey?" Mary Bet shook her head and said that, no, there wasn't.

∽ CHAPTER 13 ∾

1903–1905

WHAT SEEMED TO have changed was that Cicero didn't look quite as well turned out as he used to. It was hard at first for Mary Bet to put her finger on the difference, but once she began to look for things, she could see them plainly. Essie was now coming only twice a week; she did the laundry, some light cleaning, and as much cooking as she was able. It was all the help they needed. One day Essie said, "I don't want to complain about a light load, but your daddy ain' puttin' as many shirts and collars in de basket as he oughta." She held the wicker laundry basket on her hip, her bulky frame only a little more hunched over the years but her face sagging with age. "Either he throwin' things out, or he ain' wearin' 'em to begin wid."

How could she ask her father if he was wearing a fresh shirt and collar? If he'd changed his underwear? That she'd noticed he was bathing every three or four days now, instead of every other?

"Daddy," she said one day at dinner, "have you been to see that new barber, Mr. Clegg? I hear he has a new joke every day."

"What do I want with a barber? I've been cutting my own hair for eight years, since your mother died."

"I don't think you've been attending to it much lately."

He gave her a hard look, then nodded slowly. "So you're at the age where your father's an embarrassment, is that it?"

"No, Daddy," she said, trying not to show how angry she was. He had never raised a hand to her, had not punished any of his children after his wife died. Mary Bet had yelled at him only once—a year back, when he was questioning her on how much time she was spending with Joe Dorsett—she'd only raised her voice, saying it was her own business. She couldn't bear to see him hurt, and so she had learned how to guide him to a new topic. He was as easy to steer as a well-schooled horse, and so she felt she had to be gentle with him. She would always be his baby girl, the last of the nine, and could do no wrong in his eyes. "No," she said, "you're not an embarrassment. I just think you could spruce up some more than you have."

He chuckled and leaned back in his chair. "I don't reckon a weekly haircut is all that important for an old man."

"Sixty-two's not so old, Daddy."

He got up and went out to his sitting room, and there was no more discussion of his hair or his appearance. The next day he cut his hair in front of his mirror and did such a poor job it looked worse than before—tufts of gray-white hair sprouted from the sides and back of his head, while his sole concession to vanity was to leave a few long strands hanging from the thinned-out top like vines seeking better ground. If he'd bothered with his beard, it didn't show.

One Sunday Mary Bet came from the Dorsetts' with some dried herbs and flower parts in an earthenware bowl and set them in the kitchen. She strained hot water through a tablespoon of the mixture—dried bugbane stems, passionflower vines, the leaves and flowers of skullcap, and a little ginseng root—and took the tea in to her father, who was in his sitting room, a heavy book in his lap, staring out the window on a gray, blustery March afternoon. "I brought you some tea," she said. "With lots of honey in it, just the way you like it."

He nodded, glancing at her as though he hardly recognized her. "You could set it there," he said. She put the cup and saucer on the low table that held his ashtray and books, then took a seat and picked up a book and began idly reading about Charles VI of France, the Well-Beloved. Her eyes roamed the page: he was called the Mad; he suffered bouts in which he tore his clothes, broke the furniture, had fevers and convulsions, didn't recognize his own queen; he thought he was made of glass; he was locked away . . . She put the book down and looked at her father.

He took a sip of the tea and made a face. "What is this?" he asked.

"It's a special homemade tea I got from the Dorsetts." She glanced at the random pile of books.

"It doesn't taste like much," he said. "I don't care for it, but I'll drink it since you made it."

"I wish you would, Daddy. It's good for all kinds of ailments."

He sipped at the brew. "Well, I don't see where it'll hurt." He looked out the window again. "That new horse is a funny one. She just stands there watching me like she wants something."

Mary Bet got up so she could see from his angle. The horse, a brindle-gray mare, was busily grazing in the near paddock, where she'd been most of the day. "Lila? I don't think she can see in here, Daddy. Why would she do that?"

"That's what I want to know. Why would a horse stand there a-watching me like that? Sometimes I'll go out there and talk to her, and she pricks her ears up like she's paying attention to every word."

"What do you say to her?" Mary Bet asked, wondering if this was the sort of behavior she should be asking Dr. Slocum about.

"Well, sometimes I tell her about Susan Elizabeth, and how she would've appreciated her. She liked that brindle color on a horse."

Mary Bet thought perhaps she should remember to write down what her father was saying. For one thing, he never referred to her mother by her Christian name; it was always "your mother." But lately he'd slipped sometimes and called her "my wife" or "Susan Elizabeth."

"She once told me something that stuck with me."

"The horse?"

"No," he said, with a little laugh, "though I wouldn't be surprised. No, your mother told me, long about the time you were born, that marriage was like an old coat that never quite fit right, but she was determined now to wear it anyway. There were places that would never soften, but it was hers." He opened his hands and looked at them. "I expect she meant marriage in general, since she was only ever married to me. And then our boy died, and then Annie and Willie, the twins. But it was Ila that killed her, I think. She loved Ila more than anything—everybody did."

Mary Bet nodded, but she was thinking how little she had known Ila, except near the end. It was Myrtle Emma whom she had loved the most, and before her, Annie. But to her parents the younger children must've seemed almost like a second family.

"I kept having a dream after Ila died. I was back with my outfit, and I had both of my legs. We were marching along some high ridge somewhere, with blue hills rolling off to either side. And that ridge kept getting narrower and narrower, both slopes just falling away. All you could do was keep moving forward."

He finished his tea, and said it wasn't bad once you got used to it. She started bringing him a cup every day, and she thought she did see an improvement in his mood. Once she came in and found him laughing at something he was reading. They sat drinking the concoction—both of them, for she thought him more likely to keep drinking it if she joined him—and talking, as had become their late afternoon routine.

One day he told her that Mrs. Edwards had taken a fancy to him, which piqued Mary Bet's interest because she'd heard nothing about it from Clara. Mrs. Edwards had been dropping by the store of late, buying things she couldn't need and sometimes bringing little gifts. "I expect she's lonely and wants somebody to pay her court," Cicero said, "but I told her the ladies I'm interested in are too young to be interested in me."

"You did no such thing, Daddy."

"Ask Thad Utley if I didn't. I told her I was interested in creating something new, and that did the trick. She was slam gone."

"What did you mean?"

"There's something I want to do."

"Oh?"

"I thought I might put a new fruit tree out in the orchard."

"Good, Daddy," she said. "We don't have but one good apple tree left, and one plum."

"Yes, but I'm not thinking about apple or plum trees. I want to put a banana tree out there."

"Banana tree?"

"Yes, I like to eat them, about as much as any fruit, and you can't get them around here, unless you order them special. Then half the time they're rotten, and you still have to pay three times as much as you would for the same amount of apples. But, you see, if we had our own tree . . . And for the cold weather, I'd build a little glasshouse over it, a greenhouse."

"For one tree?"

He chuckled, picturing it. "Maybe I'd put three or four in there. And we'd have all the bananas we could eat, and I'd sell the rest at the store. Make myself rich enough to travel anywhere I want, you too."

"Is there somewhere you want to visit, Daddy?"

His brow suddenly furrowed and he smacked a fist into his open book. "By God, child, you're missing the point."

She sat back as if struck. He had no right nor cause to talk to her that way. She'd only asked him where he wanted to go—the fact that he'd taken it as a way of getting at the root of an outlandish idea made her even more upset. He wasn't as crazy as he seemed— very well then, he could do whatever mad thing he wanted. She could see him watching her, adjusting his tone to fit her reaction.

"What I mean to say," he said, rubbing his beard between a thumb and two fingers and pretending to be lost in thought, "what I mean is that the money is not what interests me. It's the idea. Growing a tropical fruit here—I know it could be done. It just takes somebody to do it. Why not me? Then if we were successful—why, we could do just as we pleased. You can't make it rich by tending a store."

"We have plenty," Mary Bet said. "All we need." Cicero laughed at this, his whole face relaxed now that he could see it was not his idea that was being challenged.

Mary Bet wanted him to know that she was happy for his enthu- siasm, as long as he didn't expect her to devote herself to his project. "Daddy, I know you can do whatever you want." He'd kept his store when others failed during the panic; twice he'd been elected president of the Columbus Lodge; he'd represented Hartsoe City at the Confederate Monument unveiling. And she was sure there were other things she didn't even know about. But what came to her mind was Grandpa Samuel and his broken waterwheel, lying on its side in the grass and weeds.

"You're right about that, baby girl," he said. And the way he said it, straightening himself a little as he did, his wise old confident voice, coming from that shaggy buffalo head, now gray, made her believe him.

When the weather was warm, he sent off to the United Fruit Company in Boston for six dwarf Cavendish suckers. It seemed crazy to him that the plants had to go all the way from Honduras up to Boston before coming down to North Carolina, but headquarters was the only port where the company was willing to consider transacting this kind of business. It took him five letters to convince the sales department that he really did want the underground stems of the plants and to negotiate a price. He was certain that the back-and-forth had to do with the company's fear of competition—they'd never had such a request from North Carolina, a fact that made him proud. To convince the company he was not cutting into their market, he said he was only interested in conducting some experiments with the local soil; any resulting fruit was for his family's consumption. "How do you know they won't send you something that'll die before it gets here?" Robert Gray asked him down at the store one day.

"That's a risk I'll have to take," he said. "Besides, the United Fruit Company would never do a thing like that."

"Maybe not," Robert said, "but they could say the plants were healthy when they sent them."

Thad Utley grinned through tobacco-stained teeth and said, "You can always feed them bananas to the hogs if they don't turn out good. That's what I do with my peaches." He leaned forward to spit, nearly turning his tilted chair out from under him.

"I'll take it under advisement," Cicero said. "You boys just wait till I'm rich and famous. You'll be lining up to join my company. I might let you pick a bunch or two."

The suckers arrived as scheduled at the train station, packed in two wooden crates the size of big coffins. Cicero and the four Negroes he'd hired unloaded the crates onto two luggage carts, the stationmaster attending the process with great concern. Bystanders looked on with amusement. "Why, he's lost his mind, same as his father," was one comment. "No, he just likes bananas."

Cicero was too busy to notice. "Watch how you make that turn now," he said. "The whole thing's liable to topple."

"I didn't think bananas could weigh so much," the stationmaster said.

"It's the soil," Cicero replied.

"Well, as long as you don't spill it all over my station."

The men loaded the crates onto a heavy two-horse drag and proceeded down the Greensboro Road—newly laid with planks—into town, then across the river and up the hill to the Hartsoe place. They drove the cart right up beside the orchard, where Cicero had dug a half dozen holes, two feet deep and two feet across, spaced three feet apart in two rows. The journals he had been reading were unclear as to the optimal spacing of banana trees; the configuration he'd settled on meant a greenhouse two hundred and thirty-four square feet, which would give the trees room to spread at the top. He thought he could get by with just a glass roof and windows; still, it was a lot of glass, enough to cover two bedrooms. But if his grandfather could build the first house in the county with glass windows, he could build the first with a glass roof.

The men worked all day getting the plants into the ground, packing the holes with chicken manure, and watering them with a piggin relay. "I hear bandana taste like sweet potato with molasses," one of them said. "Yaller-skin taters on trees," said another, mopping his brow with a tattered cloth. The quietest of the workers, and also the strongest and hardest working, was a broad-chested man named Able. Cicero retained him to come back every week and help with the watering and fertilizing and weeding. He'd worked for Cicero before, and prior to the war his parents had been owned by the Cheeks, Cicero's mother-in-law's people.

Within a few weeks, green shoots began breaking the ground. Cicero and Able kept up their weekly routine. "Shore this ain't corn?" Able asked.

"You wait and see," Cicero said. "Come next summer, we'll have all the bananas we can eat."

Able shook his head and kept working. The only comment he would make about the new crop was that it was growing fast as corn and the leaves were bigger than any he'd ever seen. At the end of one day he looked at the plants, now knee-high, and said, "Look like big green ceegars." If he had any doubts about the worthiness of the enterprise, he kept them to himself.

At the end of another day Cicero saw Able looking at the plants and he asked him, "Able, you must think this is the foolhardiest thing you've ever seen."

Able smiled broadly. "Nawsuh," he said.

"I reckon," Cicero probed, "if I said I was planting magic beans so I could climb up to the clouds you'd keep working, just as long as I was paying you."

Now Able leaned on his hoe and took up a serious expression. "Nawsuh, Mr. Hahtsoe. 'F you said they was magic beans, I'd do de work fo free, long's you gimme some of dat gole you fine."

"So you'd partner with me on a long shot, but for something as homespun crazy as bananas you want your money up front?"

"Thas right, yes, suh."

"Well, I appreciate your honesty, Able. I never was a gambling man like my father-in-law, who was happy to gamble away his house if he was so inclined. But I'll make a deal with you that won't cost you a thing." Cicero looked at Able, and Able tapped his hoe against the ground, as though considering the soundness of the earth around him. "If this crop turns out nice and healthy, and you stay with it—at the same rate I'm paying you—I'll let you have all the bananas off one tree."

Able thought about it for a moment. "That mighty kindly of you, Mr. Hahtsoe," he said. "Which tree you sayin' is mine?"

"I won't tell you that, or else you'd pay more attention to it than the others. Not that you'd mean to. When the time comes, I'll pick out a nice one for you."

"All righty then," Able said. He grabbed up his tools and started back to the shed, but before long he stopped. "Mr. Hahtsoe?" he said, turning around. "What if only five of them trees is any good?"

Cicero was amused. "I didn't know you were such a shrewd man of business, Able," he said. "I expect you'll be wanting to set up a shop in town one of these days. I'll tell you what," he said. "If only four trees make it, we have the same deal."

Able wiped a rivulet of sweat from his cheek with the back of his hand. He nodded, "I preeshate it, Mr. Hahtsoe. I shore do." He shambled back toward the shed, and Cicero wondered what was in the man's mind, whether Able really did appreciate the gesture, understanding that to Cicero it was a kind of bargain with God.

Work on the greenhouse and adjoining fireplace began nearly as soon as the banana plants showed themselves. Able said he doubted they'd need such a house for some time, that a few warm blankets would suffice since there was no tree on earth could grow high as a man in six months. "It's not a real tree," Cicero told him. "It's more like corn. Just like you thought."

The first frost came early that year, the third day of October. The house was framed, with spaces for huge windows on all sides and even bigger windows in the ceiling. Cicero had decided, after consulting with all the carpenters he knew, as well as a professor of architecture at the university, to put in skylights instead of a glass roof, which, the professor said, would surely collapse without a steel frame. The work was held up by the unforeseen difficulty of maneuvering ladders and lumber and workmen around the pre-cious banana plants, which had grown to more than six feet tall and stood like a half dozen tightly wrapped pale green soldiers. There was great excitement about when they would begin to bud and leaf out, and Cicero was as worried as an expectant father, chewing through unlit cigars as he went from one worker to another trying to encourage him to work faster.

The largest pane was saved for last. It was to be fitted into the south-facing slope of the roof to catch the most light. Cicero had a scaffold erected around the structure for this delicate operation. The lumber for the scaffold and the greenhouse he had scavenged from his father's property. Now to set the pane he and his six hired hands walked the glass up the side of the building, resting it on a cushion of blankets spread along the eave while three men went up top to receive it. Then all six men were on the roof, Cicero underneath to shout directions. He reflected that if the roof were to collapse, this would be the time, and he would be crushed beneath glass, under the weight of a crazy dream, and no one would speak of it without a shake of the head.

The window fit into its frame and held, and the men began nailing the top braces around it.

There had been two nights of mild frost, during which Able kept the new fireplace going, as well as a smudge pot inside—a cauldron of red-hot coals, ventilated out the unfinished roof. With the building glassed in, Cicero decided to dispense with the smudge pot and take his chances with the fireplace. For the first few weeks, he came out periodically in the night, checking the plants and the air temperature, inside and out, logging the numbers into a little ruled booklet. In the first week of December, the overnight temperature dipped below thirty; inside the glasshouse the air was barely above fifty. Cicero got the smudge pot going again, with Able and another man to tend it in four-hour shifts. They took to covering the roof with blankets at night, and taking them off during the day, and so kept the indoor temperature close to seventy.

By the middle of the month, all but one of the plants had turned brown. Cicero continued to water and fertilize them, but it became clear that they were dead. The final plant succumbed by the end of the year. It was the one closest to the outdoor fireplace, and Cicero lamented for the thousandth time that he had not built the greenhouse up against the main house. "I thought of doing it," he said, "but all the pictures showed them standing alone. I should've known better—those were in subtropical regions."

Mary Bet had been helping spell her father with his late-night outings, putting on her boots and coat and going out with a taper, and one of their barn dogs would come wagging up to accompany her. "It's all right, Daddy," she told him. "We can just move it in the spring, and you can get new plants."

He shook his head. "The expense," he said.

"We can cut back on sweets and silk and fancy things," she told him, "and we can sell Charlie—we don't need but one horse."

"No, I'm going to let this experiment go."

"How do you know it won't work if you don't try?" What she didn't say was that she wanted more than anything for him to succeed in growing at least one bunch of bananas, so she could say to the gossips and naysayers, just one time—he did something nobody around here ever had the gumption to try.

Cicero nodded, as though it were the wisest advice he'd ever heard. "You're right, baby girl," he said. "One attempt can hardly be called a try." So in May he sent off for another half dozen plants, and this time he got a head start on the greenhouse, taking it apart piece by piece and moving it to the south side of the house, where there was such good warm light it was a shame, he said, that they'd never taken advantage of it before. He found that by keeping a tighter account of their expenditures—in the same meticulous way he ran the store and observed the greenhouse—they didn't need to sell the horse. He seemed to have forgotten about their plans to visit the mountains, and Mary Bet felt no need to remind him, or to mention the new Singer sewing machine she'd had her eye on in the Sears catalog.

Three of the new plants developed brown spots before they were three feet high. They stopped growing and died, and Cicero sent off a letter to the United Fruit Company asking for free replacements. A polite reply explained that it was not uncommon for delicate plants under stressful conditions, or in imperfect climates, to develop a fungus that could lead to mortality. They could not be responsible for what happened to the plants after they had been shipped. Cicero shot off another letter, this one with an angry tone that he regretted as soon as he'd dropped it at the station office. How could they not be responsible, he asked, for plants that probably had a disease before they were sent, or could have developed on the train, which was about as stressful a condition as he could think of. He never got a response, nor did he get one from the next two letters he sent, each more outraged and pleading.

But the three healthy plants grew fast and strong, and even though Cicero had promised to give Able the fruit of one tree out of four he amended the promise to one out of three. During this time, Cicero ordered bananas from a fruit company in Raleigh, so that they all could get a foretaste of what they were working toward. The bunches were like hands, Mary Bet thought, with big fingers. For the next few days, when she was sewing, or cooking, or cleaning, or playing the piano, or praying, she thought about her hands. She thought of men building skyscrapers that were, so they said, ten stories tall, and she thought of Siler talking with his hands in sharp little bursts and beautiful sweeping gestures.

One cold night as she was drifting off to sleep under two wool blankets and a down comforter, just feeling her body begin to float into unconsciousness, she heard the door close and a voice rise up from outside. "He's put a spell on those plants," her father said. She got up and went to the window and saw him down below, standing in his white nightgown, his feet bare, holding a lantern up to the greenhouse and staring in. "He's spelling me, that black devil. I'll spell him!"

She lifted the sash and called out, "Daddy, what are you doing?"

He looked up, holding the lantern as though to discern who was speaking. "Nothing," he said, as brightly as a child caught in mischief, "just checking the plants. Go back to sleep."

"Daddy, it's freezing out. You oughten be outside without a coat. The plants are fine, Daddy. Please." He looked at the greenhouse, as though staring at his reflection in the dark glass, then back up at his daughter. "I'll come out and check on them," she said.

"No, I'm coming in," he replied. "They're fine, I thought somebody might've—"

"What is it, Daddy?"

"Nothing." He shook his head and went back around to the summer kitchen, where he let himself in, and then she could hear the back door opening and closing, and finally the footsteps on the stairs. She decided to stay put in her room. No need to embarrass him any more. She had a friend whose sister sleepwalked outside in her nightgown, carrying a chair so that she could have a tea party. Maybe that's what Cicero had just done, though he'd never sleepwalked before that Mary Bet could remember, not even talked in his sleep.

Under her blankets and comforter again, she shivered and tucked her knees up. What would he do next? She stared into the black darkness to where her door was, and she got up and found her way there and pulled in the latchstring.

~⌐ CHAPTER 14 ⌐~

1905

T HE THREE BANANA plants held through the winter and
into the spring, and in the next summer they bore the first
known crop of North Carolina bananas, seven arms of small
but sweet yellow fruit. Cicero picked one of the two best trees for
Able to harvest for his own use—Able sold half the fruit, at a dollar a bunch. They learned that the fruit which ripened on the tree
was the sweetest, but would rot within a day or two. Cutting the
bunches down when they were green gave them a few days to get
the fruit to market before it began to turn the lemony yellow color
that meant it was good to eat.

One of the trees began to develop the telltale brown spots of
fungus. Cicero saw them one morning and felt as though a child
had developed a rash; his chest tightened with dread. The long
green fronds, never as big or healthy as those of the other two survivors, withered back, etiolated into little pale yellow wings, and
died. The new clusters were stunted and Cicero let them ripen on

the tree. They turned an odd marbled yellow color, and when he peeled one he found almost no fruit inside—it was hard and pulpy, like wood, with long brownish-red veins. The taste was mealy, and he took his butcher knife and hacked off all the fruit of this tree and threw it to the pigs.

There were now two trees left, still producing good fruit when the first autumn chill set in, and one morning Cicero went out to the greenhouse to speak to Able. He was not sure how he should put what he had to say, because the terms of their deal had never been clear to begin with in his mind. And Able had taken such pride in owning the tree. What bothered Cicero slightly, though he never put it in words to anyone, was that Able never seemed apologetic at all about owning one of the two remaining trees. It was as if he thought he deserved to have it simply because he'd been lucky enough to have one that would outlast the others. When he entered the greenhouse, he found Able checking the plants' progress.

"Stumps just keep puttin' out new leaves," Able said, "soon as the old ones die. I think these two is just the strongest of the lot. Like you and me."

"Yes, well, Able," Cicero said, "that's what I wanted to talk to you about." Since Able only glanced up, a flash of white in a dark face behind the fronds, Cicero knew he would have to just go on and speak his mind. Was the air in the hothouse always so steamy, so wet you could hardly breathe, the windows so fogged you could see nothing of the outside but a gray blur? "You see, Able, I know how you love that tree, and I've let you harvest it as though it were your own. But now that we're down to just two trees, I have another deal to propose that I'm sure you'll think is fair." He waited, but Able made no sound at all; he just kept studying the trees for dead leaves to prune.

"I'm proposing," Cicero said, "to let you keep half the fruit of that tree. That's more generous than I ought to be. It's more than our original agreement. What do you say?"

Able, his eyes uplifted to the thin green hands growing just above his head, said, "It's your tree, Mr. Cicero. You can do as you please."

"That's what I thought you'd say, Able. Just go on picking the fruit as you've been doing, but leave it for me to sort through. I'll see you get your half." He thought of saying something about how he'd make sure Able got plenty of good bunches, but he decided to leave it at that. As he was heading out, he heard Able clear his throat.

"This here's a fine tree," Able said. "You won't be disappointed, nawsuh. I've kept it in tip-top shape."

"I know you have, and I know you haven't neglected the others at the expense of that one. And I'd ask you to consider what would happen if the other tree over there were to die?"

"I spec we'd have to share and share alike," Able said.

"Yes, I'd find some equitable arrangement." He made a jovial little laugh that sounded false to his own ears. "Able," he said, "I hope you won't think I've gone back on my word. I believe if you cogitate on it, you'll come to the same conclusion I have."

"Yessuh," Able said, "I surely will cogitate."

Cicero eyed the younger man—he had never known him to be surly or disrespectful; he wouldn't stand for it from any employee. Able looked back briefly, nodded and smiled, then seeming to recognize what was being asked, said, "I've cogitated on it, Mr. Cicero. And I believes you's right. This tree is a fine tree, but I am not its master. Nawsuh, not by a sight."

"All right, then," Cicero cut him off. "Just leave out what you pick, and I'll sort it and set your pile over by the door." He went inside and it was not until that evening that he told Mary Bet the new arrangement he'd made with Able. "I don't know why I should feel guilty over it," he said. "It seems a fair arrangement, doesn't it?"

"Yes, Daddy," Mary Bet said, though she was thinking of something Joe Dorsett had said to her that afternoon. He was nineteen now, she eighteen, and he told her he had decided their secret engagement had gone on long enough; they should get married next year and he wanted a firm promise. He was saving up his money from his job at the chair factory to buy her a diamond engagement ring on credit at McAdo's jewelry store. She was not sure whether she wanted to give Joe her firm promise.

"Able's mother was a house girl for your grandmother Margaret," Cicero said. "He's a good worker, but he thinks I owe him an entire banana tree just because I—"

"Daddy, I don't care about your banana trees and your workers. It's all you ever talk about. Bananas bananas bananas. I don't want to ever see another banana." Mary Bet stopped, aghast at the words that had flown from her mouth. "I'm sorry, Daddy. I didn't mean to—" She put her napkin to her mouth, afraid she might say something else she'd regret.

Cicero sat there in silence, his hands on the table for support, his napkin dangling from his shirtfront. He nodded and smiled, but his eyes looked sad and faraway. "I guess I do go on," he said.

"No, Daddy, I had no right to speak up to you. I'll go to my room."

"Then I'll be left alone."

"In peace."

"I don't want that," Cicero said. "You know I don't. You're all I have left. You and—well, everybody thinks I belong in the loony bin, just for growing tropical fruit."

"Someday—" Mary Bet started, then wondered if this was a good time to bring it up. But perhaps a better occasion wouldn't come along for some time. "Daddy, Joe Dorsett wants me to marry him. When I turn nineteen." She sat still, listening to the sound of her voice in the silence, looking at the remains of supper on her plate.

"Well, is that what you want?" Her father's voice had gone very quiet and steady; he looked old, more like her grandfather Samuel than he ever had.

"No, Daddy," she said. But she was thinking how romantic it would be to go away on a honeymoon with Joe, off to the seashore.

"I don't see how he could provide for you. He's a good talker, but I don't know if he'll ever amount to much. What's his rush? He ought to get himself an education so he can take up something, like the law or medicine. I wish I had studied law, but the war came along and then there was no money for going off and studying."

Mary Bet nodded politely, then stood and began clearing away the dishes. She was afraid if she sat another moment with her father she would not be able to hold her tongue; she was already burning with anger at him and shame for her earlier outburst. But her father seemed lost again in his own business, that glasshouse of his that was picking his pocket like a flimflammer, and consuming every minute of his waking hours and seeping into his dreams as well. There were times when she honestly wanted to go out there and leave the doors open and put out the fire so that the banana plants would die. Then maybe her father would quit his obsession with getting rich on some fantastical scheme that made him a laughingstock around town. People kept coming to the Alliance, but the new store up the Greensboro Road was cutting into his business. Cicero was not keeping up with the latest pills and powders and housewares, and Mary Bet worried about what would become of him when he had to quit.

Over the next few weeks, the banana plant that Able had tended and harvested as his own developed the rot. Cicero saw Able bending over and carefully cutting away the brown spots near the base of the tree one morning. He said, "It's no use. You might as well let it go. Get what fruit you can off it. You can keep it all. I should've just let you have all of it anyway. I've brought this on myself."

"I don't know what make it do like that."

"Of course you don't, Able. I'm not saying you do. I can tell you what makes it rot like that. It's a banana tree, and it's not meant to grow in North Carolina soil. Look outside there and tell me how many such trees you see growing. Do you see any banana trees?"

Able looked at his boss and shook his head. "Nawsuh," he said, taking on his most subservient tone. "I don't see any banana trees."

"No, I don't reckon you do, even if you could see out these god-forsaken fogged-up windows. There's a draft in here that would kill a mule. You can't caulk up these windows. It still gets in. You might as well chop that tree down. This one too—it won't last. It's all a waste."

Cicero went over to the long worktable where they separated the arms into clusters and small bunches, and he took up his butcher knife. He came up to the tree where Able was working and grasped the nearest leaf, a man-size green leaf with brown blotches around the edge. Able opened his mouth wide. He shook his head. "They get like that sometime," he said, the beginnings of panic in his voice. "It don't mean it's gone to the bad."

"It'll be gone soon, though," Cicero said. He leaned over and began hacking at the base of the leaf, tearing it down to the fibrous stem. He kept chopping and chopping, but it was too tough to give way easily to such a small knife. "I need an ax," he said. "Or a sword." He stood up to catch his breath, a wildness taking hold of him that felt liberating, like being dunked in the Rocky River by the Reverend Lassiter when he was a boy in knee pants. "A machete would be perfect, like they use in the tropics. Do you have one?"

"I'll get one tereckly," Able said. "Wait right there, Mr. Cicero. Don't strain yourself with anymore choppin' till I'm back." Able hurried out and around to the back of the house. Instead of pausing to knock, he let himself in and walked right into the parlor and called out for Mary Bet.

She was upstairs getting herself ready for school. She came to the head of the stairs, holding the unpinned part of her hair up, took the comb from her mouth, and called down, "What is it, Able?"

"It's your daddy," he said. "He done gone crazy."

Mary Bet jammed the hairpin in so that her braid held, and came tripping down the steps and followed Able out to the greenhouse. Her heart beat high in her chest, because she had known all along that something like this was going to happen. Something bad. When they were inside the greenhouse, they could not at first see Cicero. The banana tree at the far end was stripped of leaves to head height, the detritus lying all around the base of the plant. They heard a groan and one of the leaves moved. Then they saw the prostrate figure of Cicero beneath the leaf—a long emerald chrysalis, the human caterpillar a bearded old man in stained white shirtsleeves. "Daddy?" Mary Bet cried out.

She went over and pulled the leaf off her father and took the green-smeared knife from his hand. "Are you all right?"

"Of course I'm all right," Cicero replied. "Can't a man take a nap in his own house?"

"Let's get you up and inside," Mary Bet said. She and Able came around and, grabbing him by his armpits, hauled him to a sitting position.

"I can do this myself," he complained. "I've done it since I was a boy. You needn't fuss. You should all try sleeping beneath a banana leaf—it's refreshing. I'm going to tell Doc Slocum to recommend it. Might even try experimenting with an infusion."

When he was on his feet, he looked around at the leaf litter and, shaking his head, said, "That's not a pretty sight."

"I take care of it fo you," Able said.

"I'd appreciate that," Cicero said. "I can always count on you, Able. I think I'll go in and dress for work. Mary Bet, why aren't you in school? Aren't you late?"

"No, sir," she said, "I'll be fine. Don't you want some breakfast? Essie'll be here right away."

"I've had my coffee and tomato juice. That's all I require. Why is everybody acting so softheaded?"

"We were just worried, Daddy." Mary Bet nodded to Able as she slipped her arm through her father's and walked him back out of the greenhouse and toward the summer kitchen. "You've been under a lot of strain."

She saw that he got upstairs to his room, and then she waited in the parlor, pretending to get her books together until she heard him come down again. "I'll walk with you this morning, Daddy," she said.

That afternoon she went to meet Joe as he was coming back from the factory. The steam whistle from the sawmill shrilled at four o'clock. She had thought of so much to tell him she could hardly hold it all in her head and she'd had to write it down during Miss Birdsong's French class, which was unfortunate since it was Miss Birdsong who had encouraged Mary Bet to attend this extra year of school so that she could help teach the younger students and decide if she wanted to go into teaching herself. She was thinking of this and of what she'd written in Miss Birdsong's class about how her father had begun acting like her grandfather Samuel, when she realized she was a block past the old Buckner house and nearly in view of the chair factory.

She wondered if Joe had gone home early for some reason. It was a cloudy, chilly autumn day, with colored leaves full on the trees and the air sharp with the smell of wood smoke and coal smoke. Mary Bet wrapped her brown knit scarf against the wind on her cheeks and kept walking, studying every face coming the other way.

At the bending and chair factory, a dreary three-story brick building with two chimneys and no windows except on the front and back, Mary Bet stopped and glanced around. She looked up over the barn-style double front doors to the two tall windows on the second floor—they were like sad eyes peering out toward the farm across the road. No more workers emerged from the red-painted doors. Inside on the sawdust-strewn dirt floor were a couple of sturdy carts standing idle at loading platforms, stacks of lumber, an overhead block and tackle, and some large metal machines whose purpose Mary Bet could not divine.

As she started away from the building, she heard a voice behind her. "Mary Bet!" he called out. She turned around and there was Joe walking toward her, his derby shading one eye and his hands in the pockets of his long corduroy work jacket. He looked as if everything were a little too large for him, including the building itself, and she wished she had not seen him here in his workplace.

"You're late," she said. "I thought I'd missed you."

"I had something to finish up."

They walked toward the Raleigh Road, past the prison camp and Carter's rabbit plant, to where the lots became small farms and then, on the Raleigh Road, just houses with gardens and fowl and a barnyard animal or two. "I have something I need to tell you," she said.

"I do too," Joe said. Mary Bet waited for him to speak. "I have to find a new job," he said. He explained that he'd been given the boot for fudging his time card and being late one time too many. "Maybe I should leave town for a while. I have an uncle in Raleigh who works in a glass factory. I've told my daddy I might want to go work there sometime."

"Is that what you want to do?"

"Do you think I should?"

"It doesn't matter what I think, Joe," Mary Bet said. "I didn't—. You know I don't want you to leave, but I don't want you to be without a job either. What makes you think you can't get one around here?"

"If word got out—" Joe hesitated, looking around. They were now at the farrier's across from the post office, the banging of metal spilling into the street. A black street sweeper came along, gathering the horse droppings into piles for later pickup. The wooden sidewalk began at the undertaker's, and Joe and Mary Bet stepped up onto it.

"I have to see to my father," Mary Bet said. "Good-bye, Joe."

She hurried home to her father to see if he had gotten himself into any more trouble. It seemed that she would forever be looking back on this time as a crucial turning point in her life—the loss of her first sweetheart and the certainty that her father was mentally unstable. She would put it out of her mind until she got home; until then she told herself that her life with its problems was a speck in all the universe, a mote of dust floating in a mill with millions of other dust particles and the thousands of other dusty mills falling through the heavens like leaves in autumn.

When she got home she found the house empty, so down she went to the store. There her father was, closing up the shop as he did every day as this hour. From where he stood, back in the shadows near the storeroom, he looked as he always had when she was young and would come by for a stick of peppermint on her way home from school.

She lifted the hinged counter and went back to greet him. "I just wanted to see if you needed any help closing up," she told him.

"Oh?" He looked around, glanced at the orange box in his hands, then up to the shelves stocked with big jars and cans and boxes. "I don't know that I do . . . did you think I did?"

He'd said the words automatically, as though reaching back into his mind for the proper response, and Mary Bet wondered if at that moment he could even say her name.

That night she dreamed the Devil was riding behind her, somewhere just out of sight beyond a low hill. Home lay a long road ahead, but there was a shortcut through a woods. She looked back and thought she could see his black slouch hat; she tried to push her horse, but it wouldn't go any faster. She could feel his shimmering presence drawing nearer and nearer, and she knew there was nothing she could do but let him overtake her, no matter how much fear and pain and suffering lay ahead. She awoke in a panic, her own stifled voice echoing in her mind. For a long time, she listened to see if she had disturbed her father.

1905

ATTIE JORDAN ARRIVED the day after Thanksgiving. Mary Bet had not seen her since a brief visit to Williamsboro last spring to celebrate the swearing in of her son, Mary Bet's cousin Hooper, as county sheriff. She had been cordial, even friendly, to Mary Bet, no longer the unbending killjoy Mary Bet remembered from her father's bout with pneumonia. Perhaps it was only because she was better at being a hostess than at taking charge in someone else's home, but it was Mary Bet this time who suggested to her father that they invite Cattie Jordan to stay for a while, until he was feeling better.

"I don't know what you mean exactly," her father said, eyeing her under his thick white eyebrows.

They had been sitting at dinner, Cicero with his shirt unbuttoned halfway down his chest, because, he maintained, he couldn't breathe otherwise. "I don't mean anything," Mary Bet said. "I'd just like to see her, is all."

"You can invite anybody you please. I won't stop you." He paused to scratch his shoulder with his fork. "I've got so much work to do you won't hardly know I'm here. If I stop working, you see, I'm liable to drop dead." He winced, and his face fell and went blank.

"What is it, Daddy?"

He shook his head. "Something I said to your mama one time. Told her she was a snake in the cistern. I don't know why. All the shameful things I've said and done—if only I could stop them flowing through my brain."

"It's all right, Daddy," Mary Bet said, patting his hand. He pulled it away and looked at her with suspicion. He got up, leaving half his food untouched and went out to the greenhouse to tend to the chrysanthemums and dahlias she'd bought him. He had quit going down to the store, and on his more lucid days he told her he was thinking of selling it. She said she thought that was a good idea, that she was sure Robert Gray could help him with the details, and she'd even spoken with Mr. Gray about it herself. Mr. Gray had assured her that he could help find a buyer and draw up the papers, but suggested that she first get Dr. Slocum to come out and make sure her father was compos mentis. To which she'd replied that of course he was in his right mind—he just needed some rest. Anyway, he'd been thinking for years of selling out and running a much smaller operation from his home.

"Of course, of course," Mr. Gray said. "At sixty-four, he's at an age when many have already quit work. He's driven himself hard all this time. As his lawyer, I just want to have everything square. How old are you now, Mary Bet?" She replied that she would be nineteen next June. Gray nodded and said it was too bad she wasn't already twenty-one. "I'll come pay a visit," he told her.

And then it was Thanksgiving, and Mary Bet and her father had had a lonely time of it because he decided he didn't want to have anybody over, nor go to anybody else's house. They'd eaten in haste and gone off to their separate activities—he to his reading and she to her sewing, in adjacent rooms so that they could hear each other, yet have no need for talk. Keeping him quiet seemed the best medicine. Dr. Slocum had visited twice since the episode with the banana plants and had left some Hill's sedative pills that her father threw away. She'd served him tea infused with skullcap and ginseng. Acquiring these ingredients had been awkward since she'd broken off with Joe. But Mrs. Dorsett was as neighborly as ever. Two weeks after he was fired, Joe left for Raleigh to take a job in a glass factory, the same that had supplied panes for Cicero's greenhouse. The night before he left, he came over and brought her a jar of his mother's damson preserves.

"I never gave you a ring," he told her. "But someday maybe you'll let me." She smiled and took the jar and offered him a seat. "I'm not angry with you, Joe," she said. "I don't know what happened at work, but there are people around who've said things."

"I wasn't even allowed near the shaping and framing machines," he said. "They just had me sweeping and carrying. And sometimes dusting. Like a colored boy. One time they let me take inventory of a shipment." He sat back. "How's your father?"

"He's fine. Now you go on home and thank your mother for sending this over."

"It was my idea," Joe said. "I don't want to leave you like this."

"You'll be fine. I expect you'll take up with some girl in Raleigh before Christmas."

He didn't disagree. "Won't you miss me?" he asked.

"Of course I will," she said. "You've been a good friend." She could feel the dismissive tone to her voice, like a grown-up reassuring a child, and she really did wish he would go on home, for the truth was she felt a pain of longing for him already.

Cattie Jordan's arrival a week after Joe's departure seemed to Mary Bet a blessing worth any amount of her aunt's high-handedness.

Like all children of a forgiving nature, she believed that her own people were basically good and kind, and so any slights or cruelty could not have been deliberate. Because she chose to love her aunt, she could not, in fact, recollect any particular transgressions, let alone that Cattie had constantly corrected her grammar and table manners, had banished her friends, had suggested that Mary Bet pick out heirlooms for herself, had even tried to dictate how much time she spent with her sick father. It had, after all, been a trying and tense time for them all.

Now that she was a grown woman, the lady of the house, and her father's sole heir, things were different. It was her decision to invite her aunt, and it never occurred to her that Cattie Jordan would be anything other than helpful. From her aunt she had learned what she considered an invaluable lesson—you can't be slighted if you don't recognize an offense.

Cattie Jordan arrived with no fanfare in a rockaway pulled by a single gray mare, driven by an old family retainer who stayed seated while she got herself down. She wore a heavy dark brown coat over a beige dress, a wide-brimmed black hat piled high with dried flowers in tulle, and a strand of pearls. Her auburn hair looked faded, with here and there some gray, and new lines had etched themselves around her eyes and mouth, little betrayals of her vanity. She greeted her niece and brother-in-law on the front porch, then took herself upstairs and settled right in as though she had only been gone a few weeks. Though reduced in circumstances, she was determined to establish her place in the family. Her husband had died of overwork a year back, and with her children grown she had nothing except her D.O.C. meetings and the town gossip to live for. But she had returned to a family that had changed. Mary Bet was no longer the obedient adolescent girl she had been five years earlier. She was now the survivor of a family that had once swelled the house with laughter and talk and activity, and her father was the withered tree that had somehow borne the storm, while the weaker had uprooted and tumbled away.

Cattie bustled in and immediately started ordering Essie to air out the south guest room and change the sheets, because she didn't "believe in letting linens sit unused for weeks at a time—they get musty and moldy, and mold can cause migraine, which is what killed my husband's sister." Mary Bet went out to help the driver struggle with Cattie's trunk and bags—enough luggage, Mary Bet thought, for a grand European tour.

From the first night, it became clear that something had shifted in the way the three of them got along. Cicero was now sick in his mind instead of his body, but Cattie's philosophy, it soon became clear, did not allow for sickness. She and Mary Bet had once tolerated each other to work toward the common goal of nurturing Cicero back to health. Now, Cattie's intentions were different, and Mary Bet could not at first put her finger on exactly in what way.

At supper they talked mostly about Cattie's son, the new sheriff. Mary Bet told her aunt, as she had before, that, yes, she was very proud of her cousin. Hooper Teague was a likable young man—the county had elected him by a big majority, black and white.

Then, after Cattie had taken a mouthful, Mary Bet said, "Daddy has decided to take some more time off from the store, haven't you, Daddy?" For she was not sure from one day to the next what her father would say. Just the day before, he got dressed as he had for thirty-nine years and headed down to the Alliance. He sold items to his old customers and told them stories just as if he hadn't been gone the last two weeks. When people asked how he was he said, "Never better," and everyone, Robert Gray included, had thought he was back to himself and might stay that way. But after dinner he'd gone upstairs to nap and had not come down until after four, and then he came rushing down pulling his suspenders up over his undershirt and Mary Bet told him he should go on back up. He'd said, "Nonsense, I've got to order some coffee for Thad and Oren." But he caught sight of himself in the mirror, and Mary Bet took his arm and reminded him that William Wade was managing the store for a while and would order the coffee. He went back upstairs complaining of a headache.

Now Cicero looked at his daughter and nodded, smiling in his old wise way, and it felt to Mary Bet like a blow to the heart because it was only a simulacrum of her real father, as though a lesser man were playing the part of Cicero Hartsoe. "I reckon so," he said, taking another bite of sweet potato.

"Well, I think that's just a wonderful thing," Cattie Jordan said. "I wish Mr. Teague had taken time off. It would've done him a world of good, but it's too late for that now. Cicero, you should be proud to have a daughter who looks after you so well. She's capable of running things. Why, I bet she could even run that store of yours, if you'd give her a chance."

Mary Bet wished her aunt could phrase things a little more tactfully, but she appreciated the effort she was making. She doubted Cattie Jordan had had much experience with the kind of illness her father was experiencing, but at least she was game enough to try to help out in a crisis. Anyway, her father seemed unfazed by his sister-in-law; he even laughed in a way that appeared genuine, and she wondered if his personality was undergoing such a change that he would soon become someone she no longer recognized.

"Daddy," she said, "tell Aunt Cattie Jordan what Mr. Gray said at the store yesterday."

Cicero looked puzzled. Then he brightened. "He told me he was thinking of putting a lemon tree in his summer kitchen. Said my bananas gave him the idea. He likes to chew on the peel—claims the citric acid keeps him from getting sick."

Cattie Jordan nodded and smiled politely. "That's a wonderful hobby," she said. "Growing things like that. I don't have the touch for it, or the patience. I have to be working with people—I'm down at the church all the time, or the D.O.C., going from one meeting to another. Mary Bet, have you seen to getting your papers together?"

"Papers?" Mary Bet said, trying to think of a polite way to suggest to her aunt that she had no intention of filling out an application, that she was not interested in an exclusive social club built around her father's brief participation in a lost cause.

"You know what I'm talking about. For the Daughters of the Confederacy. I understand when you were younger you hadn't time for such things, but it looks like now you'd be interested in your heritage a little more. In your father's distinguished service, if nothing else. It's really more fun than it sounds, and it would give you some prominence around town, some standing that you can't afford to pass up. You never know what people are talking about in private parlors, that's why I make it a point to be in as many private parlors as I can."

Mary Bet took all this in, and then said, "I don't much care for parties that aren't about doing things—I need to be making things with my hands, or singing."

Cattie Jordan faced her across the table, a flicker of her old sternness rippling across her face that suddenly reminded Mary Bet of her own mother. Except that Cattie Jordan in the last few years had taken on so much weight she looked like a puffed-up version of her former self, the family resemblance fainter. "Why, Mary Elizabeth, I'm surprised at how little you understand. The D.O.C. does all kinds of important work—much more important than singing, I can assure you. Why, last year our chapter raised over a thousand dollars for the veterans' home in Durham, and the historical committee is constantly busy. You can't turn your nose up at ladies' organizations for so long before you won't be invited anymore. I'd hate for you to have to learn that the hard way, dear."

"I'm all for ladies getting together for good works," Mary Bet said.

Her aunt eyed her with skepticism. "You're not being influenced by the radical element are you, Mary Elizabeth? Those factory girls who think women should have the vote and go around smoking cigars and wearing pants and I don't know what else? I expect soon they'll be wanting to grow beards."

"I don't know about smoking cigars," Mary Bet said, just to see what reaction she'd get. She realized it had been a long time since she'd had so much lively conversation at the table, even if it did verge on an outright argument. She could not help adding, "But I'm sure that it won't be long before women will have the vote."

Her aunt looked shocked, as though Mary Bet herself were the leader of a group of trouser-wearing basement revolutionaries. Cicero only glanced from one woman to the other, not apparently following the conversation. Then he suddenly said, "I don't see that would be such a terrible thing. If a Nigra can vote, why can't a woman?"

Cattie Jordan shook her head, then with a tight-lipped smile said, "Well, you have a point there." Then she winked at her niece and said, "I bet your daddy would just love to see the new pavilion down at Mount Jordan Springs. It's the cutest little thing, with green-and-white gingerbread trim."

Mary Bet looked at her father, his head bent over his plate, napkin at his throat, and thought how strong he still looked, his hair, though grizzled, still covering his head, and his neck wrinkled yet ropy. "What would you think of that, Daddy?" she said, wondering if maybe her aunt was right—an outing would be good for him.

Cicero nodded and looked up. "Yes, the springs of beauty and health," he said. "I shall drink only from the spring of health, for I can attain no greater beauty."

Cattie Jordan laughed in a way that seemed giddy to Mary Bet, and her eyes flashed as though she were studying an object of value.

"I myself shall drink from both," she said, trying to imitate her brother-in-law's rhetorical flourish, "because I can't afford at my age not to." She laughed to point out that it was a joke, and Mary Bet gave a polite little snicker, though it was difficult having to simulate gaiety for a person who could only ride on someone else's natural humor and steal undeserved laughs. Cicero glanced at his daughter as if to ask what was funny.

"We'll go next Saturday," Mary Bet said. She wanted to encourage any sign of interest from her father. She assumed that her aunt's coquettish behavior was also simply a technique for getting him up and moving.

When, a week after she had arrived, Cattie Jordan announced at dinner that she and Cicero intended to be married, Mary Bet did the first thing that seemed natural. She laughed. She laughed because she was not sure she had heard right, and she kept laughing because, her aunt's withering look telling her it was not a silly joke, she could not think of a proper response.

"Are you done?" Cattie said. She had given up calling Mary Bet "young lady" or anything at all.

"You can't be serious," Mary Bet said, looking only at her father, who was already standing up.

"Yes, we are," Cicero said, "and out of respect for your aunt and future stepmother, you might be a little more sensitive."

"Well, I—" For the first time since the death of Siler, three years back, Mary Bet felt the grief of loss. But this was a new variety of grief, swift and punishing: her father, whose love she could always rely on even through physical and mental illness, had suddenly and arbitrarily withdrawn from her. "I'm very—" She could not make herself say the words. All she could do was look at her father, tears coming to her eyes, and wonder if he had not completely lost his mind.

"I'm not feeling well," she said, and hurried upstairs to her room.

She could not stay up there for long, or she would be late to teach the afternoon sixth-grade English class. She steeled herself and walked down slowly and deliberately, giving her aunt time to get out of the way if she chose. But Cattie Jordan was standing in the dining room entryway, waiting for her. Mary Bet smiled and said, "I'm very happy for you and father. I'm sorry I was feeling unwell."

"I know it's sudden," Cattie Jordan said. "But you'll see it's for the best. You won't have to worry about him any longer. I expect you'll be wanting to make your own way in the world before too long." She smiled placidly, like a bisque doll with a painted face, and added, "Of course, you're welcome to stay here as long as you like."

The rest of that day and the next, Mary Bet tried to adjust to the idea that she was soon to be a visitor in her own house, under the sufferance of her aunt. Very soon, because the wedding was to be held before Christmas, less than a month away. She wanted to talk to her father about it in private, but he seemed never to be alone; it was as though Cattie were guarding him like a mother her child. Finally, near the end of that first week, she found him in his study when Cattie had gone out to see about her wedding dress, the idea of which so repulsed Mary Bet that she moped in her room until she realized she had an opportunity.

"Daddy?" she said, coming into the study. He looked up, his gaze vacant, and she wondered if he'd been reading or just staring at the book. "Can I talk with you for a while?"

"Of course you can, baby girl. You can always talk. And I know this has been hard on you, change always is. But Cattie Jordan and I have quite a bit in common, not just our families. I think she'll be a good wife, and then you'll be free to do as you please."

"I'm not looking to leave you, Daddy."

"But someday you may feel differently. Not that I need someone to look after me. Are you familiar with the levirate marriage rule?"

He went on. "It's a Jewish tradition whereby a man marries his brother's widow. This is a sort of levirate arrangement, it's just a woman marrying her sister's widower. There's nothing wrong with it."

"I know that, Daddy. It's just that—well, I didn't know you were so fond of Aunt Cattie Jordan. When did that start?"

"Probably back during my illness, and we've kept up a friendly correspondence. And I guess even before that, we were always fond of each other. You know, it was Cattie Jordan that I first courted, and she turned me down for Vernon Teague."

Mary Bet shook her head, trying to erase what she'd just heard. "But, Daddy, she's nothing like mother. Mother could be stern, but she was a saint compared to—"

"That's enough of that," he warned. "I won't hear anything against her."

Then came the wedding, a small affair at the Methodist church. The reception back at home was equally modest, for Cattie was not interested in wasting money on a party. There was no singer; ginger ale and water were the beverages, and there was a small cake and a bowl of hard candy. Mary Bet spent that night at Clara's house so she wouldn't have to be alone. After one night at the Mount Jordan Springs Hotel, the bride and groom came home.

$\backsim$ CHAPTER 16 $\subset$

1905–1906

T HEY WERE A family of three, then, at Christmas, and it was all Mary Bet could do not to look at her father across the table during their turkey dinner—to which they'd invited no guests—and burst into tears. The whole thing had the unreality of a bad dream from which she was bound to awaken. She had only to endure it for a while.

"Mary Elizabeth," Cattie said, "I see your posture hasn't improved much in the past five years. I suppose it's my fault for not correcting you more, once I'd spotted the defect."

Mary Bet found herself wondering why it was that people like Myrtle Emma and Siler had died, while Cattie Jordan was as healthy as a horse. She sat there happily eating her turkey and dumplings. Could she not come down with typhoid, or a bad case of pneumonia? Mary Bet pictured taking care of her aunt as punishment. Could she not meet with a freak accident—being struck by lightning, or inhaling a bee, or slipping in a hog pen? She silently asked forgiveness for such a horrible thought. She sat up straight. "No," she said, "it's my own fault. I know I shouldn't slump." Or choking? It sometimes happened.

"When I was a boy," Cicero said, "my father used to make me go out and tell Zeke and the others to hurry with the horses." He made a muffled laugh. "I didn't much care for that."

"What are you talking about, Daddy?" Mary Bet glanced at her stepmother, but Cattie paid no attention.

"My daddy had all kinds of things he made me do. He had me to sit in the outhouse until I'd memorized ten verses out of the Bible, every Sunday."

Now Cattie looked at him, her calm smile refusing to break. "Cicero, I don't believe that's a proper subject for the dinner table."

He belched and nodded. "I'd be out there hollering, 'The Lord is my shepherd, I shall not want.' And thinking, 'except I wouldn't mind some fresher newspaper.'"

"Mary Elizabeth, you may be excused. We'll finish up here."

Mary Bet had already lost interest in cleaning her plate, so she got up and began clearing away the dishes. Cattie had taken the liberty of letting Essie go, telling her new husband that Mary Bet could easily handle the work of a servant, and besides, Essie was scarcely worth keeping, her rheumatic joints making it so she could hardly get up the steps. They needed to save money, because she only had her "widow's mite" and Cicero was paying a young man to run the Alliance, a young man, mind you, who had ambitions, Cattie Jordan had heard, though she couldn't remember exactly from whom. Mary Bet wondered how small this "widow's mite" really was, but she knew better than to ask. Her main job as she saw it was to get along, helping her father as best she could until such time as she deemed it appropriate to leave. She didn't know where she would go or what she would do. Clara had told her she could come live with her and her mother. She thought she might go to

St. Mary's finishing school in Raleigh, but when she mentioned the idea at supper a few nights before Christmas, her aunt smiled placidly and asked her where the money would come for such an extravagant plan.

Mary Bet wondered if her aunt had given the matter of her future any consideration. The day after Christmas she decided to find out. The three of them were sitting in the parlor, Mary Bet arranging decorations on the spindly cedar tree she'd been allowed to drag in (though Cattie had ruled that candles were not a good idea). Cattie was putting embroidery to a cushion piece and talking about what a waste it was to spend money for a new brick building out at the prison camp. "The wooden buildings are fine," she said. "Those criminals are not going to run off."

"It's because the conditions aren't humane," Mary Bet said. "They're drafty and you can't keep things clean."

"Well, I don't know who you've been talking to, but I think the old buildings are just fine for criminals."

"Daddy," Mary Bet began, "and Aunt Cattie Jordan, I wanted to ask you what you had in mind for me to do with myself. If you don't want me going off to college in Raleigh, did you have anything particular in mind?"

Keeping her head in her work, Cattie glanced over at Cicero, who only cleared his throat and went on reading. "Most young ladies stay at home and help out until they're married," Cattie said. "I was married by the time I was your age, but you still have plenty of time. Until then, I would think you'd be happy to have a roof over your head and good food to eat and warm clothes. Consider the lilies."

Mary Bet didn't see the use in pointing out that she only wanted reassurance that she was, in fact, welcome in her own house. Her aunt's privations extended to every corner, with a few exceptions—the food was always plentiful, particularly on her own plate, and she had started ordering things from catalogs. From Raleigh and Richmond and even New York came a new walnut credenza, a turkey rug for the vestibule, brass andirons, three ceramic hens, a brass umbrella stand. Old things went up to the attic, already crammed with pieces she'd brought from Williamsboro. Mary Bet didn't know where it would end, unless it was with them all in the poorhouse.

One morning as Cattie was finishing her breakfast, she asked Mary Bet if she'd ever heard why it was that her grandfather Samuel was so bent on perpetual motion. Mary Bet shook her head. "I didn't know there was a reason for it," she said, and she could feel the hair on her arms rising, as her aunt licked her lips.

"Yes, indeed there was a reason. There's a reason for everything. You see, he went crazy, and the reason he went crazy is what his father made him do. John Hartsoe was a hard man, and he believed in a certain way of doing things. I told you about him beating Scilla's father, but what I didn't tell you was about Scilla's uncle. His name was Shorty—that was because he was short. He apparently didn't listen any too well, or he was just naturally obstinate. He was out mending a stone fence one day, and your great-grandfather rode along and told him he wasn't doing it right and that he had to take it all apart and start over. Shorty said something about how if he knew anything, he knew how to mend fence. Scilla said he used to talk to himself and probably didn't mean any harm, he was just encouraging himself to the task—'Shorty know how to mend fence'—something like that."

Mary Bet could hear her father turn a page in his sitting room. She wished that Essie were here, so that maybe Cattie Jordan would not tell tales from the slavery days. On the table the cut-crystal stopper to the syrup vase caught the morning light and made a pencil-thin rainbow against the wood. She nudged the stopper with her finger so that it rolled over; her aunt caught it and stuck it in the vase.

"Something must've upset old John Hartsoe earlier in the day for him to do what he did. He ordered his son to shoot the old slave." Cattie stopped talking and ate the last bite of toast.

"What?" Mary Bet said. "My grandfather shot Shorty?" She'd never heard the slave's name before, and now he seemed as real as anybody.

"According to Scilla, he did it without protest. After that, a Nigra named Jonas ran off. When they caught him, they nailed his foot to the barn floor with a tenpenny nail. After they let him loose, the foot swelled up. But he still could walk, so they nicknamed him Able, because he was able to walk. They still, some of the Nigras, name their chilren A-b-l-e, Able. And you can't tell them it's spelled differently. Anyway, your grandfather turned out to be no better than his father. Your daddy when he was a boy had a little black dog that he loved more than anything. Old Mr. Samuel would kick it and make your daddy cry, and then he'd laugh. At his own son. To toughen him up." Cattie clamped her mouth and stared away, as though trying to decipher the riddle of the Hartsoes, or to forget it.

That winter was colder than any Mary Bet could remember, though it could've been simply that the house was colder. She spent more time in her room than she ever had, with her books and her sewing. She wrote long letters to friends, trying to explain her situation without complaining about it. If not for Clara's friendship and understanding, she thought she might just kill herself. But as soon as the thought surfaced, she saw her brother walking along the tracks and she shook the idea away. She resolved to confront her aunt, and so she kept a mental list of everything that she would tell her. Yet it felt petty—what could she say that would not make her feel small herself? She wanted to make her aunt as miserable as she was made to feel.

But it turned out that she didn't get the chance. One morning in early spring, the first day that Mary Bet didn't see her breath when she woke up, her father had another spell. "I feel like I'm at the bottom of the river," he said, sitting over the remains of breakfast.

"What river, Daddy?" Mary Bet said. She glanced over at Cattie Jordan, who was still working on a biscuit thick with jam.

"You know what river. The Deep River, of course."

"Maybe you'd better go lie down," Cattie Jordan suggested.

"That wouldn't help atall," he said. "But maybe if I went upstairs, I'd get to some better air."

Mary Bet stood to help her father, but he was already up and looking at her as if annoyed at the suggestion he was in any way infirm. "I just don't see the point in any of this," he said. "I'm sorry, but I don't. It's all—" He shook his head and started forward, catching himself on the side table, then on the sofa.

"It's what, Daddy?"

"It's all black," he said. He maneuvered out of the sitting room and, catching himself in the doorframe, paused, and then stumped into the vestibule, rattling the tin mail plate on the credenza and the mirror that Siler had framed. "All black."

Mary Bet came out into the vestibule and watched her father pull himself up the stairs. She heard the creak of his steps overhead, and she went into the kitchen to start frying pork chops. A few minutes later he was coming back down, his stumping gait quicker than normal. Mary Bet ran out into the vestibule. "What is it, Daddy?" she said.

"I can't find it," he said, moving past her and around to the dining room. She followed him as he pushed through the swinging door and into the kitchen. Then he wheeled around and faced her. "Where did you put it?" he demanded.

"Put what, Daddy?" She tried to keep her voice calm and even, but her chest felt suddenly tight and it was hard to breathe.

"I'll find it," he said and stormed into the summer kitchen and out the back door.

Cattie Jordan came and joined her niece, and they watched Cicero stride across the yard toward the toolshed. "Has he been like this?" Cattie asked.

Mary Bet shook her head. "No, I don't know what he's after. He loses things and then thinks I've hidden them, but I haven't. The only thing I hid one time was his whiskey, and he about tore the house apart looking for it."

Now Cicero was coming back in, his face red and his eyes wild with some kind of torment Mary Bet had never seen, as though something were pursuing him. The hair on the sides of his head stood out in tufts like a fledgling. He was talking to himself, or singing, and it was not until he was on the back porch, letting himself into the parlor that they could hear a tuneless song—"Heart was all a-flutter, around the bend the number ten, peanut butter."

Mary Bet went around to the porch, and just as she stepped out, she saw her father reaching up on the shelf where they kept lanterns and old gloves and hats. And he pulled down a box of cartridges. "Aha!" he said. "I knew they were there. Can't fool me."

"What are you doing, Daddy?" Mary Bet said, her voice shaking, for now she was frightened.

Cicero brushed past her and went inside to the vestibule closet, reached in, and pulled out his gun. Mary Bet came in from the parlor just as Cattie Jordan stepped around from the dining room. "I'll go fetch the constable," Cattie said. She started out the front door, then paused. "Maybe you should come too." Cicero was fumbling with the cartridge box, trying to open it with one hand while holding the rifle with the other.

"Daddy?" Mary Bet said. "What did you need your gun for?"

He looked up, glanced at his daughter, then at his wife, who was halfway out the door. "To by-God shoot it!"

"What for, Daddy? What for?" Mary Bet came over to stand by her father. It was instinct to want to close the gap between them.

She noticed as she reached for him that her hand was trembling, and it was the strangest sensation, as though her hand were not part of her body. She felt as if she were viewing the whole scene from some distant place, some mountaintop far in the past or the future, and it all slowed down until it was a still-life painting on a wall. In the quietness of her mind she heard the word "life." And then the word became a feeling of such strange oblivion that she felt herself in perfect balance between sorrow and joy.

His back to her, he began loading shells into the breech. She touched his shoulder. "Daddy," she said. He jerked around, the gun swinging against her leg.

"I'm going to do something I ought to've done long ago," he said. He pointed the gun at Mary Bet's chest, then at Cattie's face. He looked calm, almost cheerful, his eyes distant and content, though his breathing was coming in deep gulps, as if he could never get enough air.

"I'll just step out a minute," Cattie said. The words hung in the air like holes in the silence, behind which the pork sizzled in the kitchen.

Cicero now pointed the gun at the side of his own head, holding the barrel with his left hand and moving his right down to where he could operate the trigger with his thumb. His eyes were wide in fear now, as though he'd finally awoke to what was going on, to the madness he was creating to overcome the madness in his head.

"Daddy," Mary Bet said in as calm and steady a voice as she could, "put the gun down now. It's dangerous. You don't want to hurt anybody. Put it down. Okay?"

Cicero nodded, but he kept the barrel tight to his temple. "I won't hurt anybody, just myself. I can't stand it here anymore."

"It's all right, Daddy."

"I'll go get the doctor for you," Cattie said. Mary Bet shook her head sternly, but kept her eyes on her father.

"I'll shoot him," Cicero said.

"He's not coming," Mary Bet assured him. "We just want you to put your gun down now. There's no need to shoot anybody or anything."

"But I want to so badly," he pleaded. "I really do."

"I know, Daddy, but you oughten. Put it down, please."

His lips moved, slowly as the second hand on a watch, and he said, "I have to."

"No," she said, "you don't." The words seemed to echo off the walls of the foyer and the oval mirror and the ceiling and the turkey rug. He brought the gun away from his head, as though considering. And then he was turning away and hurrying out through the parlor to the side porch, and she and Cattie Jordan went right along behind him as though they were all heading outside to shoot a rattlesnake.

He went down into the orchard and flopped beneath an apple tree, the gun in his lap. He let it slip from his grasp. Mary Bet reached down and pulled it away.

"Make sure of the safety, child," he said.

"Give it to me," Cattie said, "I'm going for the constable straightaway."

"That won't be necessary, Aunt Cattie. Please."

"Don't you know it's a sin to shoot yourself, Cicero? Even if you're . . . well it's just not right. In front of your family that loves you?" She turned to Mary Bet. "I'm going to fetch the doctor, I don't care what anybody says. Mary Bet, are you all right?"

"I won't let him in," Cicero said. "I don't want a doctor, I told you I'm fine, I just need to rest."

"He might be able to give you something for the pain in your head," Mary Bet said. She nodded at her aunt, and Cattie Jordan headed to the carriage barn. "I'm going to sit with you until Dr. Slocum gets here, Daddy, and I want you to see him as a favor to me. Okay?"

Cicero nodded.

Mary Bet ejected the two cartridges from the gun and slipped them in the pocket of her skirt. She sat with him for a while, and then they went inside. She put the gun away and knelt to collect the loose cartridges and put them into their box. "Let's go sit in the den for a spell, Daddy." She crooked her arm for him and he took it, his face gone blank and pale, and Mary Bet wondered if he even knew what had just happened. What was it like inside such turbulence?

She guided him over to his cushioned chair and sat him down. "This is a nice quiet place, Daddy," she said. "I've always liked reading in here, it's the coolest part of the house since it's on the north side." She kept talking this way, about things that required no comment, that only provided the music of her voice, familiar and as soothing as a mother. She thought she would never ever risk the unimaginable hardship of becoming a real mother—the life-draining labor, a forerunner to the years of hard work, and then if she were to lose a child, or have one that became ill—she could not endure it.

Cicero leaned back and put his hands over his face, the thin light of winter trickling through the window so that, for a moment, he appeared to be a young man, burdened but still filled with energy. "It's hard to see," he said, looking out the window at the horse grazing in the near pasture. "I can't see so good."

"I know, Daddy," Mary Bet said, stroking his arm. "I know."

Presently Cattie Jordan returned, Dr. Slocum panting along behind her, his face red as a persimmon. You could at least count on her to persuade people to do what she wanted them to. The doctor plopped his bag onto the credenza and let Mary Bet help him off with his coat. "Now," he said, "let's have a look at your father."

They went into the den and found Cicero sitting there as relaxed and affable as ever. He stood and shook the doctor's hand and said, "Good morning, Doctor, always glad to see a friend. I'm afraid you've missed breakfast, but we can scare you up something."

They talked quietly for a while, the doctor directing his questions to Cicero. But Cicero let his wife and daughter do most of the answering.

When Dr. Slocum got up to leave, the women followed him out to the vestibule. "I don't diagnose any particular psychiatric disturbance," he said, "but this is really beyond my field of expertise." He nodded toward the other room and lowered his voice. "He's perfectly calm now. I've seen cases like this in which a delusional patient will convince himself that everybody else is in the wrong, that it was all a misunderstanding and no harm was intended."

"I can hear you fine," Cicero said from the other room. "Go on, talk about me all you want, it doesn't bother me atall."

Dr. Slocum paused, his eyes going from Mary Bet to Cattie Jordan. "The main issue here is whether you fear for your safety, or his. My advice in a case like this is to go ahead and take him up to the state hospital in Morganton. They can evaluate him better than I can."

"But will they keep him there?" Mary Bet wanted to know.

"Only if they think it's best, and not if you don't want them to. I'll go up there with you. I think the sooner we go the better."

"I don't like thinking of leaving him in an asylum," Mary Bet whispered. "What if they chain him up? We wouldn't even know."

"They don't do anything like that now. They use all the most modern techniques. No more blistering and dunking in cold water. If anything, they've gone too far in not treating at all, unless they absolutely have to. There's less therapy, and more simple custodial care."

"But he'd be put in with all kinds of crazy people and welfare cases," Mary Bet said, shaking her head.

"The criminally insane," Cattie Jordan added.

Mary Bet glanced over. "I'll never let him go to a place like that."

"There are separate wards from what I understand. You get what you pay for, and y'all are lucky enough to afford proper care. Let's not get worked up about this right now. I'll make some inquiries tomorrow, and we'll see about going up there next week. In the meantime, give him a solution of calomel as a sedative." He placed a little brown bottle on the credenza. "Put two drops in whatever he drinks, morning and night. It doesn't taste like anything. If he has another episode, I'll give him a spoonful of heroin." The doctor passed a hand over his ruddy face and sighed. "And one more thing," he said, getting to his feet, "get that gun out of this house. Any and every gun."

"That's the only one," Mary Bet said, her voice barely audible, "except for his service revolver, and I don't know where he keeps that."

"Well, then, you'll have to do some snooping," Dr. Slocum said.

A week later the four of them were in the train on their way to Morganton. As the farms flashed past and gave way to woods and blue hills, Mary Bet remembered standing at the station with her father waiting to take the train to the mountains to see Myrtle Emma. And here they were finally making their first train excursion. The turns life could take. Cicero sat opposite Mary Bet, looking out in the direction they'd been, a peaceful expression on his face, as though at last accepting that his work was done. Mary Bet told herself she would not come home without him.

CHAPTER 17

1906

MARY BET AND Cattie Jordan slept in the Visiting Families wing the first night. Then, when the doctors said Cicero needed to stay on a few more days for a complete evaluation, they found a rooming house a few blocks away. The hospital was built a quarter century earlier to conform to the latest theories in treating the insane. It had a tall central portion, flanked by massive four-story wings—one for each sex, with milder cases housed on the upper floors. The many windows provided plenty of light, and the placement of air ducts allowed for health-promoting ventilation. In all, the redbrick building and its pediments and striped awnings and peaked cupolas, set amid peaceful parklike grounds, were more reminiscent of an elegant hotel than a hospital, and so Mary Bet had fewer misgivings about leaving her father than she had thought she might.

"It's only for a few days," she reassured him, as they were heading out.

"All right," he said, "but you'll come back tomorrow?" He studied her face, his own looking so much more lined and sagging and mottled than she had ever noticed.

She nodded and peered out the window so he couldn't see her eyes. "You have a good view here," she told him. "It looks like the lawn at Mount Jordan Springs, but bigger. There's people walking on the path." She watched as two men strolled along, followed by an attendant; one of the patients appeared to have his hands in a kind of muff. The trees were still bare, but there were some evergreens. She wondered what it would look like in the spring, but she kept this thought to herself. Off to the west she could see the courthouse with its fancy cupola, and beyond that the first ridges of the mountains. From the hallway at her back came the strong odor of ammonia, lemon, and resin.

"I'm sure it'll be nice here in the summer," Cattie Jordan said. She cleared her throat as though to take back the words.

The high-ceilinged room had cream-colored walls, a yellow pine floor, a low narrow bed, one spindle-back chair, and a small deal table upon which sat a Bible. They'd asked for a private room, which Cicero could afford, but now Mary Bet wondered if he might be lonely here. It's only for a few nights, she told herself. They left his brown canvas traveling bag on the luggage stand and said good-bye.

They spent the next two days going back and forth from the hospital to the rooming house to the shops on Union Street, buying things Cicero might need for his room. "We'll come back up at Easter," Cattie Jordan told her niece. This was after Dr. Eastman, who had taken charge of Cicero's case, informed them that Cicero had tried to get out and had threatened a nurse who attempted to stop him.

"I told him we wouldn't leave him here," Mary Bet kept saying. "I promised him."

"Well you shouldn't have. They seem awfully nice there. I think that Dr. Eastman is very competent, even if he is from New Jersey. If he had a little more hair and a smaller nose with less hair in it, he might even be attractive, the kind you might be interested in, Mary Bet." She eyed her niece, but Mary Bet ignored her aunt and kept looking through the bins of socks and slippers. She wished she had time to go over and pay a visit to the deaf school, just so she could lay eyes on the last place her brother had lived.

"Oh," Cattie laughed. She squeezed Mary Bet's hand and held up a pair of fuzzy rabbit-fur slippers. "Wouldn't your father look something in these?"

Mary Bet had to stifle a laugh, picturing her father wearing the slippers. She was annoyed with herself for being so amused by her aunt. She wondered if Cattie had any close friends back in Williamsboro, and for the first time she thought perhaps her aunt, besides wanting to marry her off, really did wish her some happiness.

"Well, I'll say one thing," Cattie remarked, "that doctor's no Joe Dorsett. Not that I blame you for that business—you were young and easily fooled. But you'd be a good catch for a doctor or a lawyer, I can assure you." She brushed something from her niece's shoulder and pulled back as though to regard her.

Mary Bet did not look up, though she could feel her aunt's gaze. Standing here with her, she suddenly missed Joe, missed having him to go on walks with and talk to. The weight and shape and light of his physical presence beside her she felt as an absence, and she dropped the rabbit fur slippers she was holding because they somehow reminded her of him and how she had banished him from her life and how sadness and longing had come to fill the space inside her. It struck her as strange that she should feel such sadness for a boy, a despairing heaviness of heart that was not the same as grief for her lost family members; it was a different species of sadness altogether—an unhappiness for the future, or what might have been the future. She had to move.

Out on the wooden sidewalk she adjusted her bonnet and waited for her aunt. "I just needed some air," she told Cattie Jordan.

"Are you feeling faint dear? Do you need to go lie down?"

"No, I'm better now. I think I want to go back to the hospital and then walk over to the deaf school and have a look around." They began heading back up to their rooming house.

"All right, it might do you some good to see where your brother was. I'll go with you." A cool wind swirled dust up from the road, and Cattie Jordan retied her hat ribbon tight against her chin.

At the hospital, the day somehow got away from them. Cicero told Mary Bet that "that woman"—he pointed to his wife—was a nuisance, and so Cattie went to the solarium at the end of the ward, where a patient was playing the piano; after a while, she took herself back to the rooming house. But Cicero would not let Mary Bet out of his sight. When she tried to go out, even to relieve herself, he held her hand and said, "I don't think this is the right place for me. Please don't leave me here."

"I'll be right back, Daddy," she told him, then hurried from the room, biting her underlip to hold back the tears.

Out in the hall, the nurses gave her sympathetic looks, and later in the day Dr. Eastman assured her that she was doing the best thing for her father that she could possibly do. "Many aren't as lucky. He has a nice room with a view. There are games and activities for him, and he can do all the reading he wants, as long as it's not agitating. You said he likes to read?"

"Yes, sir," Mary Bet said. "I'll send up a box of books for him. But when do you think he'll be able to come home?"

Dr. Eastman glanced at her, then down at the clipboard in his hand. His nose was unfortunately large, Mary Bet thought, and he was short and bald as well, and unlike Dr. Slocum his eyes were guarded and thoughtful. She only hoped that he was better with his patients. The whole place, with its smell of cleaned-over panic, was distressing in a way she had not anticipated. Every now and again she could hear a shout or moan from a ward down below, and even on her father's hall, with its subdued colors and sunlit spaces, there were the odd noises of patients muttering insensibly to invisible people. She just wanted to get out, into the fresh air. How could anybody stand it here? "It's hard to say," Dr. Eastman said, his Yankee-edged voice grating on her. "A psychotic case at your father's age—I have to honestly say, he may be here indefinitely."

"Can't you cure him then?"

"Miss Hartsoe, as I told Mrs. Hartsoe, we do what we can. Routine, exercise, and medication." He ticked the three pillars of treatment off with his thumb and two first fingers. "That's what we offer. A stable, predictable schedule, plenty of fresh air and outdoor exercise, if the patient is able to function outside, and a narrow array of drugs—mostly sulphonal, laudanum, potassium iodide, strychnine." He ticked these off as well, his gaze over Mary Bet's head, as though he were talking to himself, and she could not help but wonder if he were not to some degree affected by the lunatics who surrounded him.

"My father's not crazy," she said. "He just needs some rest. He's had a hard life, you see."

"Yes, I understand. But with his violent tendencies, he needs more than rest. We'll try to keep him on this ward, which allows for some freedom of movement. If he improves, he may find that a light job in the laundry or cafeteria is beneficial. And we have art classes and reading classes and lectures and chapel services. He won't be bored."

"And you won't put him in restraints?"

"It's always a last resort, and it's for the safety of the patients."

From the window, Mary Bet could just see, to the left of the treeline across the road, the brownstone top of the school for the deaf. And yet there was no time to go over there. They were leaving on the train in the morning, but she would be back up to see her father in a few weeks. There would be time to explore the school and the town, to delve into the past. She owed it to Siler, she told herself, and she wasn't afraid of what she might find. No, she thought, I'm not avoiding it.

MARY BET AND Cattie Jordan went home and tried to find a way to live together under the same roof. Except for Clara, all of Mary Bet's close friends were engaged or married, and so Clara and Mary Bet became regular guests at each other's houses. Clara had never been a pretty girl, and as a young woman she was even less attractive. To Mary Bet, she had the most beautiful and expressive eyes she had ever seen in anybody, except for Myrtle Emma, but she knew that her tall, sturdy figure and heavy dark eyebrows were not features that men would find pleasing. When they were going somewhere together, Mary Bet was often embarrassed by how Clara would praise her as they put on their shawls and jackets.

"Thank you, darling," she would say to Clara's compliment about her hair, "now if I just had your nose, I wouldn't be half bad to look at."

Her own physicality, which had made her uncomfortable, she now took as a kind of power, yet she was unsure whether and how to use it. A few young swains about town, since discovering that Joe Dorsett was out of the picture, had asked her to church picnics and young people's socials, and after she'd turned them all down—for none of them suited her quite right—she had developed a reputation as a snob, at least where men were concerned.

It was, in fact, her refusal to attend a dance with a young law student, the son of Cattie Jordan's only friend in Hartsoe City, that made her decide to move out of the only home she had ever known. When Cattie heard of Mary Bet's refusal, she sat waiting for her in the parlor, ready to pounce.

"You're a young fool," she snapped, rising as Mary Bet came in. "And I hope you'll be happy living alone the rest of your life."

"That's all right," Mary Bet returned, "as long I don't have to live with that Sloan Pickford. His breath was terrible, and he wasn't very polite—he acted like he was doing me a favor." She hurried up to her room, thinking "and here I was thinking Aunt Cattie Jordan could change somehow and not be Aunt Cattie Jordan."

The next week she moved in with Clara and her mother. She had begun forming a vague notion, an idea she turned over in her mind while falling asleep, or upon waking, of bringing her father home, no matter what the doctors up there said. How could they stop her? But then during the day, she would busy herself mending and sewing for Clara and Mrs. Edwards, and going back and forth from her house to see to the animals. She and her aunt rarely spoke to each other, though sometimes Cattie Jordan would come out to the chicken yard and inform Mary Bet about her father's situation.

And then one day in the summer Cattie Jordan decided to sell Cicero's store. She sought out the advice and help of Robert Gray and his son, and they drew up the paperwork. William Wade, the young man who'd been managing the store since Cicero's breakdown, had found two investors. The timing seemed perfect, and through Robert Gray's son he inquired whether the store might go up for sale.

Mary Bet was in a state of panic. What if her father should improve and come home? The idea of her aunt coming to such a momentous decision by herself seemed impossible to believe.

She had to speak to her father, and the only way to get to him in time was on the telephone at the post office. They couldn't hear each other very well, and he became agitated and started yelling incoherently—something about his father trying to ruin him. One phrase caught in her mind, because he repeated it—"Let it be done."

She took that as a sign that she should turn it over to God. But what did God want her to do? She had given up her childhood rituals—the touching of her chin with joined hands, the obsessive hand-washing, and even the attention to her scrapbook. But she still prayed several times a day. She asked Clara's advice and was grateful that her friend did not say, as so many had, that he was certainly going to get better.

Mary Bet did nothing, and a week later Cattie Jordan signed the papers selling the store. And a week after that, Cattie came down with a bad summer cold that quickly turned into pneumonia. Mary Bet visited her every day, and sometimes twice a day, because there was no one else, besides Dr. Slocum, to look after her. She rehired Essie, and finally she moved back in. Her aunt lay up in her parents' bedroom, her faded brown hair spread out upon the pillows, looking bewildered and afraid. "I'm too strong to catch pneumonia," she complained.

Mary Bet read to her and told her that, yes, she was strong and that her reserves of strength would see her through. She kept to herself what people said, clucking their tongues, about how strange it was that Cicero's new wife kept the house cold all winter, then took sick in the summer.

Her son, Sheriff Hooper Teague, came over from Williamsboro for a visit. He ended up staying four nights, because his mother's condition did not improve. "I don't think she's been the same since Daddy died," he told Mary Bet. "I don't know how you felt about it, Mary Bet, but I wasn't in favor of her marrying your father. I tried to tell her, but she wouldn't listen. I didn't think it was a good idea for either of them. I'm sorry if that offends you."

"It doesn't atall," Mary Bet confided. "I wasn't in favor of it myself."

"You've done so much for Mother, and I just want you to know how much I appreciate it."

Mary Bet shook her head. "No," she said, "I haven't done hardly a thing."

"If there's anything you need," he went on, "you should let me know." He patted her hand, then stood from the table to go up and check on his mother.

Cattie took a turn for the worse and Mary Bet summoned Dr. Slocum late on a Saturday night. The three of them took turns keeping vigil. Mary Bet went in as dawn was breaking and found her aunt awake and staring at the ceiling. "Come here, child," Cattie breathed. "Sit with me."

Mary Bet perched on the edge of the bed and held her aunt's hand. "Do you feel any better this morning?" she asked. Cattie Jordan shook her head. "I'll get Dr. Slocum to come check your pressure. It might be time for your medicine."

"No, just sit a minute." She said something Mary Bet could not understand, then coughed. "I haven't always been easy on you," she said.

Mary Bet felt tears sliding down her cheeks. "No, Aunt Cattie Jordan. I've been difficult sometimes. I know I'm headstrong." Her aunt smiled a little, and Mary Bet smiled back encouragement.

"I haven't always remembered how hard it was for you." She closed her eyes and nodded briefly. "That's all."

"I'll read some, if you like," Mary Bet said. But her aunt made no response. Mary Bet went out for the doctor.

Cattie Jordan never woke up again. She died early in the afternoon, and that very day Hooper went back to Williamsboro, his mother's body in a trailing carriage. Mary Bet came on Wednesday for the funeral, and as she drove the buggy she was reminded, as she had been many times, of how a straight road that gave long views could have such deep dips that you never knew what was just over the rise.

SHE RETURNED TO a house that was at last empty of every soul except her own. Clara begged her to come back and stay, telling her it was much jollier with her around. But Mary Bet didn't like the idea of her father's house sitting empty. Sometimes Clara would spend the night, but most nights Mary Bet was alone.

Robert Gray set up an account for her in the Bank of Hartsoe City and told her he'd help her manage her affairs, but what with paying for her father's care and her own upkeep she'd need to find work of some sort. It seemed that everybody was suddenly aware of Mary Bet Hartsoe's need for a job, and it was a little embarrassing in church when women she didn't even know came up and told her they could give her some sewing work, or light housework, or told her about a teaching job their cousin had heard of in some town two days' drive away, or simply invited her over for a meal. She was invited to join the D.O.C. and the Even Dozen Literary Club. One woman brought her an old pair of gloves and a hat her deceased mother had worn, saying she had no use for them anymore. Still, Mary Bet was grateful for the love and attention, thankful not to be forgotten.

When the weather turned cold in the middle of October, she wrote to her cousin, Sheriff Teague. Not long afterwards, she received a reply, telling her he could use a bright young woman as a clerk in his office. At supper one evening she told Clara and Mrs. Edwards she was thinking of moving to Williamsboro.

"You can stay with my sister," Mrs. Edwards said. "She'd be happy to have a boarder. I'll write to her directly. And if you should go up there and not like it—well, you can just come right back."

It seemed to Mary Bet that too many things were changing too fast. She'd just taken her father off to the insane asylum and his business had been sold. She thought with excitement of moving to the county seat and working for the sheriff in the courthouse. She'd always liked Hooper—he was much more fun to be around than his mother, at least he seemed that way. But there was the question of her father and, of course, the house. Could she rent it out? Should she sell it? If only she could ask her father. Moving to Williamsboro would mean moving farther away—even though it was only thirteen miles, it was still three hours by carriage or an hour by train since you had to connect with a spur line up from Hogwaller Creek. "It'd be hard to leave you all," she said. "And my house. I've never known any other home but right here in Hartsoe City."

"I'd come visit every other weekend," Clara said, "and you could come here as often as you liked."

"Home is where your people are," Mrs. Edwards said, "and you have people up in Williamsboro, and here too. We're your people."

Mary Bet smiled gratefully. "But my daddy's house—what should I do about it?"

"What do think your father would want you to do?" Clara asked.

"I think he'd trust me to do whatever I thought was right, but I honestly don't know what that is. What if he should recover and be able to come home, and there was no house for him to come home to?"

She decided, with the help of Robert Gray and his son, to put the house up for rent, and within a month they had found a quiet young couple who were looking for a place to stay while they built a little house in the new section south of town, where O'Nora and Mary Bet had lost their way on horseback. The family was from Wadesboro, the young man coming here to work as a manager in the new feed mill. His wife was pregnant, and the idea of them starting a family in her house filled Mary Bet with a poignant sense of time and loss and change—it might've been she and Joe, or she and someone else, instead of strangers.

As she stood in the vestibule with her final bag packed and at her feet, she looked around a last time and caught a glimpse of herself in the mirror above the credenza. She smiled at herself, smoothed away what appeared to be a wrinkle beside her eye, and thought, "There's still time for me, still time to come back to this very house if I want to. But it's only a shell, and now I have to cast it aside for a while and move on. The new people will like it here, and have lots of children, and they'll live long and happy lives."

She looked in all the rooms, and went to the little fireplace to see her guardian angels once more. She took off her mother's sapphire that she had pinned on her blouse that morning and went into the parlor. The jewel glistened like ice, like a rare blue beetle, in her palm. She found the crevice in the bricks lining the fireplace and pushed the pin in with her pinkie. She straightened up, blew a kiss to each of the four walls, then went out and picked up her bag and left the house.

And then she was outside and breathing fresh air again and thinking of next week, and the next. Yet she found herself looking over to the horseless pasture and, beyond, to the woods that had been the proscenium to so much of her childhood. Somewhere out there—and she knew she could find it—was the grave of George the horse, and somewhere else were the decayed bones of a small rabbit, unburied. She hurried away from the house and from the thoughts trying to pull her back.

CHAPTER 18

1906–1907

MARY BET SAT in a ladder-back chair by the window, mending a pair of drawers; a pile of other clothes in need of attention lay in a basket by her feet. It was nearly time for supper, and the smell of boiled greens and frying onions arose from downstairs, along with occasional kitchen sounds. They were not yet so familiar to her to be a comfort, nor anything but an association with nourishment for a hungry stomach. She had been homesick for weeks. Mrs. Edwards's sister, a widow named Henrietta Gooch, liked little conversation at mealtimes. She would ring a small bell that indicated it was time for the boarders to come to the dining room. After the meal, which she provided three times daily, everyone was free to sit in the parlor for as long as they liked, though no one ever stayed very long because there was an unannounced time beyond which Mrs. Gooch would begin fidgeting and looking at the clock and making suggestive glottal noises to move people along.

Mary Bet heard the tinkling bell and laid her mending carefully in the basket and went to the wash basin on her table. There was no mirror in her room, nor anything but a high, iron-framed bed, her trunk, a table and chair, and a battered old armoire that seemed to take up a quarter of the room. If she wished to write, she sat in the chair, with a book in her lap for a desk.

She squeezed between the bed and the armoire and went out to the stairs. She was greeted there by Mr. Hennesey, a white-haired widower of about sixty years, who was no taller than she; he had a dapper way of dressing that was at odds with his sad face, his cheeks and eyes in a permanent sag that made Mary Bet want to say something cheerful every time she saw him. "Hello, Mr. Hennesey," she said, "it's a beautiful evening, isn't it?"

He nodded and indicated that she should precede him on the stairs. "It's fair enough out," he said, a hint of Irish in his voice. He worked in the post office as an assistant to the postmaster, and Mary Bet pictured him drinking a drop or two in his room at night, as she sometimes heard him singing softly to himself. At meals, the only time she saw him regularly, he maintained a decorum verging on the ridiculous. She wondered if with his exaggerated politeness he was not holding something back, some great sorrow—perhaps having to do with his wife—that had become an almost physical deformity.

They went to the dining room, where Mrs. Gooch and Amanda Tomkins were already seated, the latter having anticipated the bell by several minutes so that she could unobtrusively get herself to the table and stow her braces beneath her chair. Besides having legs shriveled by polio, she had a wine-stain birthmark across one cheek and crossed eyes, her thick glasses only exaggerating the defect. She was in her middle thirties, Mary Bet judged, and she worked for the recorder of deeds in the courthouse, so Mary Bet saw her at work every day. Her father had been a railroad clerk, and there had been some scandal about him, though Mary Bet did not yet know the full story. Both her parents were dead, but she had a brother in Raleigh. She was so shy that she almost never spoke unless spoken to. Once or twice when she turned her head in a certain way, Mary Bet thought she was quite pretty, or would be if she didn't keep her hair so short and hanging loose about her face.

After Mr. Hennesey said the blessing—at Mrs. Gooch's prompting—Mrs. Gooch remarked that she was expecting another boarder soon, and then she thought it would be just about a full house. "I never expected to take in boarders atall, but after Horace died I didn't see how I could manage. The Lord didn't bless me with children, so I've had to make do."

Mary Bet looked around the table. Mrs. Gooch sat at the head, so that she could lean back and peer into the kitchen; if she needed something, she would ring for Mehitabel the cook and maid. She talked without looking at anyone, just staring past the empty place at the other end and out the window to the hedges between her house and the next. Amanda and Mr. Hennesey hardly bothered to look up. "What did your husband do, Mrs. Gooch?" Mary Bet ventured.

The table went suddenly quiet, and both the other boarders glanced up, as though wondering who in the world dared breach the suppertime etiquette. They just as quickly went back to their eating, and Mary Bet felt herself blushing in shame, though she could not fathom why. "Well," Mrs. Gooch said, flustered, "well, he was a barber, owned his own shop. And did quite well with it." She ran her tongue around her teeth to clean them, and she let her fingertips rest lightly on her cheek as though recalling something. She had pasty skin and almost no chin, and Mary Bet was certain she had never been anything but plain. Her few smiles were all gums, her hips much too large for her bust and narrow shoulders, like a bowling pin.

"But back to the situation at hand," Mrs. Gooch went on. "I'd always said three boarders was enough. Now I could turn one of your rooms into a double, but it would be a bother." Mr. Hennesey glanced sharply up at this, his gaze instinctively avoiding Mrs. Gooch and settling instead on Mary Bet, as though she were responsible. "And I've thought of turning the back porch into two or three little rooms, but we'll just have to see . . . what would you think of that, Miss Tomkins?"

Amanda looked up, startled. "Ma'am? Oh, I don't know what to think of that." Mary Bet had to lean in to hear, and she thought Amanda's birthmark darkened just a little and an almost imperceptible scowl flickered over her face.

"Well, then, maybe I'll just go ahead and do it." Mrs. Gooch ate a few more bites.

"Did you mean add the extra rooms," Mr. Hennesey asked, "or turn one of our rooms into a double?"

Mrs. Gooch thought for a moment. "I'm not sure yet."

"I'd need notice if you were to do that, because I don't think I could live in smaller quarters." He spoke with a rapid precision, like a typewriter tapping out his lines. "Even with a reduction in rent, I don't think I could."

"And you, Miss Hartsoe?"

"Me? Why, I've just gotten here. I don't—" She started to say she had no opinion, but then she remembered something O'Nora had once said about not being afraid to speak up. "I don't think it would be such a good idea," she said, again feeling sudden warmth in her cheeks.

"Don't think what would be?" Mrs. Gooch demanded. She stared at Mary Bet, her whole face squinting, as if she were trying to figure out who Mary Bet thought she was.

"Well, I don't imagine adding an extra person to the rooms would make anybody happy. Mr. Hennesey wouldn't care for it, and neither would I, now that I think of it. I grew up sleeping in the same room with my sisters, but they were my sisters. And, well, I don't know how Amanda feels about it, but she has her room set up on this floor just the way she likes it. And as for adding rooms on the porch, I don't know where you'd put all the boxes and things that're out there now." As she said all this she realized that Mrs. Gooch likely had no intention of doing anything different, that she'd just wanted to remind her boarders who was in charge, and now she'd gone and gotten an earful.

Mrs. Gooch gave her a disapproving look and said, "Well, you may be right. Though I *could* squeeze a roomer onto the porch if need be. How's your father doing out there at the hospital?"

"He's doing very well, thank you," Mary Bet said. "Much better, they say." She and Clara had gone up there a week ago and found him sitting in a chair in the solarium, his orange afghan covering his lap and his hands in a muff restraint. Two other patients were there as well, and a young male attendant in a white jacket. All four of them sat, staring patiently at the floor or the wall as though they were waiting for a train. Mary Bet had been planning to stay for two nights, but they ended up leaving after one—her father had seemed so far away in his mind, or on medication, that he was hardly aware she was there. When she tried to hug him, he pulled back and gave her such a look that she couldn't help but wonder how he was being treated.

"He's up there at Morganton, idn't he?" Mrs. Gooch said, glancing at the others.

"Yes, ma'am, he is. It's a lovely place out there. You should go out there sometime."

"Me? I have no business out there. The very idea." Mrs. Gooch made a little dismissive laughing noise, her chest rising and falling.

"I meant the area," Mary Bet explained. "It's pretty." But Mrs. Gooch only stared back. Dessert was a small serving of cobbler or pie; seconds were never offered, and the leftovers were locked away in a tin pie safe and the key secured in the pocket of Mrs. Gooch's skirt. Mary Bet excused herself before the others this time, even before coffee, and said she was going to take a walk because it was such a nice evening for this late in the year. Mr. Hennesey and Amanda looked at her with confusion and envy, as if sorry they hadn't thought of the same thing themselves, while Mrs. Gooch made a small joke about there now being more for them.

"Amanda," Mary Bet said, "would you like to come out with me?" Amanda glanced first at Mrs. Gooch, who was looking out the window with a frown.

"Let me get my wrap," Amanda said.

Mary Bet nodded and turned away so that she wouldn't have to see Mrs. Gooch's expression. As she headed to the front door, she heard Amanda's chair scraping and then the clattering rhythm of the braces and the turned feet, and she knew that Mr. Hennesey was sitting there twisting his napkin, wanting to get up and help, but forced by Amanda's orders to sit idle. Amanda had boarded here for nearly six months, Mr. Hennesey for a year, and he still had not adjusted to her presence, let alone to Mary Bet's.

Mary Bet sat on the edge of the rocker, the only chair on the narrow front porch. One of the spindles was missing, and the rockers were misaligned so that the chair rocked with an unpleasant bump. Presently Amanda came along and, taking both braces in one hand and the wooden railing in the other, hobbled down the three steps to the flagstone walkway.

They headed up the road past the last few houses north of the courthouse and turned left. Mrs. Gooch was convinced that she had one of the largest houses in town, but while she did have a full second story, there were larger houses about, and certainly fancier. She at least kept it in good repair, which could not be said for some of the houses off the Durham Road, where thick woods and vines curtained little bungalows and shacks, a few of them occupied by black folks who had bought or inherited property from former masters.

"What do you think of Mrs. Gooch?" Mary Bet asked, feeling the tingling delight of a potential friendship.

"I nearly froze last week," Amanda said. "The boiler doesn't work right, and she only keeps one chimney burning. But my room's on the other side of the house." They were walking so slowly Mary Bet could smell Amanda's perspiration and the lavender from her hair; she tried slowing down even more. "I shouldn't complain though."

"You have every right to complain," Mary Bet said, and when she saw Amanda brighten she added, "You oughten pay to be cold." She felt a stirring of something within her—her very newness to this town and this life gave her a strange power, a freedom to be whatever kind of person she wished to be. She had always wanted O'Nora's boldness of spirit and Myrt's gentle wisdom and poise—she didn't want to *be* them exactly, but to enfold them into herself.

"You think I should say something about it?" Amanda asked, peering briefly at Mary Bet. There was a guarded tone now, a challenge, a woman doubting a youth.

"Yes, I think you should," Mary Bet said firmly, for there was no sense in retreating to a more passive role until she had discovered her limits as a decisive person, at least with this one friend. Amanda nodded thoughtfully, and Mary Bet continued, "I think you should say, 'Mrs. Gooch, it's cold as ice in my room. If that other fireplace works, I want to light it a-nights.' Tell her I'll do it for you, that way she'll know we're together on it."

Amanda laughed, but it was a strange, whimpering kind of sound high up in her throat, as though she were unpracticed in laughter. "Aren't you cold up there at all?" she asked.

"No, I must have thick blood. But I'll say I am." And now Amanda grew quiet, and Mary Bet wondered if she had said something that bothered her. Amanda set her face in a determined way, her lips pressed together, as she struggled along.

"You don't need to say that if it's not true," Amanda said quietly. "I'll manage fine." The blotch on her face seemed to darken just a bit, though there was so little light left to the evening it was hard to tell.

"Do you ever hear Mr. Hennesey singing?" Mary Bet asked.

"Oh, Lord," Amanda replied, this time with a laugh from deeper down. "I don't understand why Mrs. Gooch hasn't kicked him out for drinking, but it's surprising what she . . . tolerates and doesn't tolerate. I was going to say 'likes,' but I don't think she likes anything, except for peppers and cold rooms."

"What about you? What do you like?"

"Oh, in my spare time I like to read dime novels—romance and Westerns. Some people think they're trashy, but I like them because I can be in my room and I'm miles away having a great adventure."

"Do you want to live an adventurous life?"

"Me? Heavens no, I wouldn't care for that. I don't think I'd like chasing Indians and camping out under the stars, and I've had my heart broken once and that was enough for me." Amanda stopped to pull something out of her shoe, Mary Bet waiting for her to tell about her broken heart, but the moment passed and just as Mary Bet thought of a way to ask about it, Amanda said, "What about you? I imagine you like going to dances and parties and that kind of thing, with boys draped all over you."

Mary Bet made an embarrassed little laugh, shaking her head; she was grateful it was too dark to see her complexion. "I don't know why you'd think that. I didn't know I seemed so frivolous."

"Who said anything about frivolous? If I was pretty I would go to dances every weekend. Or I would've at your age. At your age, though, I wouldn't have said that. I would've said that dancing was a waste of time, that it was for foolish people who wanted to look foolish." A dove called, somewhere off in the darkness, and Amanda paused to button her sweater. "We should be getting back," she said. Instead of continuing around the long block, they turned and headed back the way they'd come, Mary Bet watching the ruts in the road as carefully as if she were the one dragging her feet over them. Just taking an evening stroll could be an adventure, she thought, and she was suddenly so happy and filled with hope that she told herself she would stay friends with Amanda for the rest of her life.

Mary Bet worked in the courthouse from eight to noon in the morning, and then from one until four in the afternoon, Monday through Friday, and from eight to noon on Saturdays. Every day she walked past the Confederate Monument and through the brick arcade to the ground floor entrance, then down the hall, and to the right. At the end of this hall was the office of her cousin, Sheriff Hooper Teague. She no longer knocked timidly before she entered, for she was usually the first to arrive. She liked getting there before Toby, the errand boy, because she would be sitting regally at her desk—a pine table with one drawer—and she would tell him that when he had finished stoking the fireplaces with coal, he could see to making sure the lamps were filled with kerosene before he went and fetched the newspaper, which the sheriff liked to have on his desk every morning when he arrived. With the windows this side of the building not getting lit up good until afternoon, there was nothing worse than running out of kerosene when you were in the middle of typing up a warrant.

She had learned some shorthand in school, and it was getting better every day. She improved so rapidly, developing her own method for transcribing the letters and notes the sheriff dictated, that within three weeks she was sitting in on meetings, and old Miss Mumpford, who had been a general courthouse secretary for as long as anyone could remember and whose hearing was no lon-ger reliable, could relax and go fill the coffeepot, which she was happy to do after so many years of straining to hear every word of a meeting on tax collection policy. Mary Bet promised to relay any important gossip she overheard.

Sometimes she was allowed to write up the minutes, summonses, and judgments in the big leather-bound docket books. She picked up enough legal jargon to know what was what, and she started sitting in on the more interesting court cases. Many of them were property disputes of some sort, or a job contract one party had reneged on, and there were assaults and lots of divorces, usually because of adultery. Black and white, rich and poor, came through the courtroom, though most were poor.

Hooper's standing invitation was for Sunday dinner, and though Mary Bet had graciously accepted the first two weeks, she didn't want her cousin to feel duty-bound, and so she made up excuses. But one morning in the spring he stopped at Mary Bet's desk and said, "Mary Bet, I have a little surprise for you. There's someone coming I want you to meet."

She kept her hands poised over her typewriter and, before she had time to think of an excuse said, "Thank you, Sheriff, I'll be there." Then, just as her cousin was about to disappear out the door, she asked, "Who is it?"

"His name is Stuart Jenkins. He's the new Presbyterian circuit preacher. It doesn't matter that you're Baptist. He's a nice young man. He's living in Silkton, but he'll be preaching in town this Sunday—you know it's Presbyterian week."

"All right," she said. She wasn't thrilled, though she couldn't have said why.

"He doesn't know many people around, and neither do you. It would do you good to get out and meet some nice people, and who better than a preacher? I know his folks—they run one of the silk mills. They're very good people . . ." He paused and winked. "And they have some money. Quite a bit from what I hear."

And then, just as Mary Bet was thinking how much Hooper sometimes resembled his mother, she remembered the circuit rider from long ago. She'd thought he was the Devil, with his black boots and his red-eyed horse, coming to take her—he'd said he was coming back for her someday. Of course it was foolish, what she was thinking—he was on a different circuit, and he'd be old now. Still, she could not help but see him clearly, with his long black coat and his slouch hat, and had there not been a crow on his shoulder, or was that something she had added from one of the many times she had seen him in her dreams and imaginings? She was not afraid of him, only curious—she wanted to see his face and talk to him.

"Would it be all right," Mary Bet hazarded, "if I brought a friend along? Amanda Tomkins?"

"Of course, of course. I'm glad you've made friends with her. You know her father made off with money from the railroad safe? They never said how much. He just disappeared and never came back. I think he ran off with a Nigra woman that used to work down there, because she disappeared right around the same time."

"I didn't know that," Mary Bet said. She thought that if Cattie Jordan had told her the same story it would only have been to prove that she knew things, that she had the upper hand around this town because she knew everybody's business. But coming from Hooper, it didn't even seem like gossip—it was just something he knew and had confided to her as a friend and newcomer.

The Sunday dinner was a welcome relief from the tedium and stinginess of Mrs. Gooch's table. She and Amanda took places opposite each other, while Hooper and Mr. Jenkins sat at the heads. Hooper served tremendous plates piled with succulent roast, and told everybody to speak up when they needed more. Working away, his dark brows knit in concentration and his bushy sideburns oozing sweat, he told them that, since the blessing had already been said, they should sail in as soon as their plates were served, because there was no point in letting the food get cold. She asked Mr. Jenkins if the blessing he'd said was a Presbyterian blessing.

"No, ma'am," he replied. "Far be it from me to accept the generosity of a Methodist household and proselytize for my own brand of the faith." It was meant as a light joke, but only Amanda laughed, in what seemed to Mary Bet a sarcastic way.

"I liked what you said this morning about sinners learning how to swim . . . what was it?" Mary Bet asked.

"Ah, swimming downstream toward the lake of fire. I don't like scaring folks, but sometimes you have to paint a vivid picture to get 'em to pay attention."

"Well, I paid right close attention. Didn't you, Amanda?"

Amanda glanced up. "Yes, I did," she said. "I thought it was interesting how you said to watch out for the smooth talker, because it might be the Devil in disguise."

"I thought I saw the Devil when I was a little girl," Mary Bet interjected, surprised that Amanda had said so much, and surprised at herself for cutting her off. She started to laugh and say he was a Presbyterian minister; instead, she took another bite, feeling a little wicked.

"Did you?" he asked, smiling patiently.

"Oh, children are always thinking the most absurd things," Amanda said. "You wouldn't believe some of the things I used to think. But isn't it nice that we're all grown up now?"

"You said we oughten to fear death," Mary Bet said, because she really did want this young preacher's opinion, and something about the way Amanda stared at her made her unable to stop herself. "But I am afraid of it, and I don't know if that makes me a bad person."

"No, Miss Hartsoe," he said, his fingers going to the black cravat at his neck, "allow me to explain what I meant. What I said was that we must be prepared for the Lord's imminent arrival, because we don't know when that might be. It could be today, or next year. All we know is that he will come, and that his heavenly kingdom awaits—for those who have faith."

"It's just that some nights I lie awake worrying about things— I'm not scared exactly, but it feels all black and . . . empty. And there's nobody to talk to. Daddy's gone away now, and . . ." She glanced over to Amanda, who smiled at her now, and to her cousin and boss, the sheriff, who was quietly eating. His elongated, handsome features and gentle manners were pleasingly familiar. Yet none of these people had known even a single untimely death in their families. How could they understand? "I just worry about things I may've said and done."

"We all have things we're not proud of," Mr. Jenkins said. "He that is without sin among you, you know. But without faith in our Lord and savior Jesus Christ, we can be blameless and still be denied the kingdom of heaven."

Hooper interrupted, "I think we ought to let Mr. Jenkins rest. He's had a long, busy morning and I'm sure he'd prefer to relax."

The preacher smiled in a way that said he was giving in to the host. After the pecan pie with ice cream, Hooper invited them into the parlor for coffee. Amanda, clearly eager to be up and moving, struggled to her feet and, by putting her plate between two fingers, was able to manage the handles of her braces and hurl herself toward the kitchen.

"I do this all the time," Amanda said to Mary Bet in the kitchen. "Really." Her birthmark was a cold purple lichen, her crossed eyes large and angry in the watery depths of her glasses. She let the dish down onto the kitchen table with a little clatter, then grabbed the table's edge to steady herself. "I don't see why you monopolize his time like that," she hissed, "and then say you have no friends."

Mary Bet shook her head in bafflement; she had never seen Amanda act this way. "What in the world? I didn't say—"

"I wanted to talk to him, but I couldn't say a word. And he was so nice to me. He has a warm handshake and a nice smile."

"I thought his hands were too soft." Mary Bet could see Amanda relaxing a bit; from the dining room came the drone of the preacher's even-keeled voice. "And moist." Mary Bet wrinkled her nose. "I don't like that in a man's hand."

Now Amanda laughed a little. "Oh, you just don't know anything," she said. "He's not a farmer. I like him."

"Well, you can have him then." On seeing Amanda's stain darken, she added, "Why don't I finish clearing, and you go on in."

"I couldn't sit there with him, and your cousin. He has to be five years younger than me. I don't know what I'd say to him."

"Talk about the weather and the daffodils and how fast you can type. Or just listen. He likes to talk."

"No, it's no use. I don't know what the matter is with me today. I don't—I haven't acted like this in . . . I'm sorry, Mary Bet. Just let's go home, can't we? I'm tired, I need to lie down."

They went back into the dining room and Amanda sat silently and dully, waiting until Mary Bet had finished. Then they joined the men in the parlor and listened to them talk about politics and the weather, and after twenty minutes, Mary Bet said she and Amanda had to get on home. Mr. Jenkins glanced at them both, as though just remembering their presence. Hooper jumped up and apologized for being such a bore, and said that the next time maybe he'd have some people over to play music. "We'll have us a great time," he said.

On the way home in Mary Bet's top-buggy, Amanda told her that her reputation was ruined after an insurance salesman made love to her and promised to marry her and then left town. "There," Amanda said, "now I've gone and told you everything. Except one more thing. I was gone for a month after that to visit cousins in Virginia, and there was a rumor that I went away much heavier than I came home." She paused to wipe her brow with her scarf. "But it wasn't true, and if it was it wouldn't have been anybody's business."

Mary Bet regarded her friend, hidden behind her deformities and her suffering, and decided there was something noble about her.

~⦿ CHAPTER 19 ⦿~

1907–1916

O VER THE NEXT few months Mary Bet fell into the routine of her new life, turning twenty in June and wondering whether she would become a permanent boarder in Mrs. Gooch's house. She and Clara continued visiting back and forth, but there was always something on the weekends to keep her from going out to see her father. At last she admitted to herself that she found the trips depressed her in a strange way akin to grief for a dead loved one, except that the grief was stunted and could never fully flower into a thing that would drop from the vine. Some nights lying in bed she would talk to him in whispers, begging him to forgive her. "I failed you," she would say, tears flowing, purging the guilt and fear of eternal punishment. "I lied to you. I told you I wouldn't leave you there, and I did, and I knew I would." She tried to hear his voice, and sometimes he would say, "It's all right," though she wondered if it was only her willing him to say it. She would try to keep herself awake to prolong the suffering in her heart, but she would always fall asleep. And in the morning she would forget her lonely vigil as she readied herself for the day ahead.

Twice Mr. Jenkins invited her to church socials, the invitations coming in elegantly penned letters a week before his scheduled monthly preaching engagements in Williamsboro. Amanda was angry with her for turning down the first invitation, so she didn't mention the second.

After church following that second invitation, she tried to hurry around him in the vestibule while he was shaking hands with a garrulous old veteran named Hiram Hill. But Amanda wanted to wait and shake his hand and say how much the sermon had meant to her. So Mary Bet had to stand there and watch while Mr. Jenkins, seeming to understand that she was stuck, kept holding Hiram Hill's hand and giving him his full attention, leaning down to catch every word. Lord, the time you could spend in delicate situations.

"Ah, Miss Tomkins," he said at last, reaching out to squeeze Amanda's upper arm. He seemed now to stretch time like a rubber band, as though punishing Mary Bet and, at the same time, savoring the moment of anticipation when he would at last take her hand in his. She knew enough of lust and denial and Mr. Jenkins to understand that. When he finally did grasp her hand and speak to her, it was as though he had not known she was in line behind Amanda, yet his watery blue eyes tried to pry deep into hers, accusing her and demanding satisfaction.

"That was a right nice sermon," she said, her eyes skidding off his.

His thin eyebrows lifted; his straw-colored hair—perfectly oiled, combed, and parted—fit him like a baseball cap, and his nose was pinched and thin—he was not bad looking, just a little too girlish. And his hand was soft and clammy as he held hers, like damp laundry. "What part did you like, Miss Hartsoe?" he asked, putting his other hand atop their clasped hands.

"Well, I think that part about not judging a man by his appearance was right important," she said, her face warming.

He looked closely at her, but didn't seem to notice the blush. "Yes, I have you to thank for that. Your comment about the Devil in disguise made me go back to that passage in Matthew. I'm glad you found some comfort in it." Just as she was pulling away, he added casually, "I hope the prayer meeting this evening is fulfilling and not too onerous." She had been expecting this, so she nodded—a little fib to a preacher couldn't be any worse than a fib to a regular person, could it?

Amanda overheard and, on the steps outside the church, asked Mary Bet what he'd meant. "I didn't know you had a prayer meeting this evening."

"I don't," Mary Bet said, quietly, so no one would overhear. They moved slowly down the walkway toward the street where Amanda's buggy was parked.

"You mean you lied to a preacher, and used a made-up prayer meeting for an excuse? Honestly, Mary Bet, I'm shocked."

"No, you're not. You're just a little disappointed. I don't intend going out with him."

"Well, neither do I," Amanda said, lifting her face with an arch little smile and squinting in the sunlight. "In fact, I'm going for a buggy ride this very evening." Mary Bet was not sure how to respond, so she said nothing. "Don't you want to know who with?"

"Of course I do," Mary Bet said. "I was just waiting for you to say."

"Mr. Hennesey. He said he was a good driver and he'd like to take me in my buggy out to look at the old farm he grew up on. He's very nice and old-fashioned, and when he dresses up he looks ten years younger. I don't mind if he drinks a little—all men do."

"I didn't say anything against him."

"But I can tell you don't approve." Amanda pulled herself up into the buggy and got herself situated on the box and took the reins.

Quiet and self-effacing around people she did not know well, she managed fine on her own. She clicked her tongue, and the white-tailed sorrel leaned into its traces and the buggy rolled forward.

"I'm very happy for you, Amanda."

Now Amanda smiled faintly and her complexion lightened. "We're just going riding out in the country. It doesn't mean anything." A minute or two later she said, "I guess I have you to thank. I don't think he'd said two words to me before you came. Sometimes having another person around—having you around—livens things up. I just can't wait to see Mrs. Gooch's face when she finds out. Oh my, I just thought of something."

"What?"

"She'll think it's improper, she won't let us live under the same roof." Mary Bet started to say that she doubted Mrs. Gooch would throw out a good, reliable boarder, but she wasn't so sure, and, anyway, Amanda seemed a little thrilled with the prospect.

Mary Bet's own prospects seemed less than thrilling, at least in the romantic field, but she finally did accept an invitation from Mr. Jenkins.

It was a beautiful early summer Sunday, the soft air sweetened by lilacs and jasmine and birdsong. Since she never bought herself a new hat—she could afford it, but she thought it a waste—she decorated her black brimmed hat with a piece of light blue ribbon. She wore her navy faille dress and best black shoes, and after church she walked by herself to her cousin's house.

It was just Hooper, Mr. Jenkins, and herself, and, as though by prearrangement, her cousin excused himself immediately after the pie to go down to the courthouse. "What, working on a Sunday?" Mary Bet asked, half hoping he'd ask her to come along.

"I can't help it," he said. "I'm married to my job—it's a good thing I like it." He put on his slouch hat at the door, winked at Mary Bet and nodded to the preacher.

For a while they sat in Hooper's parlor, she listening as Mr. Jenkins explained his sermon in greater detail—after all, she had asked. Now, listening to his strong deep voice, so confident and reassuring, even if what he said seemed less than satisfying, she thought he was not a bad man at all. She smiled encouragement as he shifted in his chair, gathering his thoughts, the fingers of his right hand like tentacles feeling the air.

"A young woman of beauty, such as yourself," he said, staring ahead at the mantelpiece, "can cause a man even of Solomon's greatness to falter. Or she can be a foundation for a man's life and work."

She watched him as he talked, his erect back and thrust-out chin giving him the look of a man who does not know himself; yet his large blue eyes and delicate mouth put her in mind of a boy forced against his will to become a man. She thought: Today I won't be judgmental. "That's nice of you to say," she told him. "But I don't put myself alongside the concubines of Solomon."

"Oh, no no, you misunderstand my meaning entirely," he said. He looked both indignant and flustered, his red face brightening a shade or two, and she was ashamed for upsetting him, and disappointed as well, for she knew that now he would feel the need to explain himself in a long-winded, didactic way, as though he had to hear the sound of the elegant sentences forming in his mind as it explored every possible ramification and counterargument and parenthetical digression along the way.

Before he got too far into his response, she said, "I thought we could take a walk about town." This met with an enthusiastic comment about the value of exercise and the companionship of a bright young woman being a great boon to the weary mind of a circuit preacher.

They walked up the Durham Road, and then down around the courthouse and out a ways on the Hartsoe City Road, but the dust from passing buggies made them decide to turn off. Mr. Jenkins said hello to everyone they passed but didn't feel inclined to stop and talk, which suited Mary Bet just fine. She didn't mind that he seemed to be showing her off as a walking companion, or the possibility that a walk seemed better to him than a ride because of the impropriety of riding alone with a young lady. In both cases there was an assumption that they were courting, and she decided she didn't mind that either.

They took the apple-tree lane down past the shanties of colored town, and Mr. Jenkins said, "Whenever I can, I like to see how the Nigras are living. It gives me an appreciation for everything we have, even in the hardest of times. My father taught me that."

"My father believed that the Negroes wouldn't get anywhere without better schools."

"Ah, but where do we want them to get, Miss Hartsoe? If we're not careful, we'll be working for the black race. I do not exaggerate. I have terrible visions and dreams, let me tell you. You see that pickaninny right there, playing in the dirt with no pants on? He could be the boss of your very own son someday."

The child in question paused in his mud-pie-making to look up at them with wide-open eyes. Mary Bet waved, and the boy waved back. "That's Elvira Green's boy. They're good people. Her husband, Roscoe, works at the train station."

"Yes, but don't doubt for a minute that the boy, if given a chance, could be the sheriff."

Mary Bet laughed. "I don't see how, unless white people voted for him. He could be a teacher, though, or even a principal, if he had the proper schooling. And that's a good thing, don't you think so?"

"As long as he's principal of the colored school, then it's a fine thing. But what if he was principal of the white school?"

She laughed again and shook her head. "Now you're just pulling my leg. How can a black man be principal of a white school?"

"There's talk about that very sort of thing. The Nigras up north are organizing, and if we're not careful it'll happen right here. I believe in self-improvement for the colored race, but my question is, where does it end? The colored people of Haw County are docile enough now, but I often pray that, for their own good, they will not try to rise above their God-given station."

As they headed back up toward the courthouse, Mary Bet could feel the perspiration pooling at the base of her neck and under her arms, and she thought that it was not just the heat but the closeness of this man, who seemed very unlike a preacher when he was not in church. There was some kind of perfume he wore that she had not noticed earlier. It made him seem dandified in a way that was unattractive to her, and the way he worried about colored people—she wanted to like him, but he seemed so cautious, so worried about the future that she thought he would make a stern and unforgiving father, afraid of his children making a misstep and reflecting poorly upon himself. It was silly to have such thoughts, she told herself. They were just taking a walk.

The correspondence they kept up over the next few weeks was friendly on her part, courtly and mannered on his. Nothing in his letters had but the faintest whiff of romantic interest in her, and she could only conclude that he was either not interested or was showing such caution as he felt necessary to protect his own reputation and feelings; of course, it was possible he was only thinking of her feelings and was afraid of scaring her off.

He came again the following month, on Presbyterian Sunday, and Mary Bet decided she would hold back when the service was over so that he would have a chance to talk with her if he wanted to. He'd said he looked forward to seeing her and that "perhaps we could visit some." When she offered her gloved hand, he squeezed it in both of his and gave her such a warm look she felt a tingle run through her body. Was it the warmth of the Holy Ghost, so lately voiced in this man's sermon? Or was Mr. Jenkins genuinely in love with her? She decided to tell him the truth. "I've been looking forward to seeing you all week long," she said.

He nodded and glanced about, as though to see if anyone were listening. "As have I," he replied. "Will you be dining at your cousin's?"

"No," she nodded toward Amanda, who was leaning on her braces down on the flagstone walkway, looking miserably hot with the sun beating upon her hat. "We'll be going back to Mrs. Gooch's. But I have no plans for afterwards."

"I'm having dinner with the Fred Fikes," he said. "But then I could stop by and we might ride out to Hackett's Mill, if you'd like."

He said it casually, as if he were only offering out of kindness. She couldn't help being just a little sassy. "I'd be honored to accompany you," she said, mimicking his formal tone—he'd told her he had studied in England.

At the appointed hour she was ready and sitting on Mrs. Gooch's narrow front porch, rocking nervously and fanning her face with her navy-blue sun hat. He was only a few minutes late and she was gratified to find that he was apologetic, and even a little flustered. He helped her into the buggy, and then pulled himself up in one graceful motion and stirred the horse into movement. When she asked him questions, he seemed preoccupied, uncharacteristically quiet, until she began to think she was imposing on his time—that, or he was just being rude. Finally, she said, "I hope you didn't have something more important this afternoon, Mr. Jenkins."

"Please call me Stuart," he told her. He cleared his throat, but did not look at her.

"All right, then," she said. "Did you have something else to do today, Stuart?"

"No," he said. He glanced at her, his face so dark red it reminded her of Amanda's birth stain.

At a grove of pines before the pond at Hackett's, he stopped the horse and alighted. He helped her down briskly, as if he wanted to get the job over with, and began walking toward the pond. He turned briefly to see if she were following. "Stuart," she said, "what is the matter? You seem worried about something."

He nodded and came forward so suddenly she pulled away. His eyes were large and fearful, empty blue orbs that seemed to reflect more than they saw, and his breath was heavy and shaggy. He put his arms about her and drew her tight to himself, his body shuddering. He kissed the hair that lay flat against her neck and then her cheek, and as he tried to kiss her mouth she found herself pushing him away. She couldn't see or breathe, he was such an unknown weight on her. She just wanted space between their bodies.

He suddenly pulled back and dropped his arms. "I thought—" he stopped and put the back of his hand to his lips. "I thought you—"

"Mr. Jenkins," she said. "Stuart. I wasn't expecting you to be so, so bold like that. You caught me by surprise is all." She could see now he was deeply embarrassed and ashamed and angry; he stood looking out at the pond, his arms hanging stiffly by his sides. A bullfrog roared somewhere off in the cattails at the pond's edge, and mating dragonflies flitted about the lily pads. The dance of life seemed so simple, and yet it was so impossibly complex for people it was a wonder, she thought, that children ever came into the world.

"It's all right, Stuart," she said. "I do like you."

"Just not in that way, apparently."

She hesitated, because she wanted to get her words just right, but she could see he was reading doubt in her hesitation. He said, "I've made a fool of myself, and you must think that I'm a cad. I must tell you that I'm not only a man of God, but a man with feelings, just like every man. There's never been a man—except Jesus—without such feelings."

"Yes," she said, and because she felt pity for his misguided attempts and gratitude for how he had recoiled at himself rather than her, she said, "I think you're a wonderful man and preacher, both."

"You don't want to see me again, though, do you? And I suppose my reputation has lost some of its shine around these parts?"

"I wouldn't breathe a word about this. And I do want to see you again." But as soon as she said this she pictured saying it to Hooper Teague, her own cousin.

"Are you all right?" he asked. She nodded. He suddenly seemed like such a comical man, with his neat cravat and gray jacket still intact on a warm day. She didn't mind his attentions, and though she didn't want to lead him on she offered her bare hand for him to hold.

They stood there hand in hand staring out at the pond. Finally he ventured, "I can call on you again, then?"

"Of course you can. But I don't want to marry anybody, at least not for a long time, so I don't want you to get the wrong idea."

He nodded. "Mary Bet. May I call you that?"

"Yes, you may," she said.

"You are a very independent young woman, and I admire that, just as I admire your candor. I don't know many people, male or female, and certainly not any your age, with such forthrightness and perception. If I could venture a guess, I'd say that the difficulties of your youth have made you wiser than most."

"Well I don't know about that," she replied. "I think everybody has his cross to bear, even the people who seem to have every blessing you can imagine."

They went and sat on a wide sycamore stump and Mr. Jenkins spoke to her of his ambition to become a writer of inspirational books, filled with true stories of the wonders of God's eternal plan. He told her one such story at length, and after some time Mary Bet said that she had best be getting on home. And so they rode back together, the strain gone from Mr. Jenkins and a new understanding between him and Mary Bet, and a new uncertainty as well. For a while he told stories, and then together they sang hymns. But she was picturing Siler on the tracks again, now holding his arms up as if trying to warn her against something, as if to keep her from going where he had gone.

Mary Bet refused Mr. Jenkins's further invitations, yet she was surprised when, six months later, an invitation to his wedding arrived in the mail. He married a distant cousin, a fat, phlegmatic young woman named Helena George from Elizabethtown, and he moved to the southeastern part of the state.

NINE YEARS PASSED.

It was strange how life could move so fast and yet be unchanging in the things that mattered. Mary Bet remained an unmarried clerk at the Haw County Courthouse. She went out on a couple of raids—to apprehend a drunken brawler for stealing a wagon full of illegal whiskey that he claimed he was bringing to the authorities, and a flimflammer from South Carolina who was selling bogus burial insurance to poor folks in several counties. But mostly she stayed at the courthouse, doing a job she had been at nearly as long as anyone could remember.

She made friends, went to their weddings, saw them have babies, attended church picnics and baptisms, laughed over jokes and stories, and went out to Love's Creek once a month to decorate the graves. It seemed as though she arrived overnight from being a girl to a middle-aged woman. The years rushed by as if they were in a hurry, and the world with them. And she was caught up in the whirlwind of time whether she intended to be or not, and the past was swirled together with the present and the future like a dust devil, curling around and around and around.

There were fewer and fewer trips to Hartsoe City, though Clara kept her up on the news: Dr. Slocum bought the first automobile in town, a little two-door runabout with a fold-back cloth top. Then Robert Gray Jr. bought a similar but sportier-looking roadster, and they would chug together up the Raleigh Road, racing by the time they got past the post office. After Ila died, Robert Gray Jr. became a lawyer like his daddy and married a rich widow from Charlotte. Sometimes they came to Williamsboro, and when Mary Bet saw one of them about town her heart would skip a beat, as she remembered her sister and her own crush on him when he was calling on Ila.

Amanda and Mr. Hennesey had a falling out, then patched things up and were married, and when they moved out it took Mrs. Gooch two weeks to find suitable replacements. "You'd think they could've had a little more consideration," she told Mary Bet the night before the wedding, though they'd announced their plans three months ahead. The new boarders were sisters, both schoolteachers, and they pretty much kept to themselves. But it didn't bother Mary Bet, because she had plenty of friends around town.

She wondered if she would ever find romantic love. Or was the love of her friends not better, because it was a love that did not require as much constant attention, not a demanding love the way an animal must be tended several times a day, or the way the garden must be watered and weeded. The love of friends did not tear at you the way the love of family did—you could snip away a friend like a brown leaf on a plant and go on with your life, because water was not as thick as blood, and she needed no more blood than what was in her own veins. Water should be enough—was it not the stuff of life?

It had been ten years since she and Cattie had taken Cicero up to Morganton, an entire decade of living on her own. She no longer thought of her father with self-reproach, no longer accused herself of abandoning him. Her semiannual visits to the state hospital had become a dutiful ritual, giving her neither pain nor pleasure, for her father seemed to have drifted away, his light dimming with each passing year. For a while she wondered if it was the medication that was causing his steady decline. But the doctors had assured her what they used was minimal, and she had no choice but to believe them. She wrote him a letter a week, but because she no longer (after the first year) heard back it was like writing to herself, reminding herself of the events of the previous seven days. She had no thought now of rescuing him—where would they live? How could she take care of him? And what if he should have another, worse episode? There had been enough tragedy in her life.

She was twenty-nine. Almost in the fourth decade of her life, and she sometimes felt embarrassed for living so long unmarried. No, that was not it. Just for living so long. Her friends loved her, but she sometimes felt as if she could relieve their anxiety by finding a mate. On the other hand, was it not too late for that? Almost, almost.

～ CHAPTER 20 ～

1916

·

THERE WERE MEN who came through the courthouse that
Mary Bet found attractive, but she thought they may have
sensed that in her thirtieth year she was a little too judgmental
and hard to please and decided she wasn't worth the bother. She
never flirted with anybody, because she believed in treating everyone
with the same kindness and respect. If God intended her to marry,
then he would work it out in his own way . . . although, there *was*
the possibility that he might intend for her to take some kind of
action. In the meantime, there was plenty to occupy her attention.
One day Sheriff Teague asked if she was interested in going out with
him and a deputy on a raid. She looked up from her typewriter and
pushed her glasses back up her nose. "What kind of raid?" she asked.

"On a still."

"An illegal still?"

"That's the only kind that operates in Haw County," he said. He
stood leaning over her desk like a drawn bow, his tall, lean stature

and dark eyes giving him a hungry look. His jacket hung open and his black-stock tie matched his long mustache in dishevelment. But he was hardworking and personable and Mary Bet thought that if Hooper Teague wasn't her cousin she might be interested in him. In fact, if he wasn't Cattie Jordan's son, she might . . . even though his ears were a little big for his face. There was a woman down in Possum Creek, a rich farmer's daughter, he was known to court from time to time, but they weren't engaged that Mary Bet had heard.

"I'll have to see to finishing this pile of papers," she said.

"You can see to that later, I need you to come with Leon and me."

"Is it dangerous?" she asked, rising and putting on her jacket and black felt hat.

"Naw, shouldn't be too bad. These aren't any murderers—that I know of. They might be a little nimble, and that's why I want you with us."

Mary Bet shook her head, wondering how she could possibly be of help and wondering, too, if her cousin was just having fun educating her in the ways of Haw County law enforcement. They loaded onto the sheriff's buckboard, which was powered by an enormous old chestnut named Caesar, then went jouncing along, the varnished strips of wood at their feet creaking like springs. Mary Bet covered her nose and mouth with a handkerchief against the summer dust, but the stirred air felt good on her skin.

They stopped just north of town and picked up Leon Thomas, a young teacher Hooper deputized from time to time in addition to his regular township deputies. He was heavyset and jowly and quite a bit shorter than Hooper. His hair was light and bristly and cropped so close to his skull that he looked something like a criminal, Mary Bet thought. She didn't much care for sitting beside him, so she only nodded politely when he jabbed a hand up in greeting. Only a country bumpkin would do that to a lady. He was kind enough to go around to the other side and get in next to Hooper, and then they were off again.

For the next mile or two the men talked about people they knew in common and cases they'd worked together. There was a recent brawl down in Possum Creek between a vagrant and a farmer who'd hired him to put up and paint a fence. Mary Bet didn't like the story because it reminded her of Shackleford Davies, the murderer, and because Possum Creek was where Hooper's lady friend lived and it seemed as if he enjoyed just saying the name of the village. It was a silly name for a village—she'd never heard of anybody from there, except rich farmers and vagrants. Then they started talking about the pig rustler out along the county line to the east. Leon would glance over at Mary Bet occasionally. Why, she couldn't imagine, unless it was to include her in a conversation that she could add nothing to, or to impress her with how smart they'd been in handling the pig thief.

They turned off on the White Chapel Road and rocked along under the dappled shade of oaks and hickories, past farms with white clapboard houses set back amid groves of trees, the smells of honeysuckle and ripening corn fixed in the air, and Mary Bet half listened to the men and wondered if the world consisted of young women like herself being carried along by strong men and horses and some compelling mission, all flowing as inevitably as a river. It was not a bad feeling exactly—she was in fact comforted by the men's voices and their heavy, tobacco odor—yet the place they were going, outside of her experience, filled her with a childish fear that she tried to ignore. Nothing terrible could happen, though she had seen her cousin's holstered revolver beneath the hem of his jacket.

Her limbs, at times her entire body, trembled with anticipation, and to calm herself she thought of O'Nora. O'Nora would've enjoyed this, would've considered it an adventure and a chance to see how things were done. Mary Bet thought she had grown less afraid over the years, but it seemed the older you got the more you encountered things to fear, replacing the things of the past that had once seemed so fearful with new things you'd never imagined undertaking before.

Before she had time to fully consider this, the buckboard was turning off onto a narrow lane with deep ruts and a center stripe of weeds that grew higher the farther they traveled. In another mile they turned again, down a cart path, the horse picking its slow way among holes and embedded rocks, and then again they turned and went on and on and on, until the path was so overgrown that the limbs of scrub trees thocked against the wheel spokes and scraped the sides of the buckboard as though intent on impeding its further progress. Mary Bet was continually holding up her hands to keep from getting smacked in the face. Finally they stopped.

"We lost?" Leon asked.

"No," Hooper replied. "I reckon we can walk from here."

"Shall I stay with the buggy?" Mary Bet suggested.

"Not unless you want to. I could use you for a forward man." He smiled so that the shoulders of his long mustache lifted, but Mary Bet was not especially amused. She gathered her skirts against her legs and reached a bare hand out to her cousin and let him help her down. Her hat went crooked over her face as she landed. Hooper reached back under the seat and pulled out an ax, then went over and pushed through a screen of shrubs and trees lining the path. He studied the ground. "Yep," he said quietly. "Here's the trail. I was through here six days ago on a tip. Found five barrels of mash. With the air cool as it's been, I don't reckon they were ready to whiskeyfy till now. Cap was soft as a baby's bottom."

Leon guffawed, and Hooper turned abruptly and shushed him. "We got to be quiet now. Don't even break a stick. It's a mile or so in, but they might already know we're here. When we get closer I'll send Mary Bet in to say she's been out picking herbs and got lost. Then Leon, you'll go around behind in case anybody tries to run."

"How am I gonna stop 'em?" Leon asked. He looked from the sheriff to Mary Bet, as though he'd be happy for an answer from either of them, and it was the first time she realized he was as green as she in still busting. But he didn't look nervous or scared—he just stood there, his stocky legs and torso as solid as a bull, fanning his sweating face with his slouch hat. She didn't mind the country way he had of speaking, and now that she could see him close up, his gray-green eyes sharp and focused, she didn't think he was all that bad-looking either, even if he was a little chunky.

"Just tell them to stop," Hooper said.

"What kind of herbs?" Mary Bet wanted to know. She watched as Leon took a pinch of snuff from a tin and packed it under his lower lip.

Hooper shook his head. "Any kind you can think of."

"What if they have guns?" she asked.

"They won't shoot us. It's just old Strickland Sugg and some of his lesser kin."

"Is Harlan Junior with 'em, you reckon?" Leon asked.

"Why, is he a friend of yours?"

"We went squirrel shooting a week ago. He knows every single creek and cranny and holler in the north part of the county. But I've heard old Sugg's liable to be unpredictable."

Hooper shook his head. "I'm not overly concerned. They're just trying to beat the revenue." He glanced thoughtfully at Leon as though reconsidering. "Of course, it *is* against the law."

"Shoot, Hooper," Leon said. "You got the reputation of being so dry you have to drink water just to spit." He then expectorated around clenched teeth, the brown gob instantly coating a little purple wildflower, and Mary Bet decided he had poor manners in front of a lady.

It was impossible to walk in the forest without snapping twigs underfoot, nor without snagging one's dress on unseen briars and nettles. Every so often she stooped to pick a flower or little plant, putting the posy in her sweater pocket so that she could prove she'd been out gathering herbs. Her heart was beginning to thump quicker and louder and higher in her chest, though she tried to be brave and ignore it. The next time Hooper suggested she go out on a raid, she would simply say she was too busy, or she wasn't feeling well—it was okay to lie like that when you had nothing to gain. She brushed the loose hair back from her brow and walked on, pretending to be O'Nora, pulling her shoulders up, swinging her arms along, eager to meet these strange backwoods bootleggers and to see their hive of illicit, foul-smelling depravity.

After a while Hooper held his hand up, and they stopped. The trickling of a nearby creek sounded through the woods, and Mary Bet could smell wood smoke and a faint yeasty odor. Hooper leaned down to whisper to Mary Bet. "You go on ahead. Ask for directions to the road. We'll be right along. Don't spook if you hear a shot. It'll just be a lookout warning the cookers."

Mary Bet headed forward through the forest, which seemed darker now. Clouds had obscured what little sun had found its way through the thick trees. She forced herself to take one step after another, looking back every few seconds to make sure Hooper wasn't calling her off. Leon had already disappeared. I won't fail you, she told herself, I won't fail you. Even if it was just a test of her nerves, she wouldn't let her boss down. I won't fail you, she thought, and the image of O'Nora's red-cheeked face came so clearly to mind she almost called out. "I won't fail you either," she whispered, and her heartbeat steadied itself and she found that she could breathe. She walked on toward the gathering sound of voices and didn't look back.

A little ways on she stopped behind the thick ridgy trunk of a chestnut tree. The voices had gone suddenly quiet, and in the backwash of silence she could hear the creek again, louder and more urgent. But her heart was resolved and she moved out from behind the tree. A bugle blared out three strangulated notes like a startled goose, followed by the barking of dogs. She stopped and peered through the tangled spring growth of creeper and sapling, between the gray uprights of trees unbranching until they were clear of some preordained growth that only pertained here in the primitive deep of the woods. The dogs quit barking, as if they'd been hushed, and though she kept shifting her head like a deer to see forward, the tree-on-tree weave obscured her view.

She decided they knew of her presence and that it was best to continue on—she was lost and needed to find people. A few steps farther she saw a black hairlike line at her feet and thought how odd to find a spiderweb of such color. Bending down, she saw that it was a long piece of thread running between two trees— how strange these people must be, how superstitious, she thought, stepping over the thread and reminding herself to ask them about it. She thought she would not be surprised or scared by anything now—a bear even, or a wild boar.

At the limit of her sight a man was standing beside a tree. Or what looked like a man. She came on forward now, more sure of herself and trusting that the sheriff was somewhere close behind. The man wore stained nankeen trousers and a long brown canvas jacket; his hat shadowed his face, and he leaned on a carved stick, the handle at waist level. As she drew closer he lifted his eyes to glance at her, and she saw that one eye was dead. He scanned with great care the woods behind her as though reading and rereading a passage for some important line.

"Hallo," she said, coming forward.

He nodded, his stringy beard dipping a mere inch. "Who's with you?" he asked. His voice was low and gravelly, not unfriendly, just cautiously threatening; he was perhaps seventy, or a little older, around her father's age, and she suddenly felt sorry for him and guilty for pretending to be other than the law. She imagined he was posted here because he was too old or incompetent to do the real work.

"I'm lost," she said, for she could not bring herself to say she was alone. "I was out looking for herbs to make tea with." She pulled the plants from her pocket and held them out in her palm. "Do you know which way the road is from here?"

"What was you looking for, precisely?" Again his good eye only flickered across her, taking her in and then swiftly moving on to the woods behind. But it seemed that the dead eye continued to hold her.

"I mostly was after cohosh. You don't know where any is, do you?"

"How'd you get in here, if you cain't get out?" His teeth were stained and one of the two front ones was twisted so that the side was forward.

She laughed in a limp way. "I walked from the road. I guess I'm not much good with directions."

"You're not from around here. Where're you from?"

"From over in Williamsboro," she said. "Well, I'm really from Hartsoe City."

"What's your name?"

She hesitated. "Mary Bet Hartsoe. You might've heard of my people." She looked him in the eye, and then, as though another voice were taking possession of hers, for she'd never asked a man to introduce himself, she said, "What's your name?"

"Otis Sugg," he said. A breeze carried the smell of cooking mash, heavier now, and Otis appraised her as though for a sign of comprehension. And because she could think of nothing more to say, Mary Bet finally lost her nerve and looked back. She thought of Lot's wife losing her faith and paying with her life. As she turned back around, she cried out, because she saw that Otis Sugg had pulled a pistol from his belt. He lifted it in the air and fired. Then he said, "Your friend's a-comin' yonder. I's just lettin' him know we was here."

Mary Bet looked around again, but still could not see the sheriff. She was not sure whether to believe Otis Sugg, but her heart was pounding and she felt bold enough to quit lying. "You were not," she said. "You were warning the other bootleggers. They're over there somewhere distilling whiskey, and we're going to shut you down."

"You are, huh?" He chuckled as though he were talking to a five-year-old.

"Yes, we are. That's Sheriff Teague coming with the ax right now." She thought he looked as if he were considering something, but the sadness in his face made her say, "Aren't you going to run?"

"What's the use?" he said. "I can't run no more. If that's the sheriff, he'll tell me I owe the United States government a hundred and fifty dollars. My brother'll pay it, and that'll be that."

She shook her head. "You should be ashamed, out here making liquor."

And now he gave her a harsh look, his eyes narrowing. "You don't know what you're sayin', missy. Your people don't know a thing about my people. You live off in some great big mansion with a coach and white horses, and you come traipsin' out here like you're huntin' turkeys."

"I didn't mean anything by it," she said. "I just—" She saw him looking into her eyes, understanding that she was young and full of wrongheaded suppositions, and he nodded.

"That's all right," he said. "I don't reckon making liquor's such a good thing, but people'll be wantin' to drink it no matter what. You shut this still down, anothern'll pop up somewhar else."

Mary Bet could hear footsteps behind her, the leaves and twigs of the forest floor giving notice of a man's tread. And then Hooper was beside her, his gun out and hanging at his side. "You don't mind putting that away, do you, Otis?" he said.

Otis glanced down at his gun, an old long-barreled pistol, as if he'd forgotten it. He tucked it back into his belt and said, "What can I do for you, Sheriff?"

Hooper smiled and replied, "C'mon, Otis, let's go see what you and your brother have brewing today. It dudn't smell like coffee." He started off, then said, "And you might as well hand me that pistol for safekeeping." He took the pistol in his free hand and looked at Mary Bet as if considering, then led the way down toward the creek.

They crossed on stepping stones, the hem of Mary Bet's dress already so bedraggled from the walk that she didn't bother holding it away from the water. She thought she'd be able to wash the dirt out, which for some reason put her in mind of the teacher Leon Thomas. She wondered who did his laundry and his mending and if he still lived with his parents. Hooper lived by himself like a bachelor, but she didn't think he would be for long, not that it was any of her business. She had to admit a fondness for him, even though he was her cousin and her boss and had a tendency, like his mother, to say whatever was on his mind.

Mary Bet thought all these things while crossing the clear creek and making her way up the root-plugged bank, following the bootlegger Otis Sugg, who was following Sheriff Teague as the creek took a bend to the right and past a thicket of briars, pines, and pawpaws, the ground spotted with little white bloodroots. They went around a jumble of snags that provided a kind of wall sheltering a clearing not far off the creek. And here was the bootleggers' lair, with its motley arrangement of wooden barrels and odd-shaped devices. There was no one about, but a man was approaching from the opposite direction.

Leon came into view, shouting a warning, "It's just me. Don't shoot."

Hooper called back, "All right." Then he went over to a big, squat, hammered-copper pot that was sitting on a fire, a stack of fresh logs beside it. On the top was what looked like a kettle with a long spout coming out one side, with a clear liquid dripping from the spout into a barrel. Hooper pushed his ax head against the kettle until it fell onto the ground, and then grabbed a wooden paddle leaning on the pot's side and gave the contents of the pot a stir. Mary Bet glanced in at the thick, dark brown mixture, the fermenting smell so sweetly pungent she wondered if she could get drunk breathing.

"Hmmm," he said, "first run mash."

Otis nodded and smiled a little. "Shame to waste it," he said.

Leon came into the clearing. "They all ran off. I saw one, but I couldn't tell who it was."

"It dudn't matter," Hooper told him. "Otis here'll be responsible for the fine, won't you, Otis?"

"Yessir, I reckon I'll have to." Otis suddenly looked ancient, his face gone hangdog and blank.

"All right, Leon and Otis, you'll have to help me here. We've got to turn this mash out and chop everything up."

"Everything?" Otis mourned.

"Every barrel and bottle and copper worm on the premises, and this turnip pot is the first to go. But we got to be careful with it."

"Bottles too?"

"Yep."

"Can't I just pay a granny fee?"

"Granny fee? I've never heard of such a thing. I didn't hear it from you either. You didn't just try to bribe a county sheriff, did you?"

"No, sir, I didn't."

"I didn't think so. Now give us a hand here."

Mary Bet stood back while the three men, mostly Hooper and Leon, cleared away enough embers to make room for their feet.

Then they used sticks to tilt the pot over until the concoction oozed from the lip. It sizzled as it ran down the side and into the remains of the fire, and Mary Bet watched the steam rising from the ground as though the ground was angry, scorched by the Devil's cauldron. Just beyond lay the fallen top with its queer spout, where she knew the whiskey had been issuing forth like the essence of evil spilling into a barrel for desperate people to buy and sell and get crazy drunk on. She appreciated that the sheriff didn't insult Otis Sugg, didn't call him "boy," didn't say he was a dirty, lawbreaking moonshiner, though she herself had thought up that phrase and a few more besides. But that was before she'd met Otis. Not that she'd want to have him over for tea, and the thought of him sitting down in her living room with Flora, her new housemate, almost made her laugh out loud.

"That's a lot of moonshine," she said, staring at the golden froth, trying the word out on her tongue.

The men pushed the emptied pot over to the side. Leon nodded, glancing at Mary Bet, and then chuckled. "It sure is, Miss Hartsoe. That's a funny thing to say, though." He looked at her with amusement, and Mary Bet noticed now that he had a slight cast to one eye, the right one looked off a little to the side, but perhaps this was only in certain situations. He looked less like a bumpkin now, even with a stirring paddle in his hands, than like a bright, lively young schoolteacher. He and Hooper went to work chopping and smashing, Otis joining in halfheartedly and Mary Bet thought he was maybe trying to get to some pieces before the other men did, but she saw that they weren't going to leave anything with just a dent.

"This'll be good for scraps and not much else," Hooper said, "time we're through with it. You could make a cup or two, maybe a tin hat if you fancy one. And the rest you can sell to the junk man. How long you reckon before you're back at the coppersmith, Otis?" Otis looked up from where he'd been dropping jars, watching sadly as they broke; he shrugged. Hooper said, "I reckon there's two or three more stills just like this out in the woods somewhere. I know where one is, and you could save me the trouble by showing me the others."

"I'll think on it," Otis said.

There was not much for Mary Bet to do except watch the men tear the operation apart. Hooper went about the job with no particular relish—he smashed the still and the barrels and the cooling boxes and condensing coils just as though he were chopping wood. Leon Thomas seemed to take more pleasure in the job, but it was a robust pleasure instead of a mean one. His movements were quick and sprightly for a short, stout man. His eyes were keen, his cheek muscles tight with the vigor of exercise as he clutched an abandoned hatchet and looked about for something else to destroy.

Mary Bet went over to a crude little shelter, a canvas tarpaulin stretched between three trees. Underneath stood a few oak rounds for sitting. A Bible lay on one of the rounds, turned upside down, as though the reader had just left off. There were crates of apples and peaches under the tarpaulin, and pots and pans hanging from nails in one of the trees. On a low table—a board stretched over two adzed logs—lay some banged-up tin cups and bowls, one of them still steaming with some kind of thin vegetable stew. A neatly folded blue wool jacket with tarnished gold buttons and a forage cap lay on one of the log seats at the little table; it didn't necessarily mean these people came from Yankees—more likely they'd scavenged the woods up around Durham, or traded with deserters way back.

After a while, Hooper leaned against a tree to catch his breath and said, "That's good enough, boys. Otis, I'm going to do you a favor this time and leave the slop in the turnip. You got hogs to give it to?"

"No, but my brother does, and he'd appreciate it."

"Doesn't make them sick?"

"Naw, they love it," Otis said. He'd been sitting on a stump the past several minutes, not apparently seeing any point to making himself sweat. "Best pot-tail we ever give the stock was the coon lot."

"The coon lot?" Hooper said. Leon came away from a pile of splintered barrel staves and spat.

"That was the time a raccoon fell in the mixtry."

"What? In the still?"

"Yessir, while it was a-brewin'. I don't know how it come to get in there, less it crawled up the paddle to get a taste. We didn't know about it till Thumkin Moss clanged into it while he was stirrin'. Got the tongs and pulled out a hairless critter 'bout the size of a big cat."

"How do you know it wasn't a cat?"

"Well, I don't, exactly. Thumkin speculated that it was a raccoon, because he'd known them to knock the slop barrels over so the tops'd come clean off."

"Was it dead?"

"Yep, there won't nothin' to it but skin and bones."

"What about all that hair left in there? You couldn't sell the whiskey, what'd you do with it?"

"We did too sell it. That was good double-rectified moonshine, one hundred proof."

"What'd it taste like?" Leon wanted to know. Mary Bet looked at him askance—why did he want to know, unless he was a connoisseur himself. She wished they would just go ahead and outlaw the sale of whiskey everywhere so people wouldn't be tempted, but, then, maybe they'd be more tempted and there'd be even more moonshiners.

"God's truth, I don't know. Warn't made for drinkin'. 'Twas made for sellin'. I don't remember gettin' any complaints. Fact, one customer said it was the best busthead he'd ever drunk. That's the truth." Otis couldn't help but laugh, his mouth opening in delight and showing his twisted tooth and a mottled fringe of rotting gum.

Hooper took his hat off and fanned his face. His shook his head. "I don't doubt it," he said. "All right, we've done all the government business here we can for one day. Otis, I'd give you a ride, but we've got a full load, with my two deputies here."

Mary Bet looked at her cousin, expecting him to wink at her, but he was straight-faced, and she suddenly felt more important than she ever had in her life. The men touched fingers to their hats in token of farewell, and then they began walking out of the woods, leaving Otis behind to sort through the piles of broken glass and wood and metal.

The sun was lower now, painting the trunks of trees so that they seemed to pulse with their own light, and the heat of the day was giving way to slips of cool air that rose from sinks in the forest floor as if from lost icehouses. Mary Bet listened to the tread of the men upon the leafy duff, over which the sound of her own exhilarant breath was like a new voice coming to life.

And yet from all around the darkening woods, like a rising chorus of winged insects, long-dead voices tugged at her, at her terrible guilt and unworthiness. They would never let her go, if she lived to be a hundred. She had committed the worst of sins possible—how could she ever be forgiven?

~⊃ CHAPTER 21 ⊂~

1916–1917

MARY BET HAD moved into a little cottage west of the court-house in the early spring with her best friend, a thin, angular woman named Flora Whitson. There were two bedrooms, and she had no intention of turning the study into another bedroom, even though she could have taken in another boarder. "We'll be just fine by ourselves," she told people.

And so they were, she and Flora, a woman with no attachments and a self-declared old maid. Flora was as skinny as a broom handle, Mary Bet thought, watching her at her work in the evenings, the way she leaned, straight-backed over the machine, feeding the hungry needle, her dress front puffing open off her flat chest, her bare, bony arms working and working the cloth in an expert way that Mary Bet admired. "I could never in a million years do like you do," she said. "You're so fast, and you never make a mistake."

Flora looked up again, a faint smile on her lips—the only part of her that was fleshy and sensual—then shifted her eyes back to her work. "It's just sewing, Mary Bet."

"But I wish I was that good, you're a natural. I'm not a natural at anything. I wanted to play piano once—" she hesitated, then, deciding it was okay to bring the dead into their cozy little communion, said, "like my sister."

Flora glanced up again, even more briefly, as she fed the fabric with her hands into the biting needle, her foot busy on the treadle. She nodded and said, "You're smart as a whip, Mary, that's enough."

"I reckon it's all right." Mary Bet turned back to her darning— the ripped socks and blouses in a basket at her feet would not be finished before there'd be more to mend.

Being smart was all right, but was it enough? A new world was coming, people said, and Mary Bet tried not to think of it with fear but with hope. A world in which the railroad was no longer king, a world where unmarried women weren't pitied and humored as eccentric aunties, a world of peace and electricity. But now there was a great war in Europe, and everyone prayed and hoped that it would end soon.

She wanted to be as drawn to the future as Flora, who seemed to have no reason for it. But it was not the future that drew Mary Bet. Even something as simple as a warm breeze on a cool day, something quivering and unaligned that seemed to come from a deep pocket of earth, from beyond the edges of dusk and the places where pasture gave way to meadow and woods, illuminated a way back into the world of childhood and the Devil and incantation. It was a world of candlelight, of muddy roads not macadamized, the sound of iron-rimmed carriage wheels crunching sand and gravel across a stream, the froth of horses cantering an open field to a stone fence at the far end.

The balance of her days could not be rectified against the weight of what she had lived already. There was too much . . . and yet if she could free herself, could find her brother's secret sorrow and her father's, she might be light enough to step across into another part of life. If she could be borne into the bright new world, the shadows of the old might no longer determine where she put her feet.

Sometimes she wanted to have no past, to be as a child, to be an idiot, deaf as her dead brother to the rock hardness of her memories, which were as fixed and unyielding as the shape of the land, the X of the crossroads where she was born, the granite in Love's Creek Cemetery, the words in the Book, which she knew as well as her own voice. Then there would be time enough for play and laughter and kissing her friend. There would be time for the moon to cast its orange light across the Haw River and across her pale skin and to feel its warmth and the touch of a boy, not her brother, but a boy whom she knew from far back in her mind with its ceaseless clamoring.

But her mind would give her no peace, nor would her father's mind give him peace, and so on back through the generations like the turning of the leaves in the Book. Why must it always be so, the already written fighting with the yet-to-be written?

She saw herself an old crone, sitting amid the ashes of her memories and her drooled thoughts, thin and wasted, her ripeness gone to seed, her hair white as the eyes of dead crows, hands withered like the skin of gone mushrooms. She saw herself alone and teetering, in a rocking chair far out at sea, the smoke of her ship the final thing she knew of humanity and love.

LEON THOMAS HAD become principal of the Elisha Springs School and it was rumored he was being considered for superintendent of public instruction. He was so full of boundless energy and enthusiasm he could light up a room with his voice and his broad

smile, offering his meaty hand all around, his body in near constant motion as he talked, as though his mind moved to a different
rhythm from regular people. And he had such ideas—he wanted
to improve the Negro schools and consolidate the white schools so
there would be more teachers per student; he wanted to get state
loans and float district bonds for more brick buildings; and he
wanted to add vocational teachers and implement state standards
so that Haw wouldn't be limping along like a country ragamuffin,
but leading the charge.

He was all the time reading things. Mary Bet would see him
coming into the courthouse on school business, walking past her
office to the superintendent's down the hall. Half the time he'd
have his nose in a book or pamphlet of some sort. And it was kind
of a large nose, even larger than her own, which somehow endeared
him to her. He'd be padding down the hall early in the morning,
and she'd scrape her chair or clear her throat so he'd look in. He'd
tuck his book under his arm and poke his head in and say, "Why,
Miss Mary Bet, how fine you look this bright morning."

She'd glance up as though she had no idea who it was and say, "It
doesn't look any too bright to me, Mr. Thomas. I've heard they're
calling for rain."

"Who's calling for it? I think it's a fine day for going out on a
raid. What do you say we go catch us a bootlegger or two?" He'd
tilt the upper half of his body in a comical way and then step into
the door. As soon as he was in the anteroom where she worked,
though, he became the polite gentleman, and it was up to her to
keep the conversation going.

She'd shake her head, trying to keep from touching up her hair.
"Mr. Thomas, you do carry on so. I don't have any intention of
raiding another poor soul and destroying his property. Even if his
property is illegal and sinful."

"You'll leave that to the men, will you, Miss Mary Bet?"

"Yes, I believe I will."

"I expect that's the right thing to do."

"Right or not—" She thought it best not to speak her mind too forcefully if she wanted to make a good impression on him, then she thought it was foolish of her to worry about what impression she made. And yet, she couldn't help thinking that he liked her, that he responded to her more adroitly than he did to other women, as though he enjoyed showing her his cleverness and kindness, both, and that he wanted to make a good impression on her.

"And how is your father doing?" he asked, because he would not let her sit there with an awkward half-finished sentence hanging in the air.

"Tolerably, thank you. The weather's been good out there." She liked that he asked about her father; so many people acted as though he were dead.

"I need to get myself up here more often. There's not much exciting going on down in Elisha Springs."

She smiled in a tolerant way and said, "Well, there's nothing exciting here in Williamsboro either, unless you count Flossie Pinkley getting married next month, and Mrs. Pendergrass's daughter Ella Jay having a fifth baby." Then she blushed because she didn't want him to think she was only interested in weddings and babies.

"That's a lot right there," he said. And the way he looked into her eyes made her think he wanted to say something more personal. "You always brighten my day, Miss Mary Bet."

When he was gone it was as if he'd taken the air out of the room with him. She looked at the writ in her typewriter and the handwritten version beside her, trying to figure out what she was supposed to be doing. In a few minutes she was back at work.

The weeks went on, and Leon was busy running his school. And though the thought had not bothered her for some time, Mary Bet wondered anew if she was to be a sheriff's clerk indefinitely, a person whom Leon Thomas and other men stopped by to chat with but never took seriously as a woman to court. But if they felt that way about a working woman, then she didn't want their courtship.

And then one day she heard that Leon was courting a young woman from Cotten named Ann Murchison. The news of his attachment to a woman she'd never heard of from a place she hardly knew—and the woman having the same name as her grandparents—came as such a surprise that Mary Bet felt physically ill. She went home early, sick to her stomach, and stayed in bed for two days feeling so anxious and blue she thought she must have some terrible ailment. Flora made her chicken soup.

"I hate to see you like this," Flora said, feeling her forehead. "You don't feel hot. Of course, that doesn't mean anything. My cousin's husband, Joe Funch, went to bed one night complaining of bowel trouble, no fever or anything, and woke up the next morning . . . well, he didn't wake up, because he'd passed away. He'd just come home from Washington, where he was working in a fancy restaurant, and he had to wait on a black couple. I think the shock is what killed him." She laughed.

Mary Bet said, "It must be the poor ventilation. I can't believe there's no sewerage system, and we've had pipes in town for—what has it been? And the plaster's falling down in the sheriff's office, and those beat-up old cork mats. It's a wonder everybody in there isn't sick all the time."

Flora studied her face as she lay in bed, the covers pulled up to her chin. "You're not sick that way, are you?" Mary Bet shook her head. "It's not even your time of month, is it?"

"It's that Leon Thomas," Mary Bet said. "I don't care for him atall. Well, I kind of like him, and I hate to see him tangled up with a rich woman who just thinks he's a good catch."

Flora smiled tightly and perched on the edge of the bed. She stared at the wall in a disappointed kind of way that did not help her looks any, Mary Bet thought. "I should've known it was some man you were pining for."

"He's not just some man, Flora. He's a good man, and I'm not pining for him. He's my friend, and I want what's best for him."

Flora sighed. She patted Mary Bet's covered legs, then rose. "Well, other men are available."

"Anyway, I'm not getting married. I like it here just fine."

"I know you do, Mary Bet. But you're different from me." She stood in the doorway, hands on her narrow hips. "I didn't think you'd always want to live here with me."

Mary Bet lay there after Flora had gone, thinking of Leon Thomas walking arm-in-arm with some woman named Ann Murchison—from what she had gathered a beautiful blonde with charm and sophistication, who'd been to St. Mary's and knew how to speak French and play the violin and talk about Cervantes—and she suddenly felt so down, so sick in her soul, she thought she never wanted to get out of bed again.

She thought of her poor father festering away out in the asylum so far from home, spending his days playing checkers with lunatics and staring out at the changing seasons—would she end up like that? Here she was almost thirty, and with no prospects for any sort of life other than that of old Miss Mumpford, filing papers at the courthouse and going home to her cat and her overweight niece. Or penny-pinching Mrs. Gooch and her boarders. But she did have Flora, who seemed content to live as they did, and she wondered if she too could be happy that way.

Her cousin Hooper seemed happy enough going through life a bachelor, but he was a man. Besides, it was rumored that there were ladies in his life, just no one special in Williamsboro. The way he looked at her eyes sometimes when they were alone, or touched her shoulder when he'd say good night, made her wonder what he thought of her. But he was her first cousin, and though you could marry your first cousin—unless he was a double first cousin—it was unheard of among people of any standing.

IN THE FALL the local and national elections were held, and there was much talk of the war and whether America should get involved. Sheriff Teague asked Mary Bet to help with the voter registration in the week leading up to election day. He was running unopposed, as were the clerk of court, county coroner, and surveyor, but there were two open spots for commissioner and a tight race for state senator and representative. It was doubtful the Republicans could win, but it was close enough to make for many lively dinner conversations.

Mary Bet sat at the registration table in the mornings with Miss Mumpford and the clerk of court, an old man named Mr. Witherspoon, who had brown spots on his bald head. The first day was busy with young men, eager to register so that they could vote for the first time in their lives. By the middle of the week, few people were coming by, and so Miss Mumpford went back to her corner of the office.

Late on Thursday morning an elderly man came in leaning on a cane. He was dressed in a brown suit with suspenders, shiny black shoes, and an old gray fedora, which he removed on entering the building. His glasses reflected so much light that at first Mary Bet did not realize he was actually a light-skinned colored man. His shaven face sagged into an expression of weariness and endurance. He came without hesitation to the table and said, "My name is Rufus Rathbone from Golding. Born in June of eighteen and forty-one. I'm here to register to vote for the President."

"You're not already registered?" Mr. Witherspoon asked.

"Nawsuh."

Mr. Witherspoon sighed. "Have you paid your poll tax?"

"Nawsuh, but I have it right heah." He reached in his pocket and pulled out a soiled and wrinkled one-dollar bill and placed it on the long pine table.

"Can you read?"

"Yassuh, my daughter taught me to read. And write. I can do both tolably, though my eyesight ain so good no moh."

Mr. Witherspoon shook his head and said, "Didn't think I'd need this. But here you go. Read this here. Just this first paragraph." He opened up a pocket version of the Constitution and pointed to Article I, Section 8, then squinted up, his mouth hanging open in anticipation and incredulity.

Mr. Rathbone leaned over so that he could see the small print. He tried to pick the book up, but Mr. Witherspoon bound it to the table with a mottled, veiny hand. "Cain't you see any better than that?" he complained. "You oughten to be allowed to vote for being blind."

The colored man now hunched and leaned so far down Mary Bet thought he might topple onto the table. She caught the odor of sweat and overdone greens, mixed with some kind of sweet soapy smell. He began reading slowly, "The Congress shall have. The Power. To lay and collect. Taxes, Duties, Imports—Imposts and Excises, to pay the Debits and provide foh the common De-fence and—"

"All right, Mr. Roscoe. What do you expect it means?"

"Well, suh." Mr. Rathbone straightened himself up and looked at both Mary Bet and Mr. Witherspoon. "So far, it means de Congress can lay down taxes."

"Taxes for what?"

"For de common de-fence."

"Meaning what, exactly, Mr. Ratbone?"

"It mean for fightin' wars and such." Mr. Rathbone held his hat close to his chest, his graven face unchanged and staring at Mr. Witherspoon as though he were just a stone in the river. But once or twice his eyes flicked over to Mary Bet, and when they did she looked down at the registration forms in front of her.

"And how does Congress collect those taxes?"

"The way they always do, I 'spect."

"Who asked you to come in here like this?"

"Nobody but me and the Lord."

"The Lord, huh? You sure nobody put you up to it, nobody's paying you? Mr. . . ."

"Rathbone. Nawsuh, Mr. Witherspoon. Just me, like always."

"Who did you plan to vote for?"

"I was plannin' on votin' for . . ." He paused and put a finger up to scratch the side of his thin, graying hair. "Mr. Woot-row Wilson."

"Were you now? You sure you weren't here to vote for Hughes?"

"Nawsuh, it was Mr. Woot-row Wilson fo sho."

Now Mr. Witherspoon seemed to be enjoying himself. "Why'd you want to vote for him?"

"Well, suh, he kep' us out of the war."

"So far he has." Mr. Witherspoon nodded and smiled wanly, then, recollecting himself, said, "Well, despite that, your answers are inexact, to say nothing of impertinent, and as a clerk of court sworn to uphold the laws of the state I have to deny your petition. You study up that Constitution and come back again next year. Here's your dollar."

Mr. Rathbone took the dollar and bowed. "I will, and I thank you." He walked slowly out, touching his cane upon the floorboards, his hat held lightly in his hand. He turned the handle of the door and opened it, then held it while another man about his age came in.

This man shuffled up to the desk, as though his knees were too stiff to bend. He had a grizzled beard, and his eyes were small and sunk deep into wrinkled pouches of skin. He wore dungarees and an old string tie and a slouch hat that he took off when he saw Mary Bet. "Name's Bobby James McAllister, from over to Pastures."

"Can you read and write, Mr. McAllister?" Witherspoon asked.

"Not so good."

"All right, since you come from folks eligible before 1867, you're grandfathered in. Miss Hartsoe'll fill your form in. How come you never registered before this?"

"Never cared to vote. But now my son tells me I got to vote for Hughes."

"Hughes? If that don't beat all. You folks out there ought to be for Wilson if you know what's good for you. He's all for the farmers. You expect Hughes'll be giving out loans? He's just like Taft. How do you like the income tax? Or do you not bother with it?" His laughter turned into a throat clearing.

"I don't know about that, but my son tells me Wilson's not our man. He's had enough of a chance, and things aren't any better."

"If I'd known what you were up to, Mr. McAllister, I wouldn't have let you register." Witherspoon looked genuinely annoyed, and he glanced over at Mary Bet as if she could come up with an answer.

"But you said I was automatically grandfathered in."

"Yes, but this is an abuse."

Mary Bet looked up and said, "What about the poll tax?"

"He doesn't have to pay any if he's grandfathered in." Mr. Witherspoon shook his head as though he could make the farmer and his petition go away. "All right, Mr. McAllister, she'll fill your form in and you can sign it. Can you do that?"

"Yes, sir, I can."

When he'd made his way out of the building, Mr. Witherspoon turned to Mary Bet and said, "How do you like that? Uppitiest damn nigger in the county comes in wanting to vote for Wilson, and a white man wants to vote for Hughes. We have to turn down the one and let the other pass through. That's just not right. If I'd known he was voting for Hughes, I'd've maybe forgotten that grandfather rule."

"I 'spect women'll be voting soon, Mr. Witherspoon," Mary Bet said.

"Fine," he said. "I'd even vote for a woman. But I've seen what happens when the coloreds get in office. Now there's lots of good, smart colored folks. I'll be the first to admit. But if we're not careful, this county'll be run by and for the niggers. And it won't be pretty. I've seen it in a dream and it was so terrible I woke up hollering and pawing at the sheets. My wife asked me what was the matter, and I said, 'The end of the world. A black man with a badge was riding down the street on a white horse, and a posse of pickaninnies tagging right along behind.'"

It was change that Mr. Witherspoon worried about, but not Mary Bet—she was much more afraid of growing old and never changing.

THEY WERE LAYING the water pipes to the courthouse in early spring when Leon was appointed superintendent of the public schools. He would share an office in the courthouse with the county tax assessor, and on the morning when the water was turned on in the lavatory, he came by Mary Bet's office and hollered for her and Miss Mumpford to come watch. "It's a historic event for Haw County," he said, his bulky frame filling the doorway, "you wouldn't want to miss it, would you?"

Mary Bet looked up from her typewriter and over her glasses. Her jaw went slack, because she could not think of one smart thing to say to him. It was his first week in the building and here he was acting as if he'd been superintendent all along. There was a rumor that he and the Murchison girl had broken off, though she didn't know if it was true and was too proud to make inquiries.

And then he was gone and Miss Mumpford said, "What did he want?"

"He says they're about to test the water lines and we should come watch. I've seen water run out of a pipe before. I don't know what he's all excited about."

"It's the first public building in the county on public water," Miss Mumpford said, "so they say."

"I know that." Mary Bet stood up, and when she could see that Miss Mumpford was not going to join her she said, "I'll just go see what the fuss is." Miss Mumpford glanced up as Mary Bet was turning away. "I'll be right back," Mary Bet added.

When she got to the washroom, she could see Leon half in and half out, concealing the entrance. She peered around his wide shoulders. Inside the little room was the mayor, the editor of the weekly newspaper, the clerk of court, and a worker in overalls—four and a half people in a room barely big enough for one. "You missed it," Leon said.

"Then it wasn't much to see," she replied, and was pleased and surprised when he seemed amused.

"There'll be more, just wait."

The worker reached up and pulled a chain dangling from a metal cistern, and there came a clunk-clunking sound and then the rush of water running through the vertical pipe and down into a ceramic commode that had been installed just that morning. "Flushes fine," the man said.

"I do know," Leon said. "Our very own water closet." He backed out, and Mary Bet had to move quickly to get out of his way. "How did you like that, Miss Mary Bet? Isn't that something?"

"Well, it's an improvement, I reckon," she said. And when he laughed at this, she was a little put out with him—maybe he didn't take her seriously, that or he would laugh at anything.

He walked back down the hall with her a ways, and she listened to him holding forth on the coming of electric current in Haw and how the automobile was more than a novelty. "We're gonna get trucks to bring the country children in to the schools. More trucks, fewer and bigger schools. We'll save money and educate more children, Miss Mary Bet." He glanced at her, one eye looking slightly away.

"That'll be another improvement, Mr. Thomas."

"Yes, it will," and this time he didn't laugh, because he was really thinking out loud instead of talking to her. But Mary Bet was thinking about automobiles and trucks running all over the streets, scaring the horses into turning over their carriages. She didn't like the picture and she said, "I expect some day we'll be traveling to the sun and the moon."

"Yes, I expect some day we will," he said, and nodded to her and disappeared down the corridor, lost in some thought of his own. He reminded her a little of her father, when he was deep into one of his books. He had a funny, duckfooted way of walking that was more of a strut, with his blocky middle pushed forward like a penguin or a circus bear. But she thought he was right handsome in his way, and he had strong shoulders and arms and a confident shine in his gray-green eyes.

A few days later, Mary Bet discovered that Leon had in fact broken off with Ann Murchison of Cotten.

"Does that come as good news to you?" Hooper asked. He was sitting at his desk, reading a report on the movement of state agents to close down a still in the western part of the county. His long legs, crossed at the ankles, were stretched out beneath the desk, creating a gradual, inclined plank up to his rolling chair. He didn't look up.

"What, no, I don't care one way or the other," Mary Bet said.

Hooper now turned his dark eyes on her in a way that melted her insides every time. He reached over and squeezed her hand, then shook his head and sighed. He let her hand go. "You don't mind that people say we're kissing cousins, do you?"

"I've never heard it said," she snapped. Then in a softer voice, she added, "I don't care what people say." She closed her eyes a second, wishing that her cousin would go ahead and pull her to him. But she knew he wouldn't. He wanted to, she knew that, but she knew that something made him stop himself. She thought that were she a man, she wouldn't stop herself. She'd tell her cousin that she loved him.

"What do you think of Jeannette Rankin?" he asked.

Mary Bet laughed and shook her head. "A congressman and women can't even vote."

"A congress*woman* is what they're calling her. So you don't think women are responsible enough to vote?"

"Most people aren't responsible enough to vote, Sheriff. But I'd say that, on the whole, women match up right well with men on the important things."

"So do I," he said. "I wonder what Leon Thomas thinks. He's pretty old-fashioned."

"I don't care what he thinks about it," Mary Bet replied, "nor anything else."

She decided to make herself a new dress, and that very day she went to the mercantile and bought a pattern and three yards of robin's-egg blue (for she was tired of navy) medium-weight taffeta—she didn't want to spend much—and a half yard of crisp white organdy. And that night, with Flora working away on her own project, she began pinning and cutting. She had not made a dress in she didn't know how long, and the work felt good even after spending the day at the typewriter. This was a different sort of handiwork altogether—she was creating something you could see and hold and use. The two machines' rhythms of treadle and bobbin interwove in a conversational murmur of thropping and clicking, and Mary Bet found herself totally absorbed in the work of hand and foot, her eyes focused on the stitching as she fed the cloth into the insatiable mouth of the needle. Even the smell of the new fabric, pierced again and again, had its own distinct odor, a fresh fibrous pungency that, along with the murmur of the machine, reminded her of home.

At ten o'clock Flora announced she was going to bed, and suddenly Mary Bet felt herself so sleepy that even though she was halfway up one side with a zigzag stitch, she released the thread and carefully folded her work atop the machine.

"I expect that'll get his attention," Flora said. She bit through her thread and tied off a stitch.

"Whose attention?"

"Your cousin's, or the new school superintendent's."

Mary Bet clucked her tongue. "My cousin is a good friend, and that's not going to change after ten years just because . . ."

"Because there's somebody who might really care about you? Don't hurt that man's feelings by trifling with your cousin—he has all the women he needs."

"So you don't think it's too late for me?"

"It's never too late to get married. It's never too late to do anything." Flora laughed. She thought Mary Bet one of the funniest people she knew, because she was "funny without trying." But it was Flora who had the wry sense of humor, who would look out of her blue eyes and say the most strange and interesting things Mary Bet thought she had ever heard about any topic—certainly as amusing and clever as anything the men said down at the courthouse.

"I wish I had your gumption and know-how, Flora. You know more about politics than I believe the politicians do."

"I know enough to know when to shut up," Flora said. "And that's anytime a man is speaking. Unless he's wrong, and then I just can't help myself."

Mary Bet laughed and shook her head, smiling at her friend and wondering why no man had found her attractive. It didn't help that she made little effort with jewelry and makeup. She had a plain face, Mary Bet thought, studying it as critically as if she were a man, and a sharp nose with freckles sprayed across it and onto her cheeks. But her hair was fine and silky and a delicate brown, and if she grew it out it could be her finest feature. Flora was hard where Mary Bet was soft, abrasive and brook-no-nonsense where Mary Bet was likely to be forgiving and maybe a tad too permissive. Mary Bet admired her friend for the qualities she herself lacked.

She recalled one evening when they were sitting in the little front parlor after a supper that Mary Bet had prepared—she had become the cook, while Flora had fallen into the role of cleaning girl. Flora had paused in her sewing and leaned into her straight-back chair, putting a hand to her face.

"What is it, dear?" Mary Bet asked, looking up from her own work.

"Just resting my eyes. They go all crossed on me if I work too long at a stretch."

Mary Bet put her needlework down and came over to her friend's side. She took Flora's hand away from her face and began to gently massage her temples and her eye sockets, then worked her way slowly over Flora's head and neck and down to her shoulders. "You work so hard, dear," she said. "You should rest your eyes at night."

"I don't see you doing that," Flora said, her voice strangely dreamy and far away.

"That's because I do a different kind of work during the day. Typing's not the same as sewing, and I don't do it all day." She took in the soft warm smell of Flora's cropped hair, enjoying the crisp feel of the edge line and how it just touched her neck. "Flora," she said, "your hair's so nice and silky. Look how rough mine is."

"Your hair's as soft as a fawn's."

"It's not any such thing. It's coarse, or else I'd wear it short like yours." She pulled back to admire the shape of her friend's head, always the same under her cowl of fine sandy hair, and her sharp nose, shorter than her own Hartsoe beak, but every bit as odd—everything about her friend's features seemed suddenly so endearing and lovely Mary Bet wanted to give her a kiss.

Now, looking at Flora, she remembered that time, and again wondered if she herself could really live all her life without marrying and having a family. If Flora could do it, then couldn't she? The idea of sex and childbearing and child-raising sometimes seemed so difficult and unlikely that she may as well have contemplated becoming an African missionary. Flora said something about how stubborn muslin was and how she'd have to undo the stitches, and then she smiled curtly and disappeared up the stairs.

All week Mary Bet thought about the dress and how eager she was to wear it as soon as the weather turned warm again. It would be nice enough to wear in church, with a jacket and the proper hat, though she pictured wearing it to the courthouse. Vanity, vanity, vanity. And yet the work itself, the business of finishing the dress, occupied a corner of her mind during the next several days.

It was spring again and the birds were busy all day, and night as well. The chirruping of spring peepers started up in the darkness. Blossoms had returned to the crab apple trees and the crape myrtle and the lilac, and even the spindly hawthorn in Mrs. Gooch's side yard put on its finery and its sweet smell once again, as though to say there could never be enough springs.

Amanda, who had developed crow's-foot wrinkles around her eyes and the corners of her mouth, was now living with Mr. Hennesey a block away from Mrs. Gooch. When Mary Bet saw her at the mercantile on Saturday, she told her that married life must suit her because she looked no more than twenty-one—and, in spite of the wrinkles, she meant it.

"If I look twenty-one," Amanda said, "you look fifteen."

Mary Bet laughed dismissively and said, "I'm going on thirty and feel every year of it."

"Well you oughten, Mary Bet, you really oughten."

"I'm afraid the next time I turn around I'll be forty. And then what?"

Amanda put on a serious look, and Mary Bet was sorry she'd said what she had, especially when Amanda was in such a hopeful frame of mind. "And then you'll look even more beautiful," Amanda said.

After breakfast she went up and changed into her new taffeta dress, deciding to give the dress one more try before she altered it. She'd worn it only once—to church—and decided that the waist was too low and that it felt too tight around the bustline; she'd received what she'd thought were perfunctory compliments, and a couple of people had just stared, as though they couldn't make out what was wrong. She'd glanced to make sure the organdy ruffles at the wrists and hem hadn't somehow come loose.

When she got to the courthouse, she went directly to the lavatory. There was no plumbing in the house she and Flora rented, and she liked washing her hands and face in the lavatory with the warm water running and no one around. It seemed the greatest luxury in the world to spend ten minutes at her morning ablutions. Back in the office she was surprised to see Miss Mumpford already at her desk and busy. The old woman hunched over her typewriter so that her shoulders nearly met her pendulous ears; she glanced up and said, "They're talking about forming up a unit."

Not a word about the dress, not that Mary Bet had been expecting it, and then something that made no sense. "What?" she said. "A unit?"

"A reserve unit, but it won't be reserve for long." She pulled the page out in frustration, crumpled it into her trash can, and inserted another, backed by carbon paper, into the roller. Mary Bet waited for the taciturn Miss Mumpford, who enjoyed dramatic pauses when she was sharing any sort of gossip or news. "They're gonna be drilling over behind the post office, and there's a unit already drilling in Hartsoe City at the old Murchison place."

So war had returned to her grandfather's house, where he had trained a militia and sent his son and son-in-law off to an uncertain fate. Mary Bet was suddenly filled with questions: Who was joining? Where would they go from here? And, most of all, when? "It's just people twenty-one to thirty, isn't it?" she asked. Hooper was far too old; Leon was thirty-one.

"There's men fifty that want to enlist. Looking for hot food and adventure."

"I expect they'll get plenty of adventure," Mary Bet said. "But who would want to do such a thing, go over where it's dangerous like that? They're liable to get hurt. I didn't think anybody was for it."

"Now that we're in it, you see, they've changed. I never liked that Wilson, with his highfalutin ways. When did he ever fight?"

Mary Bet thought a minute. "I've got to go see somebody," she said, and she started to hurry from the office. But at that moment Leon Thomas swept in and said, "Miss Mary Bet, that is the gayest shade of blue I've ever seen in my life. It looks so—" He stopped suddenly, his eyes traveling not just all over her dress but, Mary Bet was sure, her figure.

He closed his mouth and she blushed, but then for some reason, as if she were someone else—perhaps the Ann Murchison of her imagination—she put a hand on her hip and said, "Was there something you needed, Mr. Thomas?"

He shook his head. "No, Miss Mary Bet, Miss Mumpford. I just wanted to tell you good morning. Good morning, to both of you." He was crushing his hat between his thick hands, and she had a notion to take it from him.

"Good morning, Mr. Thomas," she said. Miss Mumpford just shook her head and went back to work. Mary Bet said, "I expect you heard about this army thing?"

"Yes I did," he said. Then he smiled and put his hat back on, then took it off again and cleared his throat. "Matter of fact, I'm joining up myself. Well, good morning to you ladies," he said, so loudly that Miss Mumpford looked up again, this time with a frown.

"That was peculiar," Mary Bet said after he'd left. And then she wondered if she had made an impression upon him, or if the only reason for his high spirits was his intention to join the army. "What a crazy thing," she said. "A man his age joining up to fight a war in Europe." She pictured him, his cigar clenched in his strong jaws like a gangster, and then in military fatigues, marching around with a gun over his shoulder. It didn't seem possible. "Well, it'll all be over by the time our boys are trained up."

Miss Mumpford glanced up, her rheumy eyes hard to fathom, said "humph," and went back to her work.

CHAPTER 22

1917

MARY BET HAD taken to wearing a little rouge and lip paint, and she'd put a partridge feather in her hatband, while Flora had stopped applying any makeup and had begun biting her nails to the quick.

"You'll never know what it's like to be me," Flora said.

And all Mary Bet could reply was, "No, I won't." She smiled at her friend and thought of Amanda, who was crippled but now contentedly married, even if it was to Mr. Hennesey. Flora's affliction was that she could never marry a man. "You're good at making friends, you'll always have somebody with you." She came over and put her arms around Flora's bony shoulders. "Besides, who ever said a word about me leaving. I'm just going out on a business trip with the new superintendent of schools. That's all."

In the morning at her office, she was nervous. She had decided to wear a plain brushed cotton skirt and white blouse—this is not a date, she told herself. We're just going over to Hartsoe City to inspect the new school they're building. The door opened and she took a quick gulp of air. The first thing she saw was a bunch of yellow iris and lavender—her favorite combination; then Leon himself emerged around the door, his gray fedora in hand. "I didn't know but what flowers weren't the right gift to offer for helping me out today," he said, "but I risked it because I thought you'd like them."

"I like them just fine," she said, her hand going to her hair.

"I don't mean anything by it, it's just that seeing as how Hartsoe's your hometown and you might know what people over there need in the way of supplies and equipment and things like that, it would be a great honor for me to show you around and that way we—well, I don't know if I explained all that—"

"If you'd stop talking for a minute," she said, "I could tell you that people there don't need anything special. But you probably know that." She sat up straight, hands on her hips, and gave him an appraising look. "And since you didn't mean anything by asking me, I don't see the need for flowers." And now he looked a little crestfallen and she was sorry she'd goaded him.

He twisted his fedora like he was angry at it. "Truth is, Mary Bet," he said, "I've been wanting to ask you to walk out with me for some time. But it always seemed like you were busy with one thing or another."

"And now that you're the superintendent?"

He blushed. "I guess that makes it a little easier. I thought maybe you'd notice me more. I'm really just a country farm boy."

"I've noticed you," she said. She looked down at the flowers so as not to give away her smile.

"There's also a church picnic down to Hackett's Mill. The Baptists don't mind picnicking, do they?"

He seemed sincere, though it was sometimes hard to tell—he had such a deadpan expression when he told a joke. "Yes, picnicking is fine. Why don't we try the drive over to Hartsoe City first?

We'll get better acquainted that way." They talked for a moment about how it was a shame that Hackett's had quit milling but that at least the new owner hadn't torn the building down, not yet anyway. And then Mary Bet said she needed the next hour to finish up her work, and, no, she didn't need any help—that was just so that she could be alone with her thoughts and not have him hovering around.

Last night she'd gone home as light as air and wondered if she might just float away. She couldn't bear for Flora or anybody else to see her in this condition, and yet she wanted to shout to the sky that she was giddy with delight. Spring had never come in so full and beautiful, with so many vivid colors and sweet smells she thought she could faint in the street and be happy. "Get a grip on yourself," she thought. A carriage ride to Hartsoe City and back was perhaps not a good idea. Spending all day alone with a man might not be the proper thing to do, even though the younger girls now were going about unchaperoned as though it were perfectly normal. After all, it was just a business trip, and, anyway, might not she and Leon grow weary of each other on the way there and back?

That idea put her in such a foul temper, she wondered if perhaps she should back out of the trip. He was very forward-thinking as an educator, but his manners were a little unrefined. He seemed gentlemanly enough, but the truth was she didn't know him all that well. She could hear her mother's voice saying, "Who are these Thomases? What do you know about them?" And she thought, taking a deep breath of warm spring air, I'm twenty-nine years old and I don't care about what I know and what I don't know. I don't care how foolish I am.

It was in this fidgety state of mind that Mary Bet took from her trunk the old scrapbook she had made for her sisters. She sat in her bed, leaning against her feather pillow, the coal-oil lamp bright on her bedside table and the red leather volume in her lap. She ran her fingers over the engraved gold letters, "Remember," and then opened the book at random and began turning the pages. Here was a lock of hair, still a lustrous red-brown, tied off with purple thread, and a caption in Mary Bet's careful running hand: "O'Nora's hair when she was 13." And there was a faded rosebud orchid, flattened between pieces of waxed paper: "orchid found in woods by Mount Jordan Springs (Myrt's favorite, after gardenias)."

There were pressed leaves—a huge yellow tulip poplar and a fiery red maple—and a little wreath made from the hair of both sisters, braided tightly together ("made by Myrtle Emma–January 19, 1899"), the dark and light strands creating their own brindle color like nothing else in the world that ever had been or would be, Mary Bet had thought at the time, and still did. There were also letters from Mary Bet to Myrt and from Myrt to Mary Bet, pieces of schoolwork and notes tucked into the blank leaves.

Mary Bet flipped through the pages, one by one, and as she did so a piece of lined paper slipped out. She saw right away that it was in Siler's hand, and she could not recall ever putting any such page in the book. She was happy that she had, but at the same time her heart was surging with the thought that there was a message from the beyond tucked away for her to find. There were little penciled drawings on one side, the kinds of sketches he used to make when he was dreaming up ideas in his workshop—a horseless carriage with a stick-figure driver, something that resembled a Ferris wheel with a crank-start engine at the base, a flying machine with bird-like wings that apparently flapped.

On the other side was a note in blue pen: "Dear Sis, please please please" then the crossed-out word "forget" and above it another crossed-out word that appeared to be "forgive," and then some more crossed-out, illegible writing, followed by, "I have make a terrible mistake." It was neither signed nor dated. A scene came to mind that she had shut away, but it came back now as startlingly clear as a dream she had just woken from. Her father coming from the closet with the rifle, which he was loading. She had known somehow that he was doing it, just by the way he was talking and acting, and then his expression as he pointed the gun directly at her heart.

She remembered being unafraid, and how that realization had given her such a welling of strength that she could feel all of her soul pouring forth like a fountain from the top of her head and filling the room with the most buoyant light in the world. It was her father she was worried about and how he would feel if he pulled the trigger. The whole world was squeezed into the·tiny word "if," and it was surrounded by her blinding light. For a moment her father seemed to disappear, and then Cattie Jordan had touched her sleeve—it was silky black bombazine—and though Cattie Jordan said something, there was no sound, because her own wide, refulgent, prismatic light drowned out everything.

Now, sitting in her bed, her legs folded up in the same way her father's had been under the apple tree, she thought: Siler must've known, must've seen something he never told anybody about. The thought pressing in her mind was, *He was afraid of turning out the same way . . . He* did *turn out the same way.*

Then this morning, walking to the office after a night of tossing and turning, she'd asked herself why she had agreed to go on a long trip with a strange man. Well, not exactly strange, but she didn't want to lead him on—had she not made a vow never to get married? God would surely punish her for breaking that vow. God had kept her father from dying and had kept her from the flames of hell, and she could not now go back on her word to the highest power in the universe. If she did she would surely be punished for eternity. Was that a childish notion?

She was almost crying by the time she got to the courthouse. She thought she could be perfectly happy, and useful, as an old maid, just like Flora and Miss Mumpford. She might not be alive now if she hadn't made her bargain, or was it mere superstition on the part of a young girl? She wanted to ask someone, but the only person who came to mind was Leon.

And then he came in with flowers, and the worries of the previous night disappeared. They went on the trip to Hartsoe City, and Leon was as charming and natural as if they were strolling up the street. He was quieter than when he was around the courthouse, though, and so polite and courtly she almost hoped he would talk a little more about himself. But he only wanted to ask about her, and whether she was comfortable, or did she need a cushion or a blanket. And then he wanted to know about her family, and she told him a little about each member who had died and what she recalled about that person. "When Myrt died up in the mountains," she said, "your father was mighty kind to us." Leon nodded and said he remembered.

The trip went by in a blur, Mary Bet taking in not so much the sense of what Leon told her about the schools—though she did try to pay attention—as the tone of his voice and how patient and kind he sounded when he was talking to the principal and the teachers. They all admired him because he listened carefully to what they said, and made them smile and laugh at little jokes and witticisms. And he didn't give them any big promises, just told them he was going to do everything he could to bring in more money and improve their school, and they seemed to respect him for this.

Not until they were on the way home did she ask him what she had been holding back. "Leon," she said, "what about this army business. You're not serious about it?"

"Yes, ma'am," he said. His tone, which had been so gentle and solicitous, was suddenly firm.

"You don't think it's best to stay here where you're needed?"

"I know where I'm needed. My mind's made up."

"What if I didn't want you to go?" she said, trying not to sound coy.

"I'd say, Miss Mary Bet, I'm flattered, but I've already signed on. We're assembling this summer at home stations. I'll be up in Durham."

"For how long?"

"As long as it takes. I don't mean that in a smart way, I just mean I'm on for the duration. They say it'll take eight or nine months to train us up right."

"By then it'll be all over."

"I expect so."

"And you'll quit all that marching about like boys and come home?"

"Yes, I will."

She sat there letting the carriage wheels fill the silence. She watched the withers of Leon's bay shift right and left under the checkrein, a white mark there pulsing with the neck muscles. A motor chugged somewhere behind them, and then a black Model T duck-honked as it passed, kicking up a cloud of dust. Leon watched in admiration as it drove off. "I found a note from my brother last night," Mary Bet said.

Leon was quiet.

"He died up in Morganton a long time ago."

"Yes, I know," Leon said. "I stopped by the Alliance that day and your father wasn't there, and I thought that was strange. And Thad Utley told me your brother had been hit by a train."

"That's right, he was. This note hasn't any date on it, but he was apologizing for something. He said he'd made a mistake, and he slipped it into my scrapbook so I'd find it, and here it's been fifteen years and I discover that note. It gave me a chill, I tell you. It was like his ghost coming back."

"Maybe he was telling you it was all right to move on."

Mary Bet regarded Leon Thomas, how he was chewing the inside of his cheek, as he did when he was trying out a thought, unsure what effect his words might have. Was he only trying to get her to give up her past, or did he really mean what he was saying? "I could never forget my brother," she said.

"No, of course you couldn't. You were close to him, weren't you?"

"What do you mean?"

"I mean you loved him like any good sister would. You and he were the last left, so it's natural you would . . ." He couldn't seem to arrive at the right word, so he let it go at that. From dark clouds in the west came an eructation of thunder, like a barrow full of stones, tilted and holding a moment before rumbling forth. It suddenly felt cooler. Leon clicked his tongue and flipped the reins, and the bay stepped lively.

Mary Bet nodded, thinking, so that's what people think of the Hartsoes—survivors, clinging to each other in the storm. "You think I oughten worry about it?" she asked.

Leon hesitated, then looked at Mary Bet, his gray-green eyes searching her eyes and nose and lips, as though he would know everything about her. It jolted her so, she could feel her insides lurch. She was not sure she wanted to be known like that, by any man or woman. And she realized then that she had never been in love, and that it could be she was now falling in love for the first time in her life and that it might be the only time she would. Looking into Leon's eyes was like looking into a mirror, for he was reflecting what he saw, and seeing only her. It was such a simple giving up of the self and its heaviness that she smiled and then laughed.

"What?" he said. "Do you think I'm funny-looking?"

"No, of course not, Leon," she said. "I think you're right good-looking."

He smiled and nodded, then turned to the road to hide his embarrassment. "I think you're right good-looking too," he said.

The thunder echoed for a while, but then grew fainter, the storm passing toward the north, leaving them with just a shower that pattered on the canvas buggy top as Leon was raising it. They rode along quietly, the gentle rain cocooning them in the buggy, with the smell of watered earth rising all around. By the time they got home they were singing "Sweet Adeline," and Mary Bet didn't want the trip to be over.

CHAPTER 23

1917–1918

THEY HAD TWO months before he was off to training. They went to church picnics and on group outings with friends. Mary Bet got Flora to come along on a bicycle expedition to Siloam Springs, where it was loud with whip-poor-wills. And one Saturday they went in two automobiles, in a merry group that included Amanda and Mr. Hennesey and Clara and her husband, to a nickelodeon in Raleigh. The piano player was quite lively, they thought, but they felt uncomfortable with all the cigarette smoke and the smell of beer and the click of balls from the adjacent poolroom. Leon had been there before, and when they were out on the sidewalk Mary Bet asked him if he was a drinking man. He said he had "had the occasional drop," but, no, he was not a drinking man. She looked at his broad, strong features and let it go. Afterwards they went to a real movie theater and saw a Mary Pickford feature, and they all laughed and later crossed the street for ice cream sundaes.

During the week Leon worked hard, helping the interim superintendent, a young teacher from Hartsoe City, prepare for the coming year. The county board thought it a shame that their new superintendent should be taken off to war so suddenly, but they told him he'd come back a hero and be even more ready to tackle the job.

Every one of their fleeting weekends, Leon and Mary Bet spent at least a few hours together. They went to a croquet and watercolor party, and to a pig roast out at Leon's brothers' place, where they put big yellow onions on the coals until the outsides were black. And one time he took her to Chapel Hill to a lecture on the German Immigrant Question, in which the lecturer cautioned the audience to be on their guard but not to draw hasty conclusions. "All of our families were immigrants at one time," he said.

On the weekend before Leon was to leave, Mary Bet invited him to a musicale at Clara's house in Hartsoe. They borrowed a friend's Oldsmobile, and when they got there it was just like the old days. Afterwards, they drove across the creek and up to Mary Bet's old house. They got out and stood admiring it, the wide porch with its fancy balustrade seeming to welcome them back, and Mary Bet pointed out where such and such had happened. She was hesitant about going up to the door, but Leon went on ahead and said he'd like to look inside. He knocked and a small, friendly-faced woman in her middle thirties came to the door. Mary Bet recognized her as the wife of the couple who had rented and then bought the house more than ten years ago. Leon introduced himself, and by this time Mary Bet was at his side. The woman invited them in.

The house had a different smell, but there was something familiar about it too, a dark whiff of well-trod pine and the lingering sense of a ghost tribe that had merely moved to the corners to accommodate a new familial presence. They sat in the parlor on a tired formal sofa with a red brocade. Mary Bet said she'd heard the Dorsetts had moved, and the woman said that they had gone back to Salisbury after Mr. Dorsett was fired for mouthing off at the manager.

"You know there's a bag full of gold around here somewhere?" Leon said.

"Is that right?" the woman asked, looking at Mary Bet to see if Leon was serious.

Leon got up and went to the window. "Colored fellow that used to live here buried it out there somewhere. Isn't that right, Mary Bet?"

Mary Bet came and stood beside Leon, feeling the warmth of him through his shirt. He had kissed her for the first time only the day before, and now there was but one week until he left. She wondered if he were not a little afraid of her—did she give off an attitude of superiority that made him treat her like a piece of china? He seemed so earthy and manly with his friends; the expressions he used and the way he laughed and joked made you think he'd be more physical and aggressive. She appreciated his tact, but now she wanted him to hold her. "Yes," she said, "old Zeke buried that money of my grandfather's. We dug around but never found it."

Outside, a girl was playing in a crab apple tree that had been too small for climbing when Mary Bet was her age. These people had let the place go a bit. The old icehouse was scabbed with whitewash, and high weeds grew about the pump and its washstand, upon which lay a few grimy dishes. There was no need for the pump, since the house had running water; it also had electric current, which the power company had installed for free. Electricity was coming to Williamsboro too—it was just a matter of time.

On the wall beside the fireplace a cuckoo came out of his clock and announced the time. The pinecone-shaped weights shifted, and Mary Bet remembered the sapphire pin.

Leon turned to the lady of the house. "Shall we go out and tell your daughter about the buried treasure?"

When the woman began leading Leon through the side porch, Mary Bet held back. She went over and ran her finger along the crack beside the fireplace. Still there. She thought she'd take it out now, but she couldn't make herself do it. It felt like stealing. The pin was no longer hers, never had been—it was her mother's, and then Myrtle Emma's.

She went out with the others, and around to the back where the yard was nearly a meadow, its high grass concealing a choir of crickets and snap wings. They still had a garden, but it was much smaller, the tangle of berry bushes and briars climbing farther up out of the gully. Their hostess took them around to the front, and Mary Bet nodded at what she said, as though everything were new to her.

The woman asked, "Do you all have children?"

Leon laughed and glanced at Mary Bet, who pretended she hadn't heard. "No, ma'am," he said. "We're—no, we don't."

"We're not married," Mary Bet said.

The side yard leading to the barn was in much better condition. The grass was clipped, and edged by cheerful borders of petunias and dahlias and hydrangeas. It was as though the house had turned its back on its history, leaving a preserve where children could play. They stood in the shade of the apple tree where her father had plopped himself, his gun in his lap. Over against the summer kitchen, vines of morning glories crept up the side of the greenhouse. The windows were clean, and Mary Bet could see a profusion of hothouse plants inside.

They thanked their hostess and made their way back to the car. Leon held the door for Mary Bet, then went around and switched on the magneto. She watched him cranking the engine and wondered: Is this competent, kind, irreverent, jolly man to be my life's companion? They waved to their hostess, who was standing on the front porch. And as their hands came down, she took hold of

Leon's hand and squeezed it. He smiled at her, apparently unsurprised, though she wondered he couldn't hear her heart thumping.

They were quiet on the drive home, and as they approached her house, he slowed the car and stopped a block away. "What's the trouble?" she asked.

"I'm going to miss you, Mary Bet." He leaned over and, because she had taken off her hat for the drive and put a shawl on her head, he could only kiss her mouth. She kissed him back, wondering briefly if the neighbors were watching. His lips were soft as a woman's—of course they were. It had been so long since she had kissed a man on the mouth, but Joe Dorsett was still only a boy then. She could hardly count Mr. Jenkins, because he had not seemed like a man somehow, but a preacher. Leon was strong and yielding, he tasted like cigars and salt and warm water, and she wanted him to go on kissing her like that, though she was afraid it wasn't the thing to do, out here on the street a block away from her own church. And yet she wanted more, that feeling of the essence of all passion held in a single kiss.

She pulled back and said, "That's enough for now." She smiled and put her hand on his cheek. Life, she thought. I haven't missed it yet.

"I could come inside."

"You're a sweet boy," she said, wondering where those words had come from—was it something she'd said to Joe Dorsett long ago?

"Will you marry me when I come home?" He kept leaning in to her, as though he could hold her there just by willing it.

"I don't know, Leon. I'll think on it." She didn't mind that it wasn't a proper proposal on bended knee. She just was unsure how she felt about the idea of being someone's wife, a helpmate and friend for the rest of their lives, sleeping with him, having his children. She was afraid of being such a disappointment that he would go off to a city to find satisfaction—probably he already had. Who was he, really? He wasn't family. But wasn't that how families were made, by two strangers? It was all so overwhelming, with his big presence here in this automobile, as though she were being driven headlong into some future that could only end in worse tragedy than she'd already known. All this swooped through her mind, and then she heard her own breathing, and his, and she said, "I don't know if I can give up the love of my friends for some kind of dangerous love."

He began to laugh, then stopped himself. "You don't have to give up your friends. And I'm not dangerous." He held out his arms. "See?"

His smile was comforting and so familiar she thought he must have some sort of spell over her. Was she in love? "I'm very fond of you, Leon," she said. "But I'll need time to ponder it. I want you to take good care of yourself while you're away."

And then they kissed again for a long time, and somehow, she could hardly recall, she was in her house again. Had he driven that last block, or had they walked it? She knew that he had held her, standing outside the house—she could still feel his arms around her, the weight and shape of him, even his manhood pressing against her belly, urging her to give up everything and come with him. And here was Flora, her thin lips breaking into a tolerant smile, her foot working the treadle and her hands feeding the machine.

"Well?" Flora said, "Did you make passionate love?"

"Psssh, Flora." Then, in a serious voice she said, "I told him he better take care of himself."

"He's not that kind, Mary Bet. He'll take care of everybody else before he takes care of himself."

"I know it," Mary Bet said. And she thought, if he doesn't come back, I won't have to take the risk of marrying him—and losing everything. It's up to God. "Forgive me," she said.

"What?"

"Nothing." She came over and kissed Flora on the top of her head. "I'm just not feeling well. I'll go on up."

He was five weeks training in Durham, and she went up to see him twice. He wanted her to come again, but she couldn't bear the sadness when they had to say good-bye, the way he held her and looked at her, that confident smile making her heart flip, tugging at her deep inside. She wrote trying to explain this, and how she was praying for him, but she could never manage to say what she felt because there were things that could only be said face-to-face, not so much in the words but in the way they were said.

And then he was off to Camp Sevier, outside Greenville, South Carolina, and they wrote to each other once and sometimes twice a week, so that the conversations would get ahead of each other, there was so much they both had to say. Mary Bet's biggest news came early the next year. "You won't believe what has just happened," she wrote. "I don't think I can myself."

Congress had recently passed a law extending the draft age to forty-five, and suddenly millions of men were either in training or on their way. One day Hooper called Mary Bet into his office and told her to take a seat. "You heard about the conscription?" he asked.

"Miss Mumpford mentioned it. She keeps up with all the news."

"I've decided to enlist."

"What? You're forty-seven years old."

"I don't feel that old. Do I look it?"

"No, but—" Mary Bet looked around the office, at the picture of the President and the old governor, at Hooper's wire baskets of papers, his jacket on the door peg and the tin badge affixed to the lapel, as though for a clue to what she should say. "You can't just leave us with no sheriff."

"I'm not going to, Mary Bet Hartsoe." And now he smiled at her in a way that made her insides churn—what in the world was he planning on doing? Did he think he could be sheriff of Haw

County while running around the woods of South Carolina? "I plan to nominate you to take over while I'm gone."

Mary Bet just sat there, staring at Hooper's smooth walnut desk and thinking, as she often had, how like chocolate it looked. What had he just said to her? He'd let his walrus mustache grow so long it seemed to match the long ends of his string tie.

"Well?"

"Well, I'll have to think on it."

"There's nothing to think about, and no time to. We're meeting tonight to put it to a vote—just a formality—and you and me are drawing up the papers today." So he was not kidding her. "You're up to it, Mary Bet. I've never seen a more capable woman, and not many a man either. You know how to get everybody to agree, and you don't suffer fools—it's just what we need for a peacemaker. If you change your mind by this evening, we'll talk about it."

"But I haven't said anything to change it from."

Hooper laughed at this. "I like your attitude, Miss Hartsoe, Sheriff Hartsoe. Don't say anything that you have to unsay later on."

"There's a lot I'd unsay if I could. Hooper, you can't be serious."

"Mary Bet, I was thinking of running for state office anyway, and leaving you in charge for a few months, say, one court term. Now I'll have to put that off a while. Anyway, I don't think I'll be gone more than a few months."

"But shouldn't there be an election?"

"Next fall, next fall. You'll be fine until then. Nobody'll misbehave around here too badly, and if they do you've got fine deputies in all seven townships. The only dirt you need get on your shoes is from walking to the courthouse."

Mary Bet kept shaking her head. "But what about tax collection?"

"You don't have to do anything but stay in this office. You'll have a badge. And it wouldn't be a bad idea to keep my pistol in your desk."

"I won't shoot it."

"Good," Hooper said, with a little laugh. "It's just for safety. And you don't have to go on any raids you don't care to."

"I don't care to go on any, particularly." Mary Bet spat a blackberry seed that she'd been working free of her teeth, and she caught the wink her cousin gave her. "I haven't even said I'll do it, yet." One day gave her no time to make such an important decision. But she realized there really was no decision; the sheriff wanted her to do this job and thought she was up to it, and, besides, there was no one other than Hooper Teague whose advice she would care to seek. Robert Gray Jr. was in Hartsoe City and wasn't up on her daily life; her father, if she called him on the telephone, would only be confused and alarmed. She thought of Leon Thomas, but of course he would only say to do as her cousin recommended.

"Look at it this way," Hooper said, "you'll be making history—first woman sheriff in the state. Maybe first in the country."

Mary Bet sat back. "Pshaw, I didn't want to make history."

"The best don't."

Mary Bet went back to her office, feeling as though she'd just received a piece of bad news. Everything looked different, even Miss Mumpford, who was pulling another page out of her typewriter and crumpling it into the trash can. Mary Bet said, "I'm going to be the sheriff."

Miss Mumpford glanced up, squinting behind her glasses as though she couldn't make out who was talking. "Huh," she laughed, expelling a lungful of air, then went back to her work.

Mary Bet felt a smile creasing her cheeks, the prick of tears behind her eyes. "My father always wanted to work in the law," she said. Miss Mumpford paid no attention.

THE FOLLOWING DAY in the courthouse, in the presence of Sheriff Teague, Mr. Witherspoon, the three county commissioners, the clerk of the superior court, and a half dozen other men, including the former sheriff, Mary Bet put her hand to the Bible and said, "I, Mary Elizabeth Hartsoe, do solemnly swear that I will support the Constitution of the United States, so help me God."

She knew ahead of time she'd be called on to swear that way and she didn't care for it, because it seemed a blasphemy to swear to God, even for something so solemn. The gravity of it made her feel woozy, and she wanted to sit down and maybe drink a glass of water and rethink the whole thing. She went on, "I do solemnly and sincerely swear that I will be faithful and bear true allegiance to the State of North Carolina, and to the Constitutional powers and authorities which are or may be established for the government thereof; and that I will endeavor to support, maintain, and defend the Constitution of the said State, not inconsistent with the Constitution of the United States, to the best of my knowledge and ability, so help me God."

Two constitutions to support—it all seemed a little too much, and she had spent the previous night reading them both over carefully. The state constitution didn't let a person run for office if he denied the being of Almighty God. It shocked her to think anybody would deny God—surely such a person would never be voted in anyway, so what was the point of such an article?

Finally, she said, "I, Mary Elizabeth Hartsoe, do solemnly swear that I will execute the office of Sheriff of Haw County to the best of my knowledge and ability, agreeably to law, and that I will not take, accept, or receive, directly or indirectly, any fee, gift, bribe, gratuity, or reward whatsoever, for returning any man to serve as a juror or for making any false return on any process to be directed, so help me God."

She signed the three copies of the document, ones that she herself had typed up earlier in the day, then she went in to say goodbye to Miss Mumpford. The old lady got to her feet. "Are you the sheriff now?" she asked.

"I reckon I am."

"Well, I've seen it all." Miss Mumpford reached over and shook Mary Bet's hand. "Are you moving into his office?" She tilted her head.

"We'll worry about that later," Mary Bet said. Then she left the courthouse and headed back to her house to fix supper.

CHAPTER 24

1918

E VERYBODY WANTED TO see the badge, almost, Mary Bet thought, as though they needed proof. She and Flora celebrated that night with a bottle of muscadine wine that Flora had been saving for a special occasion. Flora raised her glass, her thin nose flaring, "I'd like to make a toast. To the first woman sheriff in North Carolina."

Mary Bet reddened, feeling the wine's warmth. She shook her head and said, "There's nothing to it. Anybody could do it." But secretly she felt proud of what she'd been asked to do, and she only hoped and prayed she was up to it. Then, before she knew it, she drank an entire glass and felt so light-headed she started to pour herself some more.

"We might as well," Flora said. "It won't keep."

"It won't? Well, I hate to see it go to waste." She poured herself a half glass, and her friend a full one. They talked and sang, and then they were dancing around their little kitchen, the lantern light swaying and flickering like firelight on the walls. In the morning she awoke with a headache and when she came downstairs and saw the bottle nearly empty, she poured the rest out and threw the bottle in the waste bin.

Mary Bet started her term with the expectation and fervent hope that nothing much would happen in Haw County until the fall elections. After the first month the routine of sitting at the sheriff's desk instead of her own had set in. She had to send warrants over for the judge to swear out, then ask one of her deputies—usually Lloyd Everett, because he lived a block away and rarely built houses anymore—to go serve the papers.

And she had to talk to all the people who stopped in and wanted one thing or another, though most of them just wanted to chat, even after the novelty of having a woman for sheriff had worn off. For the first few weeks there was a lot of ribbing and winking out in the hall, and sometimes right to her face about her being "near 'bout the prettiest sheriff in the state." Old Thad Utley from Hartsoe City stopped by one day and told her that judging by her looks there should be a law that all future sheriffs wear skirts. She told him that he had no business saying such a thing in the courthouse and if he had nothing more, he should go on and let her get back to work.

There were those who wanted more than just a look at the first woman sheriff in the state. Some of the requests fell within her jurisdiction, others did not, and she began to have a better appreciation for the kind of work Sheriff Teague had done. One farmer wanted to know what she planned to do about the drought, because his corn and peaches couldn't survive much longer. A miller came over from Hartsoe to tell her that she ought to enforce the law requiring customers to pay their bills within thirty days, or else get rid of the law altogether the way people ignored it. "I don't make the laws, Mr. Horne," she told him. "But if somebody's not paying up, you can bring 'em to court right here." He grumbled something about lawyers and left.

It was in late June, just before her thirty-first birthday, that Mary Bet got a letter from Leon saying he was in England, on his way to France. She didn't want to think about what danger he was in. Every time she pictured him coming home on the train, leaning out and waving his hat, the image dissolved and she saw the Devil minister in his swallowtail coat leaning for her from his gray horse, and she knew without knowing how that Leon was not coming home.

He would not be afraid. She prayed instead that he would not suffer; she could not bear to think of him dying alone on some bleak field far away.

If he and Hooper and the others were willing to go over there and fight, certainly she could do her duty here at home. A string of complaints about petty thefts began coming in. "I can't find my good hoe," one disgruntled man told her, just as she was leaving for the day, "and I know exactly where I put it in my shed—same place as always. That hoe cost me a sawbuck." When Mary Bet asked if he had tried locking the shed, the complainant only stared as though she'd asked if he had tried wearing his pants on his head; he repeated how much he'd paid for the hoe.

"I left my good linen tablecloth on the line and went out in the afternoon. *Pffttt*—it was clean gone. What do you make of that?" This grievance from the dried lips of Mrs. Gooch. She seemed to hold Mary Bet accountable, eyeing her with a tilt of her shorn gray head, the way a bird will. "I don't know what to make of it, Mrs. Gooch," Mary Bet said. "I'll get my boys to look into it directly."

"You do that then," Mrs. Gooch said. Then, remembering whom she was speaking to, added, "I thank you for it." She nodded curtly and left, and Mary Bet felt no particular satisfaction in being recognized for her badge.

She sat down at Hooper's desk writing up the latest report, from her old landlady. There had now been nine such complaints in the past three weeks. If the thefts were related, could the thief be taunting her—challenging her authority to act as sheriff? She thought: turn this over to Lloyd Everett, who has far more experience in law enforcement, and let him do what he does best—go snooping around, asking questions. He loved having an excuse to get away from his house and his wife.

The complaints continued over the summer, and then in the heat of early August, with a sluggish sun melting the sky, the case turned. Mary Bet was walking to work, crossing streets to stay in the shade for the entire four blocks so that she would perspire as little as possible through her layers of undergarments, light cotton shirt, and navy cambric skirt. A colored boy named Willis Ramsey came up to her in the street, his dungarees giving off a faint odor of manure, and said, "Miz Hartsoe, ma'am?"

"What is it, Willis?" she asked, continuing at a good clip. "I can't be dawdling."

"Well, Mr. Foushee—" Willis curled his little finger into his ear and pulled out something he began examining while walking alongside the sheriff.

Mary Bet wondered if he was nervous, or just forgetful, or if he maybe had nits. "Well, what about Mr. Foushee?" She edged farther from him, but he just sidled up next to her.

"I done some work for him, and he axed me 'bout his pickax, but I tole him, nosir, I don't know what happen to it. But I seen it two days ago."

"Where'd you see it?" Mary Bet asked, afraid she was going to have to get Deputy Everett to haul Willis in for questioning. And then what? Whether he was guilty or not, Judge Lane would send him off to the county reformatory for minors where he'd spend the next year and a half learning how to steal and curse and lie, if he didn't know already.

"I seen it in Miz Cantilever's backyard," he said. "Cross my heart and hope to die."

"Mrs. Cadwallader's?"

"Yes, ma'am."

"What was it doing there?"

"Just sittin' there, mindin' its own bidness, propped on a stump."

"And what were you doing there?" Mary Bet slowed down and regarded Willis, his rich brown skin the color of coffee grounds, his rounded boyish cheeks bunching when he smiled at her in a way that he'd learned to do for grown-ups and white folks.

"I wudn't doin' nothin', 'cept mindin' my own bidness, cuttin' crost the yard to get down to the creek to hunt bait."

"How come you're just now telling somebody about it?"

"I didn't take it. I'se afraid if I go tell Mr. Foushee he say I took it. I don't even want no re-ward, I just want somebody to get that pickax and take it back to Mr. Foushee so he won't blame me."

"All right," she said. "I'll look into it."

She was thinking about how best to approach Mrs. Cadwallader, a woman who had had some standing in the community as a baker's wife. But her husband had taken up with another woman and moved away to Washington, D.C., leaving a ten-year-old boy and three little girls. One of the girls had died shortly thereafter, of pneumonia. And now the boy was fifteen or sixteen and his mother worked at the garment-label factory south of town, and was never seen at church or anywhere else except the grocery. Mary Bet had never spoken with her. She'd heard the boy had taken to smoking and going on long walks at night, which made her think of Siler.

Willis was still talking when they got to the veterans' memorial outside the courthouse. Mary Bet bid him good-bye and hurried on inside. She went through her morning routine, hardly aware of where she was or what she was doing. People came and went, papers were read and sorted through and signed. She still did her own filing because she knew where everything should go; she liked doing it, and didn't see any need of asking the board to hire an assistant for only a few months.

At lunchtime she went out to pay a visit to the Cadwallader house.

It was too hot for walking the half-mile out past the Presbyterian church and the squat houses of white wage earners to the east end of town, so she called for the buggy and driver that were available for her official use. Mrs. Cadwallader had moved to this part of town after her husband left. Her house was a clapboard bungalow with horizontal strips of peeling gray paint above the door, a leaning broken chimney, and a stoop of cracked and chipped cement, weeds encroaching from both sides. Off in an unmown side yard two girls were playing house beside a well and pump that were shared with two or three other neighbors—a common arrangement in this part of town.

Mary Bet alighted from the buggy, and, lifting her long skirt, climbed the two steps of the front stoop, her heavy black shoes crunching the loose cement. There being no knocker, she rapped on the door and peered around to the closer window. She shielded her eyes and made out a parlor with a rug and rocking chair, perhaps a sofa, piled with what looked like clothes.

She waited for a minute or two, then went around and called out, "Where's your mother at, chil'ren?"

One girl, with a streak of dirt across one cheek, pointed across the street, then began sucking her thumb, and the other one said, "She's not here."

"Are you a Cadwallader?" Mary Bet asked the latter. Getting a nod in response, she said, "What about your brother?"

"He's—he's—" The other girl now took her thumb out of her mouth and began laughing, and the Cadwallader girl—a pretty little thing, all bones and long waves of yellow hair—glared at her friend and said, "He's out in the garden."

Mary Bet started heading down around the back, and the girl called out, "Ma'am? I think you're real pretty." The other girl laughed again, for which she was shished by the young Cadwallader.

Mary Bet turned and said, "I think you are too," which pleased the girl. "Do you know who I am?" Mary Bet asked. Both of them shook their heads. "I'm the sheriff." The dirty-faced girl started to laugh, but caught herself, and both girls just stared at Mary Bet as though they didn't know what to make of such a statement.

"I thought the sheriff was a man," the Cadwallader girl said.

"He was," Mary Bet said.

"Where's your badge?" The voice was from a young man. Mary Bet looked down the yard past the house toward a row of head-high corn and saw a boy approaching. His hair was darker than his sister's, but he had the same high, almost Asian-looking cheekbones; he peered at Mary Bet through cautious, skeptical eyes as he came slowly up toward her, his long arms dangling, casually holding a scythe.

"I don't usually bring it with me," Mary Bet said. "What's your name?"

"Matthew Cadwallader," he said. "Or just Matt." He stopped about fifteen feet away and surveyed her with a sweep of his eyes. "You have a gun?"

"Huh," she laughed. "No, I don't carry a gun either."

"Don't you ever need one?"

"Not regularly."

He nodded, but seemed doubtful about her and her purpose here. He was skinny like his sister, but with strong muscles in his arms, shoulders, and neck, and Mary Bet could see now that he was handsome despite a blaze of acne along both cheeks. The laces on his canvas work shoes were undone, his singlet undershirt and even his suspenders were damp, and the undershirt was coming untucked from his blue dungarees. He waited for her to speak.

"Have you seen a pickax, sorta new, with some kind of grip to it?" she asked.

The boy stood there a moment, arms akimbo, his eyes moving from Mary Bet to the girls, who had gone silent, watching the proceedings as though in a theater balcony. He shook his head. "I don't think so," he said. "Why?"

"You don't mind if I have a look around, do you?" she asked, tilting her hat against the sun that was creeping around the crooked chimney.

The boy's eyes darted left and right, he licked his lips, and said, his voice now subdued, "Help yourself."

Mary Bet nodded once and headed toward the boy, who was now holding his elbows. He smiled at her as she brushed past him on the narrow strip of grass that was low enough for walking. "Why don't you show me around?" she said. Standing this close she noticed an odor of tobacco on his breath and in his clothes, and he had that musky, sweaty smell of boys his age, which reminded her of Joe Dorsett and of Siler.

The garden extended about a hundred feet down to a gully lined with a tangle of briars and high weeds. A scarecrow of straw-stuffed dungarees and flannel shirt, with an underwear head, stood in the middle of the garden. A crow, perched on its shoulder, flew off at their approach. Mary Bet looked around for a tree stump and saw a large one over by a slat fence that enclosed a neighbor's rain cistern. "Where do you keep your tools and such?" she asked.

"In the shed." The boy nodded toward a small wood outbuilding crusted in the same gray as the house. She began walking along the sloped ground, studying it for snakes that might be hiding in the high grass.

When she reached the shed, the boy came up alongside her and said, "It's not locked, cause there's nothing to hide." The door, consisting of three boarded-together planks, was closed with a bolt and hasp, as well as a staple, which had no lock. She thumbed back the bolt and flicked the metal strap open, and then she pulled on the door.

"I can't see anything in there," she said. "You'll have to bring me a light, or else start taking everything out one by one where I can see them."

"All right," Matt said, "but don't you need a search warrant or something?"

"A search warrant? What've you been reading? I'm the sheriff. Go fetch me a pen and paper along with the lantern, if you've a mind to."

"That's all right, I'll just get the lantern."

While he was gone, Mary Bet went ahead into the gloom and found that she could see well enough by the rift of daylight angling through the doorway. She brushed a spider off her face, and went over to a chinked wall, scattering a host of crickets. She picked out two wooden-handled tools and brought them out for examination. One of them was a rusty posthole spade with a long handle, the other a pickax with incised cross-hatching around the end.

The boy came along swinging a lantern with a cloudy globe. He looked square at her and said, "I've never seen that before."

"What?"

He nodded toward both tools, but then clamped his lips together.

"Let's see what else we have here," she said. The boy lit the lantern, and it fizzed to life, a sudden ember in a cave, and everything was angles and shadows. In contrast to the ill-kempt yard, the shed was an orderly arrangement of wooden crates lining the walls, hand tools hanging on nails, riding tackle, a push mower with well-oiled blades, and shelves holding jars of screws, washers, and nails in assorted sizes. The crates contained odd pieces of wood, bits of wire mesh, squares of some new kind of thin metal, and other odds and ends. Mary Bet's eye went to a short-handled froe hanging from two nails. She reached for it and at the same time said, "You ever use that mower?"

"Yes, ma'am," he said, "I hire out some."

"Where'd this come from?" she asked, holding up the froe, its foot-long blade nicked and scraped.

"I 'on know," he said. "Always had it, I guess."

"What do you use it for?"

"Splittin' firewood and stuff."

"Looks like its been used on rocks or something."

Matt shook his head and narrowed his eyes, but when she stared back at him he looked off into a corner, holding up the lantern as though searching for something. Mary Bet told him to keep the light steady, and she went over to the shelves and began pushing things around. Behind the mason jars of screws and nails she found more canning jars filled with what appeared to be preserves and relish. "I might have to take these in as evidence," she said. "And I don't mean that lightly, boy. Hold that lantern to where I can see."

"See what?"

"See what all you've got here. Where'd you put the tablecloth?"

"What tablecloth?"

"Mrs. Gooch's linen tablecloth. The one with the red stitching along the border. Don't act like you don't know what I'm talking about."

She heard him sniffling, but he was looking away from her. She reached into the bosom of her blouse and pulled out a handkerchief. "Here," she said. He shook his head, and wiped the tears with his free hand.

"How much of this is yours, and how much did you steal?"

He said nothing, just sniffed in hard, trying to master himself.

"Don't you know you can go to the penitentiary for this? This is a serious offense, young man, and I aim to prosecute it with everything I know how. Here you've got the town all upset, thinking there's a gang of hoodlums and cutthroats on the loose. What's the matter with you?"

The boy just stood there shaking his head, looking at the wall and the shelves as though for something he could show her.

She suddenly wanted to go over and put her arm around him, but she went on with her badgering. "If you don't start talking, I'm going to get my deputies out here to haul you in. You're not too young to put in jail. What were you doing snooping around Mrs. Gooch's yard for, anyway?"

"I'll get the tablecloth," he spluttered. "I didn't know whose it was, I swear I didn't." He put the lantern down and turned to go. Mary Bet twisted the wheel to extinguish the flame, then followed him out.

"You wait for me, son," she said. "I don't want you out of my sight." She followed him up a rickety set of steps to a back porch— a rectangle of studs and beams enclosed by translucent oilcloth. In the wan light inside she could make out old wicker and wood furniture, oil cans, a pump handle, and a yellow pine table where piles of folded clothes were spread. The boy went over to a rattan armchair, lifted up the cushion, and pulled out a neatly folded oblong of red-bordered white linen.

"What did you aim to do with that?" she asked.

"I was going to give it to my mother for a Christmas present."

"What in the world? Law, son, your mother wouldn't take such a thing. How much you think a nice thing like that costs?"

"I don't know. I was going to cut it up and make napkins out of it, and maybe a shawl for Betty Ann Murchison."

"Murchison, huh? I don't know any Betty Ann Murchison. But you've got no business taking people's things and chopping them up. The very idea." She gave him a chastising tilt of her head, her brimmed hat shuttering like a stern black wing. He stood before her in the murky light, hands clasped in front and his head sunk. "What have you got to say for yourself?" she demanded. "What else did you take?"

"I took some jars of stuff and some tools. That froe out there and a maul and wedge."

"What'd you need 'em both for? Looks like one'd do you as good as th'other." She snorted a little laugh. "What's the sense in stealing something you don't need?"

He shook his head. "I don't know, ma'am."

"Of course you don't. If you had sense enough to know, you wouldn't've done it in the first place. What church y'all go to?"

"Mama goes to the Presbyterian mostly, not every week."

"And you?"

"I quit going when I turned thirteen. I'm not much on church-going."

"Why not?"

He shrugged and crossed his arms in front of his chest. He bit on his lower lip, then looked at Mary Bet in a challenging way.

"Well," she said, "If you'd gone to church more you'd know what it says in the Bible about stealing. It's against the Ten Commandments, so it's a sin. You could be on the road to breaking more commandments for all I know." The boy made a curt nod of agreement, and Mary Bet said, "It's hot in here, let's go outside where I can see you better. I need to talk to you."

They went back out and stood in the shade of a massive oak. The smell of honeysuckle hung thick in the air behind them where a snarled row of vines and shrubs defined the border of the property. "What time does your mother get home?"

"Just after six, every day except Saturday, and then she gets off at one."

"You ever hear from your father?"

The boy's lips tightened. He glanced sharply at her, then away. "Not much, no. He writes letters to us, but my mother quit reading them. If there's no money in them, she just throws them away."

"Does he send money regularly?"

"I don't know."

"And the girl that died—she was your youngest sister, wasn't she?"

"Yes, ma'am. Emma. She was seven. She wanted to go to the state fair in Raleigh so she could see a lady with fish scales for skin. I don't know why she wanted to see that."

"What do you want to do?" she asked him.

"Ma'am?"

"What do you aim to do with your life, son?" She wondered why she was wasting so much time on this young man; she was liable to miss her dinner entirely, which meant a long and very hungry afternoon, with nothing but a box of raisins in her office. She could never admit she'd spent her dinnertime talking to the town thief and not brought him in, and she hated making up a story.

"I'd like to work with cars," the boy said. "If I could."

Mary Bet nodded, appraising the boy and his seriousness; she doubted he'd be able to stick with anything long enough to learn how it worked, especially something as complicated as an automobile. "Do you know where all these things that you stole belong?"

"Yes, ma'am. Am I going to jail?"

"I haven't decided yet." She cleared her throat, then spoke in as forceful a voice as she knew how, as if she were talking to a way-ward child, which, after all, she was. "The main thing is that we need to get these tools and such back to their rightful owners, and you have to make up for taking them." She waited for him to offer a suggestion, but when it became clear that none was forthcoming she said, "Son, you have about three seconds to start talking. After that I won't be in such a charitable mood."

"I'll do whatever you think I should."

"You think I should be lenient with you?"

"I don't know if you should. I shouldn't have taken them things. I just—I just saw them and I had to have them. I can't explain it right." He smiled at her in what she thought was a put-on sheepish way.

"I don't reckon you can explain it right, because there's nothing right about it. I'm thinking if I brought you into the lockup I'd save you some trouble, since you're bound to land there sooner or later. I'll let the judge decide what to do with you. He's out on the circuit, he'll be back next Wednesday."

The boy stood there, leaning on one leg, hands in his pockets, staring at the ground as if for an answer, or because he couldn't look squarely in the face of the law when it was threatening to lock him away. Mary Bet felt her legs prickle with the heat, and her underarms were slick in perspiration. "Well?" she demanded. "Why shouldn't I do that?" She really did want him to come up with a good answer, and she watched as it finally dawned on him, with the awareness of one who has found a missing item after a long search, that he might talk himself out of a bad scrape.

"I could come work for you," he said.

~ CHAPTER 25 ~

1918

June 11
American Rest Camp
Winnall Downs
Winchester, England

Dear Miss Mary Bet,
This may be the last chance I have to write for some time, as we
are heading to France tomorrow. The voyage over was nothing
to speak of, meaning it was not quite a luxury cruise. I am sorry
I have not written you these past weeks, but as you will see there
has been little time for anything personal. Also, I didn't want to
presume that you were hanging on my every word. Believe me,
though, when I tell you that you have been in my thoughts every
day, for you are one of the best and truest friends I know.
*   We boarded the S.S. Portadown in Long Island for the voy-*
age across. It was an old British steamship for transporting beef

and served well enough for transporting 2,500 soldiers—all of our regiments and parts of others as well. We went in a convoy with thirteen other ships, including one battleship. For the entire twelve days there wasn't much to see except fog and gray water, but we entertained ourselves as best we could. There were plenty of inspections and drills to keep us on our toes. When we got to the cold zone we stood watches looking for icebergs. We never saw any, but the life belts were good added protection against the cold.

The men don't much care for British food, and I don't blame them. We ate mutton and more mutton, and some men in my battery said they wouldn't care if they never saw or heard of another sheep for as long as they lived. It got so they were saying "baaaaa" every time we got mutton. And there were always potatoes boiled in their jackets and a strange tasting jelly called orange marmalade. I didn't think it was too bad, but some people kicked about it and I'm ashamed to say that a few cans went overboard. A few fellows were lamenting so and saying that if they ever got back to good old U.S.A. rations again they'd never complain. As their mess sergeant I said that was music to my ears, and I expected nothing but praise once we were on our own mess-line again. We had a right good laugh over it, but I don't expect promises to be kept.

We were happy to be on dry land again at Liverpool, having survived the trip just fine, except for a few cases of mal de mer as everybody called it. Camp Sevier seems so long ago, though it was only nine months. And now we are a cohesive unit, full of esprit de corps, and whereas some of us were a little shy or lacking in confidence or difficult in some other way, we are now of one mind. It's a strange thing how the outfit has taken on a life of its own—we all want to see action, because that is our purpose and what we have been working so hard for all this time.

The British countryside, which we viewed from a train, is beautifully green, like a park strewn with little villages. But the people are all gloom and doom. They're happy to see us, but they say we've come too late, that the war is over and we have lost. We don't pay heed to such discouraged voices. Winchester is another lovely town, with an old cathedral that I think you would like. You see, I do have you in my thoughts, and I hope you sometimes are thinking of me. I don't want you to worry, because I'm not worried and neither are the men. We are all very confident of success. I just wanted you to get an idea of what we were seeing and doing and to tell you that you are uppermost in my mind. I wish you were here to see the sights. Unfortunately we didn't get to see as much of Winchester as we would've liked, because we spent half a day for a review by the Duke of Connaught, uncle of King George, and other nobles.

Tomorrow we leave for Southampton, and so on to France.

Miss Mary Bet, you have been so kind to me I hardly know how to tell you just how much I appreciate your friendship. I cannot understand why, but I do know that I long to tell you everything that either gives me pleasure or worry. I suppose it is because you are the most unselfish person in the world and understand human nature. Well, I will have to bid you good night before you become disgusted trying to read this long, uninteresting, scribbled letter. So hurry to dreamland, and dream that you have many friends, but none who care for you more than I—this will be a true dream. Love and best wishes,

Sincerely,

LST

Mary Bet folded up the onionskin pages and returned them to the envelope. She studied the stamps with their likenesses of British royalty. She'd never gotten a letter from overseas, and she wondered what Leon had been doing for the three weeks it took the letter to arrive. Probably he was in France somewhere, involved in something so dangerous she wouldn't want to even picture it. She tucked it into her scrapbook. Then, as she started downstairs, she took it out again. Why not show it to Flora? News from abroad was important to everybody these days.

Flora was sitting at her machine, her back straight as a board and her head bowed. The machine whirred and clicked, the bobbin and treadle in their own rhythms that sometimes intermeshed, like that great comet that had come dashing around the sun. Mary Bet said, "Here's a letter from England." Her friend glanced up briefly. "It's from Leon Thomas, with news from the regiment. Shall I read it?" Flora nodded, and so Mary Bet plopped onto the settee and read almost all the way to the end.

"Is that all?" Flora asked. She never said much, but when she did speak, her words always meant more than what was in them.

Mary Bet laughed. "Well, almost. All right, he goes on to talk about how he appreciates my friendship and he always wants to tell me things and . . . well, that's about it. And he signs it love and best wishes, and then sincerely. That's kind of peculiar."

The machine went on to the hem of the muslin sleeve, then stopped. Flora turned around, her mouth a chipmunk smile, scolding with a minute shake of the head. "Now, I have something to tell you, *Miss* Mary Bet. Just this morning one of the girls at the shop was talking about Leon Thomas."

Other women talking about Leon meant that other women were thinking about him, and Mary Bet had to fight her natural curiosity. "What was she talking about him for?" she asked, trying to keep the annoyance out of her voice.

"She was telling about when he stood up to that preacher that time." She regarded Mary Bet with a penetrating, amused look. "You know, when the boys were up training in Durham."

"I know the time," Mary Bet said. "Just what was she saying?"

"She was wondering if he was being joshed by the boys over there, once the story went round. I expect they'll keep him true to his word."

Mary Bet shook her head and pictured the men poking fun at Leon, trying to tempt him into—she didn't want to imagine what. "I don't know he ought to've challenged a preacher that a-way," she said. "What made him to do that, do you reckon?"

"You know him better than I do. Why do you think he did?"

She tried to picture him sitting in the pew, hot to the point of burning, until he felt he would burst if he had to listen to one more thing, a fire of righteousness and love for his fellows taking over and making him stand up. She smiled almost imperceptibly. "I don't know," she said. "Something got into him."

She felt for him, putting himself on the line that way, and a sudden warmth spread over her as she sat there, and a fear she had never known. She had a strange feeling, of a soft warm wind and an empty field with deepening shadows along the edge. When Flora turned back to her work, she said a quick prayer for him, a soldier far away.

"Do you think we'd hear about it, if they—if any of them got hurt over there?"

"You'd know more about that than I do, working in the courthouse."

"Nobody's said anything about it. I reckon they'll telegraph if anybody from around here got hurt. The telegraph office would get word out to Leon's brothers, and send a notice over to the courthouse. Over to me, come to think of it."

"Why do you want to dwell on such a thing, Mary Bet?" Flora was concentrating on her work now, guiding the underarm through the pecking needle.

"It eases my mind some. If I imagine the worst, then I don't see how it could turn out that way. Things always turn out different to how you imagine."

"What do you think of Leon?"

"I like him," Mary Bet said. "I don't know why he volunteered though. His father was shot in the War between the States. And here there's a war in Europe, and our boys have to go over there and fight it for them. It doesn't seem right somehow. But I reckon it's the way of things."

"Does he give you an address where you can write him back?"

"No, they're on the move." She thought about Leon, his broad smiling face and stocky body, tramping along in a mass of dark-clad soldiers in their brimmed doughboy helmets, and she wished now that she had never been coy with him. "Well, maybe they're better off over there, with the flu as bad as it is." She smiled vaguely.

Flora paused. "I heard the flu was worse over there."

"I didn't need to hear that," Mary Bet said. "Anyway, I don't reckon they'll send them to the front, as green as they are."

She had begun to realize that she did love Leon, though mostly what that word meant to her was that she thought of him in connection with family and home. She thought it likely that he had a more romantic nature than she—he had once praised her for her practicality, for how well she was able to put unpleasant and difficult things out of her mind. And though she had taken it as a compliment, she thought he had put his finger on a weakness of her character. But she also understood that since he was the more romantic, he could probably be relied upon to do as she wanted him to. She liked that about him, that he seemed gallant regarding her needs. Yet the real test lay in how he and they endured, and she thought of her parents and how her mother had said that marriage was like a coat that didn't fit quite right. Oh, what was the point of wondering about married life with Leon? He had not properly proposed, and—she could hardly stand the thought—he was fighting in a war.

Surely they would not put untested men right up at the front. She was the sheriff of Haw County, but what could she do? Her jurisdiction ended at the county line. But she had been turning an idea around in her mind. The note falling from the scrapbook had told her it was time to go, and now that she was in a position to get some answers she didn't think it would be an abuse of her power to work in a visit to a fellow sheriff, as long as she was out in Morganton visiting her father anyway. A barrier had to be breached if she was ever to get on with her life.

SHE THOUGHT OF taking the boy out with her and Deputy Everett to apprehend a bootlegger, then decided not to show him any more immoral behavior than he was already familiar with. She went on the raid, because there was no one else available, the able-bodied being off at war, and when they got out to the still and found the place abandoned and started chopping it up, one of the Sugg brothers came out from a little pup tent with a sawed-off shotgun and demanded they leave. Mary Bet told him that she was the sheriff. She showed him the badge on her jacket and he laughed, and she said, "I'm the governor's constable here in Haw County and I'm going to haul you in, so I suggest you put that thing down and start moving."

Sugg had a grizzled beard that looked as though he'd hacked it off with a knife, tried to shave it, and given up. His sloe eyes drooped in a sad way, and his overalls were caked with hops on the bib and dirt on the knees. He looked more dangerous than anybody she knew, the way he just stared, as though he were looking at a tree, or some animal he was studying how to get the better of; a scar along the side of his mouth creased his face and added ten years to his age, which she put at around forty.

Everett looked like he wanted to run. He still had his hands in the air, and he had a kind of pleading look, as though to say, "You wouldn't shoot a lady, would you?" But Sugg just shifted the gun from one person to the other, jabbing it in the air to see if he could make them turn and run.

"Why don't you get your hands in the air, little lady," he said, "like your deputy. I don't believe you're really the sheriff. I think you bought that badge somewhere and now you just want this still because it's situated right prettily here."

"I don't want any such thing," she told him. "Except for you to put that gun down. I'm going to step over to where you are, and by the time I get there, I expect that gun to be lying on the ground to where you cain't get it. Make haste now, boy." She spat what was in her mouth and started slowly forward, keeping her dark eyes on him.

He poked the gun toward her, and Mary Bet's heart leapt. But she kept stepping. "You got a gun in that skirt?" he asked.

"I might, and Deputy Everett might. We're taking you in, so unless you aim to kill us both and hide our bodies and get clean out of this state, you'd best do as I say. And if you do kill us, I'm telling you, you won't rest a night, because the Bureau of Investigation and every policeman in the country will be out looking for you for killing a woman sheriff, and they'll find you too and string you up just like they strung up Shackleford Davies. I saw him a-ridin' on his coffin. I reckon you remember that hanging?"

He nodded, looking a little less sure of himself. There were now only twenty feet between them. Everett had held his ground, and his tongue, for which she was grateful. Sugg was working his cheeks in and out like a bellows while he was studying the problem, but it only made him more sinister, as if he were a little less than fully human.

And then she was standing five feet away from him. "Don't point that at me!" she snapped. He lowered the barrel. "Set it on the ground, slow, so it doesn't go off."

He put the stock down, then picked it back up. "What happens if I just run off?"

"Then we'll come after you. I know who your people are, and we'll find you and it'll go a lot worse for you. Right now, you've got six months in the county jail, but if you run off I'll see you get put in the state penitentiary for five years." She didn't know if he would believe her; she guessed he knew more about the criminal justice system than she did. "You ever been there?" she asked.

"No, ma'am. I've been in the jail, though, and I didn't particularly like it."

"I don't reckon you did. It hasn't gotten any better. Just do what I say, and I'll tell Judge Lane to go easy on you. But if you run off, there's nothing I can do for you."

He set the stock down, then knelt to lay the gun on the ground. He stood up as Everett came slowly forward with the handcuffs.

Everett drove—Mary Bet having never learned how—and Sugg sat up front, his shackled hands in his lap. She tapped him on the shoulder. "Don't have any second thoughts on the way and try anything foolish. You'll get good food there in the jail, and I'll see that you get all the blankets you need. We'll put you in where there're new folding cots with springs—they're better than the old iron ones." She had to shout over the wind from the car's speed, and Sugg just nodded.

When they got there he was compliant. He said, "I'm never going to live down getting taken in by a woman. Can I tell people you had a gun?"

"Tell 'em what you want," she said. "It's a lie, but I don't expect it's the first you've ever told, nor'll be the last."

~♡ CHAPTER 26 ♡~

1918

S HE RESPONDED TO Leon's letters, telling him to take care and
filling him in on the details of her life. She told him that being
sheriff mostly gave her respect for the responsibility Hooper
and men like him had shouldered. "But I reckon I'm doing a right
good job of it, because the Board hasn't let me go yet." She wanted
to tell him about Matthew Cadwallader, ask him if he thought it
was graft to let the boy pay off his debt to society by chopping her
wood and painting her back stoop.

The days rushed along, and when a letter arrived she thought,
"This will be the last one, and then a telegram will come." His letters were weeks behind the newspaper reports from the front. "He's
already gone," she thought, "and there will be no time to prepare
for it and the rest of my life as a spinster."

Once he wrote that it was only the thought of her that kept
him from temptation, and she wondered what he meant. She could
picture his broad face and smile and his sparse eyebrows, but the

image was from a photograph he had sent her, posed in his green wool uniform. In her mind, he merged with a hundred other soldiers, all alike, so she tried to see him coming into her office to visit, hat in hand, jacket open.

She imagined temptresses and French prostitutes servicing the soldiers at sordid, dirty hovels and way stations in godforsaken towns. But had God really forsaken them and could the French women be so different and lacking in morals than the women of Haw County? Perhaps during a time of war everyone was desperate, and Leon was no different from anybody. He was lonely and needed to feel the warmth of another human being, poor man. He had had only one serious affair, so he had told her, and that was with Ann Murchison. She thought, "I've waited too long. He'll fall in love with a French woman for sure, and come home married." Flora told her to quit thinking such thoughts and keep her mind on her darning.

There was a letter in which he said they were heading to Toul in northeastern France. She got out her father's old atlas and found the town, located along the Moselle River. It seemed too close to Germany. She had nothing against the Germans—her people had come from Germany—and yet now they were fighting the rest of Europe. It made no sense, and nobody around seemed to have any satisfactory explanation for it. It was just a terrible war, something men seemed bent on doing.

She tried to picture a quaint little village with a Gothic church and farmhouses scattered about, but she kept seeing mud and men and horses and big guns on wheels and dirt-smeared women trailing behind in kerchiefs and aprons, and the men and horses, and many dogs as well, were all on the march toward some horrible reckoning over a road where the noise of explosions and gunfire grew louder and louder. She'd heard of machine guns and tanks and trenches and airplanes that shot each other from the sky, and it all seemed so remote and terrible she could hardly picture Leon Thomas in such a hellish mess. She preferred to think of him as he was here, leaning into her office of a morning with a big smile on his face and that cast in one eye.

He wrote to her as often as he could, he told her, but twice a month didn't seem often enough to her. Her palms would itch something fierce on mornings she was sure a letter was coming, and then there would be nothing and the whole day would feel pointless and miserable.

One day in late September when the newspapers reported Allied troops moving toward the Meuse River, Mary Bet decided it was high time for a proper inspection of the county jail and convict camp. She took along her young charge so that he could see for himself where he might be headed if he didn't mend his ways.

They started out at the jail, south of the courthouse. "You write down what I tell you in that notebook," she said to Matthew. "Write down sixteen white and nine colored inmates." She watched as his hand formed slow, clumsy letters. "Good, now let's speak to the warden."

She introduced Matthew to Warden Hargrove, a leather-faced man of indeterminate age with buckteeth and one half-closed eye. "Warden," she said, "this is Matthew Cadwallader, helping me out for a while."

"Yes, ma'am," the warden said. He nodded at the boy. It was known, but not mentioned, that she had hired the boy shortly after he had gone around returning the stolen items and apologizing and offering to work for the people he had stolen from. Only Mrs. Gooch had come asking Mary Bet if she planned to send the boy to juvenile court. Mary Bet asked her if she was pressing a charge; Mrs. Gooch said she would think about it, and that maybe she should speak to the judge first. "That's fine," Mary Bet said. Mrs. Gooch turned up her nose, said, "Well," and walked out.

"Are the inmates well cared for, Warden?" Mary Bet asked.

"Yes, ma'am. But we could use a sewerage system in here. It's more than me and Hiram can handle, back and forth with the pots all day."

"Write that down," she told Matthew. "The board'll get a full report."

"And we could use gutters. That roof water ain't fit for drinking, getting mixed with the oil in the pumps."

"Write that down."

Next they drove out to the convict camp to the north. "Now, if you're on good behavior," she told Matthew, "you'd get to work out here."

"I'm not going to prison," he told her.

"I'm glad to hear it."

They walked around the little wooden buildings, accompanied by the camp warden. There were pens with goats and pigs, and a pasture that held cattle and mules. Three men in dungarees and black-and-white striped shirts were in the pigpen at work on the stockade fence. "We could use a pasture for the hogs," the supervisor told them. He was a short man, not much over Mary Bet's height, with a thick mustache like hog bristles. Matthew was writing before Mary Bet said a word. "And you know these shacks—"

"I've been after the board to do something about it since before I was sheriff. Mr. Teague wanted brick buildings, and I think it's high time. Next meeting I'm going to tell them it's the least we can do to honor the request of our sheriff serving overseas. Besides, I can see now for myself you can't keep things sanitary like this."

"No, ma'am, we can't."

"How about the crops and stores?"

"Fine. Plenty to feed the stock and—what is it now, thirty-nine or forty, with fourteen here and them at the jail. I don't know if they'll be enough for brick buildings." He spat and then went on.

"Hundred and fifty bushels of sweet potatoes," he said, reading from a sheet, "two hundred pounds tobacco, six tons meadow hay. The pea vine's not so good this year." He went on about the wheat and corn, the stock and straw, Matthew writing it all down.

"You say there's fifty acres in cultivation," Mary Bet said. "And we've got all these woods around here. How much?"

"With the woods on the north side," he said, holding his hand out, the last two fingers of which were nubs, "near 'bout three hundred acres."

Mary Bet looked at Matthew. "Well?" she said. "Should the county put brick buildings out here?"

"If you say they should."

"It's not up to me, it's up to the Board of Commissioners. How're we gonna pay for it?"

"Looks like you could sell some of this land," Matthew said.

"How much?"

He shrugged. "I don't know. Maybe two hundred acres."

Mary Bet felt a smile coming to her face. "So you were paying attention. If there's any left over, they can buy war bonds." The supervisor nodded, and they followed him, his mud-caked boots indicating the driest way back between ruts in the road.

They thanked him and got in Mary Bet's top-buggy, and on the way home she said, "He and the warden are brothers. Mr. Sam ran his own store up past Silkton, until a few years ago. He got drunk and ran over a colored boy. Crushed his skull. He went to the penitentiary for fifteen months, and had to close his shop. Now he works for the county. Does a good job. He was happy to have a second chance. I don't know how he lost those fingers."

"Do you ever drink?" Matthew asked.

"Drink? Me? What kind of a question is that? No, I don't." Mary Bet thought a minute as they rolled along past a stubbly, sere field of cut corn. "I use to think liquor was evil. But then I thought, how could something that happens in nature be evil? Fruits decay and ferment. And the people that drink it aren't evil, mostly. It's what people do who can't resist it that's evil." She thought, I don't care if he's listening, I'm going to say what I want. "The Devil's medicine, my mother called it. Her father was a drunkard."

"What about your father?"

She glanced at the boy, high cheekbones and red skin like he was of a different race, and yet he reminded her strongly of somebody she knew well. "Reach into my handbag, will you, son? Get that round tin out. Press it open." He opened it and held it to her, and she took a pinch for each nostril. "Help yourself, but not too much." He took a tiny pinch, stared at it, smelled it, then sniffed it in.

"My father's in the asylum out at Morganton. I'm overdue for a visit. It's a hundred and fifty miles away, but that's no excuse. He doesn't even know I'm sheriff. I doubt he knows we're at war."

When they arrived at the Cadwallader house, Matthew nodded and then hopped out. He stood there a second, shielding his eyes with his hand, and Mary Bet felt the sun on her back, and the shadow of her wide hat sliced across the boy's face and spread upon the patchy ground behind him. "Why are you doing all this for me?" he asked.

She shook her head. "I don't know," she said. "Partly for you and partly for me, I reckon. I thought as sheriff I might be called upon to bring in a bad man, something big and heroic like that. But I can see there's other ways of tending the law. Now listen, I have to take a trip this week, on a matter of some urgency."

"Is your father dying?"

"Dying? Not that I know of. I need to see him though, and attend to some business of my late brother's. I'll be back in two days, and then you come over to my house and we'll go to church."

"Yes, ma'am," he said. He turned and went inside, and Mary Bet lifted the reins and turned her buggy around and headed home.

~⊃ CHAPTER 27 C~

1918

THE STEEL RAILS curved away to the east, away from the Blue Ridge and toward the gentler, rolling land of home. The sheriff stood beside the track, listening and looking, trying to re-create entire something that had happened here many years ago. That day had been cold and autumnal, much like today, the trees stark and bare, the ground high in brown grass and goldenrod, with sunbursts of yellow sneezeweed and no good path for walking except the track.

And now the sheriff did something she'd never dreamed she would. She reached down and lifted the hem of her long black skirt and began walking right down the middle of the track. So what if her driver was up there leaning against the tin lizzie, watching her with curiosity, wondering if she were in her right mind? The crossties were a little far apart for her stride, so she had to step on the gravel in between, her heavy lace shoes alternately crunching and stepping up, crunching and stepping up. Dew beaded the late-blooming buttercups brave enough to grow in the gravel at the very edge of the track, and the tarry smell of creosote from the crossties rose in the early morning air.

He'd been walking east, her brother. Why?

She had never done anything so foolish, she thought, as she picked her way over the crossties. Her driver had warned her against walking down through the thickets to the track, had offered to help her, but she had to be alone here with a clear, quiet mind. If her brother had done it then she could too. What was he thinking as he walked along here? Was he thinking of her? Of his girl? Of his family, dwindled down to so few? Or was his mind clear of noise, clear of any fear or guilt or sense of responsibility to anyone on earth?

There was nothing beyond but a few shacks, and a store that was new since then. No reason to come out here that the sheriff could see. She remembered the local police saying something about students taking walks just for exercise, but while it was true her brother was always one for long walks to think his own thoughts and see what he could with his sharp, cunning eyes, there were other places back in town he could have chosen for walking. Was he walking just to tramp along in the direction of home, though home lay a hundred and fifty miles away, the crossties like an endless ladder one could lose oneself in climbing?

If she could figure out this one thing, perhaps all the rest would make sense. If she could find out the reason and meaning behind one tragedy, all the others might open up to her like a curse lifting at last and the sun shining through sorrow . . .

She'd come at this time knowing there was a morning train— she had to know what it felt like from right here. That was more important than anything in the world she could think of.

Could he feel it coming?

What she didn't care to think about was what she wanted the answer to be. Of course she wanted there to be no vibrations, though that wouldn't explain why he had not constantly looked around to see what was coming. She scanned along the edges of the track as if there might still be something of his, some last token—a handkerchief she might recognize, or a torn piece of his sleeve, some clue to what happened here. She could see that his foot couldn't have gotten stuck in the rails. Did he have an enemy nobody knew about? She wished she had made this journey earlier, but so many things had gotten in the way . . .

. . . The train was coming. She saw the signal flash at the road crossing far down the track, heard the bell clang before there was any hint of a train. She looked behind her. Nothing but empty track. She fought against the urge to get off. Another step into the gravel, and then up onto the next gummy crosstie. Then onto the gravel. Again, she looked around. Nothing. She kept going, straining her ears for the terror that was coming behind her as sure as the sun. It was coming but there was no sound. She was deaf to everything around her, even the bell that must be clanging again down the track—for she could see the red light flashing. Her mind was filled with a crashing sound, as if the mountains behind her were at last crumbling and rushing in waves to the sea.

She heard her driver yelling before she heard the train. Then as if from a long-forgotten dream came a searing, urgent whistle, the high clang of bells, and finally a shuddering rumble. And still, as she turned now and stepped off the track and into the dusty weeds, the track was empty where it curved into the side of a hill and disappeared. She could have walked on a minute or two—surely there was time, if one wanted to get up to . . . She looked down both sides of the track trying to find some goal—a trail leading up the embankment, a landmark of some sort. But one side was too steep for easy walking and the other was even more dense with Queen Anne's lace and pinwheel sumac trees. Maybe this had not been the exact place after all.

And then it was upon her, the steam billowing from the smoke-stack. The bell clanged again, and the higher bell from the crossing down the track. Sixteen years ago there would've been no lights and bells at the road crossing. Nothing but the striped whistle post and, facing the road, a cross.

She stood well away from the track, weeds over her ankles, catbrier clawing her hose. The train blared past, the freight cars flashing by with a terrible scissoring sound of steel on steel. A cloud of grit and soot was stirred up along the tracks, and Mary Bet pulled her silk shawl up to cover her face. There were fifty-two cars. Then, as the train rattled on down the track, she imagined the scene sixteen years ago. The train would've stopped just a little way beyond where she was standing, the engineer springing out and running back to see if there was any hope of saving the young man's life. Then the call for medical help, and shortly thereafter a small crowd of onlookers and a carriage for an impromptu ambulance. By then, of course, if she remembered the story correctly, he was gone, and they would've all known it. She went back up the track to the little game path she'd followed from the car. "Let's go up the road yonder," she told her driver.

"Yes, ma'am," he said, his white eyes and yellow teeth like screams in the dark burnt blackness of his face. She didn't know many people as black as this man—maybe Morganton had a population of people from some place known for that . . . you couldn't call it a color so much as a condition. Light on his skin, she imagined, would be swallowed up like snow falling into a pond.

"I want to see what those houses are up there," she said, looking at him for an answer. She retied her shawl around her neck. "What are they?"

"I don't know, ma'am," he said, shaking his head, his hair cob-webbed with gray. He moistened his oddly thin purple lips and said, "They was a roadhouse yondah." He stopped and stared off toward the shacks, as if waiting to be invited to continue.

"What kind of roadhouse?"

"Young folks'd come there to drink and dance and carry on. White and colored. Man got shot there one time."

"What for?" the sheriff asked, her face wrinkling up. Nosing out human folly and indiscretion was not something she enjoyed doing in her spare time, especially in another county.

"A card game, they said. But probably they was a woman in it somewhere. Always is. I been in there. Then it burned, and they closed it down."

"Let's go have a look," she said. They got in the car and the driver headed back out toward the main road, which was the only way around to the side street where the shacks stood. He pulled up beneath a spreading oak, its yellowing leaves fluttering silently.

"I don't reckon it's safe to go in there," the driver said, opening the door. "Floor's liable to collapse."

Mary Bet alighted and took a look at the roadhouse. There was a wide front porch, the ends of the planks nail-sprung and curled up, some of them. The windowsills unprotected from rain sagged, all the windows appeared broken, and strips of white paint hung like scales on the clapboard, with nothing but climbing vines to hold them. Old ruined things had never appealed to her. Death and decay she cared not to dwell on; you lived with them like you lived with the turning of the seasons from one year to the next. An owl hurrooed out in the woods.

The sheriff turned to the driver and said, "Do you remember hearing about a deaf boy getting hit on the tracks along here? A young man from the deaf-and-dumb school?"

The man's eyes fixed her like beams of white light, then shifted to some point in the woods as he thought. "I've heard about more than one deaf person getting hit on these tracks. They can't hear the train coming, and they still walk down there, risking life and limb, just to save time. They only save time getting to heaven."

"This was about sixteen years ago," Mary Bet said. She studied the man. "You said you lived not far from here, so I was a-wondering."

"That's right, I live a mile by the crow, next to Muleshoe Creek." He gazed off in that direction, pulled at his navy blue necktie. "I think I do recollect a boy around nineteen and two. Because my daddy died in nineteen and one, just after that big storm that flooded the house. And somebody was killed up here after that, or before it, I disremember exactly."

The sheriff nodded and then headed up the overgrown path to the ruined roadhouse. There were flat places where flagstones had lain until, she guessed, being stolen. Given time, people would steal anything that wasn't nailed down. But there were still people she could trust to act like they ought to. Some people could be fooled by those closest to them, but not she. But if that was the case, then what was she doing out here by the railroad tracks in Morganton? If she understood her own people, her own beloved brother, why was she standing on this creaking porch that could cave in any second?

THEY WENT TO Camp Coetquidan in Brittany for artillery training, working sixteen hours a day, except Sundays. It took two weeks for the actual guns to arrive, and it became a great joke among the men that the French field artillery had done wonders, considering they had no guns. Then a shipment of brand-new French seventy-fives arrived, slim and camouflaged, and the men were eager to fire them. They were as different from the American three-inchers as an English saddle from a Western, but the men were quick to learn. Their instructor, a brisk little man named Lieutenant Gallimon, praised them in the classroom and on the target range, trotting from one gun to the next.

Then the horses came, 1,106 in all. But they didn't seem as strong as American horses, and the rumor was that they could not withstand the work because they were pampered, living indoors and wearing fur robes and waterproof blankets. And as the summer wore on they began contracting pneumonia and dying by the score. What made it worse was the French slat-wagon, a heavy, cumbersome affair that was forever getting stuck in the mud. The men called them horse killers. But most of the other French equipment was good.

There were French ration carts and water carts, but the rolling kitchens were American. Leon got to know these kitchens better than he knew his own house out in the country north of Williamsboro. He had four cooks, none of them from Haw, but all of them decent men, and he was pretty sure he could have the best detail in the regiment by inspiring his cooks to outperform the other seven batteries. He had a hundred and eighty-one mouths to feed and, at least for now, two rolling kitchens to do it with. So much of army life was about numbers and time, he had quickly realized, and if you could keep ahead of the numbers in the allotted time you could manage your job reasonably well. But Leon wanted to do more than just manage. Already the men were pleased to be back on American beef and bacon, beans, and bread with jam. They were even more pleased when Leon began going out on "chow details" into the surrounding villages, and returning with French bread, eggs, cheese, *vin rouge* and *vin blanc*, cognac, and sometimes even fresh vegetables.

When the other batteries heard about it, they began sending out their own scouting parties, and it became quite a contest among outfits to see who could procure the finest provender.

"You know you're ruining our men," Captain Pugh told Leon one day.

"I know, Captain," Leon said, smiling, "but they love it. And you never know what we'll be eating tomorrow." It became a favorite phrase, and then a guiding philosophy. Feed the men well whenever you can. "You can't live on hard bread and corn willie."

His best cook was a man named Corn Koonce from up in the

mountains. He had a terrible weakness for the *vin rouge*, but Leon forgave him because he'd figured out omelets and French soups. They would sit around after dinner smoking cigarettes and telling stories, and there was always a nervousness in the air and an excitement as well, as news trickled in from the western front. It seemed to Leon that the men most outspoken about their eagerness to get there were the most afraid. But all of them, except a very few, wanted to hurry up with the training and keep pressing forward to whatever climax or disaster awaited, because nobody knew what it was and yet they all sensed that what they were most afraid of was their own unknown nature.

They would belch and shout after a particularly good dinner, and then the guilt would set in when somebody wondered aloud what the men in the trenches were eating. Then, since they didn't want to imagine the trenches in great detail, they'd talk about what they'd already done. "Tell us again what you told that preacher, Leon," somebody would say.

"I don't remember exactly," Leon would reply.

"Well, I do," Captain Pugh said, the night before they entrained for northeastern France. "I was there, so I'll tell it. We'd heard about this little country church out east of Durham, and some of the boys wanted to go there one Sunday. When we got there, Leon said it made him feel right at home because it was just like his own church. And the preacher, a Methodist preacher if I'm not mistaken, started going on about how the army was a den of corruption and how the young men who enlisted were blinded into false patriotism."

"They serve a false god," Leon imitated. "They fight overseas so they can come back ruined in mind, body, and spirit."

"Go on and tell it, Leon," the captain said. The men, a dozen or so, sitting on camp stools in the officers' tent, smoking and drinking, urged him on as well.

"No, you're doing fine."

"So Leon sat there fidgeting and stewing, and I could tell something was the matter, because I was sitting just behind him. And then I reckon he couldn't take it any longer, and he stands up and says, 'I'm sorry to interrupt you, Mr. Cockerel, but I have something to say about the army and I'd be happy for anybody who cares to hear me to stick around.' Of course, everybody, including the preacher, stayed, and Sergeant Thomas here told them that he thought patriotism was no sin atall, that it was in fact close kin to religion itself."

"You tell 'em, Leon!" one of the men said. "We ain't so bad, are we, gentlemen?"

"Naw," came a lieutenant's reply, "we're as good as the next people, as good as sheep."

"Then," the captain went on, "then, he said it was a shame the army should be accused of breeding vice, and that if the church felt that way they ought to see about providing a remedy for the evil instead of trying to keep men from performing their patriotic duty by enlisting. He said, 'I'm thirty-three years old, too old for the draft, but I enlisted. I'm as good a man as anybody here, and I don't expect to be any the worse when I get out of the army. And anybody that says so is guilty of slander.' His exact words: 'guilty of slander.'"

"And then what?" asked one of the more by-the-book officers.

"Well, the preacher was routed. He went off, and he never came back. And the church had to find a new preacher."

"And now," said the lieutenant, "Leon has no choice but to live the model life. That's why he can't drink and cuss and chase mademoiselles." He winked at Leon, who drained the last of the *vin rouge* from his tin cup, but refused to take the bait.

"No, I'm not much on swearing," Leon said. "My daddy played cards and drank, but I have a lady friend who doesn't much care for it. Her grandfather pretty near ruined himself with drink."

The lieutenant shook his head. "Not even your wife, and you can't get away from her here."

"Maybe that's *why* I can't," Leon said, and the men laughed. But he wished he hadn't brought her into it.

August 22
Camp de Coetquidan
Guer
Morbihan Province
France

Dear Miss Mary Bet,
We ship for Toul tomorrow, so I may not be able to write you again for some time. We've enjoyed exploring the old town of Rennes, about 30 miles from here, which you can get to on a narrow railway for 25 cents. It seems that every town around here has a very pretty church or cathedral, and the one in Rennes has the most beautiful stained glass I believe I've ever seen.

I wouldn't be honest if I didn't say I was excited about Toul and what adventures lie in wait for us there. The truth is that we're also a little nervous. I don't want you to worry about us, though, just to know that you are in my thoughts. This has to be a short letter because I was up late with the cooks, giving the boys a big feed before we ship out tomorrow. It's late here, so I know you're already in dreamland and I hope dreaming happy and peaceful dreams.

With love and best wishes,
Sincerely,
LST

They were two days getting to Toul, in boxcars, forty men or eight horses to the car. They slept in shifts on the rough wood floor, jostling in the dark, the smells of men and animals thick in the stale air. For the first time they could see that they were in a nation at war as they passed mile after mile of munitions factories, aerodromes, and vast artillery parks, and they began hearing, faintly over the racket of the train, the low thumps of heavy guns. At the stops the sound was unmistakable.

They passed trains sidetracked at little field hospitals, tent cities, and men unloading wounded soldiers. And the shelling grew louder the farther east they traveled. They were heading to the front at last.

Leon thought that he had never known such happiness, such purity of purpose and joy in the company of his fellow man. They were singing boisterous, jubilant songs as they arrived in Toul. It was a beautiful sunny afternoon, and the sky was buzzing with Boche planes, the black crosses on their wings more vivid even than they had imagined. They watched in amazement as an antiaircraft battery felt out a plane, and they gave a collective sigh of disappointment as it droned away unharmed.

There was some confusion about the billeting for the night. The villages around Toul were already full with other units, and even though Leon's regiment had sent horse feed and rations in advance to one of the villages and much negotiation in high-school French had appeared to promise decent accommodations, the regiment was commanded to camp on the road outside town, finding what shelter they could. The men took it well. It was all part of army life, and, anyway, they were so close they could smell the front.

Leon made sure his men had all they could eat, especially of bacon and beans, and, his big surprise, an apple betty made with fruit they'd brought from Coetquidan. From now on it was to be canned rations. They rested a few hours, until darkness inked the eastern sky, and an eerie quiet settled over the men as the light faded in the west. At pitch dark they began hiking north and east.

They climbed for hours, up through the Forêt de la Reine, until they came to a clearing that afforded a view some twenty miles wide. It was a sight so magnificent and stirring Leon was sure he would never forget it. The front at last. On the far horizon rockets shot into the black sky, and now and then a flare would arc up, warning of a trespasser in no-man's-land. Sometimes, only a few miles away, the brilliant flash of a nearby battery would boom and rumble the ground, but the steady noise was the distant thunder of the real front, like the sound of drums the size of ponds. And as they marched, paced by the wagons and limbers and caissons— the horses, unperturbed in their dumbness, steadily rattling their harnesses—the men knew what it was to feel at once thrilled and terrified. There was little talking.

The trucks and wagon trains and men moved with no light, not even cigarettes, a long black snake sliding through the dark. Gone too were the usual blaring horns of the heavy vehicles. Only once that first night did they hear a distant Klaxon, and they knew it was a gas scare but they didn't know if it was real. At the edge of the forest, in the shelter of tremendous oaks and beeches, they pitched their pup tents. "If I can sleep here," one of Leon's tentmates said, "I can sleep anywhere."

"I'm so tired," Leon said, "I could sleep standing up."

They spent thirteen days on the edge of the forest, and though the batteries went into action, it was a kind of seasoning period, allowing the regiment to taste battle from a safe distance. They even retreated farther into the woods for better cover, and when the rains came in the second week the forest roads became a bog, swarming with fifteen hundred soldiers and a thousand horses. They'd finally discovered a source of water that wasn't entirely punk, though it still had to be chlorinated. Too many men had already gone down with terrible retching illnesses. Dehydrated water was what they called the chemical stuff, and it was barely palatable in sugared coffee. But the men had the comfort of a YMCA hut with hot water and soap for showering, and, even better, a Salvation Army house where two stout, merry beauties baked the best pies and doughnuts the men had tasted since leaving home. And sometimes there were bowls of Hershey's Kisses.

"War's not as bad as Sherman said it was," Leon remarked one morning to the captain after breakfast.

"Don't count your chickens, Sergeant," the captain warned. "I expect we'll look back on this time like it was home."

Leon nodded. "I expect you're right," he said. "It's just that I tell my boys things like that to keep their spirits up."

∿ CHAPTER 28 ᗄ

1918

T HE DOOR OF the roadhouse stood slightly ajar. Mary Bet could make out the words "orgie tonite" and "jazz" and some initials. Would he have come here to a place where there was loud music and liquor, and people who might make fun of him? Would he have brought his girl here, or might he have come here to meet someone, a hearing girl? He'd liked music, the vibrations, the sense of motion he got from his hand on the piano. If she could picture clearly those last days and hours, she could, in her mind at least, get to him and warn him away from the tracks, away from whatever was urging him on to his own destruction. A lizard glinted in a shard of sunlight on the window frame, and disappeared through a crack. She suddenly had the feeling that this had not been a bad place, a den of vice and iniquity, but a place where lovers could escape to, and she felt herself relent a little. People younger than she had met here—yes, black and white, as hard as that was to believe—not to sin, but because they had to cleave to each other in a lonely world.

She went back outside and told the driver to take her to the courthouse. On the way over she opened her compact to adjust her hair.

"Wait here," she told the driver as she got out. "I don't expect to be long." She would speak to the sheriff on business—introduce herself and tell him she was up paying a visit to the state hospital. She knew that you couldn't just say what you wanted, because most men would find some way to jolly you out of it if they didn't want the bother. You had to play their own game—be friendly, in no particular hurry, and then firm of purpose.

She was pleased that the courthouse here was not quite as impressive as Haw County's. It had an ornate cupola, and the pediments and pillars were fine too, but the whole thing looked like a miniature of what she was used to. Perhaps because the green around this one was bigger. She straightened her shoulders, put on her most businesslike look, and strode up the walkway.

Inside, she was directed down the hall to the sheriff's office. The doors here were heavy and substantial with titles printed in bold block letters. Back home, there were no titles. They had more state money here, with the hospital and the school for the deaf. She hesitated, took a breath, and knocked on the door.

Nobody answered, so she went in. A mousy woman wearing thick glasses, her hair pulled back to her scalp line and caught in a tight bun, sat hunched over a magnifying glass reading a typed document. She reminded Mary Bet of what she herself had been like, would end up being again after her term expired. The woman's desk was neatly arranged, papers stacked in a wire basket, rubber stamps lined up just so. On the wall behind, above a black iron safe, hung framed portraits of Woodrow Wilson and the new governor, while another wall was occupied by a bookshelf and a telephone, its brass bells staring out like breasts. Mary Bet almost laughed, imagining what this woman would've made of the office back home—the old governor staring down from the wall, papers and books littering desks and floors, last year's calendar getting mixed up with this year's.

She rapped her knuckles on the door, and finally the woman looked up. Mary Bet drew herself erect, letting the woman take her in—the tilted hat and half-veil, the long sable coat, the purple scarf fastened in front with a silver brooch. She introduced herself and asked if the county sheriff was in.

The woman repeated what she'd just heard, then, the words sinking in, a light came to her eyes and she said. "Oh, you're the one from over in Haw they put in while your sheriff was away."

Mary Bet eyed the woman, judging her to be a good ten years older than she, and said, "I am. I'm sheriff until there's an election, and if I run and win I'll still be sheriff."

Now the woman pulled back, and a little smile of admiration broke out around the corners of her pinched mouth. "Wouldn't that be something?" she said.

The woman suddenly remembered her place and said to Mary Bet, "I'll go tell Mr. Upchurch you're here." Then, sotto voce, "He's not busy today."

Mary Bet took a seat in a wooden armchair and waited for her counterpart, trying to think of him as a counterpart instead of a man with a badge. What was she, really, but a deputy, a clerk authorized by the county to fill in until a real sheriff could be put in office? But she had solemnly sworn to support, maintain, and defend the Constitution of the United States and to execute the office of sheriff to the best of her knowledge and ability, so help her God. Away from home, she was a young woman—at best, a lady with a sterling reputation—but she expected to be treated like any visiting dignitary. Just let Mr. Upchurch try to shift her around here—she'd handle him, so help her God.

She felt as if she were embarking on a journey that she had meant to take long ago, and that she had caught the last train leaving the station. Whatever she uncovered, she felt that she must know, or be forever stuck in some waiting room, while life went on all around her and the bitter taste grew stronger. If she found nothing, she would return home satisfied. As soon as she had this thought, she knew that she was only fooling herself. What she'd already found had brought her this far. The note: "I have make a terrible mistake," the ambiguity of "have make" tearing at her, standing halfway between the past and the present as though challenging her to believe he'd intended to say exactly that.

The clock on the wall ticked and the quarter hour chimed, and still Mr. Upchurch kept her waiting. The mousy woman came back and said that the sheriff would be out in a few minutes and asked her if she'd like some coffee. Mary Bet shook her head, her lips pressed together. She didn't much care for coffee or any stimulating drink. She didn't see the point in being stimulated beyond what you already were—if you were tired you should go take a rest. Alcohol—that was a different thing. It could make people say things they ordinarily wouldn't. She folded her gloved hands in her lap and waited.

Presently, the secretary stood and said that Sheriff Upchurch would be happy to see Mary Bet now. She stood and followed the woman to an inner office, where a large man with a large empty holster stood studying some papers in the light of a sash window that gave onto a shrub-enclosed courtyard. The sheriff, standing before a massive rolltop desk, looked up from his papers and said, "Ah, Miss Hartsoe, it's a pleasure. I've heard so much about you." He had a wen the size of a grape on one side of his forehead, and a thick brown mustache that looked as neatly combed as his hair. He bowed his head and indicated an armchair for Mary Bet to sit in. "Looks like we might get some of that rain we've been needing," he said, taking a seat and glancing out the window. "How've y'all fared over there?"

"Tolerable," she said. She decided to get right into her business here. "Mr. Upchurch, I had a brother who was killed on the train tracks outside of town here sixteen years ago. He was brought to the sheriff's office, where your predecessor got a coroner to declare him dead. I wondered if you could show me the paperwork on that case?"

Mr. Upchurch had been listening with an open mouth, which he now closed. "Well," he said, trying to collect himself. He leaned back in his chair and sighed, his big belly rising and falling. "Well, I don't know anything about that. Sixteen years ago, you say?"

"Yes," Mary Bet said.

"Sheriff Meacham would've filed that report, and he's been at the state hospital for a long time, so he wouldn't recollect anything about it."

Mary Bet started to tell him that her own father was at the same hospital, but it was never something she told strangers, never talked about with anyone, unless they asked, and she didn't see how it could help her here. She decided to play poker with Upchurch, let him go on and explain where the paperwork was.

He rubbed his chin and regarded her a moment, and she merely smiled. "What were you looking for, exactly?"

"I want to see what it says about cause of death and time of death. It bothers me that I've never seen that report." She realized the only way she'd get anything here was to relieve his suspicions and lay everything out for him to see. "It bothers me that I've never understood what caused him to be walking along those tracks like that and then not even feel the train a-coming."

Mr. Upchurch nodded now, his second chin pouching. He stood and went to a wooden filing cabinet in a corner of the room. He opened and closed two drawers, then at the third he pulled out a large manila file folder and began thumbing through the contents. "Dr. Bone may have his own reports. I don't know how long he keeps them. But they're probably less detailed than what we have here. Here we go, we're onto the right year now. Deaths. What was the month?"

"November."

"All right. Demsey, Given, Hartsoe. Siler. Here 'tis."

At his name, Mary Bet's heart flipped. Here he was, filed away for sixteen years, and might've disappeared from the record altogether if Burke County had not been so careful. The thin pages were bradded together into an inch-thick sheaf, and Upchurch was folding them over for easy viewing, reading as he did so, when he paused. "You're not going to do anything with this, are you?"

"What do you mean?" she asked.

"Well, I don't know. You're not going to bring a case against us, are you? Heh, heh," he laughed.

"I don't reckon I'd have any cause to." She reached over and took the sheaf from him and read the report like she was drinking water after a long hot day. The report was typed, with signatures by Sheriff John Meacham and Dr. J. Trimble Bone. Her brother's name appeared at the top of the report. She gulped in the text and its significance: "Cape Fear and Yadkin Valley Railroad . . . Turkey Run crossing approx. 1 mile southeast of town . . . Siler Hartsoe, 20-year-old student at the North Carolina School for the Deaf . . ." And then the words that swam up from the page and into her brain: "Accidental Death, poss. Suicide."

"What does this mean?" she asked, showing Mr. Upchurch the line.

He shook his head. "It means there was no way to determine what happened."

"But why would they list suicide if they had no reason to suspect it?"

Again Mr. Upchurch shook his head, glancing at Mary Bet and then down to his desk. "I don't know, Miss Hartsoe. Honestly, I wasn't there. I can tell you that since I've been sheriff, lots of people have committed suicide in Burke County—something around seventeen—and three of them were on the railroad tracks."

"Were any of them deaf?"

"Not that I remember."

"I just don't see why they'd write possible suicide, not having anything to go on."

"Could've been a lot of explanations. I'll tell you the truth, I don't remember that case. I was thirty-one years old then and living with my daddy on his farm up near Turnip. But they used to have deaf people getting hit on the tracks regular, until they macadamized the road out to the fairgrounds."

"But the fairgrounds is north of town, isn't it?" Mary Bet asked.

"Yes, they used to walk the tracks partway up there and then cut through on a trail. They'd go up there to the carnivals, and there's a place where folks like to picnic."

"But would they ever have gone east?"

"There was a roadhouse down there until it burned long about five or six years ago. Maybe he was going down there. You must've come across cases like this where it's not clear what happened. How do you fill in reports like that?"

"We don't speculate on what might've happened," she replied, "unless there's a good reason for it."

"Well, I don't either," he said, pulling his shoulders back. "But I can't tell you about Sheriff Meacham. They say in his last year—a year before this event here—" he tapped the report, "he was very forgetful."

Near the bottom of the report, the words "killed instantly" had been scratched out and "deceased on site" penned in above. "Why does it say this?" Mary Bet asked.

"Probably he was still alive when the conductor got to him." The sheriff hesitated, tucked a thumb into the pocket of his open vest, then said, "Maybe even after the doctor got there."

"I thought he was the coroner."

"He's both. I expect in this case, he died shortly before or after the coroner arrived, and that's why they didn't take him straight off to the hospital, you see. That's not uncommon. And you needn't worry about the suffering—he was probably completely unconscious."

Mary Bet was not reassured, but she would not let herself picture her brother in agony, trying to live. Instead she thought of her father—all along he knew what was in this report and had never told her. It still didn't make complete sense. "I can't understand it," she said. "Why would somebody go walking on the tracks like that and not get off?"

"Could be he was distracted about something, or he didn't care one way or the other what happened to him. But I know if a person doesn't want to live, he'll find a way to die. There was a fellow here a while back that tried to cut off his own head with an ax, and when that failed he threw himself off the railroad bridge at low water. Took him a week to die. Should've been at the insane asylum. Many's tried up yonder, but they keep them from it, mostly. I'm telling you this because you seem to be in need of something, but I'm afraid I can't give any more than stories."

Mary Bet started to ask him what could've distracted her brother, but of course he wouldn't know. "I have to make a visit to the state hospital," she told him.

"I don't expect you'll find much out there. Old Meacham's not even likely to know he was sheriff. I wouldn't bother if I was you."

"I'm not going to see the sheriff," she said.

~◯ CHAPTER 29 ◯~

1918

S HE BID THE sheriff farewell and got back in her hired car to go over to the hospital. It was hard to believe that only this morning she was waving out the window to Flora and the others who had come to see her off. During the whole trip she tried to picture her father, but she was afraid of what he might look and sound like this time, and afraid she might not even recognize him, nor he her.

And now she had come away from the tracks convinced that Siler had killed himself because he was every bit as crazy as their father, and more. But she had to see if her father could shed any of his fading light on it. The driver pulled into the long, tree-lined drive of the hospital's grounds, and she remembered the peaceful feeling it had inspired the first time she visited. And yet as they approached the massive hand-cut gray stone building with its august clock tower and symmetrical wings, its huge doors and small fenced-in exercise yards, she recalled that feeling of being trapped inside, of feeling desperate for air.

She walked the long corridor to her father's ward and opened the glass-paneled swinging door. The young nurse sitting behind the desk was new since Mary Bet's last visit. Mary Bet introduced herself and asked if this was a good time to go see her father.

"He's just had his supper," she said. "He should be reading in his room."

"Reading?" This was new. He had not picked up a book in years.

The nurse flushed and smiled in a confused way. "Yes," she said. "Well, he likes to have a book with him wherever he is."

Mary Bet nodded and went on down the hall to her father's room. It was the same room he had been in since he moved here, but there was now another bed with another patient. Two years earlier, Cicero had asked if he might have a roommate, and after a couple of failed attempts, the staff had found a gentleman of about Cicero's age, a former miller from Asheville who was blind in one eye and had lumpy arthritic hands. The last time Mary Bet visited he'd said very little, except every now and then he'd stirred in his chair, where he sat covered by blankets, and murmured, "The good Lord looks after the child."

She went in and greeted them both. "Hello, Daddy," she said. "Hello, Mr. Cane." They were sitting side by side in Adirondack chairs, the tilt of the seat and back providing little incentive to get up. Cicero held a book, his glasses far down his nose, his lips moving. He glanced up, then kept on with his reading. Mr. Cane, who looked more withered and shrunken since last time, his white beard more patchy, stared at her and smiled. He said, "I can't see a thing."

"Maybe it's the light," she said. "I'll see if I can get them to adjust the lamp in here." She glanced up at the sconce on the wall and saw that it was lit by an electric lightbulb and so could not be adjusted.

Mr. Cane shook his head. "They won't do it." Then he stared out into the hall and said, "I can't see a thing."

"There's not enough daylight to read, Daddy," she said. "Do you want me to read to you?"

Cicero looked up at his only daughter, his eyes bleared and glassy, his neck a ruin of cords and turtle skin. He said, "I had nine children, and all of them perished in a fire."

Mary Bet shook her head. She perched on the edge of the closest bed, its white counterpane draped neatly over the end. The men wore overalls, because belts and suspenders were not allowed, nor were any sharp or heavy objects, and so the room was a soft, muted nest of hollows and curves and lines that met in distant corners. Even the windows, high on the wall and as vertical as castle loopholes, were part of the illusory effect, their thick, unopenable panes casting a dull yellow light as though from a distant sun. Heavy drapes could be drawn to adjust the light. She felt suspended in time here, as if she were at the far edge of the world where the normal rules of physics did not apply, and to keep herself from the despair of the place she had made her visits shorter over the years. Oh, people told her, your father won't care either way. But he does care, she thought, he does.

"Daddy, it's me," she said, "Mary Bet, your daughter. Do you want me to get you a pillow for your back?"

He shook his head.

"Daddy, I'm sorry I haven't been out lately. My work at the courthouse has kept me busy. Are you getting my letters?" It was just something to say; she knew the nurses read him her weekly letters.

"They told me you were coming," he said.

Then he knew who she was. She felt encouraged enough to say, "Yes, I wanted to see you. I wanted to ask you something important." His eyes caught hers and widened a moment as though in recognition—though of her meaning, her identity, or simply her existence, she was not sure. "I wanted to ask if you remember me telling you about a girl Siler was going with, a girl named Rebecca Savage. She was Jewish, and he was afraid of telling you. Did he ever say anything about her to you?"

Cicero shook his head. He slumped into his shoulders and seemed to retreat back into himself, no longer making the effort to understand.

"It was a long time ago, Daddy. Sixteen years, but it's important to me, you see, because I think he may've thrown his life away. There was something he couldn't live with and I need to know what it was."

Cicero cleared his throat and tried to say something. Then, "That boy was the cleverest of all my children. He couldn't hear a sound, not even a train whistle right in his ear. His mother called him God's child. Not just deaf, though." Cicero regarded his brown-spotted hands, folded on the blanket covering his lap, as though marveling at their crepey texture, forgetting that he was old.

"Not just deaf?" She leaned forward so that she had to catch herself from slipping off the bed.

"The Lord saw fit to take all my children. I believe there was eight of them, or nine. In a fire. And I expect to go in a flood." He paused, rubbing his dry, withered lips together for moisture, his mouth sunken over nearly toothless gums.

"What was the matter with Siler," Mary Bet insisted, "besides his deafness?"

"I had a deaf boy, that's right. He was afflicted like me. He seemed all right, but he was troubled in his mind. Not until he was grown did I see it. I thought it was just his deafness. He cut himself with a saw, just stood there watching the blood on his arm like it was a red spring. I saw him do it, and I came to him and scared him off. He died on the railroad tracks." Cicero started moaning and rocking back and forth, gripping his upper arms, and now there were tears edging from his eyes.

The young nurse came in and stood in the doorway. "Is everything all right, Mr. Hartsoe?"

"I can't see a thing," Mr. Cane said. "I want some water."

"I'll get you some. Miss Hartsoe? Do you need anything?"

"We're fine," she said. She didn't want to upset her father, but if there was anything else he had to say, she wanted to know what it was. There might never be another such chance in her life. It seemed as though the suspended time of this place had suddenly budded open, like a moment expanding into a million smaller moments, each one of which contained a message of great importance. When she and Leon had kissed in the car, she had felt a similar opening up of time, a desire to fall into the place where nonexistence joined with existence, and all the lost moments that had surrounded her and tried to suffocate her with her nonexistence had finally given way and let her breathe as freely as when she was little and did not know that death was not the thing to fear, but memory.

She looked at her father, his mind all but annihilated, and she saw that that was something to be feared as well. The knowledge jerked her from the edge. *Remember this always*, she told herself. *Remember this as a gift, and don't throw your life away because of what you remember.* "Was he afraid, then," she said, "of losing his mind?"

Cicero shook his head. The nurse came farther into the room, twisting her hands together now as if undecided whether to intervene. Mary Bet ignored her.

"Do you think Siler was afraid, Daddy?"

"There were two named Siler. She wanted to do that. I didn't think it was a good idea, replacing one with another. And he was deaf, and I told her it was a judgment."

"It wasn't a judgment, Daddy. It was just bad luck. All of it, all the sickness."

"I'll just go get the doctor," the nurse said, and hurried out.

And then Mary Bet saw as through a membrane her father throwing the glass at his reflection, God yelling at God and pointing his finger, "Shut up," and all she could think to do was run out into the pasture and step between the rails of the fence and go into the woods where it was quiet in her head. There was a baby rabbit, and it sniffed her hand.

It was alive.

It was alive. But it could die.

There was a big rock beside the burrow. She picked it up with two hands and held it above the rabbit. Its ears twitched, and it sat very still. What was it afraid of? She held the rock high and dropped it. The rabbit made a little whimpering noise. It did not move, but it was still alive. She could see it breathing hard. And now she was more afraid than she had ever been in her life. She dropped the rock again, and again, and again. Each time she picked the rock up, she saved the rabbit and was amazed at what it could survive. Finally it made no more little noises. It had crumpled onto its side, and its eyes were closed.

She stared in awe at what she had done. She threw the rock into the high weeds and found some leaves to cover the rabbit with—because its mother had left it uncovered—and then she went running back up to her house, pausing every few steps to look around behind her. When she got to the pasture, she stepped through the rails and slowed to the slowest walk she could, and she thought that if she walked even slower she might never have to get back to her home and to her self.

It wasn't until that night that she cried. She thought she might choke on the tears, it was so hard to keep quiet; she coughed and her sister asked if she was all right, and she nodded in the dark and said, "yes," and then came the sound of O'Nora's heavy sleep-breathing and Mary Bet prayed quietly for God not to send her away to the Devil but to take her quick to heaven.

"I killed a rabbit," she said now to her father. He looked at her through glassy, uncomprehending eyes as though trying to fathom what she was saying. And suddenly she realized that all the years she had dammed back the memory she had been mistaken. She had thought she was eight and had connected the killing of the rabbit with the death of Ila and the memory of her mother dousing her father's head. But, no, she had been much younger.

"It was after Annie's death," she said. "I must've been five." Old enough to know better, she thought, but a much younger child than her mind had told her for so long. Why had she accused herself all this time? *Because I'm guilty of killing a living thing, and it doesn't matter how old I was.* And yet, hadn't she wanted to suffer more and more over the years, to make it a worse crime than it was? *There is nothing worse than hurting a defenseless creature, and then hurting it some more . . . and not wanting it to make another accusing noise on this earth, and knowing that I could silence it forever by pounding it with the rock until it stopped.*

Was it not pity that she had felt, had taught herself? Or was it only a primitive fear? Maybe they were the same thing at their roots. She could feel the tears hot on her face now, and she wiped them away and said, "Daddy . . ." She had started to ask his forgiveness. But she got off the bed and, kneeling by his side, took his hand. She knew it was pointless to tell her father anything at all, much less something as important as what she had to say. But of all the people in the world, he was the one she most needed to confide in.

"Daddy," she said, "didn't you want to punish God? I know you did. Didn't you ever just want to do back to him what he had done to you?"

Mr. Cane called out toward the hall in an agitated voice. "I can't see a thing."

"You can see fine," Mary Bet told him.

He glared at her, then softened and asked, "Will there always be water?"

"Yes, Mr. Cane," she said, "there will."

Cicero squeezed her hand and said, "Don't leave me just yet."

"I won't, Daddy," she said.

The doctor came in now—a tall, lanky man with sloped shoulders and a drooping face to match—followed by the nurse. Mary Bet rose to her feet and went over to introduce herself. "I want to thank you for taking such good care of my father," she said. "You might check and see if he has enough blankets. His feet get cold at night. And he might could use another pillow to prop up in bed."

The doctor nodded in agreement, giving the nurse a droll smile that said, "I'll let it go this time."

"Is he eating all right?" she asked. "He's lost two more teeth, looks like." The doctor assured her he was getting the proper nutrition, having his food mashed properly and fed to him, and that he was still walking up and down the hall without assistance. He wasn't getting outside so much anymore, because it seemed to upset him.

"Well," Mary Bet said, "I wish there was something y'all could do about that, because I think the fresh air would help him. But I know you're doing all you can." The doctor and nurse seemed like honest people, and in such cases it was always best to be complimentary and so encourage their better natures to prove you right.

The nurse said, "I think we could try him again now it's not so hot out. He won't tolerate the muffs, or anything on his hands. But we could try him again." The doctor nodded in agreement, and Mary Bet felt only a little guilty for showing up here just to order them around.

"Here's a necklace he made in crafts this week," the nurse said. "He's right proud of it, aren't you, Mr. Cicero?" She showed Mary Bet the string of what looked like long insect legs alternating with blue celluloid beads. "They make those by snippin' out oval shapes from magazines, then rollin' 'em up and shellackin' 'em. Then they string 'em with the beads, like 'at."

Mary Bet went to the window with the beads so that she could see them better. The sun was going down behind the swooping profiles of Tablerock and Hawksbill off in the far distance, and over to the left she could make out the central tower of the deaf school, rising above the trees. She heard a train coming, the low rumble just audible, with the tracks a mile away. Out there, just over the trees—that was where he had decided. For she told herself that it was in a moment that he had made the decision, no matter what he had been thinking about in the days before. It was but a moment.

That night in the tiny guest room, Mary Bet began writing a letter to Rebecca Savage. She didn't know the street address, of course, but Wilmington wasn't likely to hold more than one Rebecca Savage. What could she say to a person she'd never met, a person her brother may've loved more than anyone on earth? Could she say, "I don't know you, but when Siler died I thought I couldn't go on—I loved him more than I expect to love anybody again." Surely she could not say, "We have to trust in God's mercy. If he wants us to burn in hell for eternity, he'll let the Devil have us. If he wants to redeem us from hell, it's his choice. Everybody has a conscience and everybody has to be judged."

She wrote, "Dear Rebecca, I am writing to you because my brother . . ." She held the pen over the letter, wondering why it was so hard for her to write her brother's name, to put down on paper a name that, even in her mind, brought him back into this very room. She went on,

because my brother Siler spoke fondly of you the year before he died. I'm sorry I never got to meet you. I am the last of a family of nine children. My father is still alive, here at the state hospital where I am visiting and writing this letter. I've never been to Wilmington, but I imagine it's warmer there than it is up here, where it's mighty cool, even for October.

But that's not why I'm writing. I am writing to you because I wanted to know if my brother seemed worried or agitated the last few days before he died. His last letter home didn't seem out of the ordinary. I have to know if he was troubled, and I don't know who else to ask. I don't know if my father ever made any inquiries, and now he's too far gone in his mind to ask. Siler's teachers at the deaf school have left, except for one or two, and they don't remember anything unusual about his mood. Did he seem sad to you? Did he say anything to you about taking a walk along the tracks, and where he was going? I wonder if he was blaming himself for something, and trying to free somebody else from blame. If he was doing that for me, I'll accept it as a gift, but I feel I must know. If it was a private matter, maybe something between you two, I'll accept that too. But could you please just tell me what you can, even if you know nothing, can you write me and tell me that?

Yours sincerely,

Mary Bet Hartsoe

She thought of mentioning that she was sheriff, but decided she'd have more chance of a reply, and an honest one, if there was nothing official about the letter. She sealed the envelope and addressed it "Rebecca Savage, Wilmington, N.C."

The next morning Mary Bet went back up to her father's room and kissed him good-bye. "I love you, Daddy," she said. She could not remember ever having told her father she loved him, but the words came easily to her lips. Her father's eyes were vacant as he held her hand, not wanting to let it go. Mr. Cane reached over from his chair, and so she offered him her left hand, which he took in both of his. She had the feeling of being tethered by these two ancient men, lost and wandering in their minds.

"Good-bye," she said. Her father waved to her as she stood in the doorway. He was seventy-seven years old.

~⌒ CHAPTER 30 ⌒~

1918

IN THE FOREST, they were still a long way from the front line, but they slept with their gas masks beneath their heads. There were many false alarms, and Leon was amused at how the fellows so readily became a strange tribe of elephant-men. One night German shells shrieked overhead and an ammunition dump less than half a mile away burst into flames. It was shortly after this that something big began happening.

It was the first time in his thirty-four years that Leon realized he was unafraid. He was robust and vivid, when so many around him began to seem pale and scared and vague, as if they'd caught some disease that was slowly wasting them. They came to him to warm themselves on his cheer and good humor, and he never tired of dispensing it. At home, he'd resisted being the one to set the example for his two younger brothers, and after their father died—when Leon was fifteen—he became even more distant, as though to punish his father for dying and leaving him in charge. He did what was called for, but took no particular interest in his brothers and their concerns. They seemed content to become farmers just like their father, while Leon had a notion of doing something different; he wasn't vain enough to imagine he was after something more important, he simply was not interested in scratching a living out of the soil.

And then one day he'd had a spiritual conversion, though he didn't think of it that way, because it had nothing to do with church or God. To Leon, it was more a change of heart. He was twenty-two years old and still living at home with his mother and brothers, managing the farm until Sid, the middle boy, should become legally capable of running the farm on his own. In another year Sid would be twenty-one, at which point Leon planned to go off to Chapel Hill and earn a degree that would eventually lead to law school. Their mother had been battling illness for a number of years, leaving more and more of the farming business to her sons. Her hope was that Leon would marry, settle down on the farmstead, and leave off his idea of going to college.

There was nothing special about the day that Leon became a changed man. He was riding up from the lower field, where he'd been overseeing the digging of a new drainage ditch. The laborers he'd hired, both of them white men in their middle twenties, he'd known nearly all his life. They'd attended the same rural school he had, but had dropped out after sixth grade; it was unclear whether they knew how to read more than their own names. The sun was high overhead, hot for April, and Leon suddenly felt a twitch in his cheek, just as if somebody'd poked him with a piece of straw. He jerked around, half expecting to see some child down below, playing a joke on him. The horse plodded on.

One full stride. And one more. The skin on Leon's neck tingled. He knew what he was meant to do with his life.

He kept it a secret for more than a week, taking it out every so often to examine like a found gem. Then one evening at supper he announced that he was going to become a teacher. His brothers, husky boys who looked so much alike they were often mistaken for twins, glanced at each other with wry smiles, and, as if they'd exchanged some comment only they understood, kept on eating. His mother said, "What about lawyering?"

"No," Leon said. "It has to be teaching. And I might open up a school, to run just as long as the private schools. But there'd be no tuition, or almost none."

"Sounds like a good way to the poorhouse," his mother said.

But Leon didn't mind. It was another two years before he was able to get the money together for college and to turn the management of the farm over to his brothers. During that time he began at last to understand and love his brothers, no matter how different they were from himself. He felt as though he was in a hurry to teach them everything he knew about the plants and animals around about, the underground aquifers, the way the foothills rose into mountains to the west but dropped to the sandy, coastal plain east, how there was a great comet coming that would light up the night sky like day, why it was that a machine with wings and a man inside could fly—little things that he'd studied on and read about, but kept to himself as if it were arcane knowledge that only a privileged few should have. To his surprise and delight they actually listened; he knew because he sometimes heard them repeating what he'd said.

He went off to the university, and it didn't bother him that he was six or seven years older than his fellow students. He was at last on the path of his chosen life. One thing he knew very little about, that his brothers seemed far more advanced in, was women. He had only kissed two girls, one of them in Williamsboro after he lost a debate held by the Prolific and Erasmian Literary Society on the topic, "Resolved, that the Government of the United States has reached its Zenith." He'd won on the affirmative position, but was unconvincing on the negative. He hardly knew the girl, but she told him he was handsome and a fine orator. The letters he sent to her later, his heartsick love for her overflowing the pages, were never answered.

Until his early thirties, Leon thought of women as exotic curiosities, like stereoscopic photographs of the Sphinx and the Taj Mahal. They were best appreciated from a distance. He hadn't enjoyed sex until he met Ann Murchison, a well-to-do landowner's daughter from Cotten. He'd been surprised to find such an open, freethinking, modern woman, a real flapper, in Haw County. Shortly after he started seeing her, he met Mary Bet Hartsoe, who worked in the courthouse. He couldn't have said why, but he felt himself drawn to Miss Hartsoe, perhaps because though she was much like Ann Murchison, he knew she would never give herself to him the way Ann had. He felt more comfortable around her than excited, and he thought she was more beautiful and intelligent than any woman he had ever known.

Now on the western front, no one knew exactly what was happening, but for three days the roads were crawling with wagons, motorcycles, trucks, guns, tanks, and all the other modern machines of war, beside which the horses and long line of doughboys seemed incidental. The rumor was that a great push was on for Metz. But at any rate the army was in forward motion and the men could taste the excitement in the air. One afternoon Colonel Fox and his staff rode by Leon's camp, and the commander touched his open hand to his campaign hat. Leon saluted. He thought he'd never seen a finer, more dashing man, tall in the saddle and as confident as if he were out surveying his crops instead of moving his headquarters for an assault on the Hindenberg line.

Midnight. Leon and his buddies waited outside their tents, smoking, watching, sometimes saying a quiet word, but mostly listening. It was like waiting for the end of the world, or the beginning of time. "If the Huns get me," Koonce said, "it's all right, as long as I get to see this."

And then the ground began shaking, the trees rumbling as if they would come loose and topple. Night became day. The thundering and blasting was like the explosion of a thousand thousand furnaces. For four hours the hammering went on. The smoke and the earth-quavering noise and the smell of burnt sulphur were for a while a bright cocoon for Leon and his mates as they stood transfixed. This was the world's wound, and they were here to witness it and do what they could to see that history had a certain outcome and not another. They understood this without speaking it.

Around five o'clock the shelling stopped, and they also knew what this meant. Somewhere at the front, the infantry was preparing to rise from the trenches and advance over the shredded wires. Leon thought of Colonel Fox, and how if he ordered him to the front, he would happily go, would be proud of such an honor. Not until the shelling stopped did Leon and his friends realize it was raining.

Later in the morning, while Leon's cooks were preparing lunches to send forward in marmite cans, the prisoners began coming back. There were hundreds, maybe thousands, marching along toward the pens, young and old, looking oddly content. And then the American wounded. And carts bearing the dead. There were three dead in Leon's battery—a lieutenant, a corporal, and a private first class. All of them fine fellows. The private was from Haw, and Leon wondered when word would get home. He briefly thought of his mother and his brothers, who had been turned away because of a heart condition they hadn't known about—he felt sorry for them. And he thought of Mary Bet and hoped she sometimes thought about him.

The next day the entire regiment was on the move, north toward Thiaucourt. It was a monumental undertaking, the muddy roads seemingly designed to slow the progress of a thousand men and their overtaxed horses. The valiant beasts died by the score along the way, the sound of mercy killings ringing out every mile or so.

It was chilly and damp, and Leon began singing a song that Mary Bet had sung for him before he left for the training camp. She'd been embarrassed, saying she only liked to sing in a group. They were leaving the courthouse at the end of the day, and he pleaded with her to sing, telling her it would be something to hearten him in the coming months.

They camped in a valley and feasted on some cows and pigs that the Germans had left behind. Two cows joined the regiment, and were given their own gas masks. Captain Pugh took Leon and a few other favored men on a tour of the Germans' abandoned concrete dugouts. "Underground mansion," Pugh said, as they poked their heads into rooms that held feather beds, heavy tables and chairs, a grand piano, electric lights, hot and cold running water, a bowling alley. There was a dairy with gleaming tiled walls, a poultry yard, and a summer pavilion with chaise longues and paper lanterns hanging from a trellis.

Before it had hardly settled in, the regiment was moving again, propelled by an invisible motive that seemed to arise from within itself. On toward the Argonne Forest, the fields strewn with corpses and the lines harassed day and night by black-cross airplanes. "If we can just keep moving," Leon would say, for there was the illusion that they made easier targets standing still. That sickening rise-and-fall drone coming from somewhere off to the right or left, and nothing to do but keep rolling onward, offering what encouragement he could.

"Those mosquitoes won't hurt us, boys."

At one encampment, Leon and Corn Koonce went forward as usual with their ration cart. Everybody knew them, because Leon would always wave and have some snappy remark to make about how his food was the best in the regiment, better than anything in France. They made their delivery, and an MP directed them to use a different road back. It was dark.

"What you reckon they'll make of prune apple pie?" Corn said.

"They'll think it was the best they ever ate," Leon said.

They went on a ways, for an hour or more, the sound of shelling appearing to grow louder. The only light they had was from the clouds, sporadically lit by rockets and flares. "I don't know but what we're on the wrong road," Corn finally said. He sucked in his caved cheeks and put a hand to his stubble.

"Yep," Leon agreed. "The MPs don't know from one day to the next."

They kept jostling along, the horse as content to go toward the firing as away. There was one pitch of road solid enough to keep the wheels from getting mired. "I don't like the looks of it," Corn said.

"Ssh now, Corn, it'll be all right. Don't get all hollow-eyed. We'll run into somebody before long."

"That's what worries me."

"We've got these nice woods here."

"But over yonder's all clear, except the brambles. What do you reckon's on the other side of that rise?"

"I reckon it's a music hall, boys gettin' illuminated, and the prettiest girls you ever saw." A shell dropped so close, up to their right, that the horse flinched and stalled. Leon flipped the reins and they plodded on. He began chewing an old cigar. He hadn't been nervous until Corn got worried, and now Corn could relax knowing he'd stirred Leon up. Leon would have lit the cigar, except that Corn would worry even more about the light. As if anybody'd waste a shell on a ration cart.

They crested a little hill and found themselves in a vast bowl from which they could see the shelling at a low angle; the ground shook almost constantly. "I don't like this at all," Corn proclaimed.

On a little knoll off to the right stood the ruins of a stone house; beyond lay a desolate plain, with a row of stumps at the farthest edge, and in the light of a flare Leon could see another plain beyond. A doughboy emerged from the ruins. "What the hell're you doing here with that damned ration cart?" he said.

"I'm looking for my battery," Leon told him.

"Well, you won't find it here, and you won't be here much longer yourself. You're practically in no-man's-land."

"You got a match?" Leon asked. He wasn't about to make a dash for the rear to please a tough-sounding private.

The soldier handed him one, and Leon took his time. He asked the soldier for directions, then drove out into the rutted field, making the widest turn he could. Shells dropped to their right and left, the air in concussion. Corn held onto his hat. "You trying to give them something to shoot at?" he yelled.

"Those are our shells," Leon said. "They're not gonna hit us."

As they drove past the doughboy, standing on guard in the ruins, Leon saluted. The doughboy saluted back and watched as they headed off into the night. It was not until they were a mile up the road that Corn could bring himself to speak. He shook his head and guffawed to himself, and then he laughed so hard he vibrated from knees to chin. "Them's our shells," he repeated, "they ain't gonna hit us."

In late September the regiment went into position at the edge of the Bois d'Esnes in the Argonne Forest. Over the next two weeks, casualties were commonplace, and horses became fodder for the drive. "There won't be any left," Leon said one morning, looking sadly at a pile of carcasses, carted there by the remaining healthy animals. "It's a shame." But he let it go at that. There was no time for thought or sleep, let alone pity. He had a battery to feed, and the battery had a regiment to serve. And the regiment, shuffled from one division to another, lived only to fight.

Sometimes they slept on the ground, other times in cootie-infested shacks, but Leon always chose to be near his wagon and ration cart over whatever makeshift comfort the battery had found. He began to see clearly that his mission in life was to fuel his men. When he thought of home and his days as a classroom teacher, it was as though he were looking through a series of muddy windows that revealed a scene he could barely discern. The only real thought he had of home was of Mary Bet, and he composed mental letters lying in his bedroll, until he could no longer stay awake.

The days were filled with cooking and carting. As the Germans were pushed back, they seemed fiercer to retaliate, and Leon's rolling kitchen became the target of machine guns on a couple of occasions. Once a Boche plane picked him out when the cart was stuck in the mud and he and Corn were gathering stones to put beneath the wheels. Finally Allied planes found the Boche with tracer bullets, and Leon watched with admiration as the German aviator dipped and slipped and, at last, looped his way out of trouble and disappeared. He and Corn pulled the cart free and went on their way. Showing up with food on schedule, no matter how impossible the situation, and acting as if he'd just gone to the store for a bottle of milk—that became the joy of his life.

They came along a track beside a desolate field that had been plowed and replowed by so many shells it seemed there were more craters than solid ground. In one crater, a bloated rat was gnawing on a corpse that was still holding a Bible. A group of soldiers had just discovered a blue-eyed German lad of perhaps fourteen hiding in another of the yellow-green craters. Leon stopped his cart and watched as the leader tried to tell the boy to drop his rifle, but the boy was too afraid to let go. The American handed his own rifle to a fellow soldier and started forward, showing his palms, talking calmly. The boy raised his gun and fired. There was an explosion of gunfire. Leon and Corn watched as the boy's right half was ripped away below his shoulder, and then they moved on.

That night Leon learned that the American soldier was hit in the arm and was fine. He wrote to Mary Bet:

I don't have time for a full letter, just a quick note to say I am thinking of you, and I hope you are well and happy. Army life has its high and low points, that's for sure. One of the low points is the bellyaching some of the men do about the food, and how much better it is at home. I'll be home soon, because we're making good progress, and I don't mind if I never have to see another can of corned beef again. I won't stop here, because the mail doesn't go out for some time, but for now, I wish you the sweetest of dreams.
    Love,
    LST

He lay there for a while, seeing the face of the German boy. He knew he would never forget it; he wondered how many nights he would see the face, the vivid blue eyes.

~) CHAPTER 31 (~

1919

L EON'S FINAL LETTER came from the forwarding camp in
Le Mans, dated February 13, 1919:

Dear Miss Mary Bet,
Now at last I can write to you and catch you up with everything
that has happened. Well, perhaps not everything, because I don't
know if I could put it all in one letter. I look forward to sitting
down with you and having a good long talk. Shall we take a pic-
nic down to Mt. Jordan Springs? I can see us now, with a check-
ered blanket spread out beneath the elms and the water trickling
in the background. When I get home, the daffodils should be out,
and I'll pick you a bunch. I know I'm presuming a lot, saying that
you'll still be interested in riding out with me, but it helps me to
get through this last ordeal.
First, to go back to the war. I didn't explain properly about
how it ended on the morning of the Armistice. It seemed that just

the day before, we were getting showered by those infernal propaganda leaflets from Hun aeroplanes. I saved one to bring home. It says, "WHAT BUSINESS IS THIS WAR IN EUROPE TO YOU ANYHOW? You don't want to annex anything do you? You don't want to give up your life for the abstract thing, humanity. If you believe in humanity, save your own life and dedicate it to your own country and the woman who deserves it of you. If you stay with the outfit, ten chances to one all you will get out of it will be a tombstone in France." It was pure rubbish, I expect just as a last-ditch effort to stave off disaster.

On the morning of the Armistice the order to cease firing came just as we were loading the lunch buckets for the trenches. My right-hand man Corn Koonce and me started on forward with the ration cart, because the men had to eat no matter what. We didn't know what to believe because the firing was going on just like always, thundering and whistling and thumping. It turns out, the Boche were unloading everything they had, mostly mustard shells, and a few of our boys were gassed that morning, after the cease-fire orders had been handed down. Two in our regiment died. Well we got down past the first checkpoint and suddenly the guns stopped. It was the strangest thing after eleven weeks of unending noise, to hear nothing at all. And I mean nothing. It seemed like the world had stopped. Corn said something to me, and I couldn't even hear what he said sitting right beside me, everything was so quiet.

That night there was a celebration like I never expect to see again. Both sides were shooting off flares and star rockets, and there was no fear in them—just sapphires and emeralds bursting in the black sky. And we were singing and carrying on so, men getting illuminated on French wine stashed away for such an occasion. It's hard to explain how jubilant everybody was. We wouldn't have chosen to be anywhere else in the world.

Then we were three weeks clearing out all the mines and debris. Our unit had to patrol an area half the size of Haw County. After that we were on the march to Luxemburg, and how it rained! I remember one clear day and everybody was scrambling to get a bath and shave and clean clothes. But mostly we were hiking along past muddy shell-torn fields, demolished walls, tangles of barbed wire, and rows of dead trees. There were whole towns burned because the citizens didn't pay their levy to the Germans. We hiked so much and on such bad roads, it seemed like we went out of our way to cover every bad road in France. I'll never forget the sight of one bedraggled woman passing our entire column, pushing a baby carriage loaded with a two-week bread ration from the relief commission. She said she was walking 15 miles.

When we finally got to Belgium, it was like returning to civilization. There were nice, clean little villages that hadn't been scarred by the war. I'll wait until I get home to describe everything in Luxemburg, except to say that it was deluxe living after France. Lots of our boys made fools of themselves trying to talk with the local women in what little high school French and German they had. Despite the hard sledding with the language, there were temptations, but I and many in my outfit carried a picture in our minds if not our wallets of the women we loved. I didn't need a photograph to remind me of your face and your sweet voice and the touch of your hand. There were other amusements to occupy us, and things to worry us as well. The worst thing was that Capt. Pugh, a boon companion and the best battery commander one could wish for, got pneumonia and died on Christmas day. You might already have heard of it.

As I wrote earlier, we stayed until early January as part of the Army of Occupation. Then we were loaded into unheated boxcars, 60 men to a car, for a long and trying journey back into France.

It took five days and nights, half the time on sidetracks waiting
for French trains to pass. I tell you, it was hard not to be angry,
many of us waved our fists at those trains and shouted "Is this the
thanks we get?"

Now we're at Camp Mud as we call it, waiting for our trans-
port home. The food supply is nothing to complain about, at least I
haven't heard any. The problem is the waiting and the sickness. So
many have been stricken with intestinal problems, we're worried
some won't be fit to travel. But it's the flu that is taking a toll.
Already, 5 in our regiment have died just while we've sat here
and waited, and another 60 or so are ill.

Well it's late now and I'm thinking of you and wishing you
pleasant dreams. The other night I dreamed I was walking
through the courthouse, looking for you. I opened every door and I
couldn't find you, and something told me, "She's not in here, she's
outside waiting for you." And I went out onto the grass behind
the building and you were across the street, waving at me, with
the afternoon sun behind you so it was hard to see you. There was
a long line of cars, so I couldn't get to you right away, but you
were smiling and your hair was loose, like it was coming undone.
We were both happy. And that's when I woke up. Tell me what
you think it means when I see you.

Love always,
LST

On the second day of March, four days after she'd received
Leon's letter, Mary Bet had a premonition. Just as she was waking
up, crossing the borderland from her dreams, she saw again the circuit rider in a sable suit. But this time he was riding away from her
in the other direction, toward a scarred and rutted field with mist
rising all about, and coming toward him on a big chestnut horse
was Leon. He smiled in a contented way, but he galloped past,

toward the other rider. She tried to shout and warn him away, but she could make no sound. Nor could she move. She awoke, aware that she'd been trying to yell. From downstairs rose the *throp-throp-throp* of Flora's treadle, and she wondered what on earth Flora could be doing at her machine of a Sunday morning.

Flora said she was only fixing a hem on a dress she wanted to wear that very morning and she saw no harm, since it was for church. By now they were nearly out the door, and Mary Bet said, "Flora, whether or not he comes home, I have no need to marry."

Flora stopped and adjusted her bonnet, which she preferred to a hat, not looking in the mirror, because she and Mary Bet thought it vain to primp overmuch before church. "Why, Mary, what has come over you?"

"I'm happy living here with you. What do I want with a smelly old man and his needs?" She smiled in a coy way to try to stop herself from crying.

"I've never said you did, but honestly I think something's upset you. Have you heard anything since his letter?"

"No, it's just a feeling."

"Why don't you go out and see his brothers this afternoon. It would do you good, give you some peace. They'll have the latest news."

"You and I think alike," Mary Bet told her friend. "I had the same notion as soon as I woke up." She gave Flora a kiss on the cheek, which made her friend smile and blush both. Flora then offered to come with her on the ride, but Mary Bet said there was no need.

She went out after church, the hour and a half in the buggy giving her a chance to collect her thoughts. Was he already gone and the news hadn't spread around yet? They could've gotten word this very morning. When she pulled into the dirt-and-gravel driveway and parked up close to the old house that Leon's father had built after the war, she wondered if the quietness of the place meant that there was a death in the family and they wouldn't want to be disturbed. Who was she to break in on their Sunday peace, anyway? Leon had probably not even mentioned to them that he was going with a girl, a woman, who'd become the sheriff while he was away in training. They weren't engaged. He may even have some other, closer woman friend for all she knew. She thought it best if she just kept going on around the drive and out the way she'd come.

Then Leon's middle brother, Sid, came up from the yard and rested his hands against his fat sides. "Hello, Miss Mary Bet," he said. His beard was so thick she couldn't see his mouth move. She was glad Leon didn't have a beard that like; anyway it wouldn't be fitting for a school superintendent to look like a hillbilly. She sometimes wondered how he had come out of this family, but they were so kind and gentle that she couldn't hold it against him. The younger one, Bob, was practically mute in his shyness and she didn't expect to see him, though he was probably off watching from somewhere. Sid was an incorrigible tease and jokester and he used foul language, but he wasn't mean.

Both brothers liked sweets and she had brought along half of a pound cake she had baked two days ago. "I brought you this," she said. "I just decided to drive out today, or I'd've made something special."

Sid lifted the waxed paper she'd wrapped tightly around the plate. He brought the cake to his nose and inhaled deeply. "I could eat this right now. And dinner's still in here." He patted his belly, which hung over his trousers so that his suspenders seemed always stretched to the breaking point.

Mary Bet asked after his brother and mother, and when Sid invited her in to see them, she said, "No, no. I only wanted to know if you'd had any word from Leon. He wrote me a nice long letter, but it's dated more than two weeks ago."

Sid studied her as though he was just now putting something together. He shook his head. "No, we sure haven't. We got a letter about the same time. It wasn't but about a page. He said they was just waiting on a ship to take them home. Is there something he forgot to tell us, his own family?" He raised his eyebrows in a merry way.

"What?" said Mary Bet. "Oh, no, no. 'Twasn't anything. We're just good friends, and I was concerned about him."

"Well don't you worry. Old Leon can get himself out of a predicament better than anybody I know. If he has to talk the Frenchies out of a boat, he'll do it. He one time got himself sent home for a week for speaking up to a teacher. He didn't stay no week, though. He marched right back the next day and talked her into letting him back in. Here I'm telling a tale on him." He laughed.

Can he talk his way out of the flu? she wanted to say. Can he talk his way out of the accidents that happen whenever large groups of men get together for any length of time? Instead, she just smiled and nodded and said, "I'm sorry to bother you, Sid." He assured her it was no bother at all, and seemed disappointed when she said she ought to be getting home. As she pulled the buggy around, she noticed a little patch of daffodils she hadn't seen before, the first of the season. Surely that was a good sign. But a cool March wind whipped up just as she jounced onto the White Chapel Road, and she felt a shiver through her entire body. Why had she not brought the wool blanket instead of this thin old cotton thing?

By the time she got home, the sun was low in a mackerel sky and the world felt too big. Her hands were stiff in their black riding gloves.

FOR TWO WEEKS and two days she waited, going to work at the courthouse, coming home in the evenings to Flora, mending clothes, cooking supper, helping Flora clean. They employed only a houseboy and felt themselves very modern and very industrious, and in these postwar weeks of waiting Mary Bet felt the need to keep herself continuously occupied. She removed everything from the icebox shelves and cleaned out all the compartments; she scrubbed the top of the cast-iron cookstove; she even took a scrub brush to the laundry mangle, which Flora said was the same as washing soap with soap. Why she had to keep herself thus occupied was not something she cared to dwell on, though when on some evenings they went to listen to a neighbor's Edison gramophone, her mind would drift with the scratchy music to a project left unfinished— the weekly sheets to be boiled for two hours and then ironed the way Essie used to, the walls that really could use washing—and she thought, "I must, I must be prepared."

She thought: I have been the governor's constable in Haw County. I have made a boy see the error of his ways and helped bring men to justice for operating illegal stills, and at least for a short time I have seen peace reign over my jurisdiction. I conserved food, grew a victory garden with Flora, gave up meat on Tuesdays and pork on Thursdays, and served my country the best I knew how. Why can I not now feel settled in my own home?

After the fall election, Mary Bet had asked the new sheriff if he intended to keep her on as a clerk. He told her he had given the matter some thought and wondered if she would consider a new position—office manager. "All right," she said, pleased and proud. The board voted on it and kept her salary the same as it had been as sheriff. "Of course," Flora reminded her, "that's not near what your cousin was making, nor the new sheriff either. But I guess it's better than most women around here."

One day when Mary Bet came home at dinnertime, Flora told her that a boy had stopped by saying there was a telegram waiting for her down at the depot.

"Why didn't he bring it himself?" she asked.

"He said Mr. Dalton had to give it to you in person."

Mary Bet shook her head. "I won't go pick it up. I don't want to see any telegram. I have work that needs attending to for the sheriff. I can't go traipsing down to the station." She stood in the little vestibule, undecided whether to go back into the eating room or run immediately down to pick up the telegram. She stepped into the parlor and sat on the sofa, her coat and hat still on, her handbag clutched in her lap, and stared at Flora's sewing machine.

"Let me get my coat," Flora said. "I'll come with you."

She didn't remember the ride down around the courthouse and south to the station, only the sound of Flora's voice, saying, "It'll be all right. It'll be all right."

When they got there, they saw a knot of people standing outside the office talking quietly, and one or two of them waved a greeting. Mary Bet caught bits of conversation. "It's a shame, with the fighting over, and them just waiting to come home." "Battery C." "His family'll take it hard." "I believe it was pneumonia." "I heard 'twas a bad heart, but maybe the pneumonia caused the bad heart."

Mary Bet looked down the platform as though searching for herself as a young girl at the Hartsoe City station, waiting for her father to come out of the office with the piece of paper saying her sister was dead. She tasted something like iron in her mouth and realized she'd been biting so on her lip that she had drawn blood. She felt Flora take her hand and guide her toward the little office, where she did not want to go. And then they were inside, and Mr. Dalton was standing with a woman Mary Bet knew vaguely—she lived out in the country and Mary Bet could not think of her name. The woman was crying without making a sound, her shoulders rising and falling, her breath coming in quick gulps, and Mr. Dalton in his stationmaster cap and pea-green jacket had his arm around her, patting her shoulder.

He sat the woman in a chair and went over to his desk and found the Western Union telegram bearing the name Mary Bet Hartsoe.

He smiled gravely at her. But that was the way he always smiled, Mary Bet thought. He had a serious demeanor, had maybe never told a joke in his life. He moved quickly, like a little soldier, but he had not gone to war. Hooper had gone, Leon had gone—when neither of them had to. And here was a man, his pants too short for his shoes, who had stayed at home, just to keep a few trains running and deliver bad news.

"Aren't you going to read it?" Flora said.

Mary Bet glanced at it, though she knew what it said. Her eyes were so full she could not make out the words and so she handed it over to Flora, who took it. "If all goes well," Flora read, "regiment arriving in Raleigh Saturday, March 22. Then home. Love and fond regards, Leon Thomas"

"What?" Mary Bet said. "What does it mean?"

"It means they're coming home," Flora said.

Mr. Dalton glanced at the woman sitting in the chair, her gray head bowed, her shoulders stiff, as though she were an animal trying to avoid detection. "Let's go outside," he said.

Mary Bet went over to the woman and bent down. "I'm so sorry," she said, resting a hand on her shoulder. "I'm so sorry." The woman nodded and sniffed, and then Mary Bet went outside onto the platform where Mr. Dalton told them that there was to be a reception and parade in Raleigh. The telegrams had been coming in all morning; Sid Thomas had been in earlier to receive one nearly identical to Mary Bet's.

The noon sun was bright on the concrete beyond the hard shadow of the metal roof. The air was crisp and new and full of the stirrings of life out in the fields behind the station and the brambles and woods across the track. Mary Bet could feel herself breathing, her lungs filling and the breath going out and her lungs filling again. She glanced back through the window of the station office, but Mr. Dalton was in there now and she could not see the grieving woman.

She folded the telegram, then folded it again. But instead of putting it away, she kept a tight hold on it. "We'll go home now," she said to Flora.

THE PARADE IN Raleigh was the grandest she had ever seen, with four brass bands supported by booming bass drums. She stood with Flora and the Thomas brothers and some others from Williamsboro who had driven over in a caravan, and they waved as the top officers drove slowly past in fine open-top cars. Then came the color guard, flags rippling in the brisk air. And now the soldiers came, marching in their peaked caps and olive-drab jackets past the shops and department stores of Hillsborough Street.

It was Flora who spotted him first. They called out and waved, and he smiled and saluted and marched on with his unit. Mary Bet didn't know him. He was nearly in the middle of a row, a face that was somewhat familiar, a little less rounded, the deep-set eyes older, more distant. It seemed the strangest thing to wait all this time for his return, and then see him march past until he was indistinguishable from a hundred other uniformed soldiers, as though they were only replicas of men performing a ceremony instead of real men with lives waiting for them at home. She didn't want to see him there, she just wanted to go home and think about whether she wanted to see him at all. The smells of engine exhaust and horses, the excitement of the crowd on this cool and wonderful day of homecoming was almost more than she could stand. She could feel her heart banging high in her chest with the echoing drums.

But it was a trifling thing to wait and say hello. After everything the boys had been through. The crowd surged upon the reviewing stands along Edenton Street, and Mary Bet's group found a place beneath a bare maple, where they could see the capitol, with its giant stone pillars and green dome, bright in the afternoon sun, and they could hear the speakers if not see them.

They found him afterwards in a clump of green-jacketed compatriots. He was saying something, and then the men were laughing, and Mary Bet held back as the others went forward to shake hands. She watched Leon grip his brother's hand in both of his. Then Leon was rising in the air in Sid's bear hug, his face opening in surprise and delight. Bob stepped up quietly to shake his big brother's hand, and then the three cousins who had joined their group, one of whom was a big-talking, gum-chewing twenty-year-old girl that Mary Bet didn't much care for. She went up and practically jumped into Leon's arms.

"Go on up there," Flora said.

"She just threw herself at him," Mary Bet said.

"Well, don't do that, but if you don't say something he'll think you're stuck-up."

"Maybe I am, a little."

"I've never known you to be."

And then, with his cousin still clinging to his neck, he saw Mary Bet. She felt old and unattractive, standing there in her thick-soled walking shoes and her winter coat. She smiled but didn't move a step forward. He slung his cousin over to the side and came up, removing his cap. "Hello Flora," he said. "Did y'all have a hard time getting through all this crowd?"

"No," Flora said. "We were happy to."

Now he looked at Mary Bet. He opened his mouth, but whatever he had prepared to say stood still on his tongue. "Did you get my telegram?" he asked.

Mary Bet bit her lower lip. She nodded, feeling a bigger fool than she ever had in her life. Why could she say nothing? All this time waiting for her soldier to come home, and now not one word in greeting. She started to say something just as he did, and he laughed and said, "No, no, please, what were you going to say?"

She shook her head. "I thought you'd— I didn't think—" She sniffed in, ashamed of herself, and he reached over with his thumb and wiped the tear from the outside corner of her eye. "Well, you're here," she managed. "And I reckon that's a good thing."

He bent down and kissed her on the cheek. Then he turned to everybody and said, "We just got word we don't have to go down to Columbia for the demobilization. I'll be home in two days." Everybody came up again and patted him on the back and said how good he looked, and Sid tried to bear hug him again but Leon wrestled him to a standstill. Then Sid said they'd have a proper wrestling match at home and the biggest dinner he'd ever seen. "I'll eat anything," Leon replied, "as long as it's not corned beef. If I see another can of corned beef I'll send for the sheriff." Everybody laughed, and he nodded slyly at Mary Bet.

"Don't look at me," Mary Bet said. She suddenly wished Hooper were there. He had been assigned a different regiment and was coming home in a few days. She thought, here I've built up seeing Leon again—I'm just nervous.

Then he was back among his fellows, and Mary Bet's group wended their way through the crowd and out Hillsborough to where they'd left the cars. All the way home they talked about what a fine parade it had been and how good Leon and the others had looked, and Mary Bet could feel the kiss on her cheek and she wondered if it was real and if it was possible that she would soon become a man's wife.

∾ CHAPTER 32 ᗡ

1919

A WEEK LATER LEON proposed. She thought about it for two weeks, and then on Palm Sunday she said yes. She had spent the fortnight staying up late with Flora, talking, laughing, crying, and then, alone in her bed, praying to God and sometimes talking to her father. "I don't have a good reason for saying no," she told Flora.

"That's no reason to say yes," Flora responded. "Are you in love with him?"

"I think so. And I think he loves me and will make a good husband and father."

"All right, go on then, or you'll end up like me."

Mary Bet came and put her arms around her friend, tears starting. "I'd be lucky to end up like you, strong and independent. I admire you more than anybody I know. I just don't think I could— well, this may be my last chance for a family of my own. I don't know if it's the right thing, but I've let Leon wait long enough. I love him about as well as I think I can let myself love anybody. For now."

"He can wait, if you're not sure." Flora turned back to her machine, her foot hovering above the treadle, waiting for a response.

"I'm not sure, but tomorrow I'll tell him one way or the other. If I do get married, I'm going to buy you an electric machine."

Flora shook her head, the treadle and needle already clanking and bobbing. "What makes you think you'll be able to do that?"

The next day after church, she and Leon went out for a ride in Leon's new Model T, paid for with an advance on his salary, and they ended up almost in Hartsoe City. When they stopped at Love's Creek Cemetery and Mary Bet asked him if he knew her folks were buried there, he said he'd heard that, but that he just wanted to stop at a quiet place and take a look at the river. They got out and walked a ways, and she glanced at the graves of her family but didn't point them out. Beyond them lay a newly plowed field, and then the rocky river's edge.

"I'll marry you," she said.

The words had come from somewhere beyond her, and she felt herself shimmer with the certainty that she was part of something much larger than herself, a force untethered to her comprehension, from deep within the ground and the trees and the river and the blue sky. A closed loop, her grandfather had insisted. Yet he had been wrong. With no outside energy, the wheel would stop. She felt the strength of her legs and her bones on this tilted ground, and when Leon took her hand and they began walking back to the car she felt herself giving up some of that strength to him and gaining back something unknown. She hoped. She hoped, but dared not put a name or a face to the hope.

They wanted to have a small wedding, but they kept having to add more and more guests to their list, until people were saying it was the biggest event since the electric lights were turned on in

Williamsboro last fall. It had all come and gone so quickly, she was left with a handful of images colliding in her mind. She wanted to sit down with everyone so that she could piece together the scenes into a kind of mental scrapbook, but for now she would have to content herself with a few random snapshots: the way Flora had smiled with tears in her eyes, standing there in her pale yellow dress, her maid of honor, and Clara a bridesmaid, and Amanda and Mr. Hennesey, and Mrs. Gooch and Mrs. Edwards seated together, and Mr. Witherspoon and Miss Mumpford, and the Cadwalladers, and, of course, Hooper Teague, looking so sharp and proud in his gray morning suit. Her uncle Crabtree had walked her down the aisle. And there was a man she didn't recognize, a man wearing a black suit with an old-fashioned cut to it, and a black-stock tie, his hat clutched in his hand, watching from the back row of the church. Who was he? She would have to remember to ask Leon.

They decided to honeymoon for a week in Wrightsville Beach, which meant taking a train to Wilmington. The day before they were to leave she received a letter from Wilmington, which she took to be a sign, though good or bad she couldn't tell. She sliced it open with the silver letter opener that Clara gave her for a wedding gift, with her initials engraved, "MHT." The letter was brief.

Dear Miss Hartsoe,
I am sorry not write before. Please excuse bad writing. Thank you for sending the letter about Siler. I cried when I read it, but good tears. I loved him very much. Yes, he was sad. I don't know where he was walking. He sayed nothing about walking on the tracks. I wonder about it and now I hope you are not sad in your heart about your brother. He was good and sweet, but could not marry me because I am a Jew. I tell him I know this and I can not marry him. We laugh about this and cry. Maybe someday, we sayed, we will marry in heaven. But I am a wife now with

a little boy. I am happy, thank you for writing, come visit us in Wilmington!
   Love,
   Rebecca Savage Teller

It would have to be enough, then, to know, as her father did, that grief lasts as long as memory, though the tissue of life grow around it like a wound protected from the world and shielded from the heart. Grief and love are the only things that endure.

The train for the East Coast left at five thirty in the morning. A dozen or so well-wishers met them at the platform to see them off, including Flora and Amanda and Mr. Hennesey, and even Mrs. Gooch, who had finally seemed to forgive Mary Bet for not bringing the Cadwallader boy to justice. The weather had turned cool for late May, but as the train made its way into the flat coastal plain and the sun rose, it became very warm. They slid open a window and watched the land flatten into long fields of new corn and hay, stretching to tree horizons.

As they pulled into Wilmington, Mary Bet was amazed at how big it was, with brick warehouses and factories and wide streets lined with tall buildings and shoppers and more automobiles than she'd ever seen. There were two cotton exchanges and a wholesale fruits and vegetables market, and at least a half dozen steeples punctured the skyline, which gave her some comfort. She wondered that her letter to Rebecca Savage had ever made it. They switched onto a smaller train for the short ride past the wharves and out over the causeway to Wrightsville Beach. The landscape grew even softer, with marsh grasses rippling in a breeze and actual palm trees, and Leon told her there was a pavilion where you could watch movies and go bowling and dance to a band into the small hours of the morning. There was even a movie screen out in the surf, and people waded in their bathing suits to watch. She could hardly imagine it—it all seemed too lush somehow to be good. And seeing the worry in her face, Leon assured her that they didn't have to go dancing into the wee hours unless they wanted to, but that they were sure to eat and sleep well because they were staying at the nicest hotel in town.

She had not slept well the night before, worrying about the trip and what she'd forgotten to pack, and now her impressions became dreamy and fractured as she and her new husband, this strange man beside her, moved through an alien landscape. She watched a man shoving a skiff up a creek with a long pole until he was hidden in the reeds. They got off the train amid the excitement and bustle of holiday-makers, and a driver from their hotel met them and led them to a two-horse coach that could hold eight people and all their trunks and baggage.

And then they were driving beside a trolley line down a tunnel of big green trees from which Spanish moss dangled like hair, and she thought, "Just let him be gentle with me." She felt his shoulder against hers and she sighed and relaxed into it. He was unusually quiet, almost nervous. "Just let him be gentle." A warm noon breeze ruffled the tree beards, the air heavy and somnolent and briny. On the side of the road grew little purple flowers with waxy dark green leaves, and bushes with bright red flowers somebody said were oleanders. A dinner bell tolled somewhere behind them. Now they could catch glimpses of the ocean between the dunes, rippling green out to the edge of the sky. It was nothing to fear, yet her heart rose in her chest, and she felt herself swooning, resisting, swooning. She took Leon's hand in hers, and he squeezed back. It'll be all right, she thought, it'll be all right.

Her mind turned to the wedding. All the people and the music and the food. The nervousness in the air because everyone wanted them to start out with a blast of happiness. It had been like life distilled, so swift and sure of its course—only later could you look at it and say that it was held together by each person there.

Now Leon struck up a conversation with the man beside him, and discovered that he and his wife were from Weaverville in the mountains and were also on honeymoon. Mary Bet knew he'd been eager to talk to the others and she liked that about him. She wondered if this was how they were to be as a couple—he going out into the world and she giving him permission. She wondered for the hundredth time if it was going to be hard to give up her independence, but then she thought of Mrs. Gooch and her new boarder, a pale young man with some kind of heart condition.

They pulled up to the Ocean Hotel, an L-shaped building of three gleaming white tiers; a turret rose from the corner, with three balconies where tourists stood under fancy arches taking in the view. In the greensward opposite the portico, a flag bearing the hotel's name hung limp in the noon stillness.

They had a good dinner that night in the hotel restaurant—fried flounder with lemon butter, mashed potatoes, creamed sugar corn, and peach cobbler with ice cream. She let Leon order for her, telling him she wanted the same thing that he was getting. She thought she could never get used to a restaurant as fine as this one, nor did she want to, though it was all right for a vacation. The couple from Weaverville seemed to enjoy their company—they looked genuinely disappointed that Mary Bet and Leon would not be joining them in the ballroom later. Mary Bet had already told Leon she was tired and wanted to go to bed after dinner. She told him she had only danced a few times and wasn't much good at it. "That's fine, Mary," he said, "I'm not much of a dancer. Maybe tomorrow we'll just watch awhile."

They climbed up the stairs of the turret to the first balcony and took a look at the dark ocean. Lights from the hotel cast a pale glow over the beach and the edge of the water where it frayed into foam. Music from the pavilion down the strand rose and fell in the night air, and Leon pointed past a pier to a light down the beach that he said must be the movie screen. The stars were out, but not as many as back home, on account of the hotel lights. The air was cool and damp, and not as fragrant as it had been on their arrival. She shivered a little, and Leon put his hand on the small of her back, and though she could barely feel it through her heavy sweater, it made her shiver again.

"The tide's out," Leon said. "You can see the line where it comes in high."

Mary Bet looked, but she was not sure what to look for—in the darkness it was just sand and more sand. But she was glad Leon knew about such things, and that he always had something to say. They went back to their room and she undressed in the bathroom. She thought that if she weren't so nervous she would be amazed that each room in the hotel had its own private bathroom.

Under the covers he reached for her, and she lifted up her long nightgown to let him know it was okay. She was unafraid of him because they were both strangers here, adrift together in their strangeness. It was as it should be, and she was surprised to find that she was curious. She had not dwelt on it overmuch, even when Clara had given her unasked-for advice. She wondered if it was the first time for him, and she thought maybe she would ask him sometime.

She recalled the sweetness of her gardenia corsage, the clanging of the church bell as they stood there at the church door posing for the photographer and all their friends getting backed up, waiting to get out into the sun. The laughter and nervous excitement, the young girls looking up at her, thinking of themselves someday wearing their own wedding gowns, not knowing how afraid she was, how afraid all brides must be. Life was strange, rich, terrible, wonderful. Everything that had brought her to this point—it would never go away. Her memory was too good, and that was her blessing and her curse. She believed her future was written, and though she was afraid of it she still wanted to see what was going to happen.

He fumbled a bit, but she didn't mind, because he was gentle and he murmured to her that he loved the smell of her hair and how soft her skin was. His breathing came hard as he went rigid inside her, and then the pulsing wet warmth in her core spread out through her limbs. *Of course it was like that. Of course it was a good thing, not a sinful thing to be afraid of.* Was she to be his now with no freedom to do as she pleased, had she not given up a perfectly good life for another go at the terrible burden of family love? "God, please help me," she whispered. Already she could hear Leon's heavy breathing, a sound that she must get used to. What if she couldn't stand living with him, she thought, almost in a panic.

She fell asleep and dreamed she was big with child, a child that was not moving within her, but growing and growing. Somewhere far beyond the window of her room where she slept between her sisters, the Devil was looking for her. But he was so far far away and she so deeply tucked in the warmth of her sisters that he could not see her.

In the morning the sun tipped its golden light through the sheer curtains, and she opened her eyes and heard the soft breathing of her husband, asleep beside her and already familiar. The air was pungent with the smell of damp cedar and the fertile backwater of the sound. She tried to remember her dream, but she could only chase it into the shadows of her mind. The sunlight painted a pattern across the hills and valleys of the bedspread, a pattern as mutable and unpredictable as the beginning of her new life. She smiled. She knew that marriage was not the end of sorrow, only a patch of sun through the window.

Dear Lord, she prayed, *help my father with his suffering, which must still be a burden to him* . . . She stopped. *Lord, I will not ask you for any more favors, you have done so much already. You have brought Leon home safely, and that is enough. But only this: Please forgive me, and help guide me along the right path. And if it be your will to take me, please let me go unafraid. Amen.*

Acknowledgments

I am indebted to Paul Kozlowski, Judith Gurewich, Sulay Hernandez, Sarah Reidy, Yvonne E. Cárdenas, Terrie Akers, Marjorie DeWitt, and the rest of the Other Press staff. Their unfailing support and guidance, their consummate professionalism, and their friendship have enriched my life.

For her tireless reading and her know-how, thanks to my agent, Ellen Levine.

I thank my parents, brother, and sisters for sharing stories over the years that have worked their way into my fiction. And I am much obliged to my cousins Nancy Ann and Gaines Hunter, keepers of the old place, for wonderful stories and hospitality.

Among the many friends who continue to encourage me, I offer special thanks to Steve Keach, Ted Corcoran, Leonard Phillips, Katie Henderson Adams, and Joy and Burkhard Spiekerman.

For their careful and insightful reading, thanks to Alanna Ramirez, Mary Rice, and Margo Browning. And to Margo: thanks for the title and for decades of inspiration and love.

I drew background material from the following books: Wade Hadley, Doris Goerch Horton, and Nell Craig Strowd, *Chatham County 1771–1971* (1971); Rachel Osborn and Ruth Selden-Sturgill, *The Architectural Heritage of Chatham County, North Carolina* (1991); Fred J. Vatter, *Tales Beyond Fried Rabbit: Chatham's Historical Heritage* (2009); and Arthur Lloyd Fletcher, *History of the 113th Field Artillery 30th Division* (1920).